HOT PROSPECTS

Out of the corner of her eye, Magpie saw Raven suddenly stiffen, missing a note, and hissed to him, "What is it?"

He shook his head. When the music allowed him to lower his bow, he whispered to her, "Could have sworn I saw that scrawny little priest running around backstage, the fellow I chased off his street corner a few weeks ago."

She frowned in puzzlement. "What would *he* be doing here? All the other priests left."

Raven shrugged, and evidently decided to dismiss it. "Must have been mistaken. Hey, don't miss your cue!"

Magpie raised her flute and began to play, but Raven's words troubled her. It couldn't have been the priest, she told herself. Raven must have seen one of the stagehands; it was shadowy back there, easy to mistake one face for another, even when you had two good eyes and not one. The play was almost over now, the prince about to go hunting for his own true love. Surely nothing could go wrong now.

Ah yes, here we were, the big dramatic climax: the prince had at last realized that Flora and Florian were the same person. The music swelled up in a grand crescendo as, with a joyous cry of recognition, he pulled his one true love into his embrace—

And a scream rang out from the back of the house.

"Fire! Fire! Run for your lives!"

Bardic Voices

Bardic Voices: The Lark & The Wren
Bardic Voices II: The Robin & The Kestrel

Bardic Choices

Bardic Choices: A Cast of Corbies

A CAST OF CORBIES

A Novel of

BARDIC CHOICES

MERCEDES LACKEY
JOSEPHA SHERMAN

BAEN

A Cast of Corbies

This is a work of fiction. All the characters and events portrayed in this book are fictional, and any resemblance to real people or incidents is purely coincidental.

A Baen Books Original

Baen Publishing Enterprises
P.O. Box 1403
Riverdale, NY 10471

ISBN: 0-671-72207-7

Cover art by Darrell K. Sweet

First printing, February 1994

Distributed by
Paramount Publishing
1230 Avenue of the Americas
New York, NY 10020

Printed in the United States of America

"O for a Muse of fire, that would ascend
The brightest heaven of invention:
A kingdom for a stage, princes to act,
And monarchs to behold the swelling
scene!"

—William Shakespeare
Henry V, Prologue, 1

CHAPTER ONE

THE FLOCK GATHERS

This bright summer day was fair as a maiden's dreams, the air washed clean by last night's rain. That rain had sprinkled the narrow country road with just enough moisture to keep down the dust without turning it to mud, and the Free Bard called Raven found himself whistling the cheerful air of "Come Midsummer." Normally he did not particularly care for *morning*, as such, but this morning was particularly fine, and he no longer regretted the need to rise before the bells of noon. It helped that his only company on this road was a bird or two, and not a crowd of taciturn farmers, or a shepherd and his bleating, bumbling sheep. A most amazing morning; not too hot, plenty of shade from startlingly emerald trees, the scent of flowers and fresh grass in the air.

The kind of morning you hear about in sentimental ballads and scarcely ever see.

Soon enough he'd be joining the main road into Kingsford, that most important city in the Kingdom of Rayden, and the usual stream of travellers, but for now, at least, he was able to enjoy an illusion of being out in the middle of nice, green Nowhere, travelling he Knew Not Where.

Exactly like being in one of those sentimental ballads. Next thing, I'll see a milkmaid with hair of flax and rosy cheeks, lips like cherries and teeth like pearls. And darlin' dimples. And if this is going to turn out to be a bawdy ballad, she'll have no will of her own. . . .

It was difficult on such a day to find any reason to worry, or to believe the rumors Raven had heard ever since crossing the borders into this Kingdom, the hints of trouble stirring for Free Bards—for indeed, all non-Guild musicians. Strange rumors, those; rumors he would have put no faith in, had they not come from the mouths of people he knew to be reliable. In each small town or village through which he'd passed, the story had been the same: "No one would dream of bothering any musicians in *our* village, but we've heard dark things about what's been happening in the *next* town. . . . "

There had been something of the sort last fall and early winter, but the troubles had been confined to Gradford and thereabouts—something about religious mania and a High Bishop gone rather bad. He didn't know all the details, only that Robin and Kestrel had "taken care of it."

Something about a ghost or spirit or some such . . .

But that was supposed to have ended the troubles for musicians—yet here they were again, the same rumors, the same warnings, the same dire predictions.

Free Bards and ordinary musicians alike had heard the rumors and were passing them on, yet Raven had found nothing to substantiate them. So far, whispers notwithstanding, everything had been much the same as usual; he had been able to pick his inns and play as he pleased in them, and the innkeepers had shared in the profit and rewarded him with meals and a bed, gratis. He hadn't had a spot of trouble, not a soul had tried to harass him or any other musician who happened to be with him in any way. But the rumors he'd picked up in the last village had bothered him, and more than a bit:

"It's Kingsford that's having the problem, Kingsford where the Guild is setting out to ban all non-Guild performers."

That had come direct from the lips of a Free Bard named Thrush. And wouldn't *that* be a major disaster for Free Bards were it true! Particularly since he and just about every other Free Bard was headed towards Kingsford right now: more specifically, towards the annual Kingsford Faire. His whistling faltered, as he mused over the possible outcome of such a ban at this moment of Faire-time. That Faire provided a major source of income for wandering musicians, and as importantly, it was the informal annual gathering place of the Free Bards.

Since when have you started worrying so much about rumors? Raven jibed at himself. *The Faire's too big, too vital a source of income for the city folk for them to allow any nonsense about it.*

Even those hidebound, so-very-proper-and-dull Guild members would hardly have enough influence to keep the Free Bards out of Kingsford Faire. The Free Bards were too popular with the common folk— the folk the Bardic Guild ignored in their concentration on those with power, wealth, or both.

Ah well, it wasn't as though he had any hard

evidence of trouble. Resolutely, he put the thought out of his mind. A morning like this one was not to be wasted on fretting. Time enough to worry when he was actually in the city. And worry, Raven suspected, he most certainly would. Up till now, he'd always looked forward to the Faire, and the chance to chat with old friends, perform before a monied audience, and perhaps woo a few women who found his dark Gypsy looks alluring and his eye patch nicely mysterious.

But even without trouble from the Guild, this Faire wasn't going to be *quite* like those before, not without the strong, calming presence of Talaysen to keep everyone in line. Understandable that the man wouldn't be here; he and Rune were expecting their first child, after all, and neither one of them wanted to do any traveling.

Ah, Rune. Raven smiled slightly, thinking of the first time he'd seen her, back when she'd been little more than a child, all awkward lengths of arm and leg, but with the love of music burning in her like a flame. Even had he not been sent by the Free Bards to keep an eye on her, Raven knew he would have had no choice but to teach her.

And now she was both a full-fledged Free Bard and Talaysen's wife. And in a condition which precluded travel, and left Raven to stand in Talaysen's stead as the unofficial leader of the Free Bards at the Faire. *Why me?* Raven complained silently. But then he shrugged with true Gypsy fatalism. No hope for it; Talaysen had been disgustingly firm about the whole thing. Until this moment, the last thing that Raven had ever wanted was to have to worry about anyone but himself; but if this was the way the wind blew, so be it.

He took up his whistling once more, working out the intricate twists of "The True Lady and the False

Knight." Behind him, the donkey carrying his belongings—all save for the precious fiddle safely strapped in its case on his back—added a sudden chorus of braying, and Raven broke into laughter.

"Everyone's a critic!" he said, speaking right at the large, furry ears that swiveled forward at his first word.

That earned him a sharp snort, making the bard laugh again. The donkey swerved at the sound, and Raven swerved with it, moving deftly to keep the animal away from his blind side. After all these years of living with only one eye, the bard had pretty much adjusted to his lessened depth perception, but he'd already had one startling donkey-nip hit him out of the darkness, and he wasn't about to indulge the beast with another chance at him.

Hey now, here was the main road, nice and wide, its packed earth gently banked. And at last he was overtaking some other travellers, a wagonload of them.

Travellers who'd had some bad luck.

In the ditch, hmm? Bad luck for true! Or maybe bad driving. Or a little too much ale?

They must have been travelling at quite a clip to have gone right off the road and so far down into that ditch. Two men muttered curses that drifted back to him, shoving manfully at the rear of the caravan, while a woman handled the reins of the two-mule team, trying to urge the reluctant animals forward.

Ha, wait a minute, he knew these folks, or at least one of the men, the tall, lanky fellow who kept having to stop to brush unruly hair out of his eyes.

"Heron!" Raven called out. "Having a bit of trouble?"

The Free Bard, face red with strain, glanced up in surprise. "A bit," he agreed wryly as Raven moved to the lip of the ditch. "Don't suppose you'd care to lend us a hand?"

Raven grinned, and rocked back on his heels. "Might."

Heron snorted, and waited for Raven to join him and his fellow in the ditch, but Raven had other ideas about "helping." Raven strolled casually to the front of the wagon. Murmuring to the mules, he pulled their heads down to him, blowing gently in their nostrils and whispering in their ears.

"What do you think you're doing?" the woman asked indignantly.

Raven glanced up at her. She was younger than he'd first thought, not all that many years from childhood, fine-boned as a sprite, with a feminine, bird-graceful figure, a narrow, elfin face. . . .

And impatient brown eyes. Belatedly, Raven swept down in an intricate and showmanlike bow. "Why, persuading these stubborn beasts to follow me, of course. Come, my friends," Raven said to the mules, then lowered his voice to the soothing murmur he had used a few moments before. The mules swiveled their huge ears to catch his words, then obligingly followed him, straining against their harness and the weight of the wagon behind. The stuck wagon shifted, stirred. Then the mules gave a mighty lurch, and the wagon came free, with a rattle that must have shook the driver's teeth, clattering back up onto the road.

She gaped at him, all impatience quite gone. "How did you *do* that?"

Raven grinned up at the young woman. "Gypsy magic. Or rather," he added, seeing the irritation at him glinting in her eyes, "the Gypsy gift of knowing just how to sweet-talk creatures." Leaning on the wagon, looking slyly up at her, he added, "Works with humans, too."

She wasn't accepting that; he could see that in the slightly sour twist to her smile. "Heron, do you know this man?" she demanded, as Heron pulled himself up out of the ditch and came alongside the wagon.

Heron chuckled. "Raven, fiddler, Free Bard, and full-fledged Gypsy scoundrel. Free Bard Raven, meet Free Bard Magpie."

The young woman dipped her head in wary courtesy. Raven grinned anew and swept down in a melodramatic bow. Straightening, he found himself being eyed by the second man. He was a rather scruffy-looking young man, of Gypsy blood, Raven guessed, lanky black hair falling about his shoulders, slightly unfocused brown gaze not quite staring at him. "And you?" Raven asked.

"Crow," the youngster mumbled. "Drummer."

Never yet met a drummer who wasn't strange, Raven thought drily. "Happy to meet you, Crow, drummer," he said, and turned to Heron. "Just what were you doing stuck in a ditch?"

Heron gave a short, sharp little laugh. "We didn't have much say in the matter. A wagonload of Guild musicians came barreling along towards Kingsford and forced us right off the road."

"They didn't even look back," Magpie cut in. "We could have been hurt, even killed, but they just kept going. Just the sort of thing," she added fiercely, "I've been running into on this whole journey."

"And not just because she's a woman," Heron continued quietly. "I've been running into trouble, too, ever since crossing over into Rayden."

"Me, too," Crow muttered. "Lousy Guild's been shutting out everyone not one of them. Some of the big cities aren't even letting a non-Guild musician get a busking permit. Stupid excuses: too many performers already, outsiders take away money from locals, all sorts of nonsense like that."

"Oh, I got into the cities," Heron said. "And I got a busking permit. But then I couldn't find any decent place that would let me perform."

Raven raised a brow. Perhaps by concentrating on the smaller towns and villages, he had been missing a great deal of trouble. "The streets—"

"Ha. Nobody's performing on street corners anymore, either. That's why I could get a busking permit; I could stand on a corner and play all day without collecting more than a handful of pins. I wound up having to play in a few really disreputable taverns just so I could eat." Heron sighed. "What's happening is that Guild apprentices have taken up a whole new venue; giving nice little concerts of mild, acceptable music, in brand new theaters, small, but *oh* so stylish, don't you know."

"Don't forget the dancing halls," Magpie cut in, her eyes full of bitter frustration. "That's what I kept coming up against."

"The . . . ah . . . what?" Raven asked, completely bewildered.

Magpie grimaced; her hands tightened on the reins, and the mules stamped in protest. "Oh, they're something new, just like these pocket theaters that have sprung up. The Guild has been buying or building these things in every city I've been in. The theaters are done up to look like a reception hall in some great noble's house, and the dancing halls are made to look like ballrooms. All cheap gilt and flocked shoddy, of course, but they pass for gold and velvet. Makes the common folk feel important, as if they'd been invited to a fancy party by the King."

Heron took up the tale, patting the mules absentmindedly to steady them. "They buy small buildings or put up painted tents; there's a stage, and either cheap benches, or a dance floor. Then they bring in groups of Guild musicians or apprentices. Folks have to pay a small entrance fee to get in to hear the music and dance to it—assuming anyone would *want* to dance to that dull stuff—but even though they've been grumbling about it, people have been paying."

"Of course," Raven murmured, as Heron and Crow swung up into their places, Crow going inside the wagon, and Heron perching on the seat beside Magpie. "City folk like standing about in the cold and wet even less than those who are used to hardship. A roofed hall would give them shelter to enjoy their music, even if they had to pay for it. And given that, I suppose they'd be perfectly ready to put up with Guild so-called music instead of something with real life to it."

He tied his donkey to the tail of the wagon, then took a place beside Heron, without waiting for an invitation. Heron grinned and scooted over closer to Magpie. The woman frowned, but it was a faint frown; as the Gypsy had calculated, she had more now to worry about than Raven inviting himself along for a ride. "What if Kingsford's like that?" Magpie wondered uneasily. "What if they won't even let us into the Faire?"

Exactly what I was thinking.

But he couldn't tell them that. "They will," Raven said with far more confidence than he felt. "Come, my friends, the road's not getting shorter for the waiting."

And he turned the topic of conversation to less worrisome things, as Magpie clucked to the mules and got them back on their way.

As they travelled, the road grew more and more thickly packed with other Faire-goers, folks on foot, on horseback, in wagons and carts and just about anything that could be rolled, pulled, or carried. The noise was overwhelming, and so were the smells of animal, human, spices, and a dozen other less recognizable things. But not as much dust as there might have been; last night's sprinkle had damped down the main road as well as the side roads.

But after the conversation died, Raven allowed it to stay dead. He had a great deal to think about, and most of it followed the mental question: *How would Talaysen deal with this?*

He was so lost in thought that he did not pay any kind of attention to the passing landscape. "There's the palisade," Heron said suddenly, startling him. "We're here."

Raven straightened in the wagon seat; but the glint of sun on the water caught his attention first—and then, the huge bulk of Kingsford itself. As always, he thought Kingsford looked like a great cat, curled up smugly along the farther bank of the Kanar River. The city looked fascinating and inviting behind its walls on this sunny day, giving him tantalizing hints of neat slate roofs and the elegant towers of the Ducal Palace behind them.

Money, adventure, romance, money — the city called to him, like a lovely maid, with a sly hip-twitch and a glint of promise in her eye.

But the city itself was not their goal. On the opposite side of the Kanar River from the city—this side—was the wooden wall surrounding the Fairegrounds, towards which the human river was flowing, as slowly and inexorably as the Kanar itself.

They arrived at the Faire gates amid a swarm of merchants, food sellers, actors, jugglers, and musicians. To Raven's relief, the guards of Kingsford Faire were totally indifferent about the fact that their little party was composed of all Free Bards. In fact, they seemed too harried to do more than issue them proper busking passes without more of a comment than a "Here ye are, mind the rules, hurry up, ye're blocking the gates."

At least things *looked* normal in here, Raven decided, glancing about at the bustling crowds. The Faire was technically due to start tomorrow, but that wasn't stopping anyone from selling food or clothes or pottery. Those just arrived today jostled those already set up, hunting good places to erect their own stands, unpacking merchandise and trying to get everything neatly placed as quickly as possible.

"We can sell the wagon at the livery stable I used last year," Heron said. "You can get rid of your donkey there, too, Raven."

He nodded absently, casting his eyes up and down the rows of tents for familiar signs or faces. "Good enough for me," he replied. "Ha, look at tavern row. Old Merchan has set up his travelling version of the Flying Swan!" The more permanent version, the inn within the city walls, was a Kingsford institution, at least for wandering performers. "When we're all settled, we'll gather at the migrating Swan, eh?" he finished with a laugh. Magpie cast her eyes up, but Crow and Heron both chuckled.

He continued to scan the crowd, feeling more optimistic by the moment, and buoyed up by the excitement all around him. Rumors notwithstanding, this looked as though it was going to be a good Faire after all!

Merchan had, of course, stayed in Kingsford to run his permanent inn, but he'd tried his best to make this version of The Flying Swan look as close as possible to the original, imitating the dark, smoke-stained walls with equally dark canvas, on which were pinned a few tattered banners. A tired lute leaned against one side of the bar, two flutes against another. *Atmosphere*, Raven thought wryly.

The Swan, migrating or otherwise, was always a magnet for musicians. Merchan welcomed them with great enthusiasm, whether or not there were paying customers about. He'd been looking forward to a few cheerful drinks with those friends he hadn't seen since last year's Faire. But as Raven looked about the small common room, eyes adjusting to the dimness, he frowned; this was not an atmosphere of calm, as he'd first thought. There was such a weight of gloom hanging in the air, it felt like a funeral.

And the place was so empty that if the walls had been wood instead of canvas, it would have echoed. Where was everybody? There were perhaps half the number of musicians, Free Bards or other itinerant minstrels, than should be here the day before Kingsford Faire opened. The crowd—such as it was—appeared to be mostly merchant types; small peddlers and other tradesmen.

It was several long moments before he even saw anyone he knew. "Hey now, Owl!" Raven said in relief, spotting a familiar gray-bearded face. The middle-aged Free Bard was a levelheaded sort, not the type to be easily panicked, and if anyone knew what was up here, without exaggeration and without jumping at rumors, old Erdrick, called "Owl," would. "How goes it, man?"

Owl looked grimly up at him as he approached the table. "Terribly. Come, join me. You've heard about the troubles here in Rayden?"

Raven slid into the chair beside him, rocking a little on the not-quite-level ground. His earlier cheer evaporated, like dew in the midsummer sun. "For Free Bards, you mean? I was hoping what I heard were just rumors, or the reports of isolated incidents. Not everyone likes us, after all."

Owl grimaced. "An understatement. And what you heard were hardly isolated incidents. You took your usual route through the little villages, I take it?"

Raven nodded, and flipped a coin at the serving wench who approached them as soon as he took a seat. She scampered off and returned with a mug of small beer, leaving it in front of Raven without a single word exchanged.

That had always been one of the things he'd liked about the Swan. They served you as if they could read your mind.

"I like them, small villages, I mean," he told Owl. "Nice, simple, friendly people, easy to please, good cooking in the inns. I didn't have any trouble at all, but I kept hearing horrible rumors about dreadful things happening elsewhere. They never happened to me, so I figured they were just echoes of that business in Gradford that Kestrel and Robin got themselves mixed up in. But Owl, I came into Kingsford with Heron, Magpie, and Crow. They told me some pretty alarming tales."

"True tales," the older man said shortly. "Times are hard for any performer trying to make a living in this kingdom, and thanks to the Bardic Guild, they're getting harder." Owl shook his head moodily. "Look how empty this place is. Half the folk I know haven't even bothered coming to Kingsford, and that includes Free Bards as well as common musicians. Ha, I've been hearing even some of the local folks saying they're planning to move out of Rayden altogether."

"To where? Birnam?" That kingdom, home to Rune and Talaysen, was nicely open to non-Guild practitioners of all kinds, but how many musicians could one small kingdom support? "What about the Duke here . . . what's his name . . . Arden. Doesn't Duke Arden see what's happening?"

Owl shrugged. "I don't doubt that he does. He's always been a supporter of the arts. But thus far, he doesn't seem to be willing to do anything about it."

"He is a supporter of the arts," someone muttered. Raven turned to see a very young man sitting behind them, a youngster with a pale, thin, beaky face topped by dishwater-blond hair; the neck of a lute protruded over his lean back. The young man gave a nervous little grin and a dip of the head. "Jaysen," he said. "Free Bard. Lute player."

A babe. A mere babe, Raven thought with a flash of amusement. *Was I ever that young?*

Then he had to laugh at himself. What nonsense. The odds were that Raven wasn't more than ten years the youngster's senior at most; he only *felt* as if he must be a hundred years older than this callow stripling. He politely introduced himself, then added, "You know something about the Duke being a supporter of the arts?"

"Oh yes!" the boy said enthusiastically. "He even has his own theater troupe, the Duke of Kingsford's Company. But the restrictions on non-Guild musicians are coming down from the King himself. What can Duke Arden do? He can't defy the King's edicts. What could anyone do?"

Raven had been enjoying the trained beauty of Jaysen's voice, thinking, *Lucky. When his voice broke, it broke into such a nice, clear tenor.* Caught off guard by the young man's impassioned, if rhetorical, question, he added hastily, "What, indeed," then got abruptly to his feet. "This is ridiculous. I'm going for a walk to see how matters here are for myself."

Owl said not a word, but held up his flask in a wry salute.

But Jaysen had a word of his own. "You won't like what you find."

The first thing Raven noticed as he wormed his way neatly through the crowds was a rather conspicuous lack. In every available corner of the Faire, every niche, there should have been a performer of some sort, a minstrel or juggler or magician. Instead he found no musicians of any kind, not even the most amateurish of street singers, although there were jugglers, mimes, and other entertainers in plenty. A little chill began to steal up the Free Bard's spine, particularly when he came to a plain, precisely square building labeled in prim, clear script, "Harp and Flute Dancing Hall."

So-o, the enemy! Raven thought, only half jesting, and moved forward to investigate, approaching the closed tent flap with trepidation.

"Not so fast, my fine lad." A meaty hand falling heavily on his shoulder brought Raven to a sudden stop. "If you want in here, you gotta pay."

Raven pulled away as the man ran eyes full of contempt over him. His own response was to raise an angry eyebrow at the bully. Oh, he'd seen this type a hundred times before in his travels! This big lout, jammed into a livery of purple and gold that was far too small for him, was the sort of bully who assumed every Gypsy was a common thief or scoundrel. Stupidity combined with a narrow and parochial mind guaranteed hatred for anyone who was at all different from himself. Sadism fairly radiated from him. The Free Bard did not react to the lout's obvious antagonism; instead, he merely smiled. "And what," he purred in his finest accent, "might the fee be?"

The elegant voice clearly put the bully off balance. "Three copper pennies, this time a' day."

Raven's eyebrow rose again, a little higher. "This time of day? The fee goes up at more fashionable hours, I take it?" *At prime shopping times, I imagine, when there are more folks to lure inside? Or after dark, when there are more people abroad looking to be entertained? Probably the latter. . . .*

The bully was now clearly uncomfortable. "Uh, yeah. Dancing halls are real popular these days, real . . . uh . . . fashionable."

And there, Raven realized, was the real problem. Combine the comfort of a roof over your head no matter what the weather with the irresistible lure of the new and stylish, and there went the take of the average street musician. Folks were going to save the pennies they used to toss into the hat to get into one of these stylish new dancing halls. Their pennies would buy hours of entertainment, not merely a few songs. And if they didn't have as good a time inside as they might listening to one of those street musicians—well, no one said fashion had to make sense!

For that matter, the folk who paid to get inside this tent might well convince themselves that they *were* having just as good a time as they had dancing in the "street" of the Faire. After all, they had *paid* for this privilege and sheer determination would ensure that they had a good time, whether or not the musicians were any good. Just the atmosphere would make people who paid to get in feel superior to those who had no pennies to spare. There would be no small brats underfoot, no livestock or shoppers, and an environment that would counterfeit the parties held in nobles' private portable "manors." How could a street musician compete with that?

Wonderful. Just wonderful, Raven thought. *Thank you, Talaysen, for your trust in me. The only trouble is, I haven't the vaguest idea of what to do!*

The bully frowned, becoming impatient when Raven did not produce the required pennies. "Well, lad? You gonna stand here all day?"

Raven took a deliberate step back. Sheer frustration at the size of the problem facing him made him irritable and inclined to take his frustration out on the nearest target. Sheer recklessness made him challenge, "What of it? This is Faire space, is it not, free to all?"

"Go on, get outta here!" the bully snarled, giving him a rude shove. Then he made a real mistake, as he added, not quite under his breath, "Lousy Gypsy."

In the next moment, he found himself pushed up against the canvas side of the hall, Raven fixing him with a deliberately manic glare. Raven had always been a lot stronger than he looked; he was probably stronger than this bully, for all the latter's bulk. "Do you know how I lost this eye?" the Free Bard purred. "Well? Do you?"

The bully gaped at him, taken by surprise by the Bard's strength and quickness. "How could I—"

"I lost it conjuring a demon. That's what the spell demanded," Raven continued with quiet menace. "My eye. A terrible price, but I paid it. I won. And now the demon does my every command." He laughed, very softly, very chillingly, and grinned evilly as the bully shrank away from him. "Would you like to meet him?" Raven demanded. "Answer me! Would you like to meet my demon?"

White-faced, the bully shook his head, his eyes wide with fear, his lower lip trembling as he held back tears of terror. Sweat broke out across his brow.

Raven smiled at him most charmingly. "So be it. A good day to you, my friend."

Turning away with a melodramatic flourish, the Free Bard stalked away. Truth to be told, his gait was a blatant imitation of the villain of one of the worst plays he had ever seen—but it did seem to impress the bully.

Now, wasn't that clever, he jeered at himself. *You can terrorize a provincial village idiot. But the Guild won't be so easily frightened.*

And the Guild would not be terrorized into shutting down the "dancing halls" and "concert theaters." The days of street-busking were clearly numbered.

What, oh what, was he going to do now?

CHAPTER TWO

BIRDS OF A FEATHER

Raven paused just out of sight of the Ogre of the Dancing Hall, and watched gloomily as several folk paraded inside. "This isn't the worst the Guild has been doing," a woman's soft voice said in Raven's ear.

A very familiar voice. He didn't even have to turn to see who it was.

"Hello, Nightingale." He turned anyway. As always an odd little pang, made up equally of appreciation, lust, and uneasiness, shot through him at the sight of her. Lovely, truly lovely, was Nightingale; an ageless woman, Gypsy-dark as he, lithe as a willow stem, and as mysterious and elusive as the bird of her use-name.

Mysterious, oh yes, indeed, even to a fellow Gypsy. Nightingale was a harpist fine enough to bring the tear to your eye, the laughter to your heart, but she was also just this side of eerie, uncanny. He often had the feeling that she was not entirely of this world; Bardic

Magic burned very clearly in those dark eyes, eyes that seemed to see far past the surface of things, deeply into both the past and the future.

Raven hesitated. He and Nightingale had at one time had a tacit understanding between them, and even though his mind knew all was over between them, his heart wasn't quite sure about it. Particularly at moments like this one, meeting her again after a long absence.

But his more practical side chided him for being so sentimental. *Ach, ridiculous, you're not some scrawny adolescent like Jaysen. No use pining after any woman, much less one like Nightingale. She's not for any man to have and hold for long. Not any human man, at least. Maybe an Elf lord, but nothing less. What's over is over.*

So instead, he addressed her remark. "What do you mean, not the worst?" Raven asked, his anxiety and a touch of embarrassment over his automatic reaction to her making his reply come a touch too sharply. "The worst of what?"

"The Guild Bards have also set up tiny theaters all over the Faire," Nightingale murmured, "exactly like the concert halls in the cities. Theaters where audiences can sit in complete comfort to hear their music, shaded in the day, and lit by night. And prettier dancing halls than this to draw in the aristocrats, and those who like pretending they're aristocrats."

Just as he'd feared. "In other words, to snatch away everyone with a taste for music—and money to spend at the Faire."

And what was he going to do about it? Raven's thoughts floundered helplessly. The Guild Bards had the advantage of a rich Guild behind them, with its huge coffers of money saved, to buy as many tents as they liked and build as many theaters and open halls as they wished. For that matter, current events had already proved the Guild had the backing of the Church, whose supplies of coin were unending. How could the Free Bards possibly compete? Their coffers weren't by any means as heavy.

Heavy? We barely have a common coffer. We don't have the backing of the Guild or the Church, we depend on voluntary contributions, and nothing more. . . . Damn.

"Nightingale," Raven said in sudden desperate determination. "I'm calling a meeting of all the Free Bards around. Help me spread the word, yes? I know it's early in the Faire for a mass meeting, but—we have to do something about all this now, if we can. We'll meet tonight in the clear space behind our big tent."

Nightingale pursed her lips speculatively. "You have a plan?"

Oh, how he would have liked to impress her with a great lie—but lies did not impress Nightingale. Facts did, as did honesty, even if they made him look the desperate fool that he was. "I . . . wish I did," he admitted. "No. But with so many creative minds crowded in together, we surely *must* come up with something."

Other than a quarrel. I hope.

She gave him the grace not to look too skeptical. "I shall," she replied. "But you will forgive me if I wish that Master Wren were among us at this moment."

He nodded as she turned away. How could he not forgive her? Particularly since that was precisely what he was wishing himself.

Raven glanced about at his little group: Heron and Owl were two solid, reliable islands of calm, made all the more so in contrast to nervous, flushing Jaysen fidgeting beside them, still with his lute slung over his back. Nightingale stood to Owl's left, seeming more mysterious than ever in the light from the torch Raven had staked beside his stone seat; Magpie, standing beside her, looked by contrast almost too young to be on her own. Crow, scruffy as ever, lurked to one side, dark eyes murky. The others, all those who had arrived early for the Faire only to find their efforts at busking thwarted by the Guild's new inventions, ranged behind the rest in postures of worry and hostility.

The muttering from the darkness sounded ominous. Not the best way to begin a meeting. "All right," Raven said, mustering his thoughts. The muttering died, slowly. "All right. You know why we're here. The Guild's pretty much taken over, and if we don't come up with a plan to combat them, we're going to wind up penniless beggars by the end of the Faire." He paused, seeing them watching him expectantly, and sighed. "Talaysen said I was supposed to act as our leader in his absence. So I called this meeting. Any suggestions?"

Silence. Then Heron began hesitantly, brushing his unruly hair out of his eyes, "What if we built our own 'dancing hall'?"

"Where?" Nightingale asked softly. "We can't hope to compete with the Guild on their own terms. We can't afford even one tent the size of theirs."

"Aye!" someone said out of the dark. "And what if they clean *forbid* us to build it? There's rules about what ye can put up at the Faire—Fairewards may say no!"

"Wait, now . . . " Owl murmured. "That's none so bad a notion. But we can't make our venue the *same* as theirs, we have to make it different! What if . . . yes. What if we build *our* hall not near any of the Guild's ventures, but *outside* the Fairegrounds?"

"Where?" Magpie asked warily. "We can't put it too far away, or no one will bother visiting it." She hesitated, as if an idea had just occurred to her. "We *could* put it near the beast-sellers, I suppose. They're outside the Faire, but there's traffic there even at night. And as for making our venue different—well, the charm of the Faire is that it's supposed to be rustic; most of these city-folk have never seen a country dance. We could set up an arena with straw bales and a platform, just like a country Harvest-fest. The beast-sellers would probably loan them."

"Ha, yes!" Raven grinned. "A good many of those beast-sellers are Gypsies, too; the rest are wanderers just like us, often as not. They'll help us; it won't be the first time we've helped each other out as a group."

"'Sides," Crow muttered, "they help us, we bring 'em business. People come t' dance, they might see a nice piece of stock, or maybe a pet for the young 'uns."

This was sounding better and better; Raven's enthusiasm grew with every word. "Exactly!" he crowed.

"But what are we going to perform?" Jaysen asked, then flushed when everybody turned to him. "I—I mean, people aren't going to want to leave the Faire. There's more entertainers than just musicians there. We've got to give them something pretty good to draw them to us."

Raven's grin widened. "That's not a problem. We've heard what the Guild Bards have to offer."

"Right," Owl cut in. "Court music. Dull, orderly, unimaginative court music. The Guild musicians wouldn't dream of soiling their precious minds with learning the dances and songs the common folk like."

Raven struck a triumphant pose. "You have it! So, what we'll do is set up a flat area, ringed with hay bales, just like Magpie suggested; put a platform at one end, and sing and play real country music! Reels, jigs, brawls, things that get the blood moving! Then when we tire the dancers out, we give them something quiet to listen to!"

"What about admission?" Magpie asked. "The Guild's going to come down on us if they think we're charging more than they do, but we can't afford to charge less."

"Oh yes, we can!" Raven cried. "Admission to our dancing-ring will be free."

There was a chorus of objections at that. "Free!" "Why?" "How can we—"

He waited for the noise to die down, then nodded decisively. "No admission, but donations will be asked for, just as if this was a large version of one of our street corner venues. We'll put a pot beside the 'door,' and put one of the kids with big, hungry eyes to sit beside it, watch it, and give everyone who goes by a look like a beaten puppy if they don't drop something in it."

Not a bad idea if I do say so myself. He preened a little as he saw the nodding begin.

"And the take?" Heron asked. "How are we splitting that?"

That part was easy; just a version of what Free Bards always did when they joined up to form a temporary consort. "We'll divide any profit equally between everyone who performs each night."

"It might work," Owl mused. "Having the beast-keepers and their charges so close should be enough to keep the Guild from bothering us. Nice big mastiffs, those drovers have."

"And nice big clubs, the shepherds have!" someone else added.

"What about musicians who aren't Free Bards?" Nightingale asked, before the murmur of discussion rose too much for her to be heard. "I don't think we should shut them out."

"No," Raven agreed after a moment. "I think we should open the venue to any and all performers. Everyone in agreement on that point? Yes? On all the others? Yes, again?" He held up a hand in mock-benediction. "Bless you, my children."

Owl chuckled. "I just thought of another angle we can use. The one thing the Guild's nice little dancing halls don't have is refreshments. What say we approach some of the food-and-drink vendors? Make a deal with them?"

Magpie gave an excited little laugh. "Yes! We can make *two* deals with them. Either they can allow non-Guild musicians to play beside or inside their tents for food and drink and whatever gets tossed in the hat, or they can send someone to sell food and drink at our dance hall. Ha, or they can do both! Just formalize what's been informal between us all these years!"

She glanced at Raven, face animated, eyes bright with enthusiasm, and he, to his amazement, felt his heart give an unexpected little lurch. *Don't be stupid*, he told himself sharply. *No time for that nonsense now.*

Not when they had the solution to their potential crisis to work out. It was early days yet; no telling how the Guild was likely to react to this move on their part, nor whether their certain opposition was going to be effective.

But he dared not let any of his doubt show. Talaysen had appointed him leader, and the others seemed to have accepted that, and a leader must never let anyone think he was uncertain. That was the quickest way to undermine his own authority. "Well now, I think it's going to work. No, no, I *know* it's going to work! Now, come, my friends," he added, "time is short and we have a busy time ahead of us."

And the complications will start as soon as we do!

❖   ❖   ❖

Jeweler's Row was a bit quieter than the rest of the
Faire; the crowds here in a mood to browse slowly and
savor subtleties. The brightly clad, dark-haired woman
who appeared at the end of the row and sat down
beside the stand of Shena the Jeweler garnered no attention at first. Seeming to cast a circle of calm about
herself, she ran her fingers quietly over the strings of
her harp. Passersby froze, caught by the gentle, tender
melody. . . .

But then, before that melody could be resolved, the
harpist flattened her hands on the strings, stilling
them. Rising gracefully, she murmured, "The song will
be fulfilled tonight. Near the beast-sellers' pens."

In a swirl of bright skirts, she vanished into the crowd.

The lanky, blond young man with the lute slung over
his shoulder stopped at the stand of Lerrin the Lute
Maker, examining a handful of bronze strings. Lerrin
beamed at this prospective customer, boasting over the
pure quality of his merchandise. The young man
smiled shyly.

"Could I try one of them on my lute?" he asked
diffidently.

Lerrin gloated; certain that he had made a sale. "Go
ahead, go ahead. Hear the sound of one, you'll want a
dozen!"

But the young man paused a moment, hand poised
over one of the strings. "Well . . . first hear what my
lute sounds like as it is, all right?"

The lute maker blinked in surprise at the unexpected response, and said the first thing that came into
his mind. "This isn't a dancing hall, boy. I can't—" But
then Lerrin fell silent, listening with delight to the
cheerful tune the boy was playing.

The tune broke off in a discordant chord as a hand

clamped on the lutist's shoulder. "You're no Guild Bard," a pompous voice declared.

"Uh, no, sir, I'm not." The boy seemed totally embarrassed at coming face-to-face with one of that elite company.

The Guildsman glared down at the poor young man, full of authority and obviously ready to call a Faireward if need be. And Lerrin could not help but note that the crowd that was gathering seemed to be murmuring sympathetic comments—sympathetic to the boy, that is. "You weren't planning to start begging for money here, were you?" blustered the Guildsman. "Bothering all these honest folk?"

Except, of course, that *last* year it wouldn't have been called "begging" or "bothering," it would have been called "busking." And no Guildsman could have stopped the lad.

"Oh no, sir, never that!" The boy's eyes were so wide with false innocence Lerrin almost choked on strangled laughter. But as the Guild Bard strode majestically away, the young lutist, face still as innocent as springtime, added to Lerrin and the curious crowd that had gathered, "I would *never* beg. But if you would care to stroll down tonight to the area near the beast-sellers' pens, you might hear some very interesting music, indeed."

Raven paced nervously back and forth. It was always like this before a performance, the worry and the stress. Would the audience like him, would the audience even come —

But tonight, that was a real and fear-making question. Ha, *would* they come? Here it was, nearly full night, their makeshift dance floor was all ready, and yet there was no one to use it, no one who —

Wait, now. Was that movement, out beyond the torches? Yes, it was, and not the beast-sellers, either!

Here came a few curious folks, strolling down from the Fairegrounds. . . . Not his idea of a good-sized audience, but at least it *was* an audience. Grinning, Raven raised his fiddle and began to play before they even reached the opening to the dancing grounds. The tune he'd chosen was an old country dance, sprightly and so cheerful that not a few toes started tapping. Once folk realized they weren't going to be asked to pay, they came closer, at last stepping through the gap in the straw bales and out onto the dance floor.

Now we have them, Raven thought, as couples began a lively circle-dance, and allowed himself to surrender to the joy that was his music.

As the handful of people grew to a full crowd, and several dances passed and the night deepened, Raven, fingers and arms aching from all the quick fingering and bowing he'd been performing, gladly gave over to Jaysen. A few of the original curiosity seekers were gone, but there were more folk to replace them. The lad offered the dancers a chance to catch their breath with a tender, bittersweet ballad, delivered in his sweet tenor with enough charm to bring tears to not a few eyes. He continued with another, a love song, and then a long story-ballad of the heroic ventures of their own Kestrel and Robin. Raven, who knew better than to let music overpower him on the night of a performance, kept enough of a clear head to realize that some of the folk who'd stolen away after the first few numbers had returned. Ha, and word must be spreading back there in the Fairegrounds, because more and more people were drifting this way.

And look at this: not a one of them seems to mind pitching in a penny or two into the "hat" to let them dance as long as they choose. Or as long as our wind and fingers hold out!

The night wore on. Jaysen gave way to Crow, who with a penny-whistle player, worked a dazzlingly intricate pattern of sound to keep the ever-increasing number of dancers happy. Crow in turn gave way to Magpie, whose flute rendition of "Sweet Flowers in the May" was as sweet and charming as the flowers themselves. Owl was next, with what Raven guessed was an original song, his voice thickened with age but the words and melody bouncy and bright enough for Raven to start plotting a transcription for fiddle in his mind. A trio took over the stage after him; tambor, lute, and harp—and after them came a lad with bagpipes and a lass with a hammer-dulcimer. Nightingale followed, matching the general good humor with her own happily exotic melody on the harp.

The dance floor was fully crowded now, with no one showing much desire to go home. More and more pennies—and sometimes better than pennies—ended up in the "hat," enough to make Raven grin. No danger of winding up as beggars at this year's Faire, not if they were able to continue this little venue!

Hey-ho, time to take over from Heron and Crow, who'd just worked out a breathlessly wild arrangement of "The Miller's Helper" for voice, dulcimer, and tabor, and were both blatantly winded when they finished. Now there were so many wanting to dance that once one dancer was too tired to go on, there were three more waiting to take his place. As Raven slipped neatly into the opening chords of the silly, happy country dance known as "Two Green Apples," he saw Magpie grin in quick delight. Raven grinned back at her, signaling with a jerk of his chin for her to join him. The young woman shrugged, as if to say "why not?" and sprang up from where she was sitting, flute in her hand. As Raven stayed with the main melody, Magpie began weaving a complex counterpoint around it, so delicious a secondary melody—and so beautifully improvised—that Raven smiled his enjoyment.

"You take the lead this time round," he murmured, and improvised his own fiddle trills and flourishes around the silver tone of the flute. Far too soon the song was ended, and only the sudden roar of applause made Raven realize with a start that he and Magpie had been staring blindly into each other's faces.

All at once aware of herself and her surroundings, Magpie blushed and turned hastily away, leaving Raven staring thoughtfully after her for a moment. Surely what had just happened between them had been only the momentary magic caused by their music? That was all it had been . . . wasn't it?

Suddenly drained of energy, he was very glad to relinquish the floor to Heron and Owl and go wandering off into the darkness. For despite all their success, he felt something in his bones . . . like the coming of a thunderstorm, or the strange weather that was reputed to precede an earthquake.

"Raven," murmured that all-too-haunting voice.

He started; it had come from his blind side. "Nightingale."

The woman quickly moved to his sighted side. "She is very pretty," Nightingale observed. No need to ask who she meant.

Raven flushed, annoyed that he had been so transparent, and embarrassed that she had noticed his interest. "*And* very young," he retorted.

"Not so many years younger than you," Nightingale corrected, amusement edging her voice. "Surely nowhere as young as Rune was when she met Talaysen." But then the woman's teasing smile faded. "That is not all bothering you."

He shrugged. No use trying to hide *anything* from her. If he felt that odd foreboding, and it was something more than simple weariness, then she must feel it threefold. She had that knack, after all. "Is it so very obvious?"

She nodded, slowly. "Indeed. You are Gypsy as much as I; you feel the sudden change in the air, the stirring of ill tidings to come."

Raven turned to stare at her, but could make nothing of her expression in the darkness. "Yes. I can. This night's been going well, almost too well. I can't shake the feeling that there's trouble to come."

"You could be wrong. We could both be wrong." Nightingale rested a carefully impersonal hand on his arm, then reached over to give him an equally impersonal kiss on the cheek. "Raven, don't worry. All may yet be well."

Then why can't I believe it? Raven thought, but said nothing.

Magpie (*Jessamyn*, she thought defiantly, *I am still, underneath it all, Jessamyn the players' daughter*) stood alone in shadow, watching Raven and Nightingale, and feeling absolutely horrid. Her stomach was upset, and her earlier elation had quite vanished the moment she had seen *those two* together.

This was ridiculous, worse than ridiculous. She was herself, complete, self-sufficient as she'd had to be ever since childhood; she wasn't the sort to find herself drawn to—to a penniless, shiftless, not-to-be-trusted Gypsy!

Oh, easily said. But Magpie had felt her gaze keep shifting to Raven all evening, no matter what she wanted.

It's the spell of the music, she told herself. *That's all it is. You don't have time for complications.*

Besides, the man wasn't at all what she usually thought of as handsome, not with that wild thatch of black hair framing a sharp, saturnine face: he looked, if she was thoroughly honest about it, like a bandit, a tricky, particularly dangerous one at that. That dramatic black eye patch certainly didn't help. Nor did the fact that he went out of his way to cultivate a rakehell manner. Magpie had overheard him telling one of the ladies who'd come to see them perform (and maybe, the young woman thought wryly, to arrange a private performance from Raven) that he'd lost his eye in a desperate, heroic battle with an evil wizard.

A wizard, ha. More likely he lost it to a jealous husband!

But . . . when he played the fiddle, that mocking face became serious, quietly intense, almost beautiful. Magpie suspected—no, knew—that while Raven might not take many things seriously, music was definitely one of the few things he did respect.

Oh, what difference did any of it make? Even if she was stupid enough to let herself be truly attracted to him, Raven, as the saying went, was already an item with Nightingale. Magpie hugged her arms around herself in a spasm of misery, forced to admit to herself that she envied Nightingale in every possible way. It didn't seem fair that the Gypsy woman should be so much of what Magpie wasn't!

Nightingale is mysterious, exotic, like a wild bird with a heartbreaking song and paintbox plumage. And I—I'm about as mysterious as—well, as nice, plain, good-for-you bread.

Nightingale was so very beautiful, with her dark, exotic looks. *And I look, well—wholesome!*

Oh, and there was more: Nightingale was so very blatantly a wielder of Bardic Magic, while not a spark of arcane powers lurked in Magpie. And Nightingale was a Gypsy, an unfettered, free, wonderful creature, the kind of woman who simply embodied all the romance of the open road. She'd probably pine away, caged up in a city.

And I—when I dream, it's about houses, cottages, a safe and secure place of my very own, and no more wandering, ever again.

Born into a non-Guild family of wandering players, Magpie had done her share of travelling, back in the days when she was just plain Jessamyn, but there hadn't been any *romance* about it. Her father had died so long ago she could hardly remember him, save as a large, warm presence. Her uncle, his brother, should have been the one in charge of everything. But he was a vague, good-natured creature who would never have dreamed of hurting a soul even when under the burden of drink. A fortunate thing, Magpie thought wearily, since she could count on her fingers the number of times she'd seen him truly sober. Magpie's mother, perforce, had been the one to run the troupe; but while she'd been a more than competent musician and actress, with scant patience for the weak of mind or will, she'd had almost no head for business, leaving such mundane matters as keeping everyone fed and clad and away from each other's throats to her daughter. *And I did it. For what good it does me now.* The troupe had drifted apart when her mother had settled down with her latest man, leaving Magpie totally on her own. *Wonderful. I can run a business or play just about any woodwind well enough to earn a living: thank you, Mother, wherever you are, for that much. But just because I am myself, not some simpering little idiot without two thoughts to spare, I scare off every man I meet.*

Well, no, not every man. There were always some who weren't intimidated by a strong-willed, independent woman, though she hadn't met any of them yet.

Or had she? What about Raven? At first he'd seemed just as empty-headed as all the other good-looking men she'd met. But . . . he didn't seem to mind her outspoken nature. And he certainly didn't seem to mind her musical talents, nor did he seem to see her as some kind of competition! Their duet had been —

No. Raven, Magpie reminded herself sternly, belonged to Nightingale. She was *not* a poacher!

But an evil little voice inside her would not let her be. It nagged at her, and ridiculed her caution. *Right. Go ahead, take the least risky choice, just as you always do.*

But even as she sniped at herself, Magpie knew that last wasn't quite true. She'd always had to worry about money, about how she was going to support herself without selling more than her music. How could she be anything other than cautious?

Enough of this. If the Guild had taken women, Magpie told herself drily, she was sure she would have joined it in a moment. And if that choice might not have made her happy, at least it would have left her *secure!*

By the time the Faire had surged through its first busy, boisterous week, Raven told himself that surely there was nothing at all to worry over. The Free Bards' improvised stage, their "dancing ground," as it had come to be called, was crowded with folks every night, and between the take there and that from the little nooks the Free Bards had set up in eating tents, it looked as though all non-Guild musicians were going to do all right this season.

That's all well and good, Raven mused, as he walked the rows of stalls and tents, resting his hands though not his mind. *But what of the long-term problems? So far we've heard nothing from the Guild, but they aren't known for their tender charity towards rivals. They aren't going to let us get away with cutting into their profits all the time. What can they be plotting?*

Then, as Raven wandered aimlessly through the Faire, for once hardly aware of the sly smiles and appreciative stares from some of the women he passed, Lerrin the Lute Maker whispered from the shadow of his stall, "Gypsy! Fiddler! Over here."

He obeyed, raising one eyebrow inquisitively. "Hey? What is it?"

"Look you," the man muttered, "you've been good for business, you and your troupe, buying lute strings from me and getting curious customers trying their hand at playing 'like the bards do.' Besides, I like your music, too. Look at the strings, will you?"

He nodded, and pretended to examine some lute strings, since the man seemed nervous enough to warrant going along with his play-acting. "Glad to hear it. But why whisper?"

Lerrin coughed. "Ah. Well. I thought you should know. The story's out: the King is about to pass a law banning street-busking altogether. They don't want you lot to know about it."

"They" being the Guild, of course.

"What!" he replied—not in surprise, really, but in dismay at hearing the worst of his nightmares come to pass.

"It's true," Lerrin said miserably. "The excuse is that your type of music . . . well . . . it's supposed to cause 'congestion, street crime, pick-pocketing and fighting.' I know it's nonsense, you know it's nonsense, but . . . "

Lerrin shrugged helplessly. "We can't go against the King's will. Anyhow, I'm sorry. Thought you'd want to know before it's too late."

"I . . . thank you," Raven murmured vaguely.

Now what? The larger taverns in Rayden could only hire Guild musicians, the Free Bards had already discovered that. But there certainly weren't enough smaller taverns or houses of pleasure to support all the musicians in the kingdom! Damnation, there weren't enough venues outside of street-busking to support even all the Free Bards!

What are they going to do? What are all the poor musicians who live in Rayden possibly going to do? And if this spreads to other lands . . . ? Birnam can't support us all!

What are we all going to do?

CHAPTER THREE

HUNTING A NEST

Jaysen scuffled his nervous way along to the Free Bards' hastily called second meeting. He had an idea, a pretty good one, he thought, to help everyone out of this sudden problem of royal edicts—but that meant telling everyone the truth. Did he dare?

What if they laugh at me? Or just refuse to listen to anything I say?

Nonsense. They'd listen. If only he had the nerve to be honest. But at first, looking around at all the others gathered beside the great tent that they all used as a place to sleep and leave their belongings, Jaysen couldn't find a single thing to say.

Don't be an idiot, he told himself sharply. *Pretend it's just another role; you can play it.*

The meeting had begun around noon, and it was halfway to suppertime by the position of the sun. Raven had been asking for suggestions for some time, and not getting much in the way of useful answers. Not one of the Free Bards seemed to have any idea of what they were going to do about the royal decree: where they could go, how they could continue making a living. Jaysen listened to their back-and-forth arguments for a time, then nervously cleared his throat at the first sign of a pause.

"Jaysen?" Raven asked. "Do you have something to add?"

Was the sun all *that* hot? Or was he blushing again? "Uh . . . yes. But first I . . . well, I have to confess something." He hesitated, licking dry lips, then burst out, "I'm not a Free Bard. Not officially."

To Jaysen's utter confusion, Raven broke into laughter. "We knew that, boy," he said, not unkindly, his one good eye twinkling a little.

Jaysen gaped at him. "How . . . ?"

Raven shook his head, chidingly. "Your name, Jaysen! Did you really think all of us had been *born* with the names of birds? Did you think it all one big coincidence?"

Actually, he hadn't really thought about it. But he couldn't let that on. "Well, no, of course not."

Raven's smile showed Jaysen that the Bard was not in the least deceived. "It's simple enough," he said, with just a hint of condescension. "We Gypsies don't particularly like folks playing high and wild with our true names, so we take public-use ones instead."

"And the Free Bards have picked up the custom as well," Heron added. "Bird names fit musicians nicely, don't they?" He gave a sudden sly grin. "Besides, bird names make it harder for the Guild—*and* the Church—to keep track of all of us and who we really are!"

"We're not making fun of you, Jay, honestly," Raven continued more gently. "With a voice and a talent like yours, you have every right to claim Free Bardship. If you hadn't—well, suffice it to say that we would have dealt with you by now, and you wouldn't be sitting here among us."

Oh dear Lord, he *must* be blushing. He felt as if his cheeks, neck, and ears were on fire. "Oh. Well. Thank you. B-but that's not what I wanted to tell you. You see, I think I have a way out of this mess." Seeing them all staring at him, Jaysen took a deep breath to steady his nerves, then began, as bravely as he could manage. "I'm a born and bred native of Kingsford. I never did much travelling, not like you folk, but I did manage to make a pretty good living performing on the streets. But then the law put a stop to street-busking. It was either starve or find some other way to survive. Some way that let me use my talents. So I turned to another venue."

He had their full attention now. Coloring hotly under the weight of all those intrigued stares, Jaysen continued as best he could, keeping his voice strong and steady, and trying to persuade himself that they were all just another audience. "You've heard of the Duke of Kingsford's Company, Duke Arden's own troupe of players? Well, for the last year, I've been performing with them."

Owl raised a skeptical eyebrow. "How's the money?"

"Well, you can't put out a hat. And the . . . uh . . . salary isn't as high as I might be making in a good year of street-busking. But it is comfortable, and it's steady, you get your pay every week, regular as the sun comes up. And I think you'd find it comfortable, too."

"Whoa, Jay," Raven cut in sharply. "What are you suggesting? That we drop our way of life and turn into nice, tame, *settled* players?"

"It's not such a bad life!" he protested, feeling stung, and defending his chosen life with indignation.

Raven's eyebrows said it all. "Ha!" the Gypsy replied, mockingly.

"It isn't!" he insisted. "Duke Arden's a good, honest man. Besides," Jaysen added cajolingly, "as members of his household—well, theoretically, anyhow—you would *not* be subject to Guild rules! Members of a noble household are only subject to their liege lord, and no one else. Why, you couldn't be arrested by one of the City Constables, even if they caught you stealing something! They'd have to take you straight to the Duke for *his* justice!"

The group erupted into a dozen frenzied, murmured discussions, ignoring him except for a few speculative glances.

He didn't mind being ignored for a few moments; it gave him some time to get his blushing under control.

"This all sounds very nice," Magpie said, after a moment, "but just how would it work? No matter how determined a patron of the arts your Duke might be, he certainly can't afford to hire every non-Guild musician in the land."

Jaysen blinked. He hadn't thought of that —

But someone else came to his rescue.

"No, Duke Arden alone can't help us all," Owl mused aloud. "But there are a good number of the country gentry who are friendly to us, to all the Free Bards."

Magpie snorted her scorn. "But they can't afford to support even one good-sized company!"

But Owl's words had already sparked another idea in Jay's head. "Th-they won't have to," Jaysen cut in, stumbling over his words in his eagerness. "Maybe they can't afford supporting whole companies—but they *can* afford to lend their names and—and the protection of their rank to anyone, Free Bards, maybe, or all non-Guild musicians, who want to form their own small theater companies."

"I like it," Raven said slowly. "That means that those who don't want to be tethered to one place won't have to be. These little troupes could travel the faires or perform in cities. . . . Yes. They could make deals with innkeepers . . . use the inn courtyards for stages for a percentage of the entrance fee for holding dances, and perform inside the inns in smaller groups just like we used to."

Heron nodded enthusiastically, his hair falling right down into his eyes. "And they couldn't be shut out of performing in the faires because they'd be members of noble households. Oh, and they could make the same bargains with the holders of eating-tents and the beast-sellers we made here."

"It will work," Jaysen said as firmly as he could, looking around at them all. "Let the King make his edicts—we will still be free to make our living as we choose!"

Flushed with triumph, Jaysen felt himself grin like an idiot as the Free Bards burst into a wild cheer of relief. But Raven held up a warning hand.

"Not so fast. First we need to call a second meeting, one open not just to all the Free Bards at the Faire, but to every entertainer not allied with the Guild. They all have to have a chance to make their own decision about this. It's only fair. If we don't give every minstrel the same chances we have to make use of this notion, we'll be no better than the Guild."

Jaysen looked at him in sudden alarm. Raven was right, of course. *But I was thinking only of these Free Bards I know. I never intended to be the start of a—a whole new movement!*

Too late for any doubts now. Like it or not, Jaysen had sparked a whole new way of life.

❖   ❖   ❖

By the next night more Free Bards, minstrels, street magicians, and other entertainers than Jaysen had ever seen together were crowded into the dancing area behind the Faire. And of course, each and every one of those independent creative (or not-so-creative) souls had his or her own opinion, and was determined to express it. At last Jaysen saw Raven leap up onto the makeshift stage, arms upraised dramatically.

"Enough!" he shouted, and then again, more fiercely, *"Enough!* Do you want to attract every guard in Kingsford and all the Fairewards besides?"

The turmoil settled down to a few grudging murmurs, and Raven nodded in satisfaction. "Now, I know not everybody's happy with the proposal Jaysen here has made. Wait, hear me out! It's fine and easy to say something's not so good. But one thing we're all in agreement about is that stupid royal edict. So far Jaysen's suggestion, like it or not, has been the only practical one. Does anyone here have any other solution?" He paused dramatically. "Well? Do you?"

"You know we don't," a disgruntled voice called out from the rear.

"All right, then. Jaysen, come up here with me and tell them your plan one more time."

Sure he was scarlet with embarrassment, Jaysen scrambled up beside Raven and repeated his plan. "N-no one knows why the King has made his ruling," he continued nervously. "No one knows how the Guild—it has to have been the Guild—convinced him to make it—"

"They bought him!" someone yelled, and got a whole chorus of approving shouts. "All kings need money—and it's the Guild that has the money!"

"If you don't say something quickly," Raven murmured

in Jaysen's ear, "they're going to start arguing again."

Oh, right. Say something. Jaysen burst out, "Why he's making the edict doesn't matter! It doesn't! All that matters is that he's signing it. We don't have time to worry about how to change his mind or combat the Guild or anything like that. It's the here-and-now we have to handle and, well, creating our own companies with our own noble sponsors does seem like the best short-term solution. Think about it. But don't think too long, because unless we do something *here*, something *now*, there aren't going to be any long-term answers for us!"

Flushed with triumph, he watched the others nod and drift away into small groups, the Free Bards among them already plotting which noble "friends" they'd contact and even starting to discuss what to name their newly forming troupes. But then he saw Raven, Magpie, and Crow starting off with the rest, and called after them, "Wait!" As they turned to him in surprise, he added hastily, "I—I have to talk to you. I . . . uh . . . have a proposition for you. All three of you. A business one."

They stopped, and turned back to him, although their lack of expression was not particularly promising. "Go on," Raven said, voice expressionless. "We're listening."

Jaysen fought the nervousness that threatened to strangle the words in his throat. "Oh. Well. The Duke's Company is looking for more musicians to form a small orchestra; four would be just about right. I—I sort of think of you as friends by now after working together here and, well . . . " To his embarrassment, he could feel himself blushing all over again. "Anyhow, what I'm trying to say is that I'd prefer the positions go to friends." He glanced hopefully at the others. "It would be a good way for all of us to do all right this season."

Raven sighed, and shook his head. Clearly, he was not particularly pleased with the idea of staying here in Kingsford. But it was equally clear that he had no other prospects at the moment. "I don't know if—" he began.

"Never mind the pretty words, Jaysen," Magpie cut in. "What, exactly, are you offering us?"

"A job!" Jay said, surprised that she should even ask.

But Magpie shook her head firmly. "Not enough. Will we be provided living quarters?"

Living quarters? Why should they —

Oh, of course. Whenever they played at inns, it was always part of the deal to get meals and a place to sleep. "Uh, no. The usual thing is—"

Magpie interrupted him, her frown deepening. "What about food? Will we be expected to find our own, or is the Company going to take care of that?"

Feeling as though he'd just been engulfed in a whirlwind, Jaysen stammered out, "S-sometimes. The Company does eat together after a performance, but —"

"So we provide our own lodging and most of our food. What about costumes? Are we expected to pay for those, too?"

At last! Something he could offer! "No! The Duke's Company has a full stock of costumes."

"All in the Duke's colors, I take it? Yes?" Magpie shrugged. "Well, I've seen his colors; blue and gold should look nicely theatrical on all of us. If the pay is good enough, I suppose we can afford to cover our own room and board."

Raven shook his head in wonder at her, plainly bemused. "You've done this sort of thing before, haven't you?" he asked her. "Worked with a theater troupe, I mean?"

Magpie nodded curtly. "I was *born* in one. And pretty much ran it from the age of ten or so."

That couldn't have been an easy life for anyone, let alone for a woman who's both pretty and competent. A bit more sympathetic, he waited for her next storm of questions.

They were not long in coming; she turned back to Jaysen and started in again, a seasoned and practiced interrogator. "What, exactly, are we going to be expected to do? I assume we're to play and sing music for the plays."

Jaysen nodded. "And provide entertainment between the acts, and before and after, too."

She nodded as if she had expected as much. "What about entertaining outside the plays? Are we supposed to do that, too? Are we *allowed* to perform outside the plays?"

Thank the Lord he knew the answers to those questions; he felt on much firmer ground here. "Yes, and yes. We . . . uh . . . are also sometimes called on to fill in for actors who aren't there."

Magpie grimaced a little, as if she understood that part all too well. "Understudying, you mean. I take it the Duke pays extra for extra duties like that?"

Jaysen stared; she'd caught him off guard again. How could he know that? He'd never had a chance to fill in yet. "I—I don't know. I never—"

"S'only right," Crow muttered, startling the others, who'd pretty much forgotten he was there. "Extra work, extra pay."

"I'm sure the Duke will agree to that," Jaysen said helplessly. "Now, as for—"

"What about other matters?" Magpie cut in, and Jaysen saw the faintest flicker of alarm in the keen brown eyes. "Will we have . . . other duties to the Duke? Besides the musical ones, I mean?"

What on earth could she mean? Surely she didn't think they'd be working as servants? The Duke's servants trained for *years* for their positions, and all but the lowest were fiercely contended over. "I don't understand—"

"I do," Raven said quietly. "Jaysen, I'm sure your Duke is a man of honor, as you've said. But some of these ventures are often little more than a way for a noble to maintain a kind of private bordello. I don't sell anything more than my music, thank you, and I'm sure Magpie and Crow feel the same way."

"No!" Jaysen cried. "I mean, yes! I mean, yes, the Duke is a man of honor; yes, his theater troupe is just that, only that. No, you will *not* be expected to—to do anything at all you don't want to do." He glanced wildly at the others. "Is that all right? Any more questions?"

But Magpie grinned, as if his reaction had relieved her. "Sounds good to me, Jaysen. Now what?"

"Now," Jaysen said with an inner sigh of relief, "you audition."

"Audition!" Magpie echoed, but with incredulity. "We're fully trained Free Bards, not amateurs!"

"Of course you are," he hastened to assure her. "But . . . well . . . it *is* a new job, and so the Stage Manager does have to hear you. It's his theater, really, after all, and you can't expect him to—Not that he wouldn't know you're professionals, you understand. But he has to decide for himself if your sound is right. I mean, he's already auditioned some Guild musicians and decided they wouldn't do. But I'm sure he won't turn down any of you."

Magpie shrugged, clearly no longer worried. "I've had to audition before this. It's not a big problem. Let's get it over with and—"

"Not so fast," Raven interrupted, looking, to Jaysen,

like a horse suddenly about to bolt. "I've been doing all right as a wandering Bard so far—wandering's part of what being a Free Bard is all about!"

"Raven's right," Crow muttered. "Don't like not travelling. Living shut behind walls—isn't right."

Gypsies, Jaysen thought with just a little touch of disgust. *I offer them a position on a platter, and all they're worried about is that they won't be slogging their way across country in autumn downpours and winter blizzards.* "You're missing the point. It isn't as though you'd be prisoners. You'd be free to come and go as you want. Besides," he added in a sudden flash of inspiration, "if you join the Duke's Company, you might be able to help all the Free Bards."

Raven tensed. "How's that?"

Oh, heavens, he'd better make this sound good! Raven was taking his responsibility as the Free Bard "leader" a lot more seriously than he let on. "Well, uh, the Company is in and out of the Ducal Palace a *lot*. If you join, we might, the four of us, be able to find out just what's going on in royal circles, about the King's edict against busking, I mean. Once we know the truth, there might be some way for us to get the edict reversed."

"That's a good many 'mights,'" Raven commented, with deceptive mildness.

"Well, yes, it is," Jaysen admitted, "but nothing's certain in life."

Raven snorted. "Except platitudes."

"Please," Magpie murmured. "Give Jay a chance."

Jaysen gave her a grateful little bow. "Well? What do you say? Are you all in on this or not?"

"I'm in," Magpie said with a sharp glance at Raven and Crow. "What about you two?"

The two Gypsies hesitated so long Jaysen was sure

they were going to up and run. Then Raven let out his breath in a long sigh. "So be it," he said.

But he said it with all the enthusiasm of a man agreeing to his own execution.

Raven nursed a flagon of small beer, and stared moodily down into the water at his feet. This little spot beside the river, upstream from the bathing-place they'd carved out of the rock, was a good place to sit and think.

Damn, damn, damn, damn, *damn*! *Why* had Talaysen done this to him? Had he been on his own, Raven knew he would have just said the devil take Rayden and its fool of a king, and gone off to more appreciative realms. But he *wasn't* on his own, thank you, Talaysen, he was surrounded by all the other Free Bards—including those native to Kingsford, those who couldn't just up and leave—and he was responsible for them all!

"I'm in," Magpie had said so lightly. But she wasn't a Gypsy, and neither was Jaysen. How could they possibly have any idea of what they were getting into?

Raven shook his head with disgust. At least most of the lesser nobles the Free Bards wanted to approach were either already at the Faire or would arrive before it was over. He would go with some of those Bards, and smile, and watch and listen. And when the nobles refused to have anything to do with the whole idiotic thing, well, he wouldn't once say, "I told you so!"

But things didn't work the way Raven had expected, no, not at all. To his growing amazement and alarm, he saw almost every one of the nobles the Free Bards approached practically clap hands in delight at the thought of granting his or her name to the new Companies.

"I think it's a charming idea," said a tall, lean, foppish fellow in stylish green and gold robes; Raven knew him only as Lord Seldan. "Charming, and such a deliciously genteel way to keep one's name in front of the people without needing to do any unfashionable boasting."

"What fun to have a Company perform under your sponsorship!" crowed Baron Valden, a plump, cheerful fellow in russet velvet, his arm about his equally plump, cheerful wife. "Why, I think I'll even sponsor *two* of them, one for myself, and one for my dear spouse!"

And so it went. As a disbelieving Raven kept count, he watched every one of the Free Bards get matched up with a noble sponsor. But wasn't this interesting? Even through his growing panic at the thought of being trapped in a city, he couldn't miss noting some very interesting reactions on the part of these country nobles. Oh yes, there'd been plenty of plain, unmistakable vanity; most of them shared Lord Seldan's pleasure at having their names spread about the countryside without any damage to their aristocratic dignities.

But it's so much more than something as simple as vanity.

Most of the nobles had seemed out-and-out gleeful at the thought of getting around one of the new royal edicts, almost as though lately they'd been having some nasty surprises from their King. Could it be, Raven wondered, that there had been one too many new laws in too short a time? Laws that were affecting not just commoners but nobles as well?

Maybe this new antibusking edict isn't such an isolated bit of strangeness after all. Maybe it's a symptom of something far deeper.

"I don't care!" Raven protested under his breath, as

he left the last of his "charges" discussing their duties with their new sponsor. "I'm a Gypsy, not a nobleman! I don't *want* to get involved in politics."

It didn't look as though he was going to have much of a choice. Reluctantly, Raven returned to the Free Bard tent, and rejoined Magpie, Crow, and Jaysen, who were waiting for word on how the negotiations had gone.

"Well?" Magpie asked wryly.

Raven shrugged. "Jaysen was right, and so was Owl. It looks as if it's all going to work out."

Jaysen and Magpie exchanged an amused glance, and he suppressed the urge to growl at them.

"Why are we all standing about?" he asked instead, loudly. "We have some performing to do before the Faire comes to an end. And after that, why, we have an audition to perform."

"Quite," Magpie drawled, with undisguised mockery.

And all he could do was give her a glare he hoped she'd never forget, and turn on his heel, to lead the way back to their dancing ground.

Glad she couldn't see his flush from behind.

CHAPTER FOUR

FLEDGLINGS

Magpie had always been a worrier; she hadn't had a choice. If she didn't worry about her troupe's problems, no one else would.

Now, though, she worried as never before, and the rest of the Free Bards seemed just as determined as those long-ago players to ignore tomorrow's problems and concentrate on today. Was this Faire never going to end? Magpie performed as best she could through the endless days, played her flute with the rest of the Free Bards, but with every passing hour, she was sure the threatened royal edict was going to be enacted, and come down on all their heads before anyone could get under the shelter of Duke Arden's name.

But at last the final day of the Kingsford Midsummer Faire came to a slow, noisy end. The Free Bards gathered at their impromptu stage for one last time, shaking hands, hugging, wishing everyone well, then one by one splitting off, presumably to then go off into their new Companies. Magpie saw Raven drawn aside by Nightingale, and tensed, positive she was about to see some grand, romantic farewell scene that would end any hope of her having a chance with him.

Oh, don't be ridiculous! she scolded herself. *You don't want to have a chance with him. You saw the way he acted with all the women who came to see us perform. He'd only toy with you, just as he played at flirting with them. Huh. If flirting was all he'd done. He can't be serious with any woman, you know that. He's just like all those handsome young actors you used to know, the ones who couldn't think beyond the next meal, the next drink, the next woman, or the next performance. They didn't even have the capacity to be serious, and neither does he.*

Except, maybe, with Nightingale?

Wrapped in misery, not at all sure what she wanted to see, Magpie stood in shadow, pretending to be cleaning her flute but actually watching, hoping with all her heart no one would catch her at it.

"She's watching us," Nightingale murmured, her voice warm with sympathy and a touch of amusement.

Raven did not even bother to look; he had other things on his mind. "Magpie?" he said brusquely. "Nonsense."

"She is," Nightingale insisted, shaking back her long, dark hair. "Probably expecting something dramatic and passionate between us, the poor bewildered youngster."

"And . . . is she going to get her wish?" Raven asked, moving a little closer and only half in jest.

Nightingale chuckled deep in her throat, sending a little prickle up his spine. "Raven, Raven, we both know there never was anything between us other than a brief exchange of joy. We are too much alike, and at the same time, much too different, for there to ever be more than that. So stop giving me that stricken-lover look, and take pity on your clever, pretty flutist. I think," the woman added thoughtfully, her eyes all at once very dark and mysterious, full of Bardic power, "you will find more to her than you ever found with me."

He snorted at the very idea. "That's ridiculous. Nightingale, I—"

But she waved her hand gently, silencing his feeble protest. "Hush. Time is passing and I have my own Company waiting for me to join them."

With that, she gave him a cool, totally impersonal peck on the cheek, the kind of farewell kiss he might have gotten from a sister. Almost, Raven thought with a flash of dour humor, as though she were putting on an act of indifference for Magpie's sake.

But perhaps she had already turned all her attention to her own newly fledged Company, and had nothing to spare for him, nor for any other man.

She turned without another word and vanished into the night. Raven whirled to see Magpie studiously polishing her flute as though she hadn't another thought in her head. Just as he'd thought; she hadn't been paying the least bit of attention to them. Nightingale wasn't always infallible.

Magpie? he mused, then nearly laughed aloud. *That obstinate-minded, sharp-edged little—Not a chance, Nightingale, not a chance.*

The Faire, Magpie thought, might be over, but that hadn't made the narrow streets of Kingsford any emptier. On all sides the city's half-timbered wooden buildings of two or even three stories loomed over

them, upper stories overhanging the bottom and
topped by slate tiles or thatching. The grander struc-
tures stood proudly alone, surrounded by a token of
unused space, but most of the buildings were
crammed in together seemingly at random, some of
them sagging against each other, looking as though
they were leaning together in drunken companion-
ship. *Wonderful for thieves,* Magpie thought, *or lovers.
You could step from one building to the next without
anyone being the wiser. But oh, what do they do in case
of fire? It would spread like—well, like wildfire.*

Hopefully, she'd never need to find out. Once,
when she'd been a little girl, her mother's troupe had
passed through a burned-out town, and the sight of
those charred buildings and empty-eyed survivors had
haunted her memory for years after. Kingsford, like
many other large cities, did have fire brigades, and
wells at every corner. And the Duke should have
mages who had fire-control spells; that was his duty,
just as maintaining the roads in his duchy was his duty.

Half the housefronts opened out into shops that had
simply been tacked onto the front of the original building. Those shops took up yet more of the street, and
were certainly not helping ease the congestion.

Kingsford swarmed with folks chatting and laughing
and hunting post-Faire bargains. In fact, there was an entire area of little stalls manned by people she recognized;
obviously small merchants doing their best to dispose of
as much as they could, so as not to have to carry it away.
Magpie caught a glint of jewelry from one makeshift
stand, and a moment's yearning shot through her.

*Don't be ridiculous. Anything left over from the
Faire has to be junk. Besides, you don't have the coin to
spare for trinkets anyhow.*

Ah well. Maybe if they got the job with Duke

Arden's Company things would be different. If they got the job. Which brought up yet another problem.

"This audition is one thing," she called out to Jaysen as she wormed her way through the crowds after Raven and Crow, one hand on her flute, the other clamped on her purse, "but whether or not we get hired, we're still going to need a place to stay. Any ideas of where, Jaysen?"

"Oh, yes," he said, just a touch too readily. "There's a—a boardinghouse not too far from the theater. I . . . uh . . . I stay there myself."

Raven chuckled. "With someone?" he asked innocently, and laughed again when Jaysen reddened. "Is that the way of it, eh?"

"No! I mean not—not really. It's just—I—" He broke off with an audible sigh of relief. "Here's the theater now." He was clearly relieved that he would not have to actually answer Raven's question.

The theater was bigger than Magpie had expected, bigger than any of the makeshift Guild dancing halls, a half-timbered building fully three stories tall, almost totally filling the square in which it was set and surrounded by a neat little drainage ditch. An equally neat little bridge led across the ditch, which was half-full of what Magpie hoped was simply clean river water. The bridge led to a paved landing in front of the grand main entranceway, which was all of intricately carved oak. Over the oaken door, which was firmly shut and bolted, hung two ornamental hooks; these, Magpie guessed, would hold signboards announcing whatever play the Company was to perform that day, just as the flagpole that towered over the slate roof probably flew the Duke's flag whenever the theater was open.

The Duke, it was becoming more and more obvious, was quite serious about his Company. A great deal of money had been poured into the building of this theater. Feeling suddenly very small against all this impressive architecture, Magpie followed Jaysen and her fellow Free Bards through a small side door, only to stop short, staring in wonder. Despite her own cynicism about players and their world, a little shiver of excitement raced through her, at the remembered inimitable theater smell of dust and paint and sawdust filling her nostrils.

She stood in near darkness in the common yard, where those folk too cheap or poor to buy a seat would pay a penny for the privilege of watching the performance on their feet. She faced the stage itself, while all around her tier after tier of seats rose up nearly the entire height of the building. The rafters were so far overhead they were lost in shadow, but everywhere else was splendor—or at least the theater's brave imitation of splendor. The floral carvings on every exposed bit of wood were real enough, but the gilding was only paint, and though those mighty columns might look like the most exquisite of marble, Magpie's trained eye recognized cleverly painted wood when she saw it.

Ah well, it was a common enough deception; the theater dealt in illusion, after all. Besides, the Duke might care about his Company, but no one working backstage wasted money on the real thing when it could be saved by clever sham!

Still, false marble or no, nothing could take away the magic that was The Theater. Staring at that deep, high stage, which was empty right now of any scenery—lit by a few flickering footlights, so that it looked almost like a shrine—Magpie felt a sudden irrational lust to be up there on it, declaiming lines wonderful enough to melt a frozen soul or playing music sweet enough to move the deaf to weep.

But only for a moment. The theater, as she knew only too well, was a trollop, promising everything and delivering nothing. *Idiot,* she snapped at herself. *One moment in here and you start behaving like a stagestruck little twit!*

Impossible to tell from Raven's carefully impassive face what he was thinking: whether he was feeling impressed, or—being a Gypsy used to open spaces—simply claustrophobic. "Now what?" he asked Jaysen, his voice betraying no emotion, his expression utterly neutral. "Where's this Manager of yours?"

For answer, Jaysen pointed towards the stage. Two actors, an older man and a boy clad in unremarkable tunic and breeches—the well-worn, easy-fitting type of garb worn by most theater folk for preliminary rehearsals—were listening intently to what a third man, perched on the edge of the stage, sheaf of paper in his hands, was saying. At his impatient gesture, they bowed and exited the stage, and Jaysen whispered, "Come on. Now's our chance."

As they approached the man, who was bent over his papers, shaking his head as though the actors had let him down, Jaysen cleared his throat with a nervous "Ahem."

The man looked sharply up, eyes wide with surprise. Then he got slowly to his feet, looking the Free Bards up and down with a blatantly critical gaze. Magpie watched their prospective employer carefully, from under modestly lowered lashes. So, now . . . middle-aged, medium height, balding, running just a bit to flesh . . . clever, deep-set, melancholy dark eyes, sensitive, downturned mouth: the sort of fellow, Magpie summarized to herself, who probably looked morose even when he was enjoying himself.

"Jaysen," he acknowledged shortly. "These, I take it, are your new candidates?"

"The, uh, Free Bards I mentioned, yes. May I present—"

But the Manager waved him to silence. His glance froze on Raven.

"You! Have you ever acted?"

"Frequently," the Gypsy said drily. "Ah, you meant on a *stage!*"

"Of course on a stage!" The Manager circled him, or tried to. Raven circled with him, keeping the man away, Magpie realized, from his blind side. The Manager stopped short. "A pity you have that eye patch. You would have made a fine Ithalo, all sleek, suave villainy, or maybe even—But you do have that patch."

"Forgive me." Sarcasm dripped from the words. "I lost that eye battling Chevenchi nomads in the Plains War. Lost an eye, but sent their war chief shrieking down to his Dark Earth Gods. You think there's something shameful about that?"

Magpie had never heard of any Plains War, or any Chevenchi nomads, and judging from the Manager's face, he hadn't either. "No, of course not. I only meant that an audience does not expect to see genuine war wounds in the theater. Surely you understand."

Don't bait him, Raven, she pleaded silently. *Stories are all well and good, but you'll lose us our jobs before we even have them!*

Raven stared boldly at the Manager and looked about to retort with yet another tale, so Magpie hastily cut in:

"But those battles were all long ago, weren't they, Raven? Long before you became a Free Bard. This good man is plainly very busy. We don't want to waste his time with old tales from our past that likely wouldn't interest him."

She deftly pinched Raven's arm as she said it. The

man glared down at her, but kept silent. The Manager glanced at him, at Magpie, then said to them all, "This is Duke Arden's theater, as I'm sure you know, but *I* write most of the plays that are performed here." *And superior plays they are*, went the unspoken words. "And I see that all runs smoothly. However, while I certainly can tell a good musician from a bad one, I do *not* write music."

He stopped short, looking sternly down his nose at the Bards. "Understand, my play's the thing. Jaysen provided quiet bits of song and music—not on that lute; you could hardly hear the thing at the back of the theater—music on guitar to underscore my dramas or delicately heighten my comedies. The only reason I am adding musicians is because the Duke wishes" — *demands*, the silent message continued— "more and more complicated music to accompany the plays, and Jaysen, professional performer though he is, is no longer enough."

And oh, how you're miffed at that! Magpie realized, and hastily set out to soothe the man's ruffled feathers. "You know how it is with nobles. *Such* a silly lot, so very easily distracted. They always think that if some of a thing is good, why, *more* must be so much better! So few of them can appreciate great theater."

The Stage Manager looked a bit mollified. "Humph. Truly said."

Magpie shook her head ruefully. "And how positively spoiled they are when it comes to any type of entertainment. They want everything bigger, brighter, noisier."

"Oh, they do, indeed." The Manager's downturned mouth quirked wryly up at one corner. "Never mind that what they want is as tasteless as gaudy brass set next to silver filigree. They *will* have their fripperies and furbelows."

"Believe me," Magpie continued gently, "we do understand. I promise you we are true professionals. We will be very careful about what we play and when." She gave the man her most charming smile. "One thing we will never do is trample all over your beautifully crafted scenes, or drown your brilliant lines with jangling and hooting."

Out of the corner of her eye, Magpie saw Raven stirring impatiently, dark face full of suppressed fury; clearly he was fuming about the way she had taken over. *I know you're supposed to be in charge,* she told him silently, *but all you were doing was antagonizing the man! I know what to do.*

The Manager did seem to think she was the little group's leader. Moreover, he was almost smiling openly now, apparently much mollified by her soothing words. "Shall we perform for you now?" Magpie asked sweetly.

He bowed; he actually, courteously bowed. "If you would."

She caught Raven's glare again; it was a little alarming to see how sinister a frown made that dark, narrow face look: positively piratical—no, like the villainous Ithalo, indeed. *Never mind. Someone had to take charge, and he wasn't going to say anything useful. At least I don't think he was going to say anything useful. And he certainly seemed to be going out of his way to irritate the man.*

Ah well. Enough time to soothe roused tempers after they had won the job. "Feast your ears with the music," Magpie said formally, then raised her flute and began to play a cheerful little dance tune. After a moment the others followed suit, Raven on his fiddle—the anger smoothing out from his face as he played—Jaysen first on lute, then on the louder, more properly theatrical guitar, and Crow, mercifully restraining himself from full drumming frenzy, improvising softly on tabor.

The four of them performed a variety of pieces after that, solo and ensemble, instrumental and vocal, in every style from broad country to the most genteel of court music. Magpie covertly watched the Manager as she played, and saw, bit by bit, his foot begin to tap, his head to nod.

" 'The Traveller's Gallop,' " Raven said under his breath, "all four of us together. If it suits your ladyship?"

Magpie ignored the jibe. The Free Bards swung as one into the wild, happy, bouncy strains of the dance, weaving together line after line of complicated melody till at last the gallop slowed to a trot, a walk, and at last trailed off to a stop.

The sound of applause startled Magpie. "Wonderful," the Manager said. "Perfect. You are hired, the lot of you, here and now. Jaysen, I trust they already know the terms of employment?"

"Uh, yes. All except for wages."

"Ah yes. The Duke has authorized me to offer each of you ten pieces of silver per week. Will that be acceptable?"

Something in his voice told Magpie this was not the time or place for bargaining. Still, she couldn't really complain. Ten silver pieces per week was a nice sum, proof that the Duke took his theater music seriously. "Oh, quite, for me at least."

"Sounds good to me," Crow muttered.

Raven shrugged. "So be it."

"Splendid!" The Manager actually almost managed to look cheerful. "I must admit," he added in a conspiratorial tone, "I had already auditioned a group of Guild musicians earlier today. But I did *not* like their attitude, I did *not* like their music—dry, lifeless stuff, suitable only for putting an audience to sleep—and I most certainly did *not* care for the amount they expected to be paid."

"Never mind the amount *we* expected to be paid," Raven murmured in Magpie's ear, and she gave him a quick glare. Maybe he *could* do better in a good week of busking, but this was safe, steady, honest work, with no uncertainty about it! And there would be no days, weeks, of going home from the street with nothing more than a few pins, because wretched weather had driven everyone from the outdoors but fools and Free Bards.

The Manager was riffling through his sheaf of papers, oblivious of Raven or Magpie. "But now," he said absently, "I have work to do, a third act that needs tightening. If that's all? Yes? Welcome to the Duke of Kingsford's Company."

Clutching his papers to him, the Manager started off, then stopped, calling back over his shoulder, "One thing more. Those Guild musicians were not cooperative in any way, nor did I think they would ever be—in fact, they left me with the impression that they considered my plays to be *secondary to their music*. And a poor second at that! Can you imagine such nonsense?"

"Outrageous," Raven said blandly. Too blandly.

The Manager missed the sarcasm completely, nodding his approval. "I see you appreciate fine theater. Which those overrated fools did not! Ah well, enough of them. I will expect you here tomorrow morning so that we may begin blocking out where and how music shall fit into my new play. Till then."

He hurried off, his final words to them trailing behind him: "I am much happier with you lot, much happier! Once again, welcome to the Company!"

CHAPTER FIVE

NEST-BUILDING

From the rear, the Stage Manager looked rather like an ancient, hunched-over squirrel; very busy, very pre-occupied. As the man scurried off, Jaysen let out his breath in a slow sigh. "All right, then. Now—"

"Now," Magpie reminded him gently, "we need a place to live. And we need to find out just how much it's going to cost us."

To her surprise, he blushed. "Of—of course. Uh, follow me."

Why was he suddenly so nervous? Magpie glanced uneasily at Raven, and frowned to see the Gypsy chuckling to himself. "Raven?" she whispered. "What ails the boy?"

"Wait," he murmured back, smiling, at his most infuriatingly obtuse. "Follow Jaysen. I suspect our little mystery is about to be solved quite predictably!"

They made their way through the crowded and narrow

streets for hours—or at least, so it seemed. Magpie's feet were beginning to hurt; she was not used to walking on hard stone pavement for so long. Where, Magpie wondered, was Jaysen taking them? This was definitely not the finest part of town, though it wasn't quite bad enough to make her truly nervous. The half-timbered houses had plainly seen better days, but the paved street was reasonably clean, if in poor repair, and the folk who passed wore clothing that was worn, often-mended, and rather shabby, but still more or less respectable. Every establishment they passed seemed to be occupied either by weavers or tailors; there were plenty of dark little shops in which dark little figures sat hunched over looms or needle and thread. Magpie had just about come to the depressing conclusion that if she'd had a choice, she wouldn't have chosen to live in such a depressing, dilapidated area, when Jaysen stopped and gestured.

"Here we are," he announced, shyly.

Here? Magpie stared in dismay, thinking wildly, *Oh, surely he's made a mistake, Jaysen can't mean* this!

The two-story building might have been nice at one time, but that time had been long, long ago. Now it sagged wearily to one side, the roof tiles cracked, and in some places, missing altogether. Magpie guessed from the flecks of white dotting its half-timbered walls that they might have been whitewashed once, but that had clearly been a good many years back. The walls themselves were so worn that here and there the boards showed through from beneath the exterior plaster.

Jaysen gave the Bards a faint, apologetic smile. "I . . . uh . . . know it doesn't look like much—"

"Correct," Raven muttered, dourly. He was clearly not amused. Well, for once, Magpie was in agreement with him.

"—but, well, I—" Jaysen floundered.

"You are infatuated with the wife of the owner." Raven folded his arms over his chest, and let the eyebrow over his good eye rise significantly.

Jaysen flushed a spectacular crimson, and objected violently. "No! Madam Shenna's a widow—and I'm *not* infatuated with her."

Raven shrugged. "The daughter, then." The boy flushed more, and looked away, guiltily. "Ha," Raven pounced. "I'm right! She does have a daughter, and you *are* in a state about the girl."

"No!" Jaysen repeated helplessly. "I mean, Madam Shenna does have a daughter, but she—I—She doesn't even know I exist, and I—I—"

As Jaysen blundered to a stop, Magpie took pity on him. "Never mind. Let's see what the place looks like on the inside and find out if there's room for the lot of us."

"Watch your step going in," Raven murmured in her ear. "The doorsill's pulled up from the floor and— Damn!" He'd walked right into a sloping, sagging beam. Glaring at the thing, he added, "Be lucky if the whole building doesn't come down about our ears. Look at the way that stairway slants."

"If it's stood this long," Magpie said, "it'll stand a little longer."

"Huh." Raven snorted. "Reminds me of the old joke: it's standing only because the termites are holding hands and—Ah, my lady hostess."

Instantly charming, he swept down in a grand bow. The girl who'd come timidly down the slanting stairway froze, hand at her heart. A pretty thing, Magpie thought, if you liked them fragile as the proverbial flower. The girl's face was heart shaped, with delicate features flushing the faintest shade of pink. The tendrils of hair straggling free from her long braids were so pale a blond they were almost white. The only color to her was her wide eyes of true, clear violet: worried, timid, weary eyes. "I'm sorry," she murmured apologetically, "I didn't hear you enter, and I—Oh. Jaysen."

His gaze was the devoted stare of the spaniel. A moment more, Magpie decided cynically, and he would be licking her hand. "Linnet, I've brought your mother some new tenants. If—if that's all right?"

Linnet. The irony of a non-Bard whose true name really was avian made Magpie bite back a giggle. "You have enough vacant rooms, I trust?" she asked, thinking, *You must; who would want to stay here?*

"Oh, yes!" the girl assured her, a little too eagerly. "But I—I have to warn you, we're a bit shorthanded, with Mother so ill and—It's nothing catching," Linnet added hastily, "but it does tire her so."

"Linnet?" a querulous voice asked sharply. "What's going on down there?"

The girl paled, and called up the staircase. "Nothing, Mother! Don't worry!"

"Nonsense." A woman appeared on the stairway, moving slowly and painfully. Both Linnet and Jaysen hurried up to help her descend. As Magpie saw her more clearly, she just barely managed to stifle a gasp. Madam Shenna's daughter's fragile prettiness was painfully echoed here as the faintest ghost of beauty.

Ghost, indeed, Magpie thought uneasily, seeing how skeletally thin the woman was, her nearly colorless skin stretched taut over too-prominent bones. *Death has already set Its hand on her.*

Raven must have realized the same thing. But with a kindness Magpie would never have expected of him, he let not the slightest hint of pity show on his face. Instead, he bowed as graciously to the woman as to a fine lady, then offered her his arm. Smiling faintly, she placed a trembling hand on it, and Raven helped her to a chair. "Madam Shenna," he said as calmly as though he'd noticed nothing wrong, "my friends and I are in need of rooms."

Her gaze sharpened. "How many?"

Raven glanced back over his shoulder. "Jaysen, I take it, already has his own room. Two, then, one for Crow and myself and one for our pretty Magpie."

Itching to take part in the bargaining that commenced, Magpie forced herself to keep silent. Let Raven have a chance to at last take charge!

He settled on a sum she thought was excessive for the condition the place was in, but she kept silent, suspecting he might have let the pity he would not show rule his decision. *I could have gotten us a better deal*, she thought, as she climbed the sagging staircase to her room. *Still, at least we'll have a roof over our heads, and a bed. When was the last time I slept in a real bed?*

But then she opened the door to the small, dismal room she'd been given, and stopped short. Its floor looked as though it had not been swept in over a year, the linens on the rickety cot had been left unaired for far too long, and a nasty draft slipped through cracks in the wall and down the tiny fireplace that probably hadn't been lit since the owner had fallen ill.

Magpie stood frozen in the doorway, thinking wildly, *No wonder there aren't any other boarders*, then turned to leave so quickly she crashed full into Raven. For one brief, startling moment they were in each other's arms, Magpie very much aware of Raven's sinewy strength —

Then they both backed off in mutual embarrassment.

"Your room's as bad as ours, eh?" Raven asked.

She nodded, frowning. "Drafty, smelly, dank—I can

hardly wait to see what dinner will be like." Her voice was sharper than she had intended—but she was not looking forward to spending a single night in this place, much less weeks or months!

Raven simply sounded resigned. "Worse than the rooms, I would think. The poor woman can hardly stand, let alone take charge of things, and Jaysen's little light-of-love plainly isn't up to running the whole place by herself."

"I doubt she knows much about cooking. And they can't afford to hire any servants." Magpie sighed. "Well, let's see just how bad dinner can get."

The answer, she thought wryly a short time later was—very. Magpie managed to choke down a mouthful of stale bread and lukewarm, watery soup, then set down her cheap tin spoon with a tiny clash.

"This," she said, "is ridiculous." As the others looked at her in surprise, and Madame Shenna and her daughter in alarm, Magpie added impatiently, "I cannot live like this, I don't think any of us can. And what's more, I don't think any of us need to!"

"Magpie," Jaysen murmured, his eyes wide with apprehension. "I don't—"

"Now, what we have to do here," she continued, ignoring him, "is set some sort of a deal." She'd been working on the details from the moment she'd sat down to . . . well, it could hardly be called dinner. "Madam Shenna," Magpie told the woman, "if you are willing to give free room and board—" At the word "free," their landlady started to protest, but Magpie had no trouble in keeping her from interrupting; she was either too submissive or too polite to do so. "Wait," she said, holding up a hand, and the woman subsided. "Please, hear me out. If you will give free room and board to anyone who will do a certain amount of work here, I think we can turn things around. Jaysen, Crow, what do you say?"

"To what?" Jaysen asked in confusion.

She smiled at him, persuasively. "If you'll hurry back to our old camp at the Faire before everyone leaves, I'm sure you'll find us a good number of volunteers to help here. I mean, not everyone can have taken up with the newly formed Companies. And there are certainly going to be some Companies that seem a bit oversized. Tell them we have a job here that will combine domestic work with some entertaining, and see what they say."

"It'll never work," Raven said flatly.

She frowned at him. "Oh, you're just annoyed because it's not your idea."

"I'm not—" he protested.

"You are." Smiling sweetly at the fuming Gypsy, Magpie waved at Jaysen and Crow; they left their seats and she settled back in her chair to wait. She looked confident, but what she was really thinking was: *If this doesn't work, oh my, am I going to look foolish!*

To Magpie's immense relief, she wasn't left dangling like the fool in "Armand's Revenge." In less time than she would have thought possible, the sorry old boardinghouse was full of lively people, all of them full of suggestions on how to fix the inn up.

Owl was first to arrive, his gray hair and solid figure looking amazingly reassuring. He appeared in the door to the dining room with a smile for all of them, and a bow for Madame Shenna. "Jaysen told me something of what was going on here, and I—Ah." He entered the dining room and surveyed the sad remains of dinner. Taking one sniff of the by now totally inedible soup, he shook his head and said, "That's it. My role in this menagerie will be to cook."

That won him the first genuine smile Raven had given for hours. "I've tasted your cooking. Feel free to take charge of the kitchen, my friend! Ah, and is that little Sparrow with you?"

The boy, Owl's grandson, peered around the man and grinned. "Grandpa said I could run errands."

"And wash dishes," Owl reminded him. "And do some light cleaning, too."

"Well, yes," Sparrow admitted less enthusiastically. "That, too."

"They're both Kingsford natives," Raven whispered to Magpie. "Guess not too many Companies needed a comic singer. Owl's probably glad to have work."

As the older man moved to Madame Shenna's side and began a low-voiced discussion with her, another set of recruits arrived.

"Brought some more folks," Crow said from the doorway, in his usual mumble. "This is Nightjar."

Behind him, a sturdy, black-haired woman nodded, her mahogany-dark skin glinting in the lamplight. "Nightjar I am, horn and hautboy player—and washer of laundry when need be. And these two delicate maidens are all set to do some heavy cleaning."

The "delicate" maidens behind *her* were both fair-skinned blondes, tall and powerfully built, though definitely female—and absolutely alike, from the coils of wheat-gold hair on their handsome heads to the red leather shoes on their feet. "We're Finch and Verdin," they said as one, then added with infectious grins, "Our parents named us Isa and Lisa."

"Too terribly sweet, isn't it?" said one, as Magpie grimaced.

"You can see why we'd rather have bird names!" said

the other. "We're both violists, but sure, we'll help out with the heavy cleaning." Finch—or was it Verdin?—chucked the embarrassed Sparrow under the chin and added, "Can't expect this handsome fellow to do all the work!"

Madam Shena tensed, her face creased with worry lines. "I can't have this," she objected feebly. "You're giving me more free boarders than paying."

"Don't you see?" Magpie leaned over the table and put on her most persuasive manner. "Now you can augment the income of the house by serving nice hot lunches and suppers—Owl will, of course, share in the profits of that," Magpie added with a quick glance over her shoulder at the startled man. "Ha, yes, and we can also operate a laundry service, right, Nightjar?"

Nightjar shrugged. "Uh, sure. I suppose. Might as well."

"Naturally you'll share in the profits there, Nightjar." Mind racing, Magpie continued, looking around at all of them. "Yes, and all we Free Bards will take turns entertaining at the suppers. For a small extra fee, of course. Which will bring in more people, Madam Shenna, and more money with them. You see? It's all very simple."

Overwhelmed, Madam Shenna weakly agreed. Magpie glanced at Linnet, but the girl was staring open-mouthed at her, too astonished to object. "It's settled, then," Magpie said in satisfaction.

"Oh, indeed." Raven's voice was so falsely sweet it could have, as the saying went, drawn flies. "Will you come with me a moment, Magpie. There's something we need to discuss." His hand clamped down on her arm, and he pulled her to her feet by main force. "Now."

"Raven, wait," Magpie gasped as he virtually dragged her up the stairs. "What are you—"

"Did you want us to have this out in front of everyone else?" he hissed, coming to a stop on the narrow second-floor landing.

She was completely bewildered. What *was* his problem? "Have *what* out?"

He all but snarled at her. "What the hell do you think you've been doing?"

"*What?*" she spluttered, taken even more by surprise at his vehemence.

"Don't give me that innocent look!" he replied fiercely. "You've been running right over the top of those people down there, taking over their lives as if you had a right to them!"

"That's ridiculous!" Magpie shot back. "I did no such thing! What did you want me to do, languish in a corner like that fragile little Linnet? Nobody down there was even trying to take charge of things, and *someone* certainly had to! Or did you *want* to go on sleeping in rooms that won't keep out the winter snows, in beds that a vagrant would disdain, eating food a beggar would pass by?"

"Oh, and is that what you were doing back in the theater?" he asked sarcastically, without answering her question. "Taking charge because we were all fragile little idiots? You didn't even give anyone else a chance to talk!"

"The devil I didn't!" she retorted, her own anger flaring. "You started off on some ridiculous tale of—of some kind of heroic battle with Chevengi or Chegeni or whatever those nomads were supposed to be—"

"Chevenchi." Raven bit each syllable off sharply.

"I don't care what they were! It was *obviously* a tall tale! There was no *reason* to have made it up, except that you were trying to prove how much better a man you were than the fellow we were trying to impress with how competent and *cooperative* we were! Going on the way you were, challenging the Manager with every word—I *had* to stop you before you talked us right out of a job!"

He stared at her for a moment, then spat, "That's the stupidest—"

"No, it's not," she cried, interrupting him, "And you know it! Just because the Manager insulted your pride —"

He looked as if he would like very much to strangle her. "Nonsense! I would never have endangered our chances of—"

"The group needed a leader!" Magpie cut in acidly. "What did you give them? A *storyteller*! And not a very convincing one, either! You know the saying, dammit, 'Lead, follow, or get the hell out of the way!' *Someone* had to be the authority back there, or the Manager would have been facing a—a pack of vagabonds, no better than the Bardic Guild says we are! He *never* would have hired us! Ha, no, he would have thrown us out on our collective ear! *You* didn't want the job, but the rest of us did, so *I* became the leader by default! If you don't like what I did, you can go find yourself another job! I'm sure that there are places in Kingsford just *begging* to employ you!"

Since there obviously was no reply to that, other than walking out and proving that she was right, Raven could only stand there and fume. "Well, I suppose that makes the rest of us a real herd of sheep," Raven snapped, "since you're acting like a pushy old nanny! A nanny butting in at every opportunity, whether or not she's wanted!"

Before the astonished Magpie could come up with a response, Raven shot into his room and slammed the door on her. For a moment she stood frozen in shock, feeling the hot blood surging into her face, then turned sharply away, fiercely blinking back tears.

Damn you, Raven, I wasn't acting like that, I wasn't! Just because you had your overweening male pride damaged—If only you'd acted like a leader when you were supposed to, none of this would have happened!

Magpie stormed into her own room and, just as Raven had done, slammed the door behind her. But the crash did nothing at all to relieve her feelings.

Raven, pacing fiercely back and forth in the small confines of his room, heard Magpie's door crash shut, and grimaced. Damn the woman! What right had she to be so officious! So stubborn and frustrating and—and—*So pretty,* whispered his mind, unbidden, *in the middle of the argument you had that sudden ridiculous urge to kiss her—*

Dammit! He shouldn't let a—a *woman* upset him like this.

Raven stopped short in the midst of his pacing, forcing himself to take deep, slow breaths, fists clenched, willing himself to be calm, calm. . . .

Be calm, dammit!

All right. He'd take this mess step by logical step. Magpie might be maddening as hell sometimes, but all in all, he had to admit she was quite an admirable person. And there was her background to consider. He knew something about it by now; that childhood, what with all the adult burdens descending on her head without rest, had been rough enough to have broken anyone not as strong as she.

Raven let out his breath in a gusty sigh, all at once feeling oddly guilty. Since Magpie had been forced to fend for herself right from childhood, never knowing if she'd have enough to eat or a safe place in which to sleep, how could she possibly assume that someone else would come and take charge of anything?

Whether she wanted it or not, she'd had to be in control all her life!

Besides . . . With a rueful grin, Raven admitted that it hurt his pride to confess this, even to himself, but she really had done a good job of taking care of what could have been a bad situation with the Manager—a better job than he could have managed himself. Raven's grin twisted with sudden sly humor. Chevenchi nomads, indeed! There were such creatures, yes, but not outside obscure myths. He never would have thought to claim kills against such bizarre creatures, not normally. But when the Manager had given him such a scornful look, condemning him and his appearance without a word, he'd had to say *something* to defend himself.

Ah well. It really *was* a fortunate thing Magpie had been there to set things right. Yes, and she'd done an amazing job of handling their lodging problem, too, with this ridiculous excuse for a boardinghouse.

To say nothing of indirectly giving Linnet a bit more time to herself, Raven thought with a chuckle. Although that had probably not been in Magpie's mind. Maybe now the silly little chit would notice poor, besmitten Jaysen!

"Assuming," he muttered with a sudden returning flare of temper, "Magpie doesn't meddle in that as well!"

Enough of that. First things first: business.

The Bard settled warily on the room's one, rickety chair, considering. When it came to music, he had no false modesty; Raven knew he was good, and knew as well that he was a better arranger and composer than any of the other three.

Particularly Crow. Ha, yes, like many another drummer, Crow just sat in the back and provided the rhythm, being perfectly pleased to stay as faceless as— as one of his drums. Raven shook his head. What drove the man? He hardly ever spoke, and almost never ventured any sort of an opinion.

It's the drumming, Raven decided wryly. *It's pounded all the sense right out of his head. Keeps him in perpetual trance.*

But Crow and his abilities were not the point here. Tomorrow, Raven decided, he was going to have to establish himself as the artistic leader of their little group. But what to do about their pretty, stubborn Magpie? Thinking it over, the Bard considered that things might not be so bad at that, even with Magpie as gadfly. He freely admitted, if only to himself, that the last thing he wanted was the chains of running a business. Or, for that matter, that he had the faintest idea of how such a thing was done! Magpie clearly did—and seemed to enjoy the challenge.

I salute you, my dear. That frees me from having to worry about money and lets me concentrate on what's really important: making music!

Grinning anew, Raven got out his fiddle and set about his daily practice. And if Magpie could hear him through the thin walls—Ha, yes, there were the sweet tones of her flute now, playing a tune that sounded teasingly familiar. . . .

Raven choked, nearly dropping his bow as he suddenly recognized it.

What Magpie was playing so sweetly, so daintily, and with every indication she knew what she was playing—and that he could hear her—was the melody to a very filthy drinking song!

"Point taken, my dear," he chuckled. "Point taken."

And just to prove it—and to prove that he *could* cooperate on the important things—he joined her on the chorus.

Take that, my dear! he thought as her flute faltered for a moment. *And let's just see what you make of it!*

CHAPTER SIX

HATCHING PLOTS

Raven figured that Magpie had good reason to feel smugly pleased with herself when the morning finally came. The Free Bards straggled down to a breakfast that Jaysen, beaming like a skinny sun, declared the finest he'd ever eaten— "the finest at this place, anyhow."

"I bet he managed to get Linnet alone for a bit," Raven murmured in Magpie's ear as they left the table, and saw a quick smile flash across her face, interrupting her determined coolness. "I heard your music last night," he added, and felt her flinch. "I deserved it."

She turned in surprise to stare at him. "I never thought I'd hear that from you."

He shrugged. "One thing we need to settle here and now, so we don't have to spend all our energy yelling at each other, is who is responsible for what. You, my dear, have the business expertise I admit I lack. So," he added, tapping her on the shoulders with a breadstick swiped from breakfast, "I hereby declare you official Business Manager."

As she gave a startled little giggle, Raven added softly, "But I shall be our Artistic Manager."

She lost her smile. "But—"

He had the upper hand now, and he did not intend to relinquish it. "Ah, here come the others," he said, before she could manage anything more. "Come, Magpie, everyone," he called. "We're off for the theater."

Early though the morning still was, the Manager was already seated on the edge of the stage, bent over the inevitable sheaf of papers, making corrections to what could only be the manuscript of a play. He got to his feet at Raven's tactful cough, his eyes still bright with the fervor of the truly creative soul.

"You are early risers, I see. Good." Hurrying towards them, he added, "Most theater folk seem to be slovenly late-to-bed, late-to-rise types."

"Paragons of virtue, that's us," Raven said under his breath, and to his utter delight heard Magpie top him with, "Assume a virtue if you have it not!"

But then he saw the Manager approaching Magpie, and Magpie only, as though the rest of them didn't exist, and Raven forgot about humor. He shot forward, shouldering Magpie aside to tell the startled Manager, schooling his face to the most scholarly of expressions, "Before we can properly orchestrate or set our music to your play, I really must see the text of the play itself."

At Magpie's look of blank surprise, he allowed just a tiny bit of smugness of his own to show. *What's the matter, Magpie? Didn't think a Gypsy could be literate?* he thought, as she blinked with confusion.

He bowed to the Stage Manager. "If you will be so kind to bring out a complete copy of the play," he added to the Manager, "we can go over it together. I think that would be the most efficient way of dealing with this, don't you? Then you can point out to me the types of music you want and precisely where in each act you wish them placed. *Precisely,* and indicate the volume as well, so that the music forms an appropriate frame for your play and your actors."

The Manager gave him a pleased smile. "I happen to be holding the complete text right here. We have, after all, already begun blocking out how each act will be performed, so you have come at exactly the right moment. Come, sit with me, up here where we won't be disturbed."

They sat in the first row of noble seats, the play spread out between them. Out of the corner of his eye, Raven saw Magpie looking both astonished and a little offended, but he resolutely ignored her, giving all his attention over to the play.

"*A Twice-Told Tale,*" he read. "Nice title; alliterative."

"Thank you," the Manager said drily.

"Mm . . . " Raven ran his gaze down the cast of characters, stopping at, "'Florian, a page' to be played by the same actress portraying the heroine, Flora." He raised an eyebrow.

"It is a breeches role, yes." The Stage Manager waited, and Raven sensed he was being tested.

"Oh, I know all about those," Raven teased. "A woman playing a boy: it's a wonderful chance for some nicely built actress to wear skintight breeches and show off her figure."

"Regina Shevron," the Manager replied, a touch severely, looking sternly down his nose at the Bard, "is not merely a pretty figure. I assure you, she is quite an accomplished actress in either tragedy or comedy."

"Ah." *Of course.* Interesting that the Manager was so adamant about his leading lady's *real* talents. "And this play, I take it, is a comedy?"

"Indeed it is. But *not* a farce. I do not write farces." Now the Manager stared at him challengingly.

"Thank you!" Raven exclaimed with genuine fervor. "Not much cleverness in farces, just drop your pants or slip on a piece of fruit, and everyone has hysterics. No good place for true music, either," he added sourly. "Unless you can use whatever instrument you play to make funny sounds, neither the director nor the audience is interested in you."

"Speaking from personal experience, are you?" One of the Stage Manager's eyebrows crept halfway up to what was left of his hairline. "Must have been a frustrating affair."

And the less said about it, the better. "Very."

Shaking his head, the Bard turned his attention back to the text of the play. And little by little he forgot everything else but that play. *A Twice-Told Tale* concerned the adventures and misadventures of Flora, a clever young woman whose noble family had become impoverished due to her father's improvidence and untimely death. Raven followed her through arguments with her brother, whom she loved, and who was anguished over not being able to put together a dowry for her.

Good place for some simple, gently plaintive music here, my fiddle, maybe, or Magpie's flute alone . . . yes, that would subtly underscore the sadness. Beautiful writing there, not heavy-handed pathos, just quiet unhappiness. Now, all we need is a complication . . . ah, here he is.

"He" was Sir Verrick, a lewd, obnoxious fellow slob-
bering over poor Flora, promising to help her brother
out of his financial difficulties if she "helped him ease a
certain constant itch."

*Right. And of course our heroine is too smart to
believe his lies. I can guess what's coming next ... ah,
yes, Flora runs away as a boy. The breeches role.*

But how nicely the Manager was handling the familiar situation, giving Flora just enough humor and a
sense of the ridiculous to keep the whole thing actually
believable.

*More bouncy music here, strings and tabor, maybe,
to portray her travels.*

Now Flora was finding herself a job as Florian, page
in a young Baron's household. Here, of course, she
promptly fell in love with the admittedly agreeable—if
not, Raven thought, exactly clever—young man.

*Good spot for some elegant court music, maybe
work in something ever so carefully mocking the Guild
Bard's dust-dry stuff. Mm, yes, I like that. Let's see
now, where are we ... ah.*

The Baron's family were after him to marry. He,
though willing to hold a bride-hunting ball, took up quite
a few lines insisting he wanted to wed only for love.

*Can't fault him there. Wonder if the actor playing
him can sing? Be a good touch to give him a plaintive
little song. Nice job by the Manager, doesn't make the
Baron the wet weakling he could be ... I bet our
romantic young Jaysen understudies the role.*

No, never mind the song. The Manager had given
the Baron a good soliloquy instead, in which he
bemoaned to his page that he couldn't find a woman
"more like you, Florian, with as much wit as hair" —
Nice line, that— "and cleverness as bright as her eyes
and pearly teeth."

Maybe we can work in a song somewhere towards the end of that, but not if it's going to come as an anti-climax to those wonderful lines. Well now, look who's here: our nasty, lecherous Sir Verrick.

He'd followed Flora up to the Baron's manor, but wasn't quite clever enough to figure out that Florian and Flora were one and the same. Yet. Between her seemingly hopeless love for the Baron and her fear of having her disguise pierced by Sir Verrick, poor Flora/Florian was at her wit's end. But, being the clever character she'd been written to be, she had her own little soliloquy deciding to ignore Sir Verrick long enough to see if the Baron really was telling the truth. Raven grinned at the intricately written passages in which Flora traded on all the favors she'd acquired during her stay as Florian to get herself a gown without once revealing her true gender.

Oh my, I know this story, I do. But how cleverly the Manager is handling it!

He read on, following Flora, now disguised as a foreign lady wearing an elegant feathered mask, as she slipped into the ball.

Now, here's where we put on a fine show: grand ballroom scene, lots of different types of dancing, maybe even a solo for Flora. Assuming this Regina Shevron can actually dance . . . if not, well, we'll work out something for her, surround her with extras who can dance, make her look good . . . yes. Now, let's see . . . no one's going to recognize Flora, naturally, not the Baron, not Sir Verrick.

The Baron, of course, could only fall madly in love with the disguised Flora, even though he had no idea who this masked stranger might be.

And of course she escapes just before the unmasking. Leaving half of her mask on the Baron's throne: nice touch, that. A good place for nice, skittery escape music, very light. Now, if the Manager holds true to the story . . . ah, yes.

Sure enough, the next scene revealed Flora discovering the next morning that the Baron was sincere. The Manager had him issue a firm decree: He will marry only the woman in the mask and promised a small fortune to anyone who could bring him the other half of the mask.

Determined fanfare here to underscore the proclamation. And how is everything resolved?

Sir Verrick, Raven read, was determined to find the missing lady for himself, leering nastily all over the place. Flora, as Florian, played a risky, delicious cat-and-mouse game with him. Just as he was on the verge of realizing who she really was—and, the Manager delicately implied, having his wicked way with her—Flora eluded him, stuffing him in a closet just as the Baron, hearing all the noise, hurried in. Flora-as-Florian boldly claimed the fortune for herself with a pretty little speech full of double meaning, then took the Baron to meet Flora—who was, of course, herself. The play ended, Raven saw with some pleasure, with Sir Verrick sulking off in disgrace while Flora and her Baron celebrated with a splendid wedding and another ball.

Perfect. More full-blown, happy music, here, and a grand finale—

"This is *good*!" Raven exclaimed without thinking. "Really, really good!"

The Manager snorted. "Did you expect anything less?"

Raven heard the pleasure in his tone at the spontaneous praise, though, and replied with a grin. "Ah, no, I didn't mean that the way it sounded. It's just—well—

it's charming and romantic and genuinely funny, the sort of thing audiences love: a familiar tale told in a beautiful new style." He smiled. "If I wasn't actually working on the music for it, I think I'd want to pay money to see it myself."

The Manager beamed at him, then. "The highest compliment, coming as it does from a professional. But I saw from your face that you were plotting where to place music, and what type of music it should be. Come, let's go over the play together, pen in hand, and make the proper notations."

It was only when he rose, annotated copy of the play in hand, that Raven realized Magpie had drifted down to the foot of the stage to join Jaysen and Crow. He hurried down there to join them.

"All right, I have the rough outlines of what we're going to perform. Now, we start with the entrance music, like this . . ."

As he filled them in on what he and the Manager had decided, Raven could hardly avoid seeing that Magpie was fuming over not having been at all consulted about it, though she kept her mouth shut.

But I can guess I'm going to get an earful later. That's the way it goes.

They settled into their places below the stage, waiting for the rehearsal to begin; Jaysen looked pleased and not at all nervous, Crow looked rather bored, truth to tell. Only Magpie seemed edgy. But then, she hadn't been in charge of *this* aspect of the job. Raven suspected she would look a lot more confident if she had been.

By now the actors were drifting in by ones and twos, most of them as plainly dressed as the first two actors the Bards had seen, some of them wide awake, others looking as though they really didn't want the day to start before mid-afternoon. A few strolled up onto stage and began doing stretching exercises; one young woman did a lithe, casual backbend that made Raven stare but which was ignored by the other actors. A mixed lot, these. There was the inevitable group of eager young things, all bright-eyed and carefully artfully clad, barely old enough to be called men and women, the sort for whom The Theater Was All. A motley group of locals of all ages and sizes stood idly about; these were the extras, good enough to carry props or serve as non-speaking characters to fill out a scene. Mixed among them wandered a few aging professionals, men and women with a weary theatricality about them, folks who probably had been acting for longer than Raven or any of the other Free Bards had been alive.

One skinny, pimply-faced young man had Raven puzzled; he didn't look or sound like an actor. Indeed, he didn't seem to have much of a personality at all.

Maybe he lives only in his roles? I've seen actors like that, all emptiness until they're given a part to play.

But then Raven blinked, and blinked again. Mist seemed to be swirling out from the young man's hands—Ah, of course! He was a very low-grade mage, the sort who could manage a few small illusions. Risky to try any sort of serious magic, what with the Church ready to jump at any practitioners of the like—any non-Church practitioners, that was.

Last to arrive in the Company was the leading lady herself, appearing amid a swirl of extras.

"She's always late," someone murmured.

"Can you blame her?" someone else answered. "Can't be easy, trying to serve two masters."

"Good point. The Duke's not a jealous man, they say, but he would hardly want his own theater to take first place in her attentions, now, would he?"

"So-o," Raven murmured. "This has to be Regina Shevron herself. And it would seem she plays another role than merely actress."

"Duke Arden's mistress," Magpie breathed. "That has to be it. Ha, I bet he created the Company and this theater just for her."

Wonderful, Raven thought cynically. *Just what we needed: a theatrical want-to-be who probably doesn't have a scrap of talent to her—but who has a powerful protector to see she gets whatever she wants.* But that did leave him a bit puzzled; why had the Stage Manager been so vehement about the lady's talent and ability if she was just using the Company as a kind of expensive toy? He would have had nothing to lose by telling the truth, and a lot to gain; by taking care with the music as well as the staging, a great deal could be done to make up for a lack of talent.

And why give her all those wonderful lines if she can't be worthy of them?

As she moved towards the stage, a stray beam of sunlight caught her, and Raven drew his breath in sharply, staring openly. Regina Shevron was hardly the sort to be called conventionally beautiful, but she was so wondrously striking he felt suddenly reduced to a gawking boy. Her glossy black hair was coiled up in braids crowning her face with its sharp, high cheekbones and dark, slightly slanted eyes. Her skin was a dusky rose, her mouth was full and sensual, and she moved with a lithe, casual grace that sent little shivers through him. Her simple gown was deep red, and Raven thought, in befuddled and wild confusion, *Yes, you should always wear red.*

"Forgive me for being late," she murmured, her voice a clear, dark alto, and a new shiver raced through Raven, this time of pure musical appreciation.

Her voice is so clean. Let her not sing like a crow!

The others were muttering various "it doesn't matters." The Manager clapped his hands sharply. "Enough lolling about. We have work to do! We've already run through Acts I and II, and blocked out Act III. But now, as you see, we have a new troupe of musicians with us. Obviously they haven't had time to work out every detail of the music that shall accompany our play, but we shall try to let them sketch in that music as we rehearse. If that is agreeable with you?" he asked Raven.

He managed to nod, and he hoped he did not look as stunned as he felt. "Oh, quite."

If he did, the Stage Manager was kind, and ignored it. Then again, perhaps he was used to the effect his leading lady had on males. "Fine. Then let us start with Act I, Scene 2. Places, everyone."

As the actors moved through their roles, gradually slipping more and more completely into their characters, Raven found himself watching only Regina. Well now, look at that. She *could* act, and nicely, too: her Flora was a living, breathing creation, full of purely human hopes and doubts and convictions, all of them expressed not through melodrama but so subtly Raven knew the average audience would say silly things like, "She makes it look easy."

The Manager clapped his hands sharply. "Thoran! What do you think you're doing? You're blocking Flora's entrance again!"

The young man, dressed as one of Flora's servants, hung his head. "I'm sorry. I—"

The Stage Manager's ears were pink with indignation. "You *should* be sorry! We've rehearsed this scene a dozen times and—Yes, Regina, what is it?"

She had her hand up, for all the world like a schoolgirl hoping for the teacher's attention. "I'm wondering," she said diffidently, "what would happen if Thoran said his lines from over here, stage right. Then it would look as if he'd rushed in from Flora's brother—and he wouldn't be blocking my entrance."

"Not a bad idea," the Manager mused. "Yes. We shall try it that way. Places, everyone!"

That was genuine respect for the Manager in her voice, Raven realized. *And genuine concern for that poor, flustered actor, too. She didn't argue when the Manager decided to cut two of her lines in the last scene, either: a professional, by all the Powers, a true professional.*

The Manager plainly didn't believe in pampering his cast. He worked them through scene after scene, but even though they grumbled, Regina among them, they obeyed. At last the Manager clapped his hands and announced, "We shall try something new. Third Act, everyone, Scene 3, Florian's ribbon dance."

They hadn't put on full costume for this rehearsal, not at this rudimentary stage, only rough approximations to let them keep in mind the proper feel of moving in character. That meant Regina appeared as Florian. And oh my, Raven thought appreciatively, she did look splendid in breeches! Only a blind man would believe she was a boy. But . . . her body language was a beautiful thing, a perfect study of a boy's mix of arrogance and insecurity; despite her undisguisable femininity, Raven found himself accepting the transformation of Flora to Florian.

"You, musicians," the Manager said imperiously. "Let us have some music for Florian's dance. Nothing finished, of course; you haven't had time for that. But we need a nice, bouncy jig here."

"So be it," Raven said. After a brief consultation with the others, they sprang into "The Shepherd's Joy," improvising a bit till they'd found the proper mix of fiddle, guitar, flute, and tabor.

"I like that," the Manager exclaimed. "We shall use it as is; if the audience recognizes the tune, it will add another element of reality to the scene onstage. Florian, take your measure. And one . . . two . . . three . . . now."

Well now, the woman really could dance! They might be taking the tempo just a little too quickly, but she kept right up with them, feet skipping lightly, hands mimicking the motion of the ribbons she would be waving during a performance. But the tempo really was too fast; Regina missed a step and collided with one of the actresses, a slight wisp of a brown-clad woman, sending them both crashing to the stage.

"Oh, Sella, I'm sorry!" Regina gasped as she got to her feet, struggling for breath. "Are . . . are you all right?"

"Sure," Sella said with a grin, brushing off her gown. "You?"

"Winded, that's all. Sir Manager—"

"Yes, yes. Take a rest. All of you. Come back in a turn of the hourglass."

One by one, the actors drifted out. "I'm for a drink," Jaysen said suddenly. "Who's with me?"

"No alcohol," Raven warned. "Not while we're working."

Jaysen blinked, as if he hadn't expected that admonition, particularly not from Raven. "Ah, right. There's an inn right outside that serves chilled fruit juice. Anyone else?"

"Not me," Raven said, studying his bow. "Have to make a few adjustments here. These strings need to be retired." The horsehair was so frayed it looked as if he was waving a plume when he played.

They sauntered off, leaving him alone in the heavy silence of the theater. Perching on the edge of the stage, he set about restringing his bow.

"Excuse me," a throaty voice said from the stage behind him.

Raven nearly dropped the bow. Twisting about to look over his shoulder, he managed a credibly steady, "My lady."

"Not 'my lady.' Just Regina." Still in her boy's breeches, Regina slipped down on the stage to sit beside him. "I enjoyed your group's playing. A nice mix of instruments, not too gaudy, not too soft."

He nodded his thanks.

"I liked that jig, too. But . . . " She gave him an apologetic little smile. "Can you possibly take the tempo just a *touch* slower? I mean, I like Sella, but not so much that I want to keep landing on her!"

Raven, struggling for decorum, lost the battle, erupting into laughter. "I think we can manage a slower tempo, yes. For—for poor Sella's sake, of course."

"Of course." She smiled, and even chuckled a little. "Raven . . . it *is* Raven?"

"Yes, indeed." He cocked his head to one side. "A Free Bard and a Gypsy, as you have probably already guessed. We tend to keep simple names."

She looked him directly in the eye, challenging him to tell her the truth. "What do you think of me?"

Staring at this exquisite creature, her face still flushed from exertion, her figure so clearly outlined by those breeches, Raven suddenly couldn't seem to catch his breath. "I b-beg your pardon? I—uh—I—don't know what to say."

Regina grinned—not the expected smile of the temptress, the siren claiming another victim, but a wide flash of white teeth, the gamine grin of a street urchin. "I'm no more a fine lady than you are a lord, Gypsy Raven." The delicious grin faded, bit by bit. "I grew up on the streets," she said softly. "I won't go into that; I'm sure you can understand what that was like. But one day I saw a troupe of wandering players and knew then and there that I'd found my way off the streets. I wormed my way into a company of actors— and it was there, a few years later, that Duke Arden saw me, and made me his mistress." She said that without awkwardness or gloating, reciting it simply as fact. "I'm sure you've already figured out that he created this Company for me."

How could he not, after all? The thing was, the jewel was certainly worthy of the setting, and not as he'd thought, a bit of flashy paste set into pure gold. "Uh, yes."

"Life is good for me right now. But I haven't forgotten where I came from—and that I might well go back there when the Duke tires of me. So," she continued quietly, gaze steady, "I have made it my business to see that the Company entertains the Duke and continues to entertain him. I have done my best to gather good actors and a good playwright, and now, good musicians as well. My friend Solan—the Stage Manager—and I have a deep and abiding respect and understanding for that mutual goal."

"Ah." Enlightenment came swiftly. "You were listening when the Manager auditioned us."

"Of course." Regina sighed softly. "I've had to ensure the Company works well, as I say. So when the Duke tires of me . . . " Her voice faltered ever so slightly, and Raven realized with a little pang of almost jealousy that she loved Duke Arden, truly loved him.

Ah, poor woman . . . she knows it will and must happen, knows that nobles tire of their toys. And she will, because she loves him, make no trouble for him when he no longer wants her.

"When he tires of me," Regina repeated more firmly, "I will be able to slip gracefully back into my role as actress and simple member of the Duke's household. The stage makeup and wigs," she added dryly, "cover the signs of aging very nicely. I shall be able to continue in my next career for as long as I care to act."

For once, he was completely at a loss for words. "Regina . . ."

But she shook her head with determination. "Don't pity me. We both survive by our wits, Raven, and we both know there's no room for sentiment in our lives. The truth will not vanish simply because we wish it to. The Company is all that stands between me and the street, and I intend to do everything I can to see that it survives."

She scrambled up. "Break's over. Here comes everyone."

As Raven got, more slowly, to his feet, he caught Magpie's glare. *Oh, wonderful. She thinks she surprised us in a secret little tête-à-tête. We really are going to have an explosion before the day is over!*

Magpie waited till they were back in the boarding-house, standing in relative privacy in the narrow hallway between their rooms. "How *dare* you?" she gasped in fury. "How dare you undermine my authority like that?"

"*What* authority?" Raven shot back. "You're no music arranger; I am! You aren't a composer; I'm that, too! Ha, you've never even conducted a group, while I most certainly have!"

She was struggling to find some verbal ammunition

for a counterattack. Before she could reply, Raven added in his most superior manner, "I told you this morning that you were our business manager. But in artistic matters, you should come to me, my dear. Business and art seldom mix."

She was so furious her voice sounded choked. "Don't take that tone of voice to me! *I'm* not the one risking all our lives!"

Where did that *come from?* "What on earth are you talking about—"

She actually shook her *finger* at him, as at an erring child! "What in hell did you think you were doing with Regina?"

Aha! But it irked him to hear that she thought he would be so incredibly stupid as to interfere with their noble patron's—ornament. "Talking, dammit, just talking!"

"Is *that* what you call it?" she exploded. "You idiot! Flirting with Regina is flirting with danger!"

"I wasn't—" he protested.

"It's dangerous," Magpie shouted over his protest, "because the Duke's not going to let anyone poach on his—his property! Not that you care about things like that," she added scornfully, "what with your so very fine reputation with the ladies. But the Duke is *not* likely to be as cavalier as you!"

"That's not—I'm not—Magpie!"

As he stammered helplessly over her unjust attack, Magpie stormed into her room and slammed the door in his face.

And all he could do was stare at it, stupidly caught off guard by the violence of her reaction.

CHAPTER SEVEN

NEW SONGS

Magpie fell back against her room's closed door, biting her lip so hard it hurt, refusing to burst into tears. This was ridiculous, ridiculous, she didn't care about Raven at all, it was just that she was worried about the safety of the group —

Oh, really? Then why did the very thought of Regina talking so intimately with Raven stab through her like the proverbial iron knife?

She spoke aloud without realizing she had. "Why does she have to be so—so damned *beautiful*?"

Magpie moved to her narrow little bed and sank to it, head in hands. It hurt, oh, it hurt to know that not only wasn't she any competition for Regina, she wasn't even a distant second. Worse, she couldn't even hate the woman! Frustrating, oh, impossibly frustrating to realize that everything she'd seen so far had made her actually want to *like* Regina. A good many women in her position would have been lazy, idle creatures, exploiting the favor of their noble patrons, using the Company as nothing more than a toy to while away a few hours in their days. But today Magpie had seen that Regina worked as hard as any two of the other actors combined, and as earnestly as any of them. She *wanted* this play to succeed, she *wanted* this Company to succeed.

How can I not admire that?

Magpie groaned. She didn't even have the dubious satisfaction of knowing the woman was stupid! Oh no, it was far too evident from Regina's discussions of her character with the Manager that a sharp, intelligent mind was in that lovely head. Magpie remembered chatting with one of the extras during a break, a skinny young woman, straw-haired as a broom, who'd told her more than she really wanted to know about their leading lady, and all of it in tones of admiration.

Some of what the woman had said was enough to break a sentimental person's heart. "You know, it's a pity Regina's a commoner. If she hadn't been of such low birth, I bet our good Duke would have wed her by now. He's smitten with her, you know, positively smitten. But of course, no one above the rank of Sire can wed a commoner and keep his position."

The Duke also seemed to respect her mind as well, Magpie thought sadly, because it was common knowledge among the players that the Duke listened to whatever Regina told him, and often solicited—and, more to the point, acted on—her advice.

"Wonderful," Magpie muttered in misery. "She's beautiful *and* intelligent. And nice, too. That really makes me feel so much better."

How could Raven not be smitten with her as well? How could any sane, whole man? Except for Jaysen, of course. . . .

Why, even Crow had pure worship in those vague brown eyes whenever he had looked up at the stage.

Every time she let her thoughts wander, they centered on the sight of Regina and Raven sitting so suspiciously close together in the empty theater. They'd been laughing like two old friends. Or maybe two new lovers. Raven had given Magpie such a guilty look when she'd approached, like a man with something to hide, a man totally under Regina's spell.

Why wouldn't he be snared? He's a man, isn't he? And she's the most exquisite—

Oh, damn. I haven't got a chance against someone like her. Look at me! I'm usually so levelheaded, so controlled, but she's got me acting like a—a shrewish little bitch! And for what? I can't even fight for my man, because Raven isn't mine!

Now that was truly stupid. What difference could Raven's romantic entanglements possibly make? It wasn't as though she really wanted him, after all.

She . . . didn't, did she?

Magpie sat with head in hands, not at all sure anymore *what* she wanted. The only comfort she could take, the young woman thought in misery, was that bitter rush of satisfaction she'd felt at the sight of Raven's stunned face just now, when she'd hit him with his own obvious infatuation and warned him how the Duke was likely to react.

Ha. Some comfort.

"This is ridiculous," Magpie said sharply, springing to her feet. She cast open one of the rickety shutters, nearly pulling it right off its rusted hinges in the process, and stared out at —

At the blank wall of the building across the narrow alleyway. Having nothing much to see did give her a chance to stop and think, though. Bit by bit her confused thoughts settled down and centered on one uncomfortable fact: Regina, Duke's mistress that she was, was likely to be the very best source of information for the Free Bards on what was actually going on with the King and the Guild.

So no matter how I feel about her, I had better restrain myself and do my best to cultivate the woman. Magpie gave a great sigh. "So be it," she muttered reluctantly.

The next day, Magpie went to the theater determined to speak with Regina and begin the "cultivation." And who knew? If Regina was as kind as everyone in her Company seemed to think she was, she might even have some sympathy for the Free Bards and their plight. As the lovely actress went through her rehearsal, blocking out Act III with the rest of the cast, Magpie followed her with her gaze, to the point of missing a note here and there and being snapped at by Raven. But at last her chance came when the Manager grudgingly granted a rest break. As the other actors and musicians wandered off for some cool refreshment, Regina plopped herself down on the edge of the stage, pulling her hair away from her neck and fanning herself with her hand, plainly drained. After a nervous moment, Magpie hesitantly sat down beside her, legs dangling. "Acting looks rougher than busking," she said.

The woman gave her a bemused glance. "I don't know about that," she replied matter-of-factly. "We have only the one performance, and once it's perfected, all we have to do is repeat each day; the toughest thing is keeping it looking fresh each time. But you have to come up with a new program every day."

Magpie shrugged. "Well, there is that."

"Besides," Regina said with undisguised satisfaction, a satisfaction that seemed just a little odd from a pampered ducal mistress, "here I am, safe and sound with an established Company. Buskers have to be out in all kinds of weather, never knowing where the next meal is coming from."

"True," Magpie said, a bit more sharply than she'd intended.

Regina glanced at her, eyebrows raised. "Ah, you've been there, too, haven't you? Out on the streets, I mean, scared and hungry and not sure what's to become of you, but determined not to let anyone know your fright."

It was Magpie's turn to stare, but incredulously. "You've been there? You?"

Regina nodded, and then chuckled a little. "Me."

Magpie felt her mouth gaping and strove to shut it. She was only partially successful. "B-but you're so—so—"

"Beautiful?" the woman said wryly. "Do you really think beauty was an advantage on the streets?"

Magpie considered, then shuddered. "No. Not if you didn't intend to be the prey of—" She stopped short. "I can't believe this."

"What? That we share something of the same background?" Regina tilted her head charmingly to one side. "Tell me, were you a street rat like me, or a traveller?"

Street rat! How could she be so—so casual about it? "A traveller, for a time at least." To her amazement, Magpie heard herself pouring out her childhood history to this sympathetic ear, the long, lonely, perilous days on the road or scrounging for food and coin in whatever town the troupe's aimless wanderings had brought it.

"Nobody cares for the children, do they?" Regina murmured when she'd finished. "The unwanted ones, the ones who get used one way or another. Ach, Magpie, we're survivors, you and I. We have more in common with each other than we have with the others. Even my actors. *They* all had one or two strong parents to help them, guide them, and protect them. We never had anyone but ourselves."

Magpie looked at her in surprise. "We do, don't we?"

"That's right." Regina nodded firmly. "Neither of us is ever going to go hungry again. Or be used. By anyone."

"You know," Magpie began uncertainly, "at first I didn't want to like you. You're so . . . you're everything I'm not."

She didn't expect the reaction she got—Regina chuckled, a low, throaty chuckle, and then patted her knee. "Oh, my dear, don't be ridiculous! Haven't you looked in a mirror?"

"Yes, but—" Magpie didn't know what to say.

But Regina shook her head. "No, I mean *looked*. Really looked? Yes, I have dramatic looks, I know that. It's an accident of birth; whoever my parents were, at least they left me that much. But you're a beauty, too, girl, even though you haven't yet had a chance to be comfortable enough with yourself to accept it, with that elegant face of yours and that lovely, graceful body."

To her utter embarrassment, Magpie felt her face starting to flame. "I'm not—I—"

"Look you," Regina said sharply, "one thing I don't do is tell stupid lies. And I've been in the theater long enough to know beauty, and the kind that lasts beyond the flush of pretty youth."

Now Magpie blushed, but with embarrassment, and she actually found herself hanging her head. "I didn't mean to insult—"

"Ay me, I know you didn't." Regina put a hand on her shoulder, and made her look up to see that the actress was smiling. "We both have a lot of prickles, don't we? Like a pair of silly hedgehogs."

That made Magpie giggle. Suddenly Regina broke into her gamine grin. "You know that peasant song, 'It's you and me, gal, against them all'?"

That wide grin was infectious. "You and me," Magpie agreed.

"Friends?" Regina asked, and there was a look in her eyes that could not have been feigned. She really meant it.

"I—I'd like that, yes." Magpie felt a warm glow begin, deep inside. "Friends. It's been a long time since I've had a friend."

"Me, too," the Duke's mistress said softly, in such a way that made Magpie certain she spoke the truth. "Me, too."

"Raven," Regina murmured from the depths of the theater, "have you a moment? This break won't be over for a short while yet, and this is the only time we'll have to talk freely in private."

In private? Raven covered his uneasy little start with a melodramatic bow. "For you, gracious one, I always have the time."

That earned him a chuckle. "You actor! Come, sit here with me, if you would."

Perching nervously on the edge of one of the noble seats, Raven asked very carefully, "What's wrong?"

Regina raised a wry eyebrow. "I'm not trying to seduce you, if that's what you're thinking."

"Of course you're not," Raven hastily agreed, and told himself it was downright stupid to feel disappointed. "But what . . . ?"

"I . . . learned a few things recently I think you should know." Her voice had lost all trace of light humor. "I have made it my business to know everything about my troupe, and I think you should do the same."

"Meaning?" he asked, very carefully.

"Meaning, I wonder if you haven't been just a touch unfair to Magpie." The serious tone of her voice left him no doubt but that she was completely serious.

He couldn't help his reaction; what business was it of *hers* how he and Magpie got along? "Oh now, your pardon, but I hardly think that's your affair!"

But her voice and her expression were as stern as a schoolteacher's with an erring student. "As long as it's something that affects this Company," Regina said with such sudden quiet ferocity Raven was astonished, "no matter how peripherally, yes, it most certainly *is* my affair. How much do you know of Magpie's past?"

Raven shrugged, not certain what he was supposed to answer. Damned annoying, being made to feel like a bad little boy not once, but *twice* in the same week! "That she was part of a troupe of wandering players. That her father is dead, her mother wasn't good at business, and her uncle was a drunk."

Regina's frown deepened. "Did she also tell you her uncle tried more than once to sell her for drink?"

Raven stared. "No," he said uneasily. Oh, he knew such things happened—but never among the Gypsies —

"Or that her mother wouldn't believe that when it happened?" Regina continued inexorably. Why was she telling him these horrid things?

He was feeling acutely uncomfortable now. "Regina, I—"

"Did she tell you how often the only reason the troupe had anything at all to eat was that she—a child barely at the edge of womanhood—played up to whatever men had coin?" Now she looked at him as if *he* was the one who had been responsible for putting a child in such a plight.

He was more than uncomfortable. And he *didn't* want to hear all this. "I didn't—"

Regina sighed, and her tense expression relaxed a little, although her patent displeasure and unhappiness were still there, beneath the surface. "She never had a childhood, Raven, or rather, she had a harsh, joyless stretch of life that's common to all too many youngsters."

Raven shook his head in confused denial. This was one thing he never had understood about the Settled Folk. His people might not always have enough to eat, but they cherished their children, they cherished all children. How anyone could prey on their own young . . .

I don't want to hear this. I don't want to learn any more.

It had been so easy to be annoyed with Magpie before he knew much about her life, about what had shaped her. Knowing people—really knowing them—made it damnably difficult to make those nice, easy judgments; you were forced to keep thinking about *why* they were acting like boneheads, and —

He tensed. There, her slim figure picked out by a stray, narrow beam of sunlight, stood Magpie, watching them, her face stony.

Oh hell. "Magpie, I . . . " Raven began guiltily, then let his voice trail off. What could he say? *We weren't having a tête-à-tête, we were talking about you?*

She said not a word. Her face still carefully blank and cold, Magpie turned around and walked away.

"Damn."

Regina shook her head and swore softly. Raven blinked a little—who would ever have guessed the lovely actress knew *those* words?

"What is it?" Raven asked impatiently.

"Nothing," she replied, though it was obviously untrue. "Raven, you're not used to being the head of a group, are you?"

He shrugged again, not sure where she was going. "I'm a Gypsy. Gypsies wander, often alone."

"Then you probably can't quite appreciate what it's like being the lead in a theater troupe, making sure all those melodramatic personalities—mine included—don't clash, keeping everyone as happy as possible without compromising the play." She looked off into the empty distance near the ceiling, her eyes unfocused. "This is an insular, artificial little world we inhabit, Raven, but we never can dare forget there's a world outside."

Raven snorted. "You wouldn't get much of an audience if you did!"

"Exactly." Regina's eyes flickered down to his, filled with wry humor. "But are you getting my point?"

"That you're the real head of this Company?" Raven hesitated a moment, then added warily, "That you're as much the real business head of it as Magpie is of my group?"

"It's the Duke of Kingsford's Company," Regina reminded him sternly, "not mine."

"You know what I meant," he said impatiently.

Her shrug told him that he was right. "And let me assure you, the Manager is very much the creative head. I have no ability whatsoever to compose plays, let alone anything remotely approaching the genius-touched plays he creates. I also have almost no talent for directing—and believe me, I am perfectly happy to have people take over their own areas of expertise!"

Odd. Raven could hardly deny that it would be—that it *had* been—very easy for him to be attracted physically to Regina. What man wouldn't be? But somewhere along the way in this strange discussion they were having, something had changed. Bewildered, he realized that though of course he could never ignore the fact that she was a beautiful woman, he had started relating to her not at all on the sensual level but as an equal colleague.

I wonder . . . can this be something intentional on her part? Not just the normal "I don't want to get involved with you" of the average woman, but something . . . more?

There was, after all, the special type of magic his people called glamorie: the ability to attract, fascinate, entrap. Might Regina be the master, conscious or not, of such a talent? Of a glamorie she could also reverse?

Well now, if that's the case, no wonder she's been able to hold Duke Arden so long!

And it was to her credit that she hadn't tried using it to bring the Duke to marry her, because such a marriage, noble to lowest commoner, would have been sure to bring disaster to Duke Arden. Gypsy though he was, Raven had seen enough of all aspects of society in his travels to know how things worked in the nobility. What an incredibly status-bound lot they were! At the best, Duke Arden, married to Regina, would become a laughingstock. At the worst—and this didn't seem so improbable, given the strange and unsettled state of politics in Kingsford right now—the Duke would be disgraced, retaining his lands and title but losing all trace of influence or power, with the King declaring that those lands and title would go at Duke Arden's death to the nearest relative in his line—but *not* to any offspring he might have by his shameful commoner wife.

Idiots.

Surely Regina was painfully aware of how things stood. And yet . . . as they continued to talk, chatting about small matters of music and acting, Raven began to wonder. He'd seen women among the Gypsies who wielded glamorie; even when not using it, they had a *feel* to them, something like the *feel* of Bardic Magic that ringed Nightingale round. Yet there was no such eerie otherness to Regina. Could it be she wasn't aware of her glamorie at all? Was her control of it a purely instinctive thing? Ha, yes, that had to be it! If she knew she possessed so much power, she would hardly be so afraid of the Duke losing interest in her!

"Regina—"

"All right, you lazy creatures!" a severe voice shouted from the stage, and both Raven and Regina started. The Manager, turned to an eerie silhouette by the footlights' glow, was clapping his hands impatiently. "All of you, to work!"

Somewhere during Raven's discussion with Regina, the other actors had drifted back into the theater. Regina got to her feet with a little smile.

"Our master's voice," she said, and headed off towards the stage without another word.

So much for that, the Free Bard thought wryly, watching her go. Rehearsal duties called. And any conversation must be continued at another time.

Their Master's voice—indeed.

CHAPTER EIGHT

DISCORDANT NOTES

At last, Raven thought, the play was beginning to look like a play. He'd been wondering just when the actors were going to act on something besides a bare stage. He'd even begun to wonder *if* they were going to have something besides a bare stage, although of course he wasn't going to make a fool of himself by mentioning the obvious fact that when an audience went to the theater, they expected to see something besides actors. In his limited experience, the more elaborate a set, the better they liked it. But the scenery designers had been hard at work for the past few days, hammering with what seemed to him like vicious enthusiasm whenever the play wasn't in actual rehearsal and filling the whole theater with the smell of fresh paint. They didn't seem to mind him watching, either, or asking questions.

Even when those questions were impertinent, or even rude.

He leaned over a painter's shoulders with interest. "What, pray tell, is *that* going to be?" he asked. The shapeless mass cut from flat wood looked like—well, it *might* be a cloud, but why make a cloud of wood, which would be much heavier than cloth? Why make a cloud at all, when the play didn't call for clouds?

The stagehand squinted up at him. "A bush for Flora's home *and* for the Prince's garden." He grinned. "Audience'll never notice the duplication. See, we cut out the basic shape of the bush from wood, like this—" his hands fairly flew as he snatched up various paintbrushes from the pots beside him, giving the "bush" its colors as he talked "—paint it nice and speckly with all these greens and a few browns and grays for contrast so it'll look properly leafy from the audience, then fix the sections together, bush and stand, and," he got to his feet with a melodramatic sweep of his arm, "there you have it, a bush as pretty as anything built by Dame Nature!"

Raven grinned, as he squinted to imagine the result from the audience. "It really does look lifelike. Ah, but what's that big panel going to be? Looks like the side of a house."

The workman nodded. "It will be, when we finish painting it: the side of the Prince's mansion for Act II, Scene 3, the garden scene."

Raven gawked. "Looks damnably heavy."

"It is! We'll rig it to a counterweight to keep it safely balanced—and help us get it on- and offstage. And then we—" He was suddenly distracted by one of the younger workers; a mere apprentice, who was carrying too many paint pots at once. "Hey, you, watch it!" he shouted. "You're going to spill that paint all over—"

And of course, the inevitable happened as soon as the words were out of the man's mouth. The boy dropped half of the pots, and the paint splattered everywhere. The workman swore resignedly. "Damn."

No use crying over spilled paint, Raven thought. *Call it a sacrifice to the gods of theater: paint instead of blood! And let's hope the sacrifice is accepted and that's the worst thing that happens!*

But, having been a professional musician for almost all his life, he'd seen enough weird accidents occur during the shaping of a performance to doubt they were going to get off so lightly.

"Nobody ever said producing a play was easy," Regina said to no one in particular and Raven laughed wryly.

Looks like the paint sacrifice wasn't enough!

Surely everything that could possibly go wrong *was* going wrong! People kept missing their cues or dropping their props or getting lost in the middle of their speeches. The scrawny little illusionist created a beautiful fog when he should have produced moonlight and lost his hold on a sunlit-illusion completely. It was just a matter of time before someone else —

Ha, yes. Here we go again.

"No, no, *no!*" the Manager shouted to two luckless extras. "You *enter* stage left, *exit* stage right, not the other way around! And you, yes, you in the blue gown, was that supposed to be a smile? It looked like the village idiot! All right, everyone, take it from the start!"

They managed to make it all the way through the scene. But in the next act, the trapdoor that was supposed to open to act as a staircase for the servants stuck midway, living up to its name by trapping an actor halfway up. "Never got stuck in a role before," he jibed while the others, grumbling, worked to free him.

❖   ❖   ❖

The next day brought new and interesting problems. Regina, trying to address her "brother" as "my lord brother," came out with "my bored lover" instead, and exploded into laughter. After that, both she and the other unfortunate actor kept getting stuck on the same spot in the same speech so many times they finally couldn't even look at each other without bursting into laughter.

The Manager was not amused. "Idiots!" he stormed. "The scene's supposed to be *tragic!*"

"We—we know," gasped Regina, wiping tears of hysteria from her eyes.

The Manager gave a gusty sigh of frustration. "Now your makeup's smearing. Mistress Marda! *Mistress Marda!* Curse it all, where is the woman?"

As Mistress Marda, who was in charge of the Company's makeup, came scurrying to make repairs, Raven murmured, "Ah, the magic of the theater," to Magpie.

But Magpie turned coldly away as though she hadn't heard him, and Raven gave vent to his own frustrated sigh. Ever since she'd seen him talking with Regina, the idiotic wench had been acting as if she had caught him stealing from his own mother. She never looked at him without looking down her nose at him, and her manner was so chill a wall of ice seemed to form every time they were in the same room.

If only that were the whole of it!

But no, Magpie was also proving herself a wonder of acidic humor, scalding him with it whenever the opportunity presented itself. Which, of course, since he was determined not to give her an opening, happened all too often.

It didn't help that the Manager had decided they were far enough along in rehearsals for the musicians to perform in the small, onstage alcove, curtained off from the view of the audience, that they would occupy during actual performances. In such tight surroundings, Raven could hardly keep out of Magpie's way.

She had him afraid to say a single word during rehearsals, for fear she'd somehow turn whatever he said into some jest at his own expense. He did his level best to give her as good as he got, of course—how not? But that only made things worse, and made her more determined than ever to make a mockery of him.

It wasn't fair, curse it all! It wasn't as if he'd actually done anything wrong. But every time Raven tried to explain that to her, Magpie found an excuse to be elsewhere.

Curse her. Curse this play. Curse this whole stupid town and every theater in it! I could be out on the road somewhere, the wind in my hair. But no, I'm stuck here, and all because Talaysen and Rune couldn't control themselves!

Oh wonderful. Now Magpie had him wallowing in self-pity. Disgusted, Raven snatched up his fiddle and raced through a series of intricate arpeggios until he'd cooled off a bit.

But of course all the problems involved with staging a new play continued. Actors went right on forgetting their lines, costumes arrived with seams ripped, and once one of the more nearsighted extras managed to fall right off the stage, and it was only by sheer accident that he didn't hurt either himself or the Manager, on whom he landed.

"It's not usually quite this bad," Regina murmured to Raven during a brief halt while an actor struggled to extricate the edge of his tunic from the nails someone had forgotten to hammer all the way in on a wooden "tree." "Sometimes I wonder why I put up with it all. But then somehow, miraculously, everything starts fitting together into one seamless whole. Or else," she added with a sharp, sardonic smile, "it doesn't. And then we have that theatrical phenomenon known so politely as a flop."

"But that won't happen here," Raven hastily assured her.

She laughed, and crossed her finger and thumb for luck. "From your mouth to the ears of whatever gods rule over the theater! Hey-ho, back to Act II!"

At least, Raven thought, his little troupe's music was holding true. The Manager had, rather grudgingly, complaining a bit about the extra expense, agreed to hire hornist Nightjar and the viol-playing twins, Finch and Verdin, to give the small orchestra a fuller sound, even if it meant rearranging and expanding their little alcove so all the musicians had sufficient room. Yes, there were the occasional wrong notes; they weren't machines, after all. And Jaysen had had two strings on his guitar snap, once during a dramatic confrontation, once, most startling and loudly, during a romantic solo. But overall, Raven thought, the orchestra sounded pretty fine.

And just when he was thinking that, Crow stepped on a stray board, lost his balance, and ended up putting his hand right through the head of a drum.

That does it, Raven thought wryly. *We've been in the theater too long. The mishaps must be contagious!*

Fortunately, life at their makeshift boardinghouse home was going a little more smoothly. Granted, there was a whole list of things that still needed major correction. As the season turned towards autumn, the walls had started leaking cold air at night, enough to make candleflames flicker and sometimes even blow out. But even though the Free Bard boarders were beginning to turn a bit of a profit with their dining and laundry services, such repairs would cost more than all

of them were making. And so people were correcting
what they could with the materials at hand; Sparrow
had found some planks "nobody wanted," and Raven
himself had shamelessly swiped a good handful of nails
from the theater for some makeshift repairs.

Ah well, Raven mused, at least, drafty walls or no,
everyone was getting good, hot, regular meals and had
a reasonably bearable bed in which to sleep, and a roof
that, even if it occasionally rained bits of old birds'
nests or the odd groggy insects down on everyone, was
almost leak-free.

Or so he thought, until after dinner that night.

For things didn't seem to be going quite so smoothly
for Jaysen. Raven went out for a bit of fresh air after
the meal and found him leaning moodily against one of
the boardinghouse's sagging walls, and bit back a grin.
"Holding up the house, lad?"

"Yes. No. I mean . . . " Jaysen shot him a glance wild
with worry. "Raven, you're a—a man of the world."

"Am I, now?"

"You know what women want. What they mean."

Raven forced back the easy, sarcastic replies and
contented himself with saying simply, "What they
want, Jay, is pretty much the same thing we all do when
you come right down to the basics: happiness. What
they *mean* . . . Linnet's been teasing you, has she?"

"I don't know," the young man said helplessly.
"Sometimes she seems so pleased to be with me. We
went for a walk the other night, you know, when the
moon was full, and it was . . . wonderful. But every
time I try to . . . well, do anything at all more than just
take her hand, she hurries off, claiming she has too
much work to do to waste time. I wouldn't hurt her,
she knows that! She knows I wouldn't ever . . . uh . . . "

Raven waited a moment, watching Jaysen's face

rapidly turn a number of shades of bright red, then suggested delicately, "Dishonor her?"

Jaysen made a face, but nodded. "Exactly! I'd never do something like that! What does she *want*?"

Green as grass, Raven thought. *Was I ever that naive? Or that young?* He chuckled, and leaned back against the wall of the building himself, arms folded nonchalantly across his chest. "Exactly what she's getting," he told the lad. "You."

Jaysen stared at him in confusion. "But—"

Raven simply shook his head. "Oh no, Jay, I'm not getting into the trap of trying to dispense advice. Whatever I would suggest would only make things worse."

Jaysen looked utterly despondent, and Raven patted him on the shoulder in a fatherly manner. "I will tell you this much. She's interested in you, lad, maybe even just a little bit in love with you, even if she's playing the 'come and get me, keep away from me' game. And you're definitely in love with her. Somehow I do think things will work themselves out!"

If only, Raven thought the next morning, everything else was as clear to read as young love. Jaysen was clearly more hopeful, and Linnet flushed a delicate pink every time she looked at him. On the other hand, Magpie was as cool as ever, and not one of his attempts at conversation met with more than a frigid "Oh? Indeed?"

I'd better not ask her to pass the tea, he thought with resignation. *She'll make it undrinkably cold if she touches it. And she'll surely sour the cream.*

He managed a certain amount of conversation with Finch and Verdin—enough to make the meal palatable, at any rate. They left in a group, but he trailed along in the rear, rather than risk accidentally getting in Magpie's way and earning another sharp set-down.

Perhaps that was why he was paying more attention to what was going on around them than to the conversation of his fellows.

Halfway to the theater with the other Free Bards, he stopped short, frowning.

Finch, who had dropped back to retie a shoe strap, nearly bumped into him. "Raven! What are—"

"Hush," he told her, nodding at the street-preacher holding forth on the corner across from them. "Listen."

"To him?" she replied, incredulously. "He's nothing but a streetcorner preacher."

"A representative of the Church," Raven corrected softly. "His accent's too fine for him to be the usual half-mad fanatic."

". . . and so I say to you," the preacher, a lean, sinewy fellow who looked as though he never laughed, said sonorously to his small, bemused audience, "the theater is a snare wherein the Forces of Evil trap the souls of those who come to see these immoral plays!"

Do I say something, or not? he asked himself. *I could only make us more trouble than it's worth—*

—on the other hand, perhaps I can turn this to our profit.

"Immoral?" Raven drawled, strolling forward. "Sir Preacher—forgive me if I don't have your title correct— what is so immoral about a play wherein true-hearted lovers are united, virtue triumphs, villainy and lechery are defeated and exposed, and everyone lives happily ever after? Not a bit of impropriety, I promise you, in *A Twice-Told Tale*," he raised his voice just enough to catch the attention of the preacher's audience, "the new comedy to open at the Duke of Kingsford's Company Theater in a fortnight."

With that, he bowed more to the gathered watchers, turned dramatically, wishing he had a cloak to snap out behind him, and walked away, closely followed by the other Free Bards. Behind him, he could hear the preacher frantically trying to regain the dispersing audience's attention with a fierce, "The demons speak beguiling words! These players are *whores*, I tell you, common *whores* masquerading as honest entertainers!"

"Now that's really going to keep people away," Raven murmured to the others. "He might as well be selling tickets to the play."

"You," Nightjar said in admiration, "have the most colossal nerve of anyone I've ever seen. Taking on the Church, turning an anti-theater harangue into an advertisement—have you no shame, man?"

"None whatsoever," Raven told her blithely, and grinned.

He stopped grinning the moment they entered the theater. The actors were clustered onstage, standing over one of the young women extras, who was huddling on the floor, sobbing.

"It's all right, dear," Regina soothed. "You weren't hurt, thank heavens."

"What happened?" Raven asked.

"A slight accident," the Manager told him. "One of the trees fell over and knocked her off her feet. Fortunately, it was one of the thin, wood pieces, hardly enough to raise a bruise. The silly girl's merely frightened."

But he waited with, for him, amazingly gentle patience till everyone was calm once more. One of the stagehands examined the wooden tree and called out, "Two of the supporting braces came loose, pulled the thing right off its base."

"Well, fix it!" the Manager said impatiently. "We have work to do! 'Sir Verrick,' get back in place. Act II, Scene 2, from the start."

This was the scene in which Sir Verrick, furious over Flora's disappearance, vowed vengeance on her and her whole family. The actor portraying him—who was, much to Raven's amusement, a nice, gentle fellow who liked birdwatching—ranted and raved his way through his speech, creating a nice, unnervingly real mix of comedy and menace.

"I will have such revenges!" he shouted at last. "What they are, yet I know not. But I do so swear it by this sword!"

With that, he ripped the weapon from its sheath —

— and wound up clutching only the hilt. There was a moment's stunned silence, then a collective roar of laughter from actors and musicians alike. The only ones not laughing were the Manager and "Sir Verrick" himself, who protested, "It's stuck! I swear, the sword is glued in there!"

"Nonsense." The Manager climbed up onto the stage to examine the sheath himself. "It can't possibly be . . . "

Evidently, however, it was. He glanced up, eyes blazing. "Is this someone's idea of a *joke*? If so, it most definitely is not funny!" Hurling the sheath and glued-in sword from him, he roared, "Prop Master! Fix it! And whichever one of you pranksters it was who did this take warning: one more such incident, and you're out on your ear! Is that understood? Now, get back to your places!"

Nothing else went wrong that day, and Raven told himself drily, *I suppose we've satisfied the imps of perversity today!*

But the imps plainly weren't finished with them,

because the next day Florian's dance ribbons turned up, after a long, frustrating search, tangled into a mare's nest of knots.

"But that's impossible!" Regina protested. "I put them away myself, and there wasn't a knot in them!"

"They didn't snarl themselves," the Manager muttered, but he could hardly call the Duke's mistress a liar. "The mask!" came a cry from backstage, and the Manager threw up his hands in disgust. "Now what?"

Mistress Gerna, the Wardrobe Mistress, came scuttling onstage. "Someone," she said dramatically, "has stolen Flora's mask!"

"That's impossible. It must have been misplaced. Just like," he added with a glare at Regina, "the ribbons."

"They were *not* misplaced!" Regina snapped. Raven recognized the look in her eyes for what it was: the warning of real anger. Regina never made excuses, and never lied—and she would *not* put up with implications that she did! "I *know* I put them into the proper trunk. Surely," she continued, her voice ringing out with full righteous indignation, "you don't think I'd try to spoil my own performance?"

The Manager yielded to her insulted fury. "No. Of course not. Someone else must have—Mistress Gerna!"

"Eh now, don't look at *me*!" the woman protested. "All I did last night was straighten the creases in a few costumes. I didn't move a thing."

Raven stepped forward, deciding that *someone* ought to intervene before the Manager or Regina said something unforgivable. Better him, an outsider, than anyone else. "Did you see the mask, Mistress Gerda? Or any sign that someone else had been in the Wardrobe Room?"

Mistress Gerna shrugged helplessly. "Didn't notice," she admitted. "Who'd want to bother mere stage costumes? They're all false fur and imitation silk. It's not as if you could actually *wear* them anywhere but onstage!"

The other actors were already searching, for lack of anything more constructive to do, although no one really expected to find the mask; Raven could tell that from their expressions, ranging from boredom to helplessness. Rather than make themselves targets for the Manager's irritation, the musicians joined the search.

"Hey, wait a bit," Nightjar said, suddenly, pointing to something. "What's that?" She gestured again, out into the area for the audience. "I think there's something in the front row, caught under the third seat from the aisle. . . ."

One of the extras jumped down off the stage and pulled out what Nightjar's sharp eyes had spotted.

The Duke's mistress cried out in mingled annoyance and relief. "My mask!"

Regina rushed to snatch it from the woman as she brought it back to the stage, smoothing its rumpled plumage, examining it with care. "It doesn't seem to be damaged, just a little dusty. But how did it—Who would—Why do such a stupid thing?"

The Manager, fairly radiating frustrated fury, whirled, his gaze stabbing at each actor and musician in turn. "These games have gone far enough!" he roared. "Now it won't merely be the street for the prankster if I catch him or her, it will be a confrontation with the Duke himself! Now, on with the rehearsal!"

"Raven, look," Magpie murmured the next morning. "Your preacher friend has been replaced."

Raven looked, and didn't like what he saw. This well-fed fellow in elegantly cut clerical robes was, without a doubt, a fully ordained priest of the Church —

And a more sly, more false creature I never saw, Raven thought in distaste. *Press his hand and feel oil, touch his honor and see tears. But underneath the slime . . . ah, I don't like the coldness in those flat eyes. Petty evil, yes, but evil nevertheless.*

Priest the man might be, but the gist of his sermon was the same as that useless preacher: the theater was the home of sinners, and honest folk, folk in fear of the safety of their immortal souls should stay away from such shameful places.

"Not going to jest with him?" Nightjar asked wryly.

Raven gave her a sour grin. "There *are* limits."

"For you?" Magpie's voice dripped with sarcasm. "Did you ever stop to think that your little jest might have sent that relatively harmless preacher straight to his superiors? And given us this full-fledged enemy instead?"

"He's not an enemy." Raven forced an insouciant grin. "Just a man with too much spare time on his hands. Remember, this is the Duke's own theater. Even the Church isn't going to want to start something with him."

"Oh, right," Magpie muttered. "Of course not. I believe that."

She doesn't believe it for a moment, Raven thought, thinking of those cold eyes, *and I'm not sure I do!*

They left the priest to his sermonizing, and moved on, but Raven caught even Magpie looking back over her shoulder uneasily. As well she might.

He tried to tell himself that this was probably only one isolated incident. A theater troupe could hardly be considered a major target for something as vast as the Church. If they kept themselves properly quiet and submissive for a time, Raven mused, the Church would surely forget all about them and go after more obvious prey.

All right, then. "To the theater," Raven said, a touch less dramatically and more softly than he would have liked. "Let us play the play!"

CHAPTER NINE

JARRING SONGS

The girl shrank back against a whitewashed wall, her eyes trying to focus on all of her attackers at once; heart pounding, clutching the broken loaf of bread to her thin body. The taunts and jeers were fewer now that they had her cornered; the cruelty in their faces said it all. Why had she been so careless, why?

This had started off in the usual way, the gang of street kids idly taunting one small girl who wasn't one of their number, shoving her, trying to snatch away the piece of bread she'd slipped off a baker's tray when no one was looking. They'd never quite managed any real harm in the past, but the promise of it was always there, lurking behind the nasty words. And always before, she'd kept an escape route in mind, gotten away from the boys before things got out of hand —

But this one time, overwhelmed by hunger, focused only on the food, she had forgotten about danger. She'd let the gang surprise her, corner her, and now that they thought she couldn't get away, they were clearly about to fulfill those promises.

They closed in on her, until she stood in a tiny clear space with only a scrap of wall at her back. A hand reached out of the mob and shoved her, into the arms of another, who tossed her at a third. She became a kind of shuttlecock, batted from hand to hand, each time with more force. They paid no more attention to the battered loaf she held; she was their target now. Despairing, she knew they were working themselves up to beating her, abusing her, crippling her, maybe even killing her. It wouldn't do a bit of good to scream; she'd learned that bitter lesson almost from the start of her short life. Not a soul in all Kingsford would care, or even notice, what was happening to one small street rat. She would be hurt, die, and no one would lift a finger to help her.

A wild surge of mingled panic and rage blazed through her. No longer thinking, she was only acting, reacting, as any cornered animal would, fighting for her life.

Dropping the bread, hands crooked into rough-nailed claws, the girl darted forward in fury, kicking, scratching, biting, screaming with fury at the top of her lungs.

The startled boys fell back from this small, fierce, crazy thing, and the girl raced off with all her might, hearing them yell behind her. They shouted to each other as if to prove no mere girl could possibly have frightened them. Through the running blood in her ears, she heard them pounding after her, hungry for revenge, promising the things they'd do to her if they caught her.

She didn't dare let that happen.

Dodging men, ducking under wagons, dashing down narrow alleyways, all she knew was that she must run, run, run —

Regina, woman now, street rat no longer, woke with a start, gasping, staring blankly up at —

At the canopy of a bed. Painted all over with a mural of fat cherubs floating among impossibly white and fluffy clouds, illuminated from below by the tiny oil lamp in the headboard that Arden kept burning all night long, in deference to her fear of the dark.

The Duke's bed. The dream was over and she was here, in his private suite, she was safe, and Arden was a warm, comforting presence beside her, snoring ever so slightly.

Regina let out her breath in a long, relieved sigh. Here she'd thought she had long ago banished the memories of what had been! But for all her determination, the past did occasionally manage to slip its way back into her dreams, reminding her of what a narrow line there was between poverty and security.

She turned her head to look at Arden, running her gaze tenderly over the strong lines of his face relaxed in sleep and framed by its neat, graying beard, and a slow, reluctant smile formed on her lips.

I never meant to love you, the woman told him silently. *It would have been far, far easier not to love you, to let this be strictly a business proposition, warmth and security in exchange for the pleasure you take in my body. But . . . ah well.*

What would be, would be. Arden loved her now, she had no doubt of that, but who could tell what the future held? Noblemen such as he seldom cared for such as she for very long.

But I will not be sent back to the streets. Whatever

else happens, Arden, I will not let you send me back.

The Duke's Company should see to that. Assuming it survived. Assuming the Church didn't—Oh, nonsense. Just because one priest decided to speak out against the theater didn't mean any real danger.

Yawning, brushing back the dark, disheveled mass of her unbound hair, Regina reached out to pull aside one of the bed's heavy, richly embroidered hangings and sighed to see pale gray light stealing gradually into the room. Reluctantly, she started to slip out of bed. But Arden's hand closed gently on her own, holding her there, her feet dangling over the edge of the massive bed as though she were still a child.

"Arden, please."

"Don't go," the Duke mumbled sleepily.

Regina wriggled back into bed enough so that she could bend over and give him a quick kiss on the cheek. "It's nearly morning, love. I have to get back to my own suite."

The hypocrisy of customs among the high and mighty made her smile wryly. As long as the Duke didn't flaunt her openly as his mistress, as long as she had her own private little suite, everyone could tactfully pretend she was merely a . . . guest, less than a noble, of course, but more than a mere servant. Everyone could ignore his reluctance to contract a marriage of state or convenience.

The Duke yawned mightily, arms flung over his head as he stretched. "I'll be attending Church services in town this morning." His voice was a little more focused as he slid back into full awareness. "Join me?"

It wasn't really a question. Regina shrugged. This was one of the Duke's customs, to visit the ordinary sites of Kingsford, show his people he was, despite his noble blood, one of them. And as for having her at his side, well as long as she wasn't actually clinging to him but acted with quiet discretion, everyone could pretend it was all perfectly respectable. Even in Church.

"If you will," she murmured. "Come, let go. I must get dressed."

His teeth flashed in the dim light. "I'd love to watch."

"I'm sure you would," Regina chuckled, getting to her feet. "But then we'd be sure to miss all the Church services. Till later, love."

The church Duke Arden had chosen to attend this morning was an elegant, solid building set back from its neighbors on a cobbled square. It stood fairly close to his theater, this Church of St. Bede. *Patron saint,* Regina mused, *of scribes, composers, and musicians. Also the church favored by the Bardic Guild. Nice, ironic choice, my love.*

Regina, hand resting ever so properly on his arm, fingertips just barely grazing it, was very well aware what a fine couple they made: he, so striking and distinguished a figure with his strong build and the graying, neatly shaped hair and beard, she, with her gleaming dark hair coiled neatly on her head, her wine-red gown modestly covered by a shawl of deep, respectable charcoal gray. There was, she admitted with an inner grin, enough of the actress in her to enjoy the stares they were getting from everyone as they entered. She sat demurely beside the Duke, playing the shy, well-bred lady for all she was worth, face schooled to piety and eyes downcast.

But the first words from the priest brought her head up again in a startled stare.

This isn't the usual priest—this is the man who's been preaching against the theater!

It could hardly be an accident. Regina eyed him in wary disapproval, wondering. Ugh, how oily he was, how smug and self-righteous! She heard the Duke draw in his breath in an angry hiss as the priest began his smooth, sly sermon and they heard the point of it.

"My children, sin is all around us. None of us would deny that. Sin is rooted strongly in this city, some of it so blatant as to make a stone weep. I will not speak of the things we have all seen and turned away from—girls barely old enough to leave their dolls painting their faces and selling themselves on every corner, boys who should be at their schoolbooks debauching themselves in low taverns. These things are easy to see as sin, and as evil. But there are other, more subtle sins against the Laws of the Sacrificed God."

The priest paused, hands clasped dramatically, his glance sweeping the congregation, making sure he had their total attention. *We're listening,* Regina thought impatiently. *Get on with it.*

"And one of the most subtle, most insidious forms of sin, my children," the priest continued smoothly, "is that of pretending to be what you are not, of challenging the will of the Creator by saying, 'No, I am not happy with my birthright, no, I am not satisfied with what I am but lust after what I am not.'"

So I should stay content as a starving, filthy street rat? Regina thought angrily. *Sell my body for a scrap of food? Is that what you preach, priest? I thought you just said that selling yourself was also a sin!*

"Do you understand what I say, my children?" he went on, a faint, pitying smile on his face. "I am not speaking merely of women, although they are the weakest and the first to succumb to such sin and temptation. I do not mean the good, modest homebodies of course—but those who do their best to deny what the good Lord gave them by covering their heads with false hair and their faces with thick, ugly layers of paint."

Sanctimonious idiot, Regina thought. *Who do you think sets those ridiculous standards of beauty? If it wasn't your fellow men who insist on their narrow ideas of what a woman should be, none of us would have to distort ourselves at all.*

"But there is more," the priest went on. "I speak of something far more dangerous than the foolishness of women. For lo, there are those Godless folk who regularly disguise their very beings with false roles! Worse, those Godless folk dare lure others into believing their pretenses are true and not the dark lies of perversion they are! In short, my children, I speak of the *theater,* of its *actors.* Now, we all know what actors are like: Godless, indeed, low, immoral creatures with no fixed homes or means of support save for their sinful trade. Actors, we all know, practice all the vices forbidden to any with a grain of human decency."

"Do we, indeed," Regina murmured, hoping to make Arden chuckle.

But just then the priest proclaimed with all his oily fervor, "But worse than any actor are those who *support* actors, who *allow* such things as actors, *as the theater itself,* to flourish!"

The congregation stirred uneasily at that. Nervous glances shot sideways at Duke Arden, at his actress-mistress.

"I'll listen to no more of this rot!" the Duke muttered in Regina's ear. But before he could rise, she clamped down on his arm with all the strength in her hand. "Dammit, woman—"

"You can't walk out," she murmured. "You don't dare let him see he's bothered you. Deal with him later, in private. Remove your patronage from this church if need be. But make no show of anger in public."

Duke Arden's hazel eyes had gone cold gray with barely suppressed rage. Regina knew he was as well aware as she that this could only be a deliberate attack. *But against whom?* the woman wondered uneasily. *Against Arden, or me, or maybe the Free Bards and the whole idea of our theater?*

The service finally ended. As the priest beamed his oily smile, Duke Arden rose with immense dignity, and left, only his stiff back and his eyes showing his rage. But he very blatantly did *not* drop his usual generous gift into the collection box as he exited. And once outside, he strode off in a fine storm of fury, fairly dragging Regina after him. His servants and bodyguards had to trot to keep up with him. "Arden, please!" she whispered after a half block of this. "I don't want to arrive at the theater looking like a whirlwind dropped me!"

He slowed, then stopped, and turned to really look at her. For all the anger still smoldering in his eyes, the Duke gave her a most gracious bow, touching his lips ever so delicately to her hand. "My anger is not with you, and you do not deserve to feel it. Till later, then, my lady," he murmured. "Servants! See the lady to wherever she wishes to go."

"Arden," she murmured. "You really must see the play for yourself. It is *your* production, after all. You should know what it is you are being taunted with."

He nodded absently. "Invite your musician friends to your suite for an evening of music, too. Perhaps I will find the time to pay a visit."

With that, he turned away, and moved on with all the grace and kingly manner of any true monarch, leaving Regina smiling after him.

Ah well. Duty called. "Come," she told the servants, and walked with them the few yards to the theater.

The Manager was waiting for her, watching up the street for her, and looking about as harried as she'd ever seen him. "Regina!" he exclaimed as soon as she came within speaking distance. "At last—"

She blinked in surprise. Had she possibly forgotten an early rehearsal? But how? "I . . . beg your pardon? I'm not late, am I?"

He shook his head violently. "No, no, I'm sorry—" he replied hastily, running his hand through what was left of his hair. "It's not that, it's just . . . I was terribly worried about you. There's been an accident. A floorboard onstage gave way, and Sella took a nasty spill."

Regina's hand flew to her mouth in dismay. "Oh no! Is she hurt?"

Again, to her immense relief, he shook his head. "A wrenched ankle and some bruises. Fortunately that's all. The woman could have broken her leg easily enough, or her neck. I've had the stage crew go over every one of the boards." The Manager wiped his brow. "You and I know there are always accidents in any theater, but there've been so many small incidents lately. . . . "

"The cast is growing uneasy," Regina finished for him. "I'll try speaking to them."

"Would you?" the Manager asked fervently. "Thank you. Perhaps they'll listen to *you*. And hopefully, hopefully nothing else will go wrong!"

They walked together into the theater; Regina's own personal servants remained, to go to her dressing room. The rest of her escort took themselves off to the nearest tavern; they would wait for the rehearsal to end before escorting her back to the Ducal Palace. As Regina climbed up onto the stage, she felt curious glances following her. She turned to see the others, actors and musicians together, watching, and for a moment couldn't find a thing to say.

But as she looked at them all, seeing in them the same dream of the theater that lived and moved within her, a sudden warmth surged up in her heart, a warmth born of mutual respect and affection.

Best start with a joke. There's nothing quite like laughter to chase fear-demons away.

"I suppose you're wondering why I called you all here today," she said, dryly imitating the Lord Mayor of Kingsford at his stuffiest.

Cast, supporting workers, and musicians all chuckled or giggled a bit nervously, but some of the tension eased at once.

"Well. I'm sure at this point everyone's nerves are quite frayed away. I know mine are." She looked around, taking care to meet every set of eyes that would meet hers. "That's the way it usually is at this stage of a production; we've just been under a little more strain than most. I know we've been having a weird string of accidents lately—but really, that's all they've been, accidents. You all know the Gypsy saying, don't you? 'The imp of the perverse only leaves when *he* is weary.' Trust me, my dears—I have lived as long as some of you and a good deal longer than many, and I can tell you that misfortunes, like pigeons, roost in flocks and leave droppings *everywhere.*"

That earned her a laugh, and this one was genuine.

She smiled at them all. "Don't think that *I* have been left out of being splattered, either. Remember the ribbons and the mask? And I just came from a Church sermon wherein I was singled out and told I was triply damned." She ticked the points off on her fingers. "First, I dare wear paint on my face." Regina imitated the oily voice of the priest, and heard an appreciative ripple of amusement.

"Then we're *all* damned!" one of the extras shouted, and won a few outright laughs.

"Exactly," Regina said. "But there's worse. I dare pretend to be what I am not. Poor me, daring to play a woman playing a boy!"

Almost everyone was laughing by this point. "Sinful!" someone called out, and "Shameless!" someone else exclaimed.

Regina let them go on for a time, each one trying to top the next, then held up her hands for silence. "And third, and worst of all, not only am I an actor, not only are we all actors, we let ourselves be sponsored by the most sinful man of all, the Duke of Kingsford who dares support the theater and all the arts!"

"Hurrah for the Duke!" an actor yelled.

"Do you dare say this?" Regina asked slyly. "Do you dare claim to be an actor?"

"Yes!" "We do!" "We are!" It was a ragged cheer, but it came from almost all of them.

"Do you dare claim to be a member of the Duke of Kingsford's Company?"

"Yes!" they shouted, this time a bit less raggedly.

And now was the time to egg them on, to bolster their courage by encouraging their spirit. "I can't hear that," she chided. "Are we all the Duke of Kingsford's Company?"

"Yes!" came the shout, with more fervor.

She stamped her foot on the stage. "Again! Are we the Duke of Kingsford's Company?"

"*Yes!*" they shouted as one. "*Yes!*"

Regina grinned. "Then let's prove it. Let's stop all this superstitious nonsense and get to work!"

She stood for a moment in triumph, watching everyone setting off to his or her work. Only one figure didn't move. Raven, face impassive, was studying her as steadily as if he was trying to solve a puzzle.

"Is something wrong?" Regina asked, perplexed by his expression.

He started. "Ah, no. Of course not." Moving to the edge of the stage, leaning on both elbows, he added with a grin, "Brilliant speech. I don't know what office you're seeking, woman, but you've got my vote."

"So glad to hear that." As Regina stepped down from the stage, she asked, "Did you know that it was our priestly 'friend' from the street corner who was speaking out against us in the Church of St. Bede this morning?"

Raven shrugged. "I'm not exactly an avid church-goer."

She studied him for a moment, wondering if all those stories that she had heard about Gypsies were true. And if they were—did he hold a solution to this run of so-called bad luck they'd been having? "Raven . . ."

He cocked an eyebrow at her. "Eh?"

"This sounds stupid, but . . . you don't really think something strange has been happening here, do you?" She hoped that he would answer "no."

To her discomfort, he didn't answer right away. "I don't know," the man said after a thoughtful while. "I'd like to think we've just been having an inordinate share of accidents, but when you add to that this sudden interest in the theater by the Church—"

She grimaced. "Or at least by one particular cleric."

"—with sermons against us by that same cleric," Raven continued, "then I do have to suspect that there might be something more going on than is . . . " He shrugged again. "Something more than natural."

Trust a Gypsy to see the occult in everything, Regina told herself drily. *I never should have asked him.* "I didn't mean the supernatural. Just some sort of plot against us."

Raven frowned slightly and turned to study the

empty house, leaning back against the stage. "Oh, I agree. The question isn't so much whether or not these incidents are magical but whether they really are related—and why. There are all sorts of charming possibilities. I think we can rule out a disgruntled employee. The Manager, for all his bluster, hasn't fired anyone, and for all his sternness he never says anything to really hurt anyone's feelings."

"Not to the point of wanting revenge, no," Regina murmured. "But there's a much larger picture."

"Oh, right. Politics." Raven spat that out as if it was an obscenity, and Regina glanced at him.

"Is this, do you suppose," she asked carefully, "a veiled threat against me? Or more to the point, against Duke Arden, using me as the way to get at him? Against the very idea of this theater?"

"Just as easily say, against the Free Bards," Raven added with a sigh. "And while we're mulling things over, is said threat coming from the Church, or from the Guild?"

She nodded. "The Bardic Guild, you mean. They don't take too kindly to you Free Bards, do they?"

Raven snorted. "There's an understatement! We don't fit in any of their neat, dull little niches, we go where we want and sing what we want: in short, we're everything they fear and envy all wrapped up in one. What makes it worse is that our nice, so-very-law-abiding Guild does often work hand-in-hand with the Church, and —

Suddenly his eyes widened. "Holy—look out!"

He pushed her aside so roughly Regina went sprawling—just as a heavy section of scenery came crashing down off the stage, landing right where she'd been standing.

The crash brought everyone running back into the

theater in alarm. Raven didn't wait for them, but vaulted lithely up onto the stage, disappearing into the wings. As Regina scrambled back to her feet, shaking, the Manager hurried up to her.

He gave her his hand to steady her as she brushed off her dress with trembling fingers. "My dear woman, are you all right?"

She nodded, too shaken for speech. Wringing his hands, the Manager moaned, "I *knew* we should have stayed with the old-fashioned painted hangings. Wooden sections are too unstable!"

"Nonsense." Regina managed that in almost a level voice. "The illusion is better with these. . . ." Her voice trailed off as she looked up. "Oh—" she breathed. "Oh no—"

The Manager tried to see what she was looking at, but he was notoriously short-sighted. "What is it?"

She pointed. "The wire holding the counterweight, the weight that would have kept the panel safely upright—"

"Yes, yes, I know what it's supposed to do," he said impatiently, squinting. "What about—" He stopped short. "Where is it?"

Regina shrugged helplessly. "The wire must have snapped. That can happen, what with all the weight it has to bear. And then only the slightest push would have been enough to—"

Just then, Raven darted back onstage, face wild with frustration. "Not a soul back there. Whoever pushed the panel must have run like hell to get away."

"But this is impossible!" the Manager protested. "No one would have done such a horrible thing; there'd be no reason. Why, Regina could have been killed!"

"The . . . wind?" Jaysen suggested uncertainly. "If

the counterweight wire had already snapped, the panel would have been shaky enough. Maybe the wind was just strong enough . . . ?"

The Manager glanced gratefully his way. "Yes. Of course that's what it was, nothing more than a—a stray gust of wind. When one of the back doors to the theater comes open, you can get quite a powerful gust blasting up off the river. You," he pointed to one of the stagehands, "go back and see if one of the doors did come open."

The man disappeared. From behind the stage came his ghostly cry: "One of the door's open, all right. Probably wasn't latched properly."

Or whoever pushed the scenery left it open when he escaped. Looking at Raven, Regina knew he was thinking the same thing. *But damned if I'm going to panic everyone all over again. The play must go on.*

The Manager threw up his hands in relief. "There we have it: it *was* the wind. From now on one of you stagehands has the added job of making *sure* those doors stay locked. And *you*—" He pointed at one particularly steady fellow. "Your job is to check those counterweights when you arrive in the morning, right after lunch-break, and when we finish in the evening. Is the panel damaged?"

The scenery crew had been worriedly studying it. *Almost*, Regina thought with a touch of amusement, *as though they're more worried about it than me! But then, they spent hours making it. And they certainly haven't made me!* The unexpected double entendre made her giggle, and the Manager glanced at her in alarm.

"Are you truly all right, my dear?" he asked in an undertone. "Do you want to lie down?"

She shook her head, still choking back laughter. *I*

am not *going to become hysterical,* she scolded herself.

Magpie moved forward to take her arm. "We're going out to the inn," she said shortly. "You need a chance to just sit down with a good, hot cup of *chai*."

"Thank you, yes," Regina admitted, willing to allow herself that much weakness. "I'm afraid you're right about that."

The Manager nodded his approval, his attention already back on the scenery. "It *is* undamaged?"

The chief designer nodded shortly, already surveying the stage for the best way to raise the piece back to its proper place again. "Just scratched a little. We can fix that with a few daubs of paint."

The Stage Manager sighed. "Good, good."

As Regina left with Magpie, she heard the Manager chattering away like a worried mother hen, fussing over the dourly muttering stagehands.

"Get the panel upright . . . careful! Don't bend it or it will break! Yes, yes, now you and you, get up there onstage. Pull the panel back up there with you, gently—*gently*, I say! Keep it straight! There, that's right. Now get it back in place . . . good! You'll take care of the rewiring? Double strength this time, you say? Fine. Rewire *all* the panels. That's right, *all* of them. We don't want another incident. Is that one stable? Yes? You're sure? Fine! That does it. We've taken care of this situation then. I'll leave it in your hands. The matter is closed."

But as Regina glanced back over her shoulder, locking gazes with Raven, she knew neither one of them truly believed that.

CHAPTER TEN

STRANGE NEW MELODIES

In the middle of rehearsing an intricate little fiddle trill from Act II, Scene 2, Raven glanced up—and froze. Into the theater was marching a whole little army, servants, most of them, he guessed from their livery of blue and gold. But in the midst of their common, pale blue plumage strode a rare bird indeed: a man of middle height and solid build, hair and beard more gray than brown. Dressed in rich, somber robes of gold-flecked maroon brocade, a gold chain of office about his shoulders, he carried himself like a prince.

Or a Duke, Raven realized suddenly. "Well, now," he murmured to the others, "this must be our noble patron himself."

So it must, indeed. The Manager, not the sort to fawn on anyone, still managed to get a good deal of deference into his polite, proper greeting. And Regina, still in Flora's frilly gown, scurried down from the stage to throw herself into the Duke's embrace with a happy cry of "Oh, you *did* come!"

Well, that certainly confirmed his identification. Raven studied the man covertly, liking what he saw. Especially liking how he treated Regina.

Still with his arm about her, Duke Arden strolled towards the musicians, apparently not at all bothered by having to look up at them where they stood onstage. "These, I take it, are the Free Bards?" he asked the Manager, and at the man's nod, gave them all a courteous little dip of the head. "You've probably gathered who I am by now."

Raven grinned, and spoke up for all of them—since even Magpie seemed too stunned to reply. "Be pretty foolish if we hadn't."

To his amazement, the Duke grinned right back at him. "You *must* be Raven. Regina's told me about you."

Raven heard Magpie's soft gasp, and felt a bit like gasping himself. "Has she, now?" he asked very carefully.

"Indeed. You've been truly professional, you and your fellows, helping my Company marvelously. And rather good at knowing the right moment for a jest, so she says. Every good leader should have that particular talent." The hazel eyes held Raven's gaze, evaluating but not at all hostile. *Almost,* the Gypsy thought incredulously, *as though he's thanking me for being kind to Regina!*

"But I'm interfering with your rehearsal," the Duke said after a moment. "Please, continue. And no," he added with a laugh, "I'm not going to say something foolish like, 'Just pretend I'm not here!'"

That produced an uncertain chuckle from the Free Bards and an easy laugh from the actors, who apparently were quite at ease with their noble patron. He

stood there in the open pit like any penniless groun-
dling, and after a moment's hesitation, Raven shrugged
and signaled to the other musicians, pulling the
screening alcove curtains into place; if the Duke
wanted to be an audience, he'd be treated like one!

"From the Prologue?" Raven asked the Manager, who
stood in the wings where both actors and musicians could
see him, and at the man's nod, broke into the bouncy tune
that began the play. Patron or no patron, he had never yet
given less than an honest performance, and damned if he
was going to give a poor one now!

They took the play all the way through the first act
without pause, and for a wonder, Raven thought,
everything went just the way it was meant to go, with
no false entrances, no broken props, no missed cues.
Regina, now dressed in Florian's breeches, gave her
determined little closing couplet:

> "Come what may, through trials of heart and mind,
> Florian shall this day his fortune find!"

She dashed offstage, boy's sword raised in her
upheld hand, and the Duke broke into applause.

"Rest, everyone," the Manager called out. "Mistress
Gerna, turn and watch the hourglass, if you would. I
wish this break to last only as long as would a proper
intermission."

The Duke strolled forward. *Here we go*, Raven
thought cynically. *Now he's going to pay us some nice,
false, patronizing compliments. Talk about the pretty
music and how splendid Regina looks in breeches.*

But the Duke promptly engaged the Manager in a
discussion of literary style, congratulating him quite
sincerely on some of the elegant, clever phrases and
cunning little plays on words in the second scene,
quoting them flawlessly from memory. "As always, you

have a masterful taste for the language, man. Down-playing the sentiment like that: the audience isn't going to know just *why* they're so moved, not without any blatant pathos to drown them, but if there is one of them who doesn't sniff a bit over poor Flora's dilemma, I'm a bird-monger! Ah, and you, Master Raven and you others, I congratulate you, too. You see," he added to the Manager, a hint of mischief in his eyes, "I *told* you adding more musicians was a good idea."

"Your wish," the Manager said with dry sarcasm, "is my command."

Duke Arden laughed. "Since when?"

"Why, my lord Duke," the Manager retorted, "who would dare to countermand you?"

The Duke only looked sly, as if he knew a secret or three. "Not you, of course," he said, with heavy irony. "Never."

To Raven's astonishment the Manager actually grinned at that, his usually lugubrious face crinkling up with amusement. They were used to these games! Commoner and noble though they were, they were old friends used to good-natured heckling. "Isn't the Duke of Kingsford known far and wide as a paragon of virtue and wisdom?"

"Just as much as you're known as a paragon of fool-ish wit!" the Duke replied sharply. "But this once, you have to admit, I was right."

"Ah well, yes."

This, Raven thought wildly, was hardly like any other noble he'd ever come up against. Oh, yes, he certainly had met nobles before, even dined as a guest of one or two of them, but few of them had ever been quite so . . . approachable!

No wonder Regina loves him. Unless the man's a finer actor than any I've ever seen onstage, he's every bit as easy and honest as she.

"Intermission's over," Mistress Gerna called out suddenly.

"So be it," the Duke said, and returned to his place as obediently as his actors.

He stayed for the entire play, all three acts, right through to the grand finale, with all the actors onstage, whirling about in their joyous wedding dance and all the musicians playing full out. Applauding enthusiastically, he gestured to Regina. As she hurried to his side, Duke Arden whispered in her ear and gave her a quick, decorous kiss on the cheek. With a final appreciative bow for the entire Company, the Duke of Kingsford exited amid his coterie of servants. Regina, smiling, returned to where the drained musicians sat.

"I would be most honored," she said formally, "if you would visit me in my suite in the ducal palace tonight for a small, informal musical performance."

At the Duke's command, Raven finished silently for her. *Now what?* But of course it wouldn't be politic to refuse, so the Bard bowed his most gallant bow. "My dear Regina, I'm sure I speak for us all when I say we would be the ones who are honored."

The boardinghouse contained, unfortunately, only two small, cracked mirrors, hardly enough for a whole troupe of edgy Free Bards, all of them determined to look their best. Raven, in control of one of the mirrors, at least for the moment, glanced up and down at his multicolored, wide-sleeved shirt, with its many-hued ribbons, and grinned. Its cheerfulness went so beautifully with the somber black of eye patch, breeches, and boots. And if Regina and her Duke couldn't appreciate true Gypsy costuming, well, that was their loss!

"Where's Magpie?" Jaysen asked nervously. "We're running late."

"Coming!" called a voice from upstairs, and Magpie suddenly appeared out of the darkness on the landing.

Raven's breath caught in his throat. Regina must have lent her the gown, or maybe she'd been hiding it away all along, but: *Lovely, oh lovely, slim and graceful in gentle rose-pink—does she know how it plays up the softness of her hair and the beauty of her eyes? But how can she not. . . .* Hardly knowing what he was doing, he stepped forward to offer her his hand —

But she, ignoring him completely, took Owl's hand instead.

Damn, damn, damn! Raven thought. Angrily snatching up his fiddle case, he set out after them. This feuding was getting to the ridiculous point—and the worst of it was, he wasn't even guilty of anything!

All the way to the elegant ducal palace gleaming like gilded snow on its hill, he continued to fume, and by the time they'd reached the fine wrought-iron gates, Raven knew what he was going to have to do to end this foolishness.

But their performance must come first.

Raven had hardly expected mere musicians to be allowed through the front door, but this side entrance was almost as fine, the door frame of smooth white marble, as though whoever had designed the palace had wanted it all of one splendid piece. The Free Bards were met by a slim young manservant, sleek in his pale blue livery, who gave them the faintest of bows, narrow face carefully impassive.

"If it pleases you to follow me?" he said quietly.

"What if I said no?" Raven asked wryly.

"Then I should know you for the wrong musicians, and send for guards to have you removed," the servant replied without missing a beat, and the other Bards chuckled.

Raven smiled. "Don't you approve of musicians?" he asked as they started forward.

The man's expression remained bland and untroubled. "It's not for me to approve or disapprove."

Raven was not through prodding him, however—like a small boy with a turtle, he itched to produce some reaction. "Like the Guild music, do you?"

That earned him a quick sideways flick of suddenly nervous blue eyes. "If you are trying to pry out political secrets from me, I fear you must be sadly mistaken. I know none. I do but serve my lord the Duke."

Raven allowed his expression to become as bland as that of the servant. "Of course."

"Nice try," Magpie muttered sarcastically in Raven's ear.

He shrugged. "It was worth a try," he whispered back.

Their footsteps muffled by carpeting worked in intricate floral designs, the Free Bards were led down quietly elegant corridors lined with wood paneling gleaming softly from years of polish. Exquisite candelabras of iron worked to look like leafy branches stood at every corner, casting a gentle golden glow over everything.

"Pretty," Raven muttered, refusing to be impressed. "Just a bit too pretty."

"Jealous?" Magpie jibed, and he frowned at her.

"Hardly. I feel as if we're in the middle of an enormous, sugar-frosted, over-decorated pastry. Just hope no one decides to take a bite!"

That pried a stifled little giggle from the sleek young manservant. Determinedly refusing to laugh, he rapped on a door carved with a delicate design of flowers gleaming softly with gilding. As a second servant cast it open, the first stood aside with the barest of bows.

"Enter, if you would." But as Raven passed him, the

servant murmured, barely audibly, "For what it's worth, I *hate* Guild music."

"So do I," Raven agreed conspiratorially, and entered.

The chamber beyond was small, but exquisitely furnished, the floor of patterned marble checkered black and white, the walls painted a soft, dusky rose. Lacquered screens focused the glance—here, to draw attention to a graceful vase—and there, to the smooth lines of a simple lounge upholstered in velvet the exact shade of the walls. At one end of the room, lacy curtains covered tall, narrow windows letting in evening sunlight turned soft and muted, glinting off the inlaid wood of chairs and dainty tables placed here and there with artful casualness. A harp stood in one corner, covered by a brocade cloth, marking this formally as a music room.

Suddenly all the sterile, quiet prettiness came to vibrant life as Regina hurried in, her gown a darker rose that contrasted nicely with the intricate coils of her black hair. "Ah, forgive me! I didn't realize you were here already. Please, make yourselves comfortable. Refreshments are on the way."

Raven held up a hand. "First, we perform, then we eat."

"If you prefer." The woman sank to the lounge with such easy grace it looked unstudied, the folds of her gown settling about her like the petals of a rose.

And where, Raven wondered as they took their own seats, *is the Duke? Watching from behind that mirror, perhaps? Or listening from behind one of the screens?* He knew enough about the ways of nobility to understand that this music room was part of Regina's private suite, separate from the mainstream of palace life; everyone probably tactfully pretended she was just another Ducal guest. One who was . . . very fond of the Duke.

Idiots. Any man should be proud to have such a woman on his arm. Or in his bed.

Dangerous thought. Because he knew he was going to say something impolitic in another moment, Raven took his fiddle out of its case and became very interested in getting each string tuned exactly right.

There, now, that should do it. Raven glanced at the other musicians, then started right in with the sweet, gently melancholy strains of "The Maiden Esme's Lament." He played it all the way through, keeping the tempo slow but not dragging it, refusing to add more than the slightest of ornamentation to the deceptively simple lines.

At last he lowered his bow, aware of his fellows' cool, professional appreciation, but looking only at Regina. "Well? Does that meet with the Duke's approval?"

For one startled moment the air hung heavy with alarm and censure. Then Regina gave her bright, gamine grin. "I knew we couldn't fool you."

Applause sounded. The Duke of Kingsford stepped from behind a screen and took his place beside Regina, one arm draped with easy affection over her shoulders. "So much for polite pretense. Raven, my thanks. That was exquisitely played."

Raven's bow held only the slightest touch of sarcasm. He and the other Free Bards had had enough time back at the boardinghouse to plot out their whole program. "Never mind the fine court music," they'd all agreed. "The Duke must hear enough of that nonsense from everyone else. We are what we are."

So, when he straightened, Raven signaled to the others, and they, without hesitation, struck up the bouncy strains of "The Oak and Apple." He saw a startled, pleased smile light up the Duke's face as though he liked the common music but heard it all too seldom, and an answering delight sparkled in Regina's eyes. Amused by their reaction, Raven let an answering smile turn up the corners of his own mouth.

The Free Bards played on, singly and together, going from dance music to ballads to simple songs, showing the Duke every variation on every instrument they'd brought till at last Raven decided enough was enough. He led the others through the grand finale music from their own play, all of them ending up as one with a dramatic flourish. Still as one, they bowed, and the Duke and Regina both broke into genuine applause.

"Splendid," Duke Arden told them. "All of you. Quite splendid."

"Please," Regina murmured graciously, "put your instruments away now and take some refreshment."

As they nibbled neat little cakes and sipped iced drinks, Raven turned to the Duke and asked sardonically, "I take it you've decided we're professional enough for your theater?"

The corners of Duke Arden's mouth quirked up. "Was this all that transparent?"

Raven favored him with an eloquently raised eyebrow. "Quite."

The Duke raised his glass in a wry toast. "You pass with highest honors, all of you."

"Better than Guild musicians?" Raven asked, ignoring Magpie's startled, disapproving hiss.

The Duke's smile thinned ever so slightly. "Now, you'd hardly expect me to answer something so controversial, would you?"

Ah. He'd gone a step too far. Raven took the warning hinting in the suddenly chill voice. "My apologies," he said at his most urbane. "I would never dream of pressuring so gracious a host."

To his relief, Duke Arden merely laughed. "Oh no, of course you wouldn't. Look you, man, I can understand why you and the other Free Bards are walking nervously these days, and I wish I could set your minds at ease. But surely you know anyone of rank *always* walks nervously. Trust me, my musical friends, I have enough problems with simply keeping life running smoothly here in Kingsford. I don't need to involve myself in anything as perilous as Guild politics, thank you."

Which, of course, sounds impressive but says absolutely nothing. This time it was Raven who raised his glass wryly. "Then let us, by all means, discuss something . . . less upsetting. To the success of *A Twice-Told Tale.*"

"To the *Tale*," the Duke agreed, and drank.

CHAPTER ELEVEN

RENEWED FLUTTERS

"Is he still out there?" one of the actors asked. No need to ask *who*, not with the suppressed anger on every face.

Raven, newly arrived with the other musicians at the theater that morning, let out his breath in an angry hiss. "Still there, that oily excuse for a priest: still on his street corner, still ranting and raving about the theater and the sinful folk who work there."

"I don't like it," someone mumbled. Raven saw, somewhat to his surprise, that the voice belonged to the nameless illusionist; until this very moment, the scrawny youngster had been as taciturn as Crow. In fact, Raven realized, up to this point he hadn't even known the man *could* talk! The illusionist reddened when everyone turned his way, but continued darkly, "People are starting to listen to him."

"Oh, nonsense," Magpie snapped. "They're listening

not because they believe a thing he's saying—I'll bet you anything you want half of them couldn't repeat one word of it—but only because he's providing something we'll be able to provide them in much better style: live theater."

"Easy for you to say," the illusionist muttered, scowling. "You're not the one in danger. *I'm* the one who's working magic. I'm the one they'll cart off first."

"They're not going to cart anyone off." Regina's quiet voice was as soothing as balm on an irritated wound. "All this foolishness will end as soon as the play opens and everyone realizes it *isn't* what he claims it is, and how much harmless fun it is. Much more fun," she added with a smile, "than standing around in the dust and the hot sun listening to an inane preacher's ravings. But they aren't going to see the play if we don't finish rehearsals."

"Point well taken," Raven said. "Once more into the fray, dear friends."

"Nicely said," came a voice from the rear of the theater. "A bit scrambled on the quotation, perhaps, but nicely declaimed, and well chosen."

Raven turned in surprise. "Ah, my lord Duke. I didn't see you enter."

The Duke grinned up at all of them. "I can move quietly when I wish. And swiftly. Don't stand there staring at me, everyone. To work, all of you!"

Raven, refusing to be cowed by authority, gave the man a low, melodramatically intricate bow. As he took his place with the other musicians in their onstage alcove, he was frowning slightly. Odd, very odd. After their performance in the ducal palace, Arden had begun showing up at the theater rather frequently.

Now, what is he about? It's one thing for a man to enjoy watching his mistress, or even to take pride in an enterprise into which he's pouring money. But this surge of interest was all out of proportion even to the fact that the Company was basically a vehicle for Regina. *Ah well, the man is paying the bills. Not for us to question his motives.*

Easy to say. But as the days passed, bringing them closer and closer to their first performance, the Duke's visits increased. And, Raven noticed warily, there seemed to be a new, brittle edge to him that hadn't been visible before.

But then, there was a brittle edge to everyone these days. The weird series of accidents had stopped as suddenly as it had begun, leaving everyone feeling strangely off balance, sure the troubles were going to continue, wondering nervously when that would be and in what form.

"The illusionist doesn't look like he's going to last till Opening Day," Nightjar murmured to the other musicians. "I mean, look at the man! He's so high-strung he's going to snap like a guitar string. I swear he's worried off so much weight there's hardly any meat left on him. And his hands are shaking so much I'm surprised he can cast any illusions at all!"

"Nerves," Crow muttered. "Be all right when the play opens."

Magpie shook her head. "It's more than that, I think. He's so scared the Church is going to *get* him, he's worked himself to the edge of hysteria."

And at last, as she had predicted, the youngster fell over the edge.

It happened no more than a week from Opening Day. Everything was going well; they were in full rehearsal now, and the boy would cast his illusions two and three times a day. He had made it through sunlight, fog, and was about to manage moonlight, when without any warning, he let out a shriek of sheer despair. "That's it! I'm not going to stay here a moment longer. I quit!"

The Manager dove down on him like an avenging fury, grabbing him by the arm. "You can't quit, man, not now!"

"Ha!" The illusionist tore himself free with a savage, "Try and stop me!"

"But you *can't!*" the Manager all but gibbered. "We're all depending on—"

"Spare me the stupid sentiment," the boy spat back, hysterically. "You don't have to listen to that—that vicious, *evil* preacher every day; you don't have to see him stare into your eyes as though he knows perfectly well who and what you are and is just waiting to see you burn!"

"We wouldn't let—"

The mage cut him short. "Oh, you'd protect me, would you? As if you *could!* What a lie!"

"It's not—"

"A lie!" the illusionist shrieked. "You don't have to see the suspicion in everyone's eyes here, either! You don't care what happens to me! If you needed a scapegoat, you'd gladly throw me to them! You all think *I'm* the one who caused all those accidents, don't you? Well, don't you?"

A few of the actors did look embarrassed, refusing to meet his terrified gaze. But Raven said calmly, "It's not possible. You're an illusionist, right? No other powers, right? It wasn't illusion that broke the board poor Sella fell into, or knocked over the scenery, either." The Gypsy reached out a gentle hand, making his expression as calming as possible. "We all know the difference between illusion and reality! So let's forget all this nonsense and—"

"No!" The illusionist slapped away Raven's hand and, before anyone could move to stop him, bolted out of the theater like a frightened deer.

There was a long, confused silence. Then the Manager let out his breath in a great sigh. "We were all wondering what new disaster was going to strike. At least now we don't have to wonder."

"We'll just have to manage without his illusions," Regina said softly.

"That's right," Magpie added. "We never really needed them anyway, not really. Oh, don't give me those sorrowful looks! What are you, true actors or just children who need pretty tricks to cover up the fact that you really can't act?"

That sparked more than a few angry mutters, but she continued fiercely, "Actors, is it? You've decided on that? Then stop complaining! If between your performance and our music we can't make the audience believe exactly what we want them to believe, then there's something very much the matter with us all!"

She wasn't a Regina, Raven thought, grinning, to dazzle everyone with glamorie, but at least she'd gotten everyone back to work!

Even so, he had to admit after they'd run through the formerly "moonlit" scene, it just wasn't quite the same without the illusion. What a shame that those lantern-like footlights couldn't cast a convincingly cool white light, no matter what colored-paper filters were placed in front of them. And what a shame there was no safe way to cast light down on the stage from somewhere up in the rafters. Raven had heard tales all his life of strange contrivances, most of them created by the mysterious race known as the Deliambrens, that allowed for such wonders—but such things were horribly expensive, and the Deliambrens were loath to part with them. Some Gypsies he knew, like Robin, had been privileged to see them, and to see their near-magical fortress-city, but most, like him, had only heard the rumors. And how could one find Deliam-bren light-bringers at such notice, anyway?

Might as well wish for the moon itself.

But the next day, Duke Arden arrived practically radiating secret delight. "We have our moonlight," he declared without preamble, signaling to some of his blue-clad servants. "Be careful with those! They were costly as the devil," he added to the puzzled actors, "but if they work, they'll be worth the expense."

"Lanterns?" the Manager asked in confusion. "But where would one place a candle?"

The Duke laughed. "You don't *need* candles. Only sunlight. And there should be enough of that," he added, craning his head back, shading his eyes with a hand, "filtering through those narrow windows up by the rafters. Is your pigeon boy about?"

"In a manner of speaking," the Manager said ambiguously, scanning the upper tier himself. "Ah." He gave a sudden sharp whistle, making everyone jump. A hand waved in acknowledgment from up in the shadowed seats.

"Pigeon boy?" Crow asked with as much curiosity as the drummer ever showed.

"He's the one," Regina explained with a grin, "whose job it is to scramble about up there near the roof, routing pigeons that think the theater would be a perfect place to nest. We certainly don't want them . . . ah . . . dropping anything on the audience. Particularly not on the noble part of the audience!"

Raven laughed. "Hardly! But—" He stopped short, staring. Up till now, he could have sworn that the slight, lithe figure scampering its way down from the rafters was a boy, maybe one about twelve years old. But as the figure came closer, Raven caught the glint of scales. "What *is* that?"

"Haven't you ever seen a Tilsani?" Magpie's voice was disgustingly smug.

"Of course I have," Raven insisted. "I was just startled for a moment, that's all."

"Of course," she echoed.

"I *have* done a fair amount of travelling, you know," he said indignantly.

"Am I denying it?" she asked smoothly.

Ach, no arguing with the woman! Raven watched the Tilsani lightly leap the last few feet to the floor of the pit, then scurry forward. *Like a lizard caught in the middle of turning to a human!*

A shy lizard. The Tilsani wouldn't come quite close to the actors, only just barely tolerating the Manager's patronizing pat on the scaly arm. "Don't be afraid," the man murmured. "Listen to what your Duke wishes of you."

Duke Arden was as casual as though he saw the lizard-like people every day. "I would like you to take these lights up to the rafters—gently, mind you!—and fix them in place where the sunlight can fall fully on them. See? These prongs fit into the wood, like this. Got that? Yes? Make sure their faces are aimed straight at the stage. Can you do that?"

A quick dip of the reptilian head. The Tilsani snatched up the first light, ignoring the Duke's sharply indrawn breath, and scampered back up into the rafters.

"He's mute," the Manager murmured. "And I suspect not quite right in his head, though it's difficult to always be sure about a non-human. I'm not even sure of his name—or if he *has* one. But he's thoroughly reliable."

So he seemed to be, setting the lights in place, one by one, in a short time. "Now," the Duke said to Regina, "I want you to get up onstage and say this phrase. I know it's a line in the play."

He whispered it in her ear. Regina shrugged, climbed onto the stage, and proclaimed, "The glowing moon!" She added a startled, "Oh!" echoed by the others, because the lights had suddenly come to life, beaming down on the stage a cool white radiance that looked remarkably like true moonlight.

"Amazing people, the Deliambrens," Duke Arden said with immense satisfaction. "Tall, beautiful, and strange—but oh, what wonderful technicians! Don't worry," he added to the Manager. "The 'moonlight' will fade again as soon as the actors leave the stage; the lights are keyed to human body warmth as well as the trigger-phrase. Exit a moment, if you would, my dear . . . there." The lights obligingly faded. "Now, come back onstage, please, and say, 'The bright sun.' That's in the play, too."

Regina did—and the lights promptly beamed yellow radiance down onto the stage. She burst into delighted wonder. "This is marvelous!"

"It is, isn't it?" the Duke agreed, and beamed as brightly as the lights. Then he turned to the Stage Manager with an arch grin. "Of course—*now* you are going to have to somehow write 'the bright sun' and 'the glowing moon' into every one of your plays to justify my horrendous expenditure!"

The Stage Manager only cast his eyes up, as if asking for patience from on high.

The days slipped away towards the date of the first performance. The cast was running through the entire play at one stretch now, and the Manager, tense as a mother hen with chicks who weren't quite to be trusted to behave, promised that soon, soon, they'd be ready for a full dress rehearsal. Fewer mistakes were being made, despite his worryings—and fewer accidents occurred.

And the Duke of Kingsford showed up to watch them almost every day. Finally Raven lost all patience with trying to puzzle out just what was going on there, and cornered the Manager.

"All right, man," he growled. "The Duke's been watching us like a duck with one egg. This has gone far beyond the casual interest of a man in his mistress or even in his financial investment. What is all this about?"

The Manager's surprise was tinged with obvious guilt. A good thing that the man wrote and directed the plays—he'd never have made an actor. "Why, what can you—"

"Oh, please," Raven groaned. "Give me some credit for brains. He's here almost all the time, watching. Watching for *what*?"

The Manager sagged in surrender. "I can only make a surmise about this, understand. But I do happen to know that some of the Royal Advisers are going to be secret attendees at the premiere."

Raven blinked. "Are they, now!"

"Indeed." The Manager mopped his brow. "You see the point, don't you? The Duke *must* be sure that his Company looks legitimate, and is not merely a toy for his favorite mistress."

"That would be a bit of a social blunder, I take it?" Raven asked carefully.

"Worse than that." The Manager hesitated an uneasy while, then let out his breath in a long sigh. "The truth of it is, there have been rumors, ugly rumors, about Regina."

Now that took him completely by surprise. "What do you mean? We all know she's absolutely faithful to the Duke, lucky man, and that he adores her."

"That's just it. You see . . . " the Manager hesitated a moment more, then said, so softly that Raven could hardly hear him, " . . . the rumors claim that Regina is a sorceress."

Raven had to stifle his yelp. "What!"

"Yes," the Manager nodded, sweat standing out on his forehead, "and that she has enthralled our Duke to the point that he will give her anything."

Raven could not help himself. He snorted. "Oh, that's ridiculous!"

"Not really." The Stage Manager's gloomy expression convinced Raven as nothing else could have. "If the Company turns out to be a failure, that will, the rumor-mongers claim, prove them right. And that, of course, would disgrace Duke Arden beyond redemption."

"It wouldn't be so good for Regina, either!" Raven said sardonically.

"Ah, no. Of course not." The Manager did not mention Regina's probable fate, but they could both imagine what it would be. At the best, she would have to be cast off. At the worst? Could the Church demand that she be handed over for trial as a sorceress? "But if the Company impresses the advisers, well then, all is fine. The Duke's reputation will be saved, and even enhanced as a genuine patron of the arts."

"Well, then, all is fine. . . ." Raven repeated softly, more shaken than he cared to reveal. There was more going on behind the scenes, as it were, than any of them had dreamed! And those rumors of sorcery . . . Oh, they were far too close to the truth for him to feel comfortable. As soon as he could convincingly get away from the Manager, Raven set out to speak with Regina.

"Raven?" she asked in surprise as he nearly backed her into a corner. "What in the world are you—"

"Is it true?" he demanded without any preamble. "Are there really rumors about you?"

"I don't know what—" she began.

"Oh, yes you do!" he snapped. "Dammit, woman, you know I'm not talking about what you and your Duke do together; that's your business. I'm talking about the rumors that you've been working sorcery on him!"

"Oh. That." She smiled, but it was a shaky smile, and not at all convincing.

"Regina, *please!*" he groaned. "The Manager has already told me about the Royal Advisers *and* the rumors, and he's not the sort to toss off idle gossip."

"Ah . . . no," Regina admitted.

"Then tell me! Is he right? Are there such rumors?" And could he convince her to confide in him?

Her gaze dropped. "I . . . have to admit it," the woman murmured. "He's probably right."

"Dear sweet gods of music," Raven breathed.

"It's not that bad, Raven," she said hastily. "The Duke isn't going to let anything happen to me—or to himself."

Raven bit back what he'd been about to blurt out. Oh, true, he hardly wanted to see her in the Church's grip, and Duke Arden, nobleman or not, seemed too decent a fellow for such a fate, either. But they weren't the only ones in peril! If Regina was charged with sorcerous intent, the entire Company could, only too easily, be taken with the very same charge! His thoughts ran round and round like frightened little mice.

Ach, yes, what an easy jump of illogic that would make for those narrow, hating little minds. Why not *condemn us all? Actors and musicians are considered lower than low anyhow!*

Worse, still worse, two of the Company, he and Crow, were Gypsies—and all those nice, Churchgoing idiots who accepted everything their priest might tell them already believed Gypsies practiced every type of sorcery!

They'll burn the lot of us!

Like hell they would. *First,* Raven told himself sharply, *they have to catch us! And if we can only stick together they're not going to be able to do that.*

Oh, right. Perfect unity. With a feud the size of an icy river running between himself and Magpie.

I should never have let it go on for so long. But, one way or another, Raven decided fiercely, *it's not going on any longer!*

CHAPTER TWELVE

SETTLING RUFFLED FEATHERS

It's been a long day, Magpie mused wearily on her way up the boardinghouse stairway to her room. *Going to be good to just sit down and relax. I wish my room had something more than that cramped little hipbath. A nice, hot soak would be wonderful. . . . I bet Regina has a bath deep enough to swim in. All the hot water she wants, too.*

She was shocked from her envious little reverie by Raven suddenly appearing out of the shadows. Magpie had time only for a startled, "What are you doing?" before he shoved her into her room and slammed the door shut behind them.

For one wild, panic-stricken moment Magpie could hardly find the air even to breathe, her mind gibbering, *He's gone mad, Raven has gone mad!* But this was stupid, worse than stupid, she was acting like any idiotic little girl in the ballads, even if he did look terrifyingly insane, with his single eye blazing like that and his face all contorted with rage —

Nonsense! Furious at herself for her weakness, she yelled, "What the *hell* do you think you're—"

"Shut up!" he hissed.

"How dare you—" she began.

"Just shut up!" he spat again. "You've already gotten us into enough of a tangle with this insane jealousy of yours."

"Jealousy!" Magpie echoed incredulously. "I'm not—"

"Oh, not much you're not!" he retorted, his face a veritable mask of anger. "You practically seethe every time I so much as mention Regina's name. Go on," Raven added challengingly, "deny it. Tell me to my face that you aren't jealous of the woman. Well?" he prodded. "Go on! You're so outspoken about everything else. Tell me you aren't jealous of Regina!"

"I won't!" She intended it to come out forcefully, but her voice broke.

He laughed, a short, sarcastic bark. "You *can't!*"

She fell back on bluster. "That's the stupidest thing —"

"Prove it," he insisted, his voice deep with sarcasm. "Go ahead, tell me you aren't jealous of her."

"I—I—Oh *damn!*" Why did she always have to be so ridiculously honest? Why did she have to be honest even with herself? "All right, curse you," Magpie said flatly. "I am."

Raven gave a great sigh of pure exasperation, and relaxed. "Now that," he said, in a more conversational tone, "really is the stupidest thing I've heard from you."

His reply left her spluttering with mingled outrage and shock. "What?"

"Look you, you little twit, you have nothing at all to

be jealous about. Regina *is* a beautiful woman; I'd be the world's worst liar and greatest fool if I tried to deny it. But she has eyes for one man only—and that man is Arden, Duke of Kingsford." The exasperation was plain in his voice now, echoing in every word. "Don't *you* have eyes, woman? Haven't you seen her when the Duke's in the theater? She plays only to him. And when he isn't there, well, she doesn't deny their relationship, but have you ever heard her say one disparaging word about him? There's not a shred of doubt," Raven continued with flat honesty. "There is no room for another man in Regina's life."

"No," Magpie admitted softly. But she refused to surrender so meekly! "That doesn't forgive the way you've been acting."

"I!" Raven yelped. "I haven't done anything!"

"Oh no." Now it was her turn to have the high ground, and she seized it, her own voice dripping with irony. "Every time I see Regina, you're hovering around her, sniffing at her, edging her into dark corners—"

But to her surprise, he looked at her as if she had just flubbed a simple harmony. "Don't be an idiot. And don't make me out to be one, either! I have more sense than to fool around with a nobleman's mistress."

"Not for want of trying! You, yourself, said she's beautiful, and—and—" She faltered to a stop, her voice unexpectedly choking. But not with tears—no—

"And so are you, dammit!" Raven shouted, and without any warning at all, kissed her full on the lips.

For one startled moment Magpie couldn't do anything but think inanely, *Nice* . . . Then she drew back and slapped him sharply across the face. Raven's hand shot up, and Magpie froze, watching, ready to dodge.

But then Raven let his hand fall and turned abruptly

away, shoulders shaking. "What is it?" Magpie asked warily. "I couldn't have hit you *that* hard, and—" She caught the sound of smothered chuckles. "You're laughing!" she accused.

He turned to face her, his mouth contorting with the effort of holding his laughter back. "Of—of course I am. We just acted like a pair of living clichés, you and I!"

"What—I—" To her astonishment, Magpie felt her own laughter start welling up until at last she had to let it free. Giggling, she admitted, "We did, didn't we? But I'm not going to apologize for hitting you."

"And I'm certainly not," Raven chuckled, "going to apologize for kissing you." He held out a hand. "Peace?"

Magpie touched palms with him. "Peace."

"Good. I don't think my poor face could stand another go-round like that." The humor slowly drained from Raven's face. "Magpie, enough games," he said quietly. "I had to settle matters between us quickly because I suspect we're going to need to stand firm, all of us, fairly soon."

"What do you mean?" She blinked at him, then a surmise dawned upon her. "Is this about the theater?"

Raven nodded. "I've been thinking about all our odd little accidents."

"You can't possibly think they're all related," she answered him uncertainly. "Can you?" The expression on his face frightened her in ways she didn't understand. "Raven . . . ?"

"Why not?" He shrugged, but his expression was a brooding and unhappy one. "The Church doesn't like us, the Guild doesn't like us, and Powers Above only know what enemies the Duke has. Ah, and then there are the rumors. The ones that hint that Regina is a sorceress. And if she's branded one, and she's always seen in our company . . ."

Magpie shuddered; suddenly this all seemed far too plausible. Certainly the Church could make it so! "But that would mean the accidents are all part of one big plot."

"Against the Duke," Raven agreed. "What better way to discredit him—and incidentally destroy us—than to sabotage the whole theater and end up blaming it all on nasty, sorcery-working us?"

Magpie opened her mouth to argue, closed it again. "Raven," she said at last, "if this is true, if there really is some sort of conspiracy, we can't possibly handle it on our own. And the Duke isn't going to believe us."

"Not without proof, no." He nodded, and waited.

He *wanted* to hear what she had to say! Well, that was a change! "Well then, I think we'd better call a convocation of all the Free Bards in the house, right here and now." She folded her arms across her chest and looked at him with challenge in her eyes.

She half expected Raven to disagree—they'd been doing so much of that lately—but to her surprise, he nodded eagerly. "If we act quickly, we can catch everyone at one time."

It wasn't difficult: Raven found Nightjar right away and got her to give a series of long, loud blasts of the horn that brought all the musicians scurrying down to the common room.

"What the hell—"

"What are you—"

"What's going on?"

Magpie held up her hands for silence. "Please. We needed to get everyone in on this meeting. It's important to all of us." She glanced at Raven, who was practically radiating anxiety. "Raven, if you would?"

Quickly, eliminating any trace of his usual flamboyant language, the man outlined all that had been happening at the theater. Before he had quite finished, the others were murmuring uneasily.

"I know what you mean," Owl said. "I've been hearing that priest on what seems like every street corner. Sometimes he contents himself with just denouncing the theater, but lately he's been expanding his diatribes to include *all* performers."

"Worse than that," Crow muttered. "This talk of sorcery: guess who's going to get blamed for that?" He pointed a thumb at Raven and himself. "Get us, they will. Anyone who's 'different.'"

"Tell me about it," the dark-skinned Nightjar exclaimed. "Huh. It's all right for the Church to work magic. But let anyone else try even the most benevolent of healing spells . . . " She shook her head. "You ask me, it's only a matter of time before the Church outlaws any magics not worked by its own priests."

"It happened in Gradford," Raven warned them all. "It could happen here. This time it isn't just one priest gone bad; it looks like a conspiracy of anyone who has reason to want to be rid of Duke Arden."

"It's more than that," Owl added. "You wouldn't have noticed this, your lives wrapped up in the theater the way they've been lately, but the Church has been butting into people's lives in more and more ways. Did you know it's now illegal to sell anything dyed scarlet to the common folk? That's right," he told the indignant Nightjar, whose bright neck scarf was a definite scarlet. "Better hide that before you walk outside. The Church has decided that unless it's worn by a Church official, scarlet becomes a sinful color. Promotes sensual thoughts."

"Ha!" she said scornfully. "They just don't want anyone mimicking them."

Owl shrugged. "Who are we to question the Church?" he asked drily. "But wait, there are other rules." He ticked them off on his fingers. "All selling of any sort must stop during the official hours of prayer. No one may wear any robe that might be mistaken for Church vestments: hmm, maybe your guess is right at that, Nightjar. No woman may display her hair unbound—more sensual thoughts," he added dourly.

"But this is ridiculous!" Magpie exploded. "Why is everyone putting up with it?"

"My dear, this *is* the Church." Owl shrugged. "Right now, the penalty for such indiscretions is only to perform some sort of penance or pay a fine to the Church—which hardly applies to us, since we never bother to attend—but I suspect it won't be long before Church law becomes *general* law."

"But—the King!" someone spluttered. "What of the King?"

"The King," Owl drawled, "seems to be most conveniently turning a blind—or perhaps a blinkered—eye to the whole affair."

"I can't believe Duke Arden's allowing this kind of nonsense," Jaysen said stoutly.

"What would you have him do?" It was Owl who replied, with all the wisdom and world-weariness of his years behind him. "Your Duke's a good man; you all must know that by now. But even though he's such a well-known populist, even though he rules Kingsford with the help of a Council of elected citizens—didn't know that, did you?"

"We're hardly active in the political scene," Raven drawled, and Owl grinned.

"No. Can't see a notorious fellow like you running for office." He lost his smile. "But no matter how well-meaning and 'for the people' Duke Arden may be, he's still only one man."

"That's right," Magpie said slowly. "If the Church could discredit him, *hey, presto,* out he'd go, neatly removed from advising the King against following their edicts."

Finch—or was it Verdin?—shook her head in confusion. "I can't believe all this! If the Church is getting so strict about magic, what will it do about all those nice, friendly, non-human creatures who live in Kingsford, the ones who simply *are* magical?"

Her innocent question faded into grim silence. As the young woman glanced about in bewilderment, Nightjar said, "Think, girl. Have you forgotten Mooncat Tribe?"

Finch blanched, shrinking back against her twin.

"All this is well and good," Jaysen said suddenly, "but what we've been doing so far is guessing, merely that. If we're going to get the Duke to believe us, we're going to have to get some kind of proof."

"We know that," Raven said. "The only problem is: how?"

Silence fell anew.

"I think," Magpie murmured after a moment, "the time has come to bring Regina in on the discussion."

The others stared at her. Then, one by one, they began to nod.

"But how?" Verdin—or maybe Finch—asked.

Raven bowed to Magpie. "My dear," he said, with just the slightest touch of mockery in his voice, "this idea is yours. And so the task, too, is yours."

Oh. Of course. Now all I have to do is figure out how to manage it. Of course. I'll start talking about acting and fashions and add "By the way, I think the Church is using dark sorcery." Right.

Magpie was still wondering about that the next day, when she and Regina chanced to meet on their way to the theater. A vendor passed them with his tray full of cakes, trailing a tantalizing aroma of honey and spice.

"Honeycakes!" he sang. "Hot and sweet, fresh honeycakes. Seedcakes, seedcakes, buy them now, buy them now. Honeycakes! Seedcakes!"

Regina inhaled deeply then gave a melodramatic sigh. "I am simply *dying* for a seedcake!"

Magpie looked at her in surprise. "Then why not buy one?"

Regina threw back her head and laughed. "Oh, I'd love a seedcake—but not at the expense of a bellyache! The street vendors here are all too well known for adulterating their products with sawdust or even nastier stuff—"

"Eeeuww." Magpie made a horrified face.

"—and for using whatever else comes to hand: rancid butter, spoiled honey. No thank you, my dear. I'll pass." But her eyes followed the vendor with longing.

"But—but you don't have to!" Magpie stumbled over her words in her eagerness to take advantage of this sudden perfect opportunity. "Owl—that's Erdric, Owl's his Bardic name—Anyhow, Owl, Erdric, whatever you want to call him, shares our boardinghouse. He's a marvelous baker, and his seedcakes are *wonderful*! Why don't you join us there? I know we'd all love to host you."

Regina was very obviously taken by surprise by this sudden invitation. *This sudden* graceless *invitation,* Magpie scolded herself. *You sounded like a little girl inviting her teacher to tea—*

"I'd love to come," Regina said simply.

She'll never— "Uh, what?"

Regina smiled. "I said, I'd love to come. It would be *so* good to have an afternoon off! An afternoon away from the ducal palace, from the court, from all those

silly, formal restraints. An afternoon just to be myself—
How about today, dear? We don't have a full day's
rehearsing scheduled. Would today be too soon?"

"Ah, no," Magpie stammered, caught totally off-
balance by this sudden acceptance. "N-not at all. This
afternoon it is."

The Free Bards had rather been expecting some
grand procession of servants and guards. But Regina
slipped in unheralded, dressed not in noble finery but
in the same beribboned blouse and colorful skirt most
of the musicians wore on the streets.

And it's not some sort of costume for her, Magpie
thought with a little thrill of approval. *It's all been worn
and used: this is the real Regina, the woman who
existed before she caught the Duke's eye.*

"I smell baking," Regina said with a grin.

Magpie grinned back. "Follow me. The rest of us
are in the kitchen, pestering Owl."

Owl, as it happened, was just drawing out a tray full of
seedcakes from the oven, filling the kitchen with such
wonderful aromas that he had to slap back snatching
hands. "You're as bad as Sparrow, you lot!" he scolded in
mock anger. "Let 'em cool at least a few moments!"

They obediently waited for perhaps five heartbeats.
"That's a few moments," Nightjar exclaimed, and
snatched up a seedcake, juggling the hot thing from
hand to hand, slathering it with sweet butter. Biting
into it, she rolled her eyes in silent ecstasy, and the others laughed and followed her lead, Regina among
them, grinning around a mouthful of cake, her lovely
face smeared with butter and crumbs.

"Mph, wonderful," she got out. "Best I've tasted
in—best *ever!* On my life!"

Owl beamed at her and bowed.

Magpie, licking her fingers free of butter, grinned at Raven. You could take the woman out of the street rat, but you couldn't quite take the street rat out of the woman!

But Raven's face was thoughtful. He was biding his time, Magpie realized, waiting for the proper moment to speak to Regina.

"Never thought to see a fine lady gobbling pastries like this," Nightjar teased with a smile.

Regina only smiled and reached greedily for another. "Believe me, one thing I am not is a fine lady! It's not much fun being one: too many perils up there in the high places!"

"Exactly," Raven cut in, seizing his opportunity. "And we've been thinking there may be more perils than usual."

Regina froze, a half-eaten pastry in one hand. "What do you mean?" she asked softly.

Raven glanced quickly at Magpie, then began, "Well, we think there may be a conspiracy being worked against us—and against the Duke. . . . "

He continued in total silence, listing all the different factors he'd discussed with Magpie. When he finished, Regina remained quiet, the pastry still dangling, forgotten, from her fingers.

"So," Magpie asked, "are we being foolish, easily frightened—or have we seen something that those in high places have not?"

Suddenly aware of the pastry she held, Regina put it down with exaggerated care on a table. "I wish I could say that you are being foolish," she said, glancing about at the others. "I think it's time for all of us to have a talk."

They went through every one of the accidents at the theater, analyzing each, trying to find a link between them. "I'd discount some of the incidents," Regina said. "Props do break without any outside intervention, actors do forget their lines. No need to be suspicious of everything."

"Masks," Magpie reminded her, "don't hide themselves under seats. Ribbons don't tie themselves into knots."

"Ah well, no," the woman admitted with a sigh. "And swords don't glue themselves into scabbards, or previously sound floorboards snap by chance."

"The thing is," Jaysen said, "is magic being involved?"

Magpie frowned, and tucked an errant strand of hair behind her ear. "Almost all the incidents could have been worked without any magic at all. I mean, any prankster could have glued 'Sir Verrick's' sword into its scabbard."

"But who?" Nightjar wanted to know. "I can't see any of the actors—and certainly none of us—trying to hurt a good source of income."

"The Tilsani?" Magpie suggested dubiously. "He *is* an odd little thing: maybe he resents humans."

That won her a glare from Crow. "Just 'cause someone looks different," the drummer muttered, "doesn't make him evil."

She licked her lips and tried to make her next words an apology of sorts. "Of course not. I didn't mean—"

"Besides," Regina added, "he's totally loyal to the theater and the Manager. Who else would hire the poor little slow-witted fellow? He's too gentle to ever want to hurt anyone—and not so slow he wouldn't go running to the Manager if anyone tried to use him as a tool."

"It still doesn't have to be magic!" Magpie protested. "Someone could have sawed the floorboard just enough so it would snap when anyone stepped on it."

"Someone," Regina reminded her quietly, ticking off the list with her fingers as Owl had done, "could hardly have easily stolen into a locked Wardrobe Room, slipped past a wide-awake Wardrobe Mistress—she does *not* sleep on the job—opened a locked trunk, and slipped back out with my mask without being seen without using *some* magic."

"The Church uses magic," Raven muttered, "deny it in others as they would. They've been denying others a lot of things lately, they and the Guild together. Streetbusking, for instance." As Regina listened intently, he explained how the Free Bards had gotten involved in the theater at all, summarizing what had happened at the Kingsford Faire, how hard they'd all been hit by the King's edict, what they'd done to escape it. "And now we're desperate to find a way to get it repealed, or at least amended."

Magpie shook her head. "It's gone beyond our little problem—"

"Little!" Raven said indignantly.

"When you compare us to the whole population of Kingsford, of the whole kingdom," Magpie retorted, "yes, our problem *is* little. What I think is that this restriction on us is only part of a bigger issue. And that's a gradual restriction on everyone's freedom."

Everyone started talking at once, but she managed to silence them before it became a row by holding up her hand. "Wait," she said. "Listen to me. The Church has been nibbling away at what people can or can't do, taking away the right to wear certain colors or sell certain things—it's been so subtle I'll wager a good many folks don't even know it's been happening. But the Church does seem to be extending its influence everywhere."

"And where it goes," Raven added wryly, "restrictions do seem to follow."

Regina nodded as though this was something she'd already realized. "Well," she said briskly, "the movements of the Great and Powerful are something we can't do much about—but we can deal with the little things that give them their power. And of course we do have our allies," she added with a slight smile. "Not *all* the Powerful are the enemy."

"Duke Arden," Raven said. "I'll give him this: he's playing a dangerous game, trying to give folks more freedom to run their own lives all the while he's keeping on the good side of King and Church. It can't be easy."

"It's not," Regina agreed flatly. "Even if I wasn't his lover, I'd do my best to support him. Now, let's get back to these accidents at the theater. Could they or could they not all have been caused by magic?"

"In my opinion," Nightjar said, "yes. Look you, I know some healing spells, I think you all know that, but I'm not making any claims about being a great mage, or even of wielding much in the way of Bardic Magic. If I was," she added softly, "I'd surely heal our poor landlady." With a sigh, Nightjar continued, "But it happens that I do know a mage, a powerful one. He's a Gypsy, and so he's on the road a lot, but this time of year he should be traveling not far from here. I can send for him if you like."

"I don't know. . . . " Jaysen said slowly. "It might be dangerous. Getting mixed up in magic, powerful stuff like that."

Raven shot him a contemptuous glare. "On the other hand, boy, if there's a mage already working against us, it would rather nice to know about it, don't you agree?"

Jaysen flushed. "Yes, of course, but—"

"But what? I vote we contact Nightjar's mage."

"So do I," Magpie added before Jaysen could cut in.

"It can't hurt just to send him a message," Owl agreed. "Especially since I think I know who you're talking about."

"Sounds scary," Finch and Verdin said as one. "But let's do it."

"Anyone else?" Raven asked, looking straight at Regina.

The woman shrugged. "Count me in," she said.

Nightjar nodded. "All right. I'll send off my message to him—his name's Peregrine and—What's the matter, Raven?"

Even Magpie had noticed his start. "Recognized the name, that's all. Send your message, Nightjar. Meanwhile, we're all going to start keeping a sharp watch for spies and saboteurs."

"And I," Regina added, "will find reasons to have you Free Bards going in and out of the ducal palace. Spies, whether they're from the Church or the royal court, are probably not going to suspect anyone as—forgive me—lowly as musicians."

Magpie smiled hesitantly. "Plots within plots within plots. Sounds like one of our songs."

Regina laughed. "It does, doesn't it?"

"Let's just hope," Raven added wryly, "that it's one of those songs that stays on pitch."

CHAPTER THIRTEEN

NEW SONGS

Raven sat perched uncomfortably on the narrow windowsill of his room, looking out into the warm spring night without really seeing anything. He'd long ago resigned himself to lonely sleeplessness, and now he stared out at nothing, patiently waiting for the dawn. He certainly had recognized the name Nightjar had mentioned: Peregrine was by far the best mage Raven knew of among the Gypsies. A good man to have as an ally, no doubt of it. But if Peregrine got an intimation of danger, he would surely stay away from Kingsford.

Can't blame him for that. But we do need his help, or someone's help. Someone with power, a different kind of power; something more than stupid, uncertain political power. Ah, Talaysen, Talaysen, what a tangle you've enmeshed me in!

Still, thanks to Talaysen, Raven thought drily, he did

have, as the gamblers might say, a secret ace to play. And he fully intended to play it, as soon as it was light enough for him to see where he was going.

The sound of soft voices below his window alerted him to the fact that he was not the only sleepless soul this night. Who . . . ?

Ah. Jaysen and Linnet, taking advantage of her mother's slumbers and the sultry air to snatch some private time together. Raven listened to their quiet courting involuntarily, trapped by his position on the windowsill into being their captive audience, his smile only slightly tinged with irony. Poor Jaysen didn't seem to have gotten much past the stage of a quick kiss, though judging from the certain overtones in Linnet's voice she really did care for him.

"Come with me," Jaysen whispered. "After all this is finished and the play's over, come with me."

There was more of resignation in her voice than delight. "Oh, Jaysen, I—" her voice broke a little. "I want to—but—I can't."

"But I love you!" he cried. "Doesn't that mean anything to you?"

Fine words, my lad, Raven thought cynically. *But despite the ballads, love warms no cold hearths in winter.*

"Don't you think I love you, too?" she responded immediately. "But how can I possibly leave?"

"Leave what? This boardinghouse?" Jaysen snorted. "It's not worth your worry. It's a prison, holding you here, caging you when you were meant to be free!"

And what ballad did you steal that from? While Raven felt a good deal of sympathy for the young lovers, he could not help but think that young Jaysen hadn't *half* an idea about what they were going to do to keep body and soul together after they'd run off. He'd never been outside of Kingsford, after all. And what of Linnet's other responsibilities?

As if she had somehow heard his thoughts, she chided him gently. "My mother, Jaysen. How can I leave her? Sh-she's so ill, she hardly ever gets out of bed. . . . " Soft sobs drowned the rest of whatever it was she was going to say.

Right on cue, he told himself ironically—but then chastised himself for being so ungenerous. Linnet might be a limp little thing, but she did care for her mother in her own weak way, and she did her best for the old woman.

"Oh, Linnet, don't cry!" Jaysen choked out. "Please, don't!"

"I—We—we never were very close, but she i-is my mother, and when she . . . when she . . . goes, I won't have anyone."

"You'll have me," Jaysen told her, and there was no doubt that he meant the words; sincerity gleamed from every syllable. "You will always have me."

You will always have me, Raven echoed silently, smiling to himself in mixed amusement and nostalgia. *What would it be like to be that young and naive again?*

No, I don't think I was ever quite that naive. But I do wish you well, the two of you, he told the couple. *Now go away before I start thinking of . . .*

Magpie? Ach, ridiculous. That pretty package held a tough, sharp-tongued, domineering spirit, someone who couldn't play second to anyone or anything. Someone who really wasn't interested in cooperation, when it came right down to it. *And yet Nightingale was so sure*— Ridiculous.

Hey now, while he'd sat here eavesdropping, the first gray light of morning had come stealing into the city. Raven got to his feet, stretching muscles stiff from sitting in one position so long, then stole quietly out of the boardinghouse, and set off, with a wry sense of irony, for the Church, the great Cathedral and the Cloisters of the Justiciars.

Going to the Church for help! So bloody unlikely that not even a Churchman would think of it. But there, inside those high, stone walls, lay his trump card. Lady Ardis was that anomaly among Church officials: someone who was both mage and priest, Justiciar—and a friend to Free Bards and Gypsies. She was also, not coincidentally, Talaysen's cousin.

I only hope she's enough of a friend to us to go counter to current Church policy. Talaysen told me she was, but what the hell, he's her blood-kin. Ha, I hope I can even get an appointment with her!

Walking briskly through the chill of early morning, passing street sweepers and sleepy-eyed servants, he crossed the bridge over Kingsford's wide river, the smell of water and fish and dank wood making him wrinkle up his nose in distaste. Below him, there were signs of life aboard the docked riverboats, hints of cooking breakfasts drifting up as well, reminding Raven he hadn't eaten yet.

Well, he'd gone hungry many a time before; it wouldn't hurt him now. He hurried on down the road towards the towering walls of the Kingsford Cathedral Cloister. A bit of searching along what at first looked like an unbroken stretch of stone—Raven freely admitted he was hardly familiar with the layout of any building associated with the Church—brought him to a small, plain door, just as Talaysen had promised. Raven glanced around in sudden caution to be sure no one was sneaking up on his blind side, then rapped on the door.

No answer. He rapped again with a little more

aggression. The Church was supposed to never sleep; surely someone was awake in there!

The door creaked open a crack. An eye peered out, whether it belonged to a male or a female, Raven couldn't tell. A voice, equally sexless, asked, "What do you want?"

Such a warm welcome. Raven gave one of his more melodramatic bows and said, "I am here to request an appointment with the Lady Ardis."

A dry cough, half a laugh, half an expression of derision. "Are you."

Raven sighed in impatience. "I was told by her cousin that Lady Ardis would see me if I needed to ask for an appointment. Look, we're not going to stand here playing games, are we?"

"No," the voice replied flatly, and the door started to creak closed.

"Wait!" Raven snapped, shooting out his hand and preventing the door from closing entirely. "Tell the Lady Ardis that Raven needs to speak with her. Got that? Raven. Tell her I'm a friend of Talaysen."

Did the eye blink at that? "So be it. Stay here," the sour voice commanded, "and touch nothing."

The door slammed shut, leaving the fuming Raven outside. "Touch nothing?" he mimicked angrily. "What does he or she or it think I'm going to do? Steal the wall?"

He waited, pacing restlessly back and forth, as the morning heightened and the sunlight began to creep down the wall. Then, just when Raven was about to give up on the whole business, the door creaked open again.

"Enter," the sour voice told him. "Follow me. Touch —"

"Nothing," Raven completed impatiently. "I know."

He followed the figure—which was so totally

hidden in its robes he still had no idea of its gender—through a maze of potted greenery. A scarlet-clad woman sat beneath a rose arbor, her blonde hair cut as short as every priest's, her narrow face and sharp gray eyes reminding Raven strongly of Talaysen. He swept quickly down in his most theatrical bow. "Lady Ardis. Kind of you to see me."

"Raven." The Lady surveyed him measuringly. "You must be *the* Raven. No one else could be quite so—full of panache."

Raven blinked, not certain whether he'd been complimented or insulted. "At your service, my lady."

The faintest hint of amusement flickered in the keen eyes. "I doubt that you came here because of a sudden attack of religious fervor," Lady Ardis murmured. "Come, sit with me and tell me what is so terrible it brings a Gypsy within these holy walls."

This, Raven decided, was not going to be easy! Watching that narrow, clever face, he gathered and abandoned a dozen hasty stories before deciding that the wisest move would be to simply tell this keen-eyed woman the truth. Dropping all melodrama, he quietly related everything that had been worrying him about the theater and the unlikely spate of accidents, and of his suspicions of a political or—he was a little wary about telling her this part—a religious conspiracy. Lady Ardis listened to his entire account without interruption, frowning slightly when he mentioned the Church.

There was a moment of awkward silence when Raven finished. "You do believe me?" he asked warily. Talaysen had told him that while her religious commitment was genuine, she was no fanatic, but nowadays one never could be too careful. . . .

The woman's frown deepened slightly. "Unfortunately, I do believe you. What you've just told me simply confirms my own suspicions. Unfortunately, it seems that someone learned the wrong lesson from the sad fate of High Bishop Padric."

He relaxed a little, and allowed his relief to show. "So-o! Somehow I doubt much gets past you, my lady!"

"I can't afford to let it," she said, quite seriously, "particularly not if it's a matter that may concern the Church. And there are enough mages in the Church," Lady Ardis continued grimly, "who believe in following the words of the Primus rather than the Word of the One. It's all too possible it is one of our mages helping to undermine Duke Arden."

That was not good news, although it was something he had already put high on his list of "probable causes." "Can you do anything?" he asked hopefully.

Lady Ardis fell silent for a time, her keen gray eyes thoughtful. "Not directly," she said at last, then lapsed into contemplative silence once more. Without warning, she got to her feet, scarlet robes swirling about her tall, slender form. "Wait here," Lady Ardis told Raven, and vanished into the Cathedral.

"Wait here," Raven echoed drily. That seemed to be all he was doing lately. He sat looking about the rose arbor, enjoying the sweet scents until the still air made them reach the cloying point, then got to his feet, stretching, wandering about the cloister garden, sure someone was going to find him and throw him out. Here, amid all the flowering and exotic greenery, was what looked like a pot of common mint, and he stooped down to pluck a leaf.

"Raven."

He sprang guiltily to his feet, the leaf caught between thumb and forefinger, certain he had somehow broken some terrible law. Lady Ardis smiled slightly at his expression of panic.

"No need to look so alarmed," she told him. "I often pick a mint leaf myself, to clear the air. Come, I have something that just may help the . . . unfortunate situation at the theater."

She held out two small, round metal objects: one of silver, on a silver chain, and one of bronze, pierced four times by holes for nails. "A holy medal?" Raven asked cautiously. "And that has to be one of those house-blessing charms I've seen nailed up beside doorways all over the city."

Ardis smiled very slightly. "Looks, as the saying goes, can be deceptive. I hardly wanted something that would look too suspicious or obvious. Give the medal to Regina, and nail this charm up at the main door to the theater." Lady Ardis shrugged wryly. "Do it as openly as you wish. It will do neither of you any harm to be thought pious!"

Raven grinned. "Somehow I think there's more to this than a worry about the state of our souls."

"Tsk, such a cynic." She shook her head with mock-regret. "But you're right in one regard: these are a good deal more than they look. Both are powerful wards. Regina's will prevent anyone from exercising magic against her; the charm will do the same for the theater."

"Amazing work, lady!" Raven said in genuine admiration. "And in such a short time."

"Not quite so amazing. If there is a Church mage active, he's almost certainly working simple curses against you, and such are easily deflected, as easily deflected, in fact, as they are to cast." She paused, studying Raven with wary eyes. "But there's something more to this matter, something you haven't told me yet."

"Talaysen was right," Raven told her with a little nod

of recognition for her abilities. "No one *can* hide anything from you." Before she could do anything more than raise a skeptical brow, he continued, "There is one thing more, something I . . . well, I didn't quite dare discuss this with anyone else. I suspect Regina of working magic, but unconsciously. She simply does not know that she is doing so."

For a moment Lady Ardis stared at him as if he'd gone mad. "What type of magic?" she asked with great caution.

"Oh, nothing darkly sorcerous!" he assured her hastily. "In fact—well, under most circumstances it would be considered harmless! Have you ever heard of something we Gypsies call glamorie?"

"The art of attracting someone to you? Or, for that matter, repelling them?" She nodded, her lips pursed a trifle. "Of course. And you think Regina wields such power?"

"Unconsciously," Raven repeated. "I am certain she has no idea that she is doing anything at all."

"Unconsciously," the woman echoed thoughtfully. "It might be so," she murmured after a moment. "You could very well be right. Ay me, just what we needed: further complications."

Raven pursued his advantage. "If I'm right, it's dangerous both for Regina and Duke Arden. Neither of them can afford even a whisper of such a thing right now."

"Indeed." Lady Ardis nodded decisively. "That is only too true, I am afraid. If someone uncovers this secret Regina doesn't know she bears, it would discredit them both—and possibly destroy Regina. So now, what do you plan to do about it?"

"Me?" Raven gulped. When he had come to this woman, he had *not* expected to have his problem thrown right back into his lap!

"Raven, you know these people better than I," she told him, as patient as a stone. "And for all your flamboyance, I doubt you're a fool."

"Oh, thank you," he said drily, and paused, not knowing what else to say.

"Well?" she persisted.

Well, what *was* he going to do about this? Shouldn't the first thing be to go straight to the heart of the matter? "Well, I think the best thing to do is to tell Regina what I guess," he said slowly. "She's an adult, and no fool, either. She has the right to make her own decision of what to do if she decides that I'm right."

Ardis nodded approval. "Then that is what you should do. Only wait a bit after you bestow these gifts of mine and see what happens before you tell her anything. If there really is magic being worked, it will reflect back upon the caster threefold." Her smile had little of humor about it. "I think you will know if any magic was cast, and soon."

Raven began to bow, then startled in surprise as she touched a hand to his head. "My blessing on you," Lady Ardis told him, "whether you will it or not!"

"It won't kill me," Raven said jauntily. "I'll accept it. Good day to you, Lady Ardis."

Whistling blithely, Raven strolled back across the bridge, dodging people on their way in and out of Kingsford, stopping briefly to wave at a child staring up at him from a riverboat. Below him, traffic was now in full flow, and the water was almost as crowded as the bridge.

"And where," a sharp voice asked, "were you?"

He came alert with a shock, staring at her. "Magpie!"

The young woman blocked his path, fists planted

firmly on her hips. "Don't 'Magpie' me! Where were you?"

Don't tell her, a voice seemed to whisper in Raven's mind. Lady Ardis's warning? Or was this merely an echo of his own sudden annoyance at Magpie's tone? "I hardly think that's any of your concern," he replied coldly.

"Isn't it?" her eyes narrowed. "When you disappear all morning, without any of us having a clue as to where you went?"

"You aren't my keeper, Magpie, my love," he told her flippantly, and pushed past her, striding onward towards the boardinghouse and the theater. But beneath his cavalier exterior, he was trying to remember whether or not Talaysen had given him permission to reveal Lady Ardis's partisanship to anyone else. He didn't think he'd been given that freedom; at least, he didn't remember it. So it would have to remain his own secret.

"I am *not* your love!" she snapped, scurrying along beside him. "But maybe you do need a keeper! Wandering off like that on some selfish, frivolous errand when there are people depending on you—"

He favored her with a glare. "What I had to do was hardly frivolous. And dammit, don't give me that look: I was *not* having an affair!"

"Oh, really?" she asked skeptically. "Can you honestly tell me you weren't with a woman?"

Raven opened his mouth, then closed it again. *One more problem, thank you, Talaysen. Your cousin would be a female! Damn.* "Who I was or wasn't with," Raven said lamely, "is none of your business."

Magpie's voice rose, as strident as her namesake. "You *were* with a woman! The rest of us were rehearsing our heads off, and you—"

"That's enough!" Raven stopped short, so furious he could hardly focus his thoughts. "Look you," he spat, "I was out on business that concerns us all. I can't tell you exactly who I went to see or why because I promised Talaysen—you *do* know who he is?—I promised him that I would not talk about this person. And if that isn't good enough for you, then maybe you should just give up on us Free Bards and take to the road by yourself! That seems to be what you want!"

She stopped dead in her tracks, frozen in place by his vehemence. "No! I—"

"Look, Magpie," he said, stiffly, "I know you had a hell of a rough childhood. But dammit, woman, the past is the past!"

It was just a good thing that there was very little traffic on this street, or they would have been terribly conspicuous. As it was, they earned no few curious glances from passersby.

Her stricken look turned to one of suspicion. "Now, what is that supposed to mean?"

"You don't trust anyone—" he said flatly. "Fine, I can understand that; a lot of us road folk aren't too trusting, we can't afford to be. But you act as if you don't think anyone can make sensible decisions but you!"

"I do not!" she flared.

"Don't you?" He leveled the accusation straight at her eyes. "You don't act as if you think anyone can behave like a sensible adult but you!"

"That's the stupidest thing I've heard!" she shouted, furious. "I don't—"

He laughed, but without any humor in the sound. "Oh, no, not much you don't! Look at the way you just attacked me."

"With reason!" she growled. "You were off playing the tomcat—"

"Do you know that?" he demanded, and saw her flush. "Do you really? Had you any proof? No, dammit, you've got it in your head that just because some men acted like scum to you when you were a child, all men are bullying children, with nothing on our minds but— but food, fun, and fornication!" *Nice alliteration,* a corner of his brain noted. "Well, maybe it's you who needs to grow up, Magpie. The heart of being an adult is knowing when to share a job, when to trust someone else to do his or her part—and curse it all, to know when to think with your head instead of—" a hasty bit of self-censoring "—instead of with your emotions!"

Magpie stared at him, so white with shock that for a moment Raven could almost pity her. No, dammit, he was *not* going to start feeling sorry for her! Instead, he strode angrily on, teeth and fists clenched as he worked to keep his anger at her alive, determinedly silent, ignoring the equally silent Magpie at his side.

A long time of soundless fuming passed, as they made their way down back streets towards the theater. And then, out of the silence came Magpie's timid, "You're right."

Now it was his turn to stop cold. "What's that?"

She glared at him. "I'm trying to say I'm sorry."

"Are you?" he demanded. "Are you really?"

"Raven, please," she begged, as the glare faded. "Don't be difficult. I . . . had no right attacking you like that. I know that whatever else you may do, you take your music seriously. You wouldn't run off like that unless it was something truly important."

Aha! Raven waited just long enough to savor the triumph, then said brusquely, "Apology accepted. Here."

Magpie took the holy medal with a puzzled frown. "What is it? Besides the obvious, I mean."

He smiled in triumph; this much, at least, he could

tell her! He checked the street for eavesdroppers, and lowered his voice to a murmur. "That is what I went to get. It has a spell on it that's supposed to get rid of curses. I want you to give it to Regina."

"Why can't you do it?" she asked in puzzlement.

"Come now! *I'm* not going to risk being seen giving jewelry to the mistress of a Duke!" He shook his head at her. "Every suspicious tongue in this town would start wagging over that one!"

"Ah. Right." Magpie flushed again; clearly she realized that one of those suspicious tongues would have been hers. "Good point. If I give it to her, no one will think anything of it."

"Tell Regina to wear it at all times—" he cautioned, after a careful look up and down the street told him there was no one coming "—and not to remove it for anything. That's important, Magpie: she must never remove it."

Magpie looked down at the medal as if it had suddenly turned into something that might bite. "She's probably going to think I've gone mad, but . . . all right. I'll do it."

They entered the theater together—and froze. The rest of the musicians and actors were clustered around a small figure lying motionless on the floor.

"Oh, hell," Raven moaned. "*Now* what?"

He and Magpie rushed forward, to find Nightjar, so drained-looking she could only have been working healing spells, crouching beside the Tilsani, his glittery eyes bright with pain and fright.

"What happened?" Raven asked Jaysen softly.

Jaysen seemed very shaken; he was nearly as pale as Nightjar. "He—he fell from the second tier. I don't know what happened; I guess part of the railing gave way."

"It's going to be all right," Nightjar crooned to the Tilsani. "You were lucky, my little friend. You've got a cracked leg, but it's a clean break and I've set it on its way to healing. There's nothing else wrong with you but a few bruises."

But the fear still glittered in the Tilsani's eyes. The Manager, with a gentleness Raven would never have expected, told the little being quietly, "Don't worry, little friend. You'll be taken to a safe, comfortable place and cared for until you are well again." And as the lizard-creature started with surprise, he added, "What, did you think we'd toss you out on the streets to starve because you can't do your work?"

The little being nodded fearfully.

"Nonsense!" the Manager said, so forcefully even the lizard had to believe him. "We do not abandon one of our own. You're one of us, lad, one of the Duke of Kingsford's Company! Without your help, we could not have placed those Deliambren lights! We need you!"

"And the Duke will take care of him," Regina added. "We certainly have enough room in the palace, and he'll get good care there."

As the little Tilsani was carefully carried out, Raven took advantage of the momentarily empty theater to climb (warily, not risking touching the railings) up to the second tier of seats. Here was where the Tilsani must have fallen, where a section of railing had broken away.

Except . . . it hadn't broken. Crouching down to gingerly run his hand over what should be rough, splintery edges, Raven frowned, a little shiver running through him. The wood was as smooth as if it had melted. Or as if a section of it had been somehow persuaded to just let go. . . .

Sorcery. Raven got to his feet, rubbing his hands in disgust, glancing about for the best place to hide the charm Lady Ardis had given him. Ah, yes, there!

He hurried back down to the theater floor and hunted for the tallest ladder he could find. Carefully, hoping none of the rungs had been magicked as well, Raven climbed up over the main door, then scrambled up to the false balcony above that, and up to the ornamental carving over that. Trying not to think about what would happen if the whole thing suddenly gave way under his weight, he nailed the charm in place behind some curlicues of wood, where no one could easily find or remove it. Scrambling back down, Raven let out a sigh of relief when he stood on firm footing once more, then craned his head back to study his handiwork.

Ah, yes, he'd done a good job. Couldn't see even a hint of the charm from down here, and he doubted anyone would spot it from the seats, either. Hopefully it wouldn't matter if anyone sorcerous sensed the charm, because that someone wouldn't be able to do anything about it.

I hope, Raven thought.

Ah well, his people didn't believe in brooding on what might or might not be. With a fatalistic shrug, Raven left the theater to go find the others.

CHAPTER FOURTEEN

CRIES OF ALARM

"I told you she meant it," Raven whispered to Magpie as the Free Bards followed their guide down the halls of the ducal palace. "I knew Regina would find excuses to get us back in here."

"But what good is it all doing us?" Magpie shot back. "I mean, the Duke seems to genuinely enjoy our music, but so far we haven't learned one word about what's going on with the anti-busking edict."

True enough. Not one of the servants—who, in a normal aristocratic household, knew everything—would exchange more than a few coolly courteous words with them, and the Duke, egalitarian soul though he was, was hardly about to gossip with commoners. But Raven, eying a buxom young servant girl who, judging from her plain, serviceable outfit, was hardly of the upper rank of servants, grinned suddenly. "I think," he murmured, "I just developed a raging thirst. Can't sing on a dry throat, after all."

"Raven, wait, you can't—"

But before Magpie could stop him, he had slipped away from the group and was trailing after the servant girl.

Raven! Magpie thought in frustration. Granted, she doubted he was after anything other than information — he wasn't, as he'd be the first to remind her, stupid — but just the same . . . Magpie straightened, realizing the others had gone on without her—and that a rather attractive young man in the higher ranking servant's blue livery was giving her the interested eye. *Well, now,* Magpie thought, *two can play at this game,* and gave him a radiant smile.

"I always get lost in this place," she told him sweetly. "I wonder . . . would you mind very much giving me a tour?"

He nearly tripped over his own feet in his eagerness to take her arm. Younger than she'd first thought, Magpie realized, barely old enough to shave, very possibly too young to have yet learned proper caution.

We shall see, she thought in amusement, *what we shall see.*

Raven sat with both elbows propped on the kitchen table, head resting on hands as though fascinated by his new acquaintance but actually struggling not to yawn. Across the table, the servant girl rattled on about one silly thing after another. Watching all that nice, healthy, richly curved woman-flesh jiggling pleasantly with every move she made, Raven thought with a touch of self-mockery that if only he were here with no other motive than entertainment he might not be quite so bored. . . .

If only he could get her to just stop chattering for a moment! He was learning more about the personal lives of the cleaning staff and the kitchen help of the ducal palace than he ever wanted to know—and not one shred of information that was of any real use. Raven leaned forward as though totally engrossed, and took one small, work-roughened hand in his own. The girl reddened most intriguingly all the way down into the top of her not-quite-concealed bosom, but kept right on chattering.

"My dear," Raven purred when she at last had to stop for a breath, "what a fascinating world-in-itself this is, this palace. What wonders you must see."

She batted big blue eyes at him ingenuously. "Oh, I do! Just the other day I was saying to Sanni—do you know her, she's the Fourth Underservant in Charge of Linens, the one with all that bright red hair (I swear it's the shade she was born with, too, fancy that)—well, anyhow, I was saying to her what weird things was going on."

"Weird?" Raven prodded carefully.

"Did I say weird? Well, maybe not really weird. But there's been so many people coming and going—but then there always are—"

"My dear," Raven cut in, just barely keeping from gritting his teeth, "I'm sure this is a nice, busy place. Your master is a Duke, after all—"

"And such a fine man he is! A true friend of the people— No, no, I mean it. He nearly got in trouble with the King's own man the other day, arguing it wasn't right to—to—" Her voice took on the abstracted air of someone trying to quote from memory. " '—take away the livelihood of poor folk.' "

"Ah! Was he talking about street-busking?"

The girl looked at him blankly. "Lordy, no. About

194   *Mercedes Lackey & Josepha Sherman*

the new tax on woolens. And isn't that a stupid tax? Folks need their woolens, but if they have to pay so much for 'em they can't afford 'em, they'll—"

"Nothing about street-busking?" Raven interrupted.

"Why, no. Not a word." She beamed at him. "Would you like another beer?"

Only if it means you'll drink one, too—and give me a few moments of silence! Raven thought desperately, and grimly kept smiling.

"And this," the young man said, "is the third-best drawing room, built one hundred years ago by the present Duke's grandfather, Alaric the Third. Note the columns of Darric marble. Such black veining is very rare, you know, and the fluting brings it out beautifully. Now, over here we have the portrait of the Duke's third cousin twice removed, Lady Senda, and beside her . . ."

Magpie barely stifled a yawn. Who would have expected such a fine-looking young man would have nothing between his ears but a passion for—history and architecture? If she heard one more word about "Ilonic-style arches" or "windows in the fashion of Tharian the Good . . ."

And gossip that was over three hundred years old was hardly going to do *her* any good!

"My," she said, before he could get started on a lecture about a series of portraits of very dull-looking people, "you really *do* know this palace."

He beamed. "It's something of a hobby of mine. I try to learn every detail about it."

"No, really?" she said ingenuously, hoping she did not sound as sarcastic as she felt.

If she did, the sarcasm went right over his head. He

nodded fervently. "There's so much fascinating material here. For instance—"

"But you haven't said anything about the people! The living people, I mean," she added hastily. "You must see all sorts of splendid folk!"

"Oh. Well, yes, I do." His tone implied live aristocrats weren't as fascinating as those who'd been dead for hundreds of years. "Just the other day, I personally took two of the Royal Advisers on a tour of the palace. Odd," he added thoughtfully, "they suddenly remembered an urgent mission only an hour into the tour."

Magpie nearly choked. *The Duke did it on purpose! He must have been trying to find a polite way to get rid of them, so he risked boring them to death!* "They must have had some fascinating tales to tell."

The young man gave her a startled glance. "Why, no. Not a thing."

"But—but I mean, Royal Advisers, what with all the royal edicts coming down and the changes in the laws—they must have had something interesting to say about that!"

He blinked thoughtfully, falling silent for so long Magpie felt hope surging through her. But then the young man merely shook his head. "Not a thing. Now, these portraits here have some *particularly* fascinating stories! It seems that Duke Alessandro's beloved fourth cousin on his mother's side was involved with a brilliant lady artist against the family's wishes. . . ."

Magpie escaped from her erudite young guide when he was summoned off to other duties. She hurried back down the way she had come, only to run into Raven. He looked as if he'd just escaped a particularly excruciating Guild concert. They stopped in the middle of the hallway, and both began talking at once.

"And so I learned—"

"—more about the kitchen staff—"

"—more about architecture—"

Raven and Magpie stopped short, stared at each other, then burst into mutual laughter. "Frustrating, isn't it?" Raven asked. "We know the Duke knows what's going on, but we can't ask him point-blank—Or can we?"

Magpie looked at him aghast. "Raven, no!"

"Ah well, no," he agreed. "I suppose not."

"So there you are!" an officious servant exclaimed, appearing around a corner. "You cannot go wandering off about the palace like that! Come, the rest of your troupe are waiting to perform. Hurry, follow me."

Raven and Magpie exchanged wry glances, and followed.

To the Free Bards' surprise, they found another group already in the music room. "Guild Bards," Raven muttered under his breath. "What are *they* doing here?"

The Guild musicians were wondering pretty much the same thing, but more loudly. "We hardly expected to have to share our recital with such street scum," one announced to the servant who had found Raven and Magpie.

"Scum!" Jaysen exploded, but Raven closed a firm hand on his arm before he could go any further. Smiling thinly, the Gypsy gave the Guild Bards his most intricate, most aristocratic bow, so precisely perfect it was an insult in itself. "There seems to have been some manner of mistake."

The man who seemed to be the leader of the Guild troupe, a slender, gray-eyed man of middle years, a fiddler judging from the case tucked under one arm, granted Raven the merest dip of the head. "There does, indeed. While your . . . noises are probably just what the swarm who attend the theater expects, I am certain the Duke of Kingsford does not wish to hear such things here in his palace."

"How strange," Raven countered, "considering he sent for us."

The leader sniffed, superciliously. "I find that rather difficult to believe."

"Did I say something too complex and difficult for you?" Raven asked ever so gently, as if to a village idiot. "Which words didn't you understand? I'd be happy to explain them to you."

The head of the Guild troupe flushed a brilliant scarlet, and his eyes narrowed dangerously. "You piece of offal! I should throw you out my—"

A gentle cough made him turn to see their hostess. He reddened again, but this time from embarrassment. "Ah. My lady." The Guild Bard bowed his finest as Regina, elegant in red-violet silks, came hurrying forward.

"I'm sorry about this," she whispered to Raven. "The King sent this group to us without warning: I suppose he thought we'd be flattered."

"Maybe we should just leave," Magpie said, uncertainly. "Save you the embarrassment."

"No . . . " Raven murmured. "I don't run from the Guild. Besides," he added in a much louder voice, flinging himself down in an elegant rose-pink chair, "I don't often get a chance to hear the Guild's finest. I'd like to see just what it is that they're so proud of." He waved a languid hand at them. "Please, don't let me stop you."

"Raven!" hissed a scarlet-faced Magpie, but he ignored her, smiling urbanely at the Guild fiddler.

Ah no. He is not a "fiddler." He is a violinist. He does not concern himself with mere fiddle tunes.

The Guild Bard, gaze never leaving Raven, took out his fiddle—*violin*—tuning it with care. Without a word, he began the precise, perfectly structured measures of "My Lady's Pleasance." Raven knew that one; it was a court tune, yes, but unlike a good deal of that type of music, this was a piece with enough challenge to it to make it interesting to any fiddler. The trick, he knew, lay in playing the music exactly as designed, without adding any additional expression yet without letting it become mechanically dull. The Guild Bard wasn't quite up to managing that last, but his technique was good enough to hold Raven's intrigued interest, better than the usual lifeless Guild perfection. The man finished with a precise flourish that was a wordless challenge, and Raven grinned and got to his feet, taking out his own fiddle.

What to play? Not the same piece, tempting though that might be; that would be too direct an insult, and Raven didn't really want to insult someone with such fine technique. With a grin, he launched into one of the melodies he'd learned as a child sitting around a Gypsy campfire. The title didn't translate into the common tongue, but the melody, a quiet, thoughtful musing on the countryside, was just deceptively simple enough that he knew the Guild fiddler would appreciate what he was doing.

As he did. Raven saw the grudging admiration flash into the man's eyes, and smiled. He played the melody through, gaze linked with that of the other fiddler, then ended with the same flourish the Guild fiddler had performed, and put down his bow.

"Enough from me for now, children," he jibed. "Play nicely, now."

As he wandered off to take a cooling drink from the tray a servant bore, the Guild fiddler followed him. As the other musicians played in the background, Guild and Free Bards alternating melodies with careful, chill courtesy, the two fiddlers drank in silence.

"A pity," the Guild musician said at last. "Such talent as yours should not be wasted."

Raven raised an eyebrow at him. "I could say the same about yours."

The Guild Bard frowned. "What I meant was that you should not be forced to waste your time playing for mere commoners. Were you properly Guild-trained—but you're not. A pity, as I say."

"Ah, but I am free to go where I will," Raven said, voice carefully light, "perform where and when and what I will."

"For now," the Guildsman said darkly.

Raven simply looked mildly interested. "Oh?"

"Surely you know of the royal edict?" the Guildsman challenged.

"Banning street-busking?" Raven shrugged. "Well, unlike you, I am not bound to one kingdom. The Deliambrens favor my sort. There is Birnam, for instance—or the fine city-state of Gradford—"

The Guildsman reddened a little, then paled, and by that Raven knew that *he* was well aware of the Guild's lack of royal favor in the former land, and the troubles in the latter. According to the word passed by Robin, the Guild might well have been involved with High Bishop Padric, at least in the beginning. If so, they had lost as much, if not more, by that involvement as anyone who had opposed him.

But this was a group supposedly sent by the King. Raven decided on a little delicate probing. "Do you, perhaps, know *why* such an edict came to be passed?"

The Guild Bard hesitated a long while. "No," he said at last, "quite frankly, I do not. As far as I know, it was none of our doing. But then," he added wryly, "I cannot speak for what all the Guild does or says. It *is* a shame, though, that such a musician as yourself should be so penalized—or sent off into other lands in search of employment. Good day to you."

He raised the glass to Raven in an ironic toast, then strolled away to rejoin his group.

"And to you," Raven murmured thoughtfully, watching him go. "None of our doing," eh? Was that true? Was the edict really none of the Guild's creation? If so, that left only the Church as foe—or a simple regal whim. Unless, of course, the musician had been lying, or ignorant of Guild affairs, or —

Ah, curse it all, they were no better off now than when this day had started!

Except, Raven added to himself with a grin, that at least now *one* of the Bardic Guild knew to appreciate a Free Bard's music!

"Places, everyone," the Manager called. "Places! This is our first full dress rehearsal—and I don't have to tell you I expect it to all go flawlessly."

"Or else," Raven whispered to Magpie, and got a quick flash of a grin in return.

"Musicians!" the Manager said sharply. "On the downbeat, and . . . five, six, seven, eight— !"

They sprang into the sprightly notes of the piece they'd chosen to open the play, a bright, happy combination of a dozen dance tunes, telling the audience without a doubt to expect a comedy. As the last notes died away, Adela, Flora's lady-in-waiting came scurrying onstage in a busy flurry of frills and laces to tell the audience, in the guise of a complaint about all the work she had to do— "a-sewing of my lady's hems when she *will* go walking in the woods or a-cleaning of her pretty shoes when she does most happily challenge her lord brother to the climbing of a tree—" the state of things in Flora's home.

In the midst of this silly, good-natured plaint, a sad-faced servant entered behind her to the slow, solemn strains of Magpie's flute. Adela obligingly squeaked and gave a melodramatic start when the man tapped her on the shoulder. Before she could get out more than a dozen of her scolding words for startling such a fine lady as herself, he delivered his sorry message:

"Oh saddest day, oh saddest, saddest day that ever sun did shine! My lord and master's dead."

"What, dead?" Adela echoed in melodramatic horror.

"Dead as Themion. Dead as Mardick. Dead, alas, as Death itself."

She mimed her startlement. "How should he be dead? Did he die in battle?"

"Not that." The servant sighed enormously.

"At sea?" The maid grew impatient as well as alarmed.

"Neither that." The servant sighed again, and wiped a tear from his eye ostentatiously.

"How, then? In church, perchance?" she urged, her patience visibly shortened.

"None of that," the servant said, face like a sad-eyed hound. "He had just sworn there was not on this earth the beast that could defeat him, when a traitorous ox did do the deed."

"Alas the day, was the poor man *gored?*" The girl was clearly horrified, and well she might be. "Oh, sorrow, sorrow, where did such sadness occur?"

"At table."

Adela stopped dead. "At table?" she repeated with comical disbelief. "What was an ox doing at table?"

"It was not what the ox did to the man, but what the man did to the ox. He choked," the servant told her lugubriously, "on a joint of beef."

And by now, Raven thought as Adela burst into artful lamentation, beating her breast and bemoaning her fate and the fate of "poor, dear Flora, left without a father's care," *the commons are laughing over the thought of a nobleman choking on his food like anyone else, and the nobles are just arriving fashionably late, so everybody's happy!*

Hey-ho, on with the play! Act followed act, with only the smallest flaw here and there, a missed line, a slip of the tongue, nothing an audience would notice. Flora became Florian, Florian made plans to become the mysterious masked lady. As she hurried about the palace, gathering the glamorous bits and pieces that would become her gown, Raven grinned at Magpie. This section, accompanied only by cheerful gittern and drum, allowed her a chance to actually watch the play, and he knew this was one of her favorite scenes.

But Flora hadn't gotten more than five lines into her nice, gloating little speech of "I shall dazzle him with damask, stun him with silk; my love shall never know me," when a sudden sharp cry of "Fire!" rang out.

For a horrified moment, actors and musicians alike froze, very much aware of being surrounded by nothing but wood. Painted and oiled wood—flammable and volatile.

The shout came again, this time more clearly from outside, closely followed by the harsh, booming sound of an alarm bell, and they all raced from the theater to look wildly about.

"No fire here on the theater grounds," the Manager

said in relief. "Nor from anything nearby. Can anyone else make out—"

"There!" someone shouted. "I see flames!"

"That's the Church of St. Bede!" Regina gasped.

Flames were already engulfing the parsonage, blazing forward with terrifying speed to envelop the church itself. Raven caught his breath at the ferocity of those flames, thanking all the Powers it was a still day, with no wind to hurl the fire to other buildings. Fortunate, too, that churches were always set back from their neighbors, like prelates drawing the skirts of their robes away from "worldly contamination."

"Here comes the fire brigade," someone said.

"Several of them," the Manager added sharply as the men came rushing up with their water-wagons. "But I doubt they'll have any luck. That fire is just too fierce to fight. I suspect they'll have to just leave it to burn itself out."

Fierce, indeed, Raven mused—almost supernaturally so. Suddenly he found himself thinking about what Lady Ardis had told him of curses returning threefold on the caster, and slid away from the others back into the theater, glancing up at the hidden little protection charm.

Not so hidden. It might, Raven told himself, be only a trick of the eyes, his coming from bright sunlight back into dimness. But he could swear the charm was glowing. Uneasy, he stepped back out into daylight, and found Regina at his side, visibly shaken.

"What did you give me?" she murmured, her tone half accusation, and half fear.

"I beg your pardon?" he said, startled.

"The medal, Raven." She was losing the fear, but there was still enough alarm in her to make her hands shake ever so slightly. "What is it, really? The moment someone shouted about the fire, it grew warm, almost uncomfortably so. And I can't seem to take it off. Oh, Raven, what have you done? And what is happening to us all?"

"Nothing to harm you," Raven tried to assure her. But Regina had already walked away.

CHAPTER FIFTEEN

FLOCKING TOGETHER

Watching that hot, savage fire blazing with all its terrifying strength, Magpie felt herself trembling, and once she started, she couldn't seem to stop.

She had never seen a fire that strong, that fierce. It had a malignant life all of its own. Flames seemed to leap into places where they had no right being; the fire spread so quickly that she was afraid no one inside the church and the parsonage had time to escape. The flames roared and shouted with obscene glee, and a huge fireball danced atop the bell tower long past the time when the structure should have collapsed. Sorcery. Oh dear Lord, it could only be sorcery.

Impossible, she tried to argue with herself in panic. *It—it's an oil-fueled fire or something like that, that's all it can be. There's no such thing as magic actually powerful enough to destroy a building.*

Wasn't there? She hadn't wanted to believe it, she

hadn't wanted to believe in curses and spells and all the rest of that perilous, perilous matter, no matter what anybody else said. The world was real, solid, material. After all, Magpie insisted to herself, up to this point, no matter how far she'd travelled, she had never seen any magic stronger than Nightjar's spells of healing or those little theatrical illusion-charms. Everything else was merely sleight-of-hand and chicanery, it had to be. Oh, the psychic effects of Bardic Magic were real enough, anybody could see that, but she didn't dare start believing in weird, unseen forces powerful enough to change all reality, forces you couldn't even control! Granted, she'd dutifully delivered Raven's medal to Regina, but that didn't mean she believed the thing had any real power; no, no, at the time Magpie had thought Raven was just being a superstitious idiot. And when Regina had just as faithfully strung that medal about her neck on a heavy silver chain the Duke had given her —

Ah yes, the medal . . .

Magpie continued shuddering. During Florian's dress-gathering scene, the musical scoring hadn't called for her flute, and so she'd been standing there simply enjoying the scene; she always did, what with its clever bits of dialogue and those funny, cunning tricks by its heroine as she assembled a ball gown out of all the bits and pieces she'd collected. Regina had been facing her fully, giving her a good view of the medal, just at the moment when the cry of "Fire!" had first rung out.

And at that precise moment, the medal about Regina's neck had flared into glowing life. There hadn't been any chance of a mistake, of it being a simple trick of reflected light: the chain and the medal had both been totally in shadow.

The medal had glowed all on its own, a warm, golden glow that spoke to something deep inside Magpie.

Magic was real.

No, no, I don't want to believe it!

Magpie hugged her arms tightly about herself. Dear Lord, dear Lord, she didn't mind the thought of an enemy she could see, but an unseen one, one that could strike without warning . . .

She clenched her jaw fiercely, fighting back tears of sheer terror, aching to just turn and run and run and run. . . .

I never even had an enemy before, not really, not someone who—who actually wanted me dead. And whoever is behind all this does want us dead, all of us.

A fire in a theater would be disaster. Everything in there was flammable, down to the very walls and roof! And if the house was crowded, or the exits happened to be blocked . . .

No, oh no, I—I won't think of that. I—I—I don't know what I want to do!

She should tell Raven enough was enough. She should just quit and head on out. After all, Magpie told herself sharply, what did she owe the Duke? Nothing! He might be a good Duke for Kingsford, but he had never done a thing for her, not herself personally.

But what about Regina? I like her.

That wasn't important, not now! Regina was a nice woman, a likable woman, of course she was.

But I don't owe her anything, either! Certainly not my life!

That was it. Anybody who wanted to pitch their lot in with this group was welcome to it, but why should she stay where her life was being threatened?

Raven and Regina know what's going on, but they probably won't even warn the rest of us. The show must go on, and all that. Even if that puts us all in peril of—of—

"All right, everyone," the Manager said shortly. "Show's over. Fire's under control. Everyone back to the rehearsal."

But as they all filed uneasily back into the theater, Regina said suddenly, "Wait. Please." As everyone turned to her in surprise, she added, "All of you, please join me in the rear balcony."

"Why—"

"We'll have a good view of the rest of the theater from there, but no one will be able to eavesdrop."

I shouldn't bother, Magpie told herself. *I should just head out while I can.*

But she found herself climbing up into the balcony with everyone else, though she couldn't have said why.

"Make yourselves comfortable," Regina told them. "This may take some time."

"Go ahead, Regina," Raven said when they'd all gotten settled. "We're listening."

"Ah. Yes. I think it's time everyone knew the truth, or at least as much of it as I know. I don't know how much of what's been happening lately the rest of you have puzzled out, but Raven and I have pretty much determined that those accidents that've been happening aren't happening by chance. They're all part of a plot."

"A plot!" the Stage Manager exclaimed—although it sounded more to Magpie as if it was in startled confirmation of something he had already suspected.

The others exploded into panicky excitement, all talking at once at the tops of their lungs.

"I knew it!"

"It's the Church—"

"—the Guild—"

"—the King. I knew he hated the idea of theater —"

"Enough!" the Manager snapped. "I said, *enough!*"

Cast and musicians both were so used to following his orders by now that everyone fell obediently silent. Regina hastily continued before anyone could start up again. "It's the fire that proved it for me. You all saw it: those were no natural flames."

There were indrawn gasps of horror, but not one voice was raised in argument. Regina paused, studying them all, very evidently dreading what she was going to say next.

"That fire was meant for us," she said at last. "Wait, wait, hear me out! I can't tell you *how* I know; but I promise you that I have never been more certain of anything in my life. We do have *some* protection, and again, I can't tell you how that came about, but it is there. I also can't order you to stay. I won't even ask you to do such a thing. But, well, there's more at stake here than just a play or a group of actors. Someone is very blatantly trying to destroy Duke Arden."

"What's that to us?" someone yelled, and was firmly hushed by everyone else.

"Please, go on," the Manager told Regina, who nodded.

"I know this is a frightening thought," she said slowly. "I admit I'm so scared I want to start running and never stop. But that's stupid. If we stay like the bunch of nice, shallow-minded actors folks think us, and act as if we haven't figured out the truth, we're going to give the Duke's enemies a target they'll find very tempting—"

"*Too* tempting!" someone yelled.

Regina sighed. "Perhaps. But we'll also be keeping those enemies from picking a target closer to him. We may even be able to gather enough evidence against them to stop them—permanently."

"Before you make any hasty decisions," Raven cut in, "let me assure you that as Regina pointed out, we aren't exactly going into this without defenses. I was the one who set part of this in motion. I . . . can't go into much detail, but let's just say we have a powerful ally, one I'm not permitted to name at this time. And that ally has given me something—again, I'm not going to discuss it, just in case—that blocks curses from this theater. That's almost certainly why the fire recoiled and hit the church rather than us."

"Well and good," one of the actors muttered, "but that hardly eliminates all danger."

"No," Regina agreed honestly, "it doesn't. I repeat, I can't order you to do anything. I can only ask that for the sake of the Duke and the future of Kingsford you all decide to stay."

That's it, Magpie thought. *I'm out of here.*

She was just about to jump up and tell them exactly that when Raven and the Manager stood up simultaneously. With a wave of his hand, Raven deferred to the Manager.

The man had never shown his age quite so clearly before. Every wrinkle, every line born of age and worry, stood out with pitiless clarity. He remained silent for a moment, plainly organizing his thoughts, then spoke in a quiet voice that was totally unlike his usual melodramatic delivery.

"I don't have to tell you how good Duke Arden has been to me. I like to consider him as my friend. But he's more than that, and more than a mere patron of the arts as well. Duke Arden has been a boon to the whole city. Think about it, you who are native to Kingsford. You know what life is like here. Imagine what the city would be like without his Council telling him what the common folk need, without him speaking out in our favor to the

King and keeping the zealots of the Church from turning this city into a mere extension of their Cloister, with all the rules and restrictions of an abbey and none of the benefits."

The Manager stood with arms folded, firm as an oak. "Come what may," he concluded, "I will not desert him, not after all he's done for us. I am staying."

He glanced at Raven, who gave him a slightly sardonic salute, then added flatly, "Think about that edict against street-busking, my friends. Think about all the other restrictions that might have crushed performers—and still might crush us if we lose our one friend in the ranks of the high and noble in this Kingdom. What happens to the Duke, my friends, is all too likely to happen to others—" he glanced significantly at the Free Bards "—if the Duke's enemies aren't stopped. Consider Gradford before you speak. I did, and I'm staying."

"Ah well." The actor playing Sir Verrick got slowly to his feet. "I'm too old to find another job. It's either the theater for me or begging. I'm staying."

"Me, too." Another actor got to her feet.

"And me."

"What the hell. Me, too."

At last only the Free Bards remained sitting, glancing uneasily at each other. Jaysen suddenly sprang to his feet. "I'm a Free Bard," he said defiantly. "I'm also a citizen of Kingsford—and I am not a coward. I'm staying."

Nightjar shrugged. Shaking out the folds of her colorful skirt, she got her feet. "I don't like the idea of anyone regulating my music, or condemning me for healing spells," she commented to no one in particular. "Raven's right. We really can't afford to let the Duke be harmed, whether we care about Kingsford or not. I'm staying." She looked casually at the other musicians. "Anyone else?"

Finch and Verdin glanced at each other. As one they stood, as one they declared firmly, "We're staying."

Crow hesitated a while, slumped in his seat as if he hadn't heard a word of what the others had been saying, then got slowly to his feet. "Don't like bullies," he muttered. "I'm in."

Magpie looked uneasily about. She was the only one left sitting. *I am a coward!* she wanted to cry. *And I—I don't care what happens to Kingsford!* But Crow's simple words had cut her to the heart. Leaving now really would mean giving in and letting the bullies win. *Letting the cruel, the powerful, have their way with her, as they had too often in her past* . . . Biting her lip, Magpie realized she had, one way or another, been running all her life, first with her family's troupe, then on her own. Yes, she'd been nothing but a child back then, she'd had no choice but to run from those who could have harmed or even destroyed her at a whim. But now she was an adult capable of making her own choices, choosing her own way to walk —

Or run. But sooner or later, I'm going to be out of places to run to. And . . . I guess even a coward has to take a stand sometime.

"I'm staying." The words sounded as if they were coming from someone else's mouth. But the look of approval from Raven was almost worth the terror blazing through her.

Almost, Magpie thought wryly.

"Enough vow-making," the Manager said suddenly. "We're not going to be able to get any more work done this day. Go home, all of you. Be here first thing tomorrow."

"So we will," Raven agreed.

Barring the unforeseen, Magpie added silently, and instantly wished she hadn't thought of that.

✧   ✧   ✧

The Free Bards walked slowly back to the boarding-house, lost in a heated discussion of what had just occurred.

"We had to stand firm," Jaysen said suddenly.

Nightjar nodded. "No one's arguing with you about that. I can't see myself ending up imprisoned or dead as a 'sorceress' just because I tried using a healing spell to help someone."

Magpie had been silent all this while, hardly hearing what the others were saying, but suddenly she couldn't keep herself from bursting out, "What do you think will happen next?"

Raven shrugged with exasperating lack of concern. "Who can say? I think that misplaced fire is going to give our unknown enemy something to consider. Whoever that enemy is probably isn't going to risk trying any more direct sorcery against the theater."

"What about against us?"

Raven glanced her way in surprise, then grinned. "What the hell, woman, what will be will be. I'm not going to worry about the future."

"Gypsy," she muttered.

"What's wrong with that?" he retorted cheerfully. "You learn to be fatalistic when your life is spent wandering from site to site, never knowing whether the morrow will bring famine or good fortune."

"How can you be so casual?" she cried, in spite of herself, and in spite of her resolve not to seem hysterical.

He shook his head at her, but for once, there was nothing of mockery in the gesture. "Magpie, there are enough real things to worry about in this world, most of them concerning mundane matters like food and shelter. Those we have, at least for now. We've done our best to protect the theater and our troupe. Anything else—well, we probably couldn't change anything else. Why worry about something you can't affect?"

She sighed, but not in exasperation. "I wish I could be that offhand about it."

"I'm not being offhand," he countered, "just realistic. Besides, why should either of us worry about —"

"Linnet!" Jaysen interrupted sharply, and raced forward to meet the young woman in the doorway. The girl looked a bit paler than usual, and definitely worried. "What is it? What's wrong? Is—is it your mother —"

"No, no, she's fine. As . . . fine as she can be." Linnet shook her head fiercely. "But you, all of you, there's a message here for you. The messenger said it was urgent."

The Free Bards exchanged startled looks. "Peregrine!" Nightjar exclaimed suddenly. "It has to be from him!"

She broke into a run, and the others hurried after her. Nightjar snatched up the intricately sealed parchment waiting on the kitchen table, then shook her head. "Does he always have to be so wary?"

"Wariness has kept him alive so far," Raven drawled.

"True enough. Well, let's see if I can figure out how this works." Nightjar studied the seal, then nodded and muttered a mysterious word over it. Magpie gasped as the seal quietly dissolved into vapor, and Nightjar shot her a quick grin.

"Peregrine taught me that one. The spell's ridiculously easy, but without it . . . The whole parchment would have dissolved if I'd tried to force the seal open, but when you say the right word—neat, isn't it?"

"Uh, sure."

"Now, let's see what he has to say . . . oh."

"What's wrong?" Raven asked sharply.

Nightjar glanced up at him, frowning with worry. "Peregrine says he isn't coming. It's too dangerous: his magics have been warning him over and over that Duke Arden's enemies have started using spells—well, we already knew that much. Hmm . . . I don't think I like the sound of this: Peregrine adds that they've also started looking for mages in the Duke's own household."

"Regina!" Raven gasped. "Aie, she'd better walk warily!"

"Oh, Regina's no fool. Now, let's see what else Peregrine has to say . . . ah." Nightjar gave them all a wry smile. "He concludes with a most emphatic 'Beware of fire.' "

Magpie gave a laugh. "Well, that's useful, isn't it? A bit on the late side, though!"

But Raven wasn't smiling. In fact, for one of the few times since she'd met him, he looked downright alarmed. "Raven?" Magpie asked warily, "What is it?"

"I know Peregrine," he said simply, "And he never sends a message that will arrive too late. He's too powerful a mage for that."

Magpie stiffened. "What are you saying?"

"That this means the 'fire' he warns against is yet to come." Raven's voice and face both were expressionless.

Magpie took one look at his face and began shivering again. "B-but that's not possible! You told us the theater's protected against curses!"

Raven hesitated, then shrugged. "What will be, will be," he said, this time putting a decidedly unpleasant slant to the adage. "Remember," the man added softly, "that the way of disposing of 'evil' mages is burning.

And the Church has a long history of incinerating folks."

Magpie cried out in denial. "But that was in the past! They wouldn't do anything so barbaric nowadays, would they?" *Oh, how ridiculous! I sound like a child crying, "Make it not so!"*

Raven sighed. "Who knows what they will or will not do? All I can do," he added, glancing about at all of them, "is simply repeat Peregrine's warning, remind you to keep it always in mind."

"Beware of fire." Nightjar said ominously. He nodded.

"Exactly. *Beware of fire.*"

CHAPTER SIXTEEN

DANGEROUS NESTING

Raven could practically feel Magpie's terror radiating from her. *Never realized you had such a fear of fire.* At least he assumed that was all it was. *I'm sorry,* Raven told her silently. *Much as I'd love to stay and comfort you, there are two people I have to warn about all this before it's too late.*

To warn them, and hopefully have a consultation with them—assuming, Raven thought wryly, the associates of one or the other of them didn't behead him first!

The fire didn't seem to have affected the general citizenry of Kingsford much, if at all. The streets were as crowded as they always were at this time of the day. Raven glanced covertly back over his shoulder, pretending he was merely adjusting the fall of his sleek hair. It had been no easy thing to elude all the others, but anyone raised in the Gypsy world knew how to steal through a crowd without being noticed.

Even, he thought in wry self-mockery, *if it goes against the grain to let my splendid self go unmarked!*

Ach, what a hot, still day this was! This summer was the worst for heat in his memory, without even a breath of wind to stir things around. Those streets that had been left unpaved were dusty as a desert, those with cobblestones were uncomfortably warm underfoot, and even the houses looked wan and colorless. Raven acknowledged that he'd been spending most of his time lately within the cool dark world of the theater, coming out again usually after sundown—*like some creature of the night!*—but now that he stopped to think about it, Raven realized he couldn't remember the last time it had rained for any length of time.

Not since the Midsummer Faire, in fact. Going to be hot and dry, I'm afraid. Bad for farmers. Means food prices are going to shoot up here in Kingsford, too. Ah well, can't do anything about that.

So now, here was the ducal palace, its marble walls looking white-hot in the remorseless sunlight, and somewhere in it was his first quarry: Regina.

Assuming, of course, Raven thought, he could find a way *into* the palace. He shrugged, then rapped sharply at the door by which the Free Bards usually entered and smiled his most dazzling smile at the servant who opened it. "Theater business," he told the man crisply, and marched boldly forward. *Always look as though you know exactly where you're going and have a perfect right to be going there.*

As always, the brazen technique worked. He left the servant standing in the doorway in confusion, not quite sure if he'd done the right thing to let Raven pass but rather dazed by that display of overwhelming self-assurance.

Now all I have to do is locate Regina's suite again

*without anyone getting the chance to stop me or ask
any embarrassing questions.* He'd been too busy trying
to worm information out of servants on his previous
visits to really notice directions. *Let's see . . . I know it
was down this way, past the stair, through these doors,
and—*

Well, close. He'd reached her suite, all right, no
doubt about that, but this was hardly the music room.

Probably should have turned left, not right. Ah well.

He was standing in a large, elegant chamber, its
walls painted a gentle, restful blue ornamented here
and there with floral reliefs in the archaic style. To his
left, a floor-length mirror touched the vanity in Raven
and made him glance at his reflection with a grin, shaking his sleeves to watch the multi-hued ribbons fall
neatly into place. Directly ahead were some brocade-
covered clothing screens, scattered with casual
artfulness, and to his right a delicate, graceful little
table covered with perfume flasks proved that this
chamber could only be Regina's dressing room.

*And through that doorway must be her bedroom—
Aie, what if she and the Duke are—*

No. To his vast relief, the elegant canopied bed was
unoccupied.

*This is not the best place to wait. But I don't dare
keep wandering about hunting a better one. Sooner or
later someone would be sure to find me and toss me
out!*

Raven settled himself gingerly on a reasonably comfortable chair, a dainty little thing that creaked
alarmingly under him, and waited. And waited. And
waited.

Sooner or later, he told himself wryly, Regina had to
come back here.

Sooner. Or later.

❖   ❖   ❖

The screened little alcove had presumably been originally intended for a Ducal aide who would whisper cues to a less alert Duke than Arden, but now, Regina thought with a faint smile, it made the perfect place for her to watch and listen unseen as Duke Arden met with his Council. This quiet observation was her choice, not Arden's; she rather enjoyed the intricate, wary game of politics—as long as it was the Duke playing it, Regina admitted, and not she! Besides, Arden had made it very clear he approved of her interest and appreciated her insights and advice afterwards.

The Council was most definitely not being cooperative today, its solid, well-fed, sensibly clad members—a cross section of Kingsford's more prestigious merchants—alike in their stubborn expressions. "But, my lord Duke, the expense—"

"Hang the expense!" Duke Arden brought his fist crashing down on the table, and all the merchants jumped. "Don't you see the danger? Kingsford is mostly wood, not stone, *wood*!"

One of the plumper merchants sniffed. "Only in the common quarters."

"Only in the *business* quarters!" the Duke corrected hotly, and all those fat, wealthy *businessmen* sat up and exchanged startled glances. "Ha, that strikes home, doesn't it? Look you, all of you, we all know the weather's been unusually hot and dry—perfect weather for fire. We cannot continue to depend only on men with a few paltry buckets!"

"But, my lord, our bucket brigades have worked well enough so far," protested a gem merchant.

"So far, yes! Against kitchen fires and the like. But what good would they be against a large fire? Or one spread by wind? Look at what happened to St. Bede's!"

The Duke rose from his chair and began to pace, gesturing fiercely. "We couldn't *put* the fire out, we had to wait for it to burn itself out, and it was only our own damned luck that there wasn't a wind to carry it further than the church and the parsonage! Dammit, man, you've seen how well the new water-wagons work! It takes only two men to pull one, and only one man to work the pump—yes, and send water squirting up two stories high! You can't do that with a bucket brigade!"

"But—" began another.

"But nothing! Yes, the wagons are expensive, yes, they're new and untried in the kind of inferno I've been warning you of, but so is the entire science of fire fighting!"

The Councilmen glanced uncertainly about at each other. "True," one man said warily. "It does make sense to train men in the use of those long grappling hooks that tear off burning thatch so the whole building does not burn. But what about that fire at St. Bede's? The water-wagon was useless there."

"Only because the thrice-cursed fire spread so fast and because we only had *one* wagon!" The Duke shook his head impatiently and flung himself back down into his chair. "The wagon *did* succeed in saving the side-chapel where it was stationed. Not even the most skilled fire fighter is going to win every time; we are, after all, only human. But I tell you, we must have a more modern means of fighting fires— and I am *not* going to pay for it all! Don't wince like that, gentlemen. You are going to contribute to my fire-stopping fund as well, like it or not, and so is everyone else in Kingsford. If needs be, I shall raise a one-time tax on the citizenry."

Two of the Councilors choked. A third simply raised his eyebrows. "My lord, is that wise?" he asked mildly.

"Of course it's wise!" the Duke roared. "We must modernize—or I promise you, we all shall suffer!"

He sprang to his feet, ignoring the frantic scraping of chairs as the Council hastily followed suit, and strode angrily from the room.

Regina slipped out through her own secret exit and followed her Duke like a quiet shadow till they were safely alone, then moved to his side to link her arm with his. "A difficult session," she murmured softly.

He grunted. "That's the problem with working with merchants. They mean well for the city, but they will not see further than their own purse strings. But we do need those water-wagons." The Duke glanced her way. "You don't think I'm being stubborn, do you?"

Regina chuckled. "Of course you are, my love. But quite justifiably so. I saw the fire at St. Bede's for myself." She touched an affectionate hand to his cheek, and felt him smile and lean into her caress. "Enough business for now, Arden. Relax, dearest."

"Ha! How?"

Regina chuckled again, deep in her throat. "I can think of one very pleasant way," she murmured. "Follow me, my love."

Was Regina never coming back? Raven got impatiently to his feet and prowled about the room, sniffing at perfume flasks, admiring the colors of a carelessly draped silken scarf, enjoying all the pretty accessories of a lovely woman and rather wishing he could enjoy the woman, as well.

Phaugh, this way of thinking was beginning to border on the indecent! Raven's restless prowling grew wider, bringing him into the doorway of the bedroom —

"What," thundered a furious voice, "are *you* doing here?"

Raven whirled in shock to see Regina—and Duke Arden beside her, his arm draped about her shoulders.

Oh hell. How was he going to explain this one? *I was just exploring your mistress's bedroom for the fun of it? I was looking for a nice perfume for myself?* The only way to get out of this one alive and . . . ah . . . unaltered, Raven decided, was to play the innocent for all he was worth.

"I *am* a member of your Company," he said cheerfully, "and I'm here on Company business. Come now, man," Raven added, "I'm hardly part of some clandestine rendezvous! If I was that stupid, I would have hidden the moment I heard anyone enter! Instead—" he threw out his arms with a flourish "—here I am out in the open, completely at ease."

And isn't that *a lovely lie?*

The Duke muttered something under his breath. But his first hot rush of anger had apparently started to cool a bit, because his voice was almost steady when he asked, "So why are you here?"

Not much choice about it. Raven shrugged at Regina, who watched him with wary alarm, and said, "To warn you. You, my lord Duke, are in definite danger."

"No news there," the man answered drily. "I usually am. Did you have some specific peril in mind?"

"Ah, this is going to sound a bit bizarre, but someone is planning to discredit you by using your patronage of the arts and your theater and Company as a weapon." The Duke's expression darkened and he scowled. "No, wait," Raven said hastily, "don't be so quick to scoff! Regina will back me up on this. Won't you?" Raven added, turning to her with hope.

Regina sighed, her hand going to the holy medal about her neck. "I'm afraid I must, Arden. You see, we've been having a strange string of accidents lately . . . accidents that some of us concluded were not accidents at all. . . ."

Midway through her listing, Duke Arden interrupted angrily, "This is ridiculous! Trying to get me to believe that a few misplaced props are part of some dark, deadly plot—just what do you two think you're doing? Regina, I warn you, even you, that if you're trying to play me for a fool—"

"I most certainly am not!" she snapped. "If you think so little of me that you'd believe I would—"

"Hey, whoa!" Raven cried, and held up a hand, forcing a placating grin onto his face as the Duke and Regina both glared at him. "Uh, if we can get back to the matter at hand?"

The Duke angrily waved him on. Raven shrugged. "Please just listen to the entire list of what's been happening in the theater, Duke Arden, and you tell me if we're being foolish to take it seriously."

Watching the man's expression slowly shift from anger to skepticism, he continued to list "coincidence" after "coincidence," as coolly and unemotionally as he could. When he'd finished, Regina continued with her own list of "coincidences," ending up with the fire at St. Bede's that had burned with such unnatural ferocity.

Duke Arden shook his head. "I can't believe—"

"And what about what's been happening at court?" Regina added sharply. She mentioned a variety of strange incidents, each one apparently accidental, each one putting the Duke in an awkward position. "We both thought the missing scroll and the lost medal were merely coincidences, too," she reminded him. "And the time that you never received the King's message *could* have been an accident. But when you combine the whole thing with what's been happening at the theater . . ."

"It does begin to look uncomfortably like a plot," Duke Arden admitted reluctantly. "Oh, but my dear, by whom? I have enough enemies."

Regina's face turned cool and expressionless. "But which ones would gain the most not just from your removal from power but from seeing you actually dishonored?"

"Ha!"

"Arden, please." Regina counted the names off on her fingers. "Duke Sesmand would certainly love your position at Court. Lord Jarreck would take a giant leap in status upward if you were out of his way. Duke Regimand would love to push you aside to get at your lands. Lord Rand has hated you ever since you made him look foolish in front of the King. And pretty Lord Menden would definitely like to see you out of his elegant, ambitious way. Just a handful of foes, fortunately—but you have to admit they are quite a nasty handful."

The names she'd mentioned meant nothing at all to Raven: well-born, well-propertied, aristocratic folk, judging from the titles, and presumably as treacherous as such a lot could be. But they certainly meant something to the Duke, who was frowning by the time Regina finished.

"There's only one problem with all this," he said to her. "That nasty handful of nobles, as you call them, are the very ones who would also be most likely to oppose my seeking to ennoble you so that I could marry you. And you know that very well."

"Do you really think I would stoop so low?" Regina murmured, and Raven saw the hurt flash in her eyes. But she continued as steadily as ever a woman arrested for sorcery faced her accusers. And she moved to the tiny shrine in the corner of her room, and placed one hand on the Holy Book that lay there. "I swear by the

One that everything I promise you is true. If you seek a title for me, I will refuse it."

"Regina," the Duke cried in horror, "don't—"

"If you offer to marry me, I will deny it, and sign a pledge to that effect in the Cathedral itself. What I want from you is something no King or title can give me." She removed her hand and regarded him steadily.

Raven stared, speechless at her act of brave self-sacrifice. Did she know what she'd just done? Regina had just completely destroyed any chances of wedding her Duke. She could never become more than his mistress now, for the oath she had just sworn was the most binding there was.

As Regina stood proudly erect, fighting back tears, Duke Arden searched her face for a moment, his expression softening. "I'm sorry," he said in a quiet, choked voice, then enfolded her in his arms. Raven turned away, embarrassed by the anguish and love shining from them both, wishing with all his heart that he was somewhere else, that he could leave them in the privacy they deserved.

But all at once Duke Arden pulled away. "There are things I must do," he said in a voice that was just a touch too controlled to be genuine, "to verify what I can and put my own gatherers of information into motion. I will return shortly."

He stopped to look at Raven, who shrugged and grinned. "I'll be gone by then."

"See to it," the Duke replied, in a voice that brooked no argument.

Regina watched the Duke leave, her eyes luminous with pain, then whirled angrily to Raven. "That was a risky bit of business you just worked!"

He shrugged. "I didn't really have much of a choice, now, did I? Regina, I—I'm sorry about what just happened. But for both our sakes and the sake of the Duke, we must talk. In private."

Her eyes flamed with anger. "Oh, must we? I—"

"Listen." Hastily, Raven told her of Peregrine's warning, and saw her start. "Ah, wait," he added, "there's more. And I—well, I'm not sure how you're going to take this. Regina, Peregrine is a powerful mage, as I've said—but it's beginning to look very much as if you have your own magical abilities. Have you ever heard of something called 'glamorie'? Let me explain—"

Her eyes widened in shock as he spoke. But rather to Raven's surprise, Regina didn't even try to deny his claim. Instead, she listened carefully, nodding now and again. As remotely as someone discussing some abstract bit of science, she murmured, "It would explain a great deal. . . ."

He heaved a great sigh of relief. "You believe me, then."

"The One help me, yes." A great shudder shook her, and Regina turned sharply away, then just as sharply back again, on her face the panic of a wild thing caught in a trap. "What am I going to do? The Church is hunting mages— Arden's enemies are hunting weaknesses— Oh Raven, please, I can't put him in danger! How can I possibly *not* use this—this glamorie?"

"Hush, now," Raven soothed. "No need to panic."

"But—"

"It's the easiest thing in the world, or so the Gypsy mages tell me, *as long as you know you have it*. All you really need to do is simply concentrate on not influencing the people you're with. Even your audience," he added hastily. "That's almost certainly when your enemies are going to be testing you, during the play. You'll have to rely only on your acting ability to win over the audience." He tried to smile, but he knew the smile was weak.

She laughed, a bit too merrily to be quite convincing. "That's all I ever asked. Raven, I do thank you for the warning, no matter what awkwardness it caused. But Duke Arden will be returning at any moment. I think you had better return to your friends."

He nodded fervently. "Oh, indeed."

With a bow, Raven left, letting himself be surrounded by officious servants and formally ushered out of the ducal palace.

One message delivered, he thought. *Now for the other. And may it be less perilous than this!*

CHAPTER SEVENTEEN

A TEMPTING ROOST

The massive stone walls of the Cathedral close didn't look any more welcoming in this late afternoon light than they had when he'd seen them the last time he'd been here. Raven hesitated, staring up at their height, then shrugged; this was hardly the time or place for foolish qualms. After a quick, cautious glance about, he rapped smartly on the same door as before— *Good gods, was it only a few days ago?*—and proceeded to wait for what seemed like exactly the same infuriatingly long time before the door opened a crack and what *had* to be the same wary eye peered out at him.

"You, again," the sexless voice said, flatly.

Biting back the urge to spit out something sarcastic, like *My, what a clever child it is,* Raven contented himself with a dry, "Me, again. And it's just as important as the last time."

The unseen figure sighed. "And I suppose you wish the same troublesome matter as before: to see the Lady Ardis."

No. I merely wanted to come in and smell the roses. "So I do. As I said, it is urgent. I would not trouble her otherwise."

"You fail to understand. Then, it pleased the Lady to grant you some moments out of her day. Now, I must warn you, we do not have the same situation as before. Thanks to urgent Church business, the Lady Ardis does not have much time to spare for visitors." The voice *did* seem to have a little more strain in it this time.

"Particularly not such lowly creatures as myself?" he asked, with a trifle less sarcasm than he wished.

"If you wish to call yourself by such a humble name," the figure said smoothly, "so be it. We are all," he or she added piously before Raven could frame a suitably sharp reply, "the children of the One."

The very *last* thing he was in the mood for was a set of platitudes! "Fine," Raven snapped. "This child of the One urgently needs to see Lady Ardis, on business that concerns her as much as me, so if we can cut back on some of this sparkling repartee maybe we can—"

But the figure, infuriatingly, had already vanished, leaving Raven's angry words hanging in mid-air. Fuming, he paced back and forth, counting off the passing moments, wishing all officious servants of any degree to whatever places of punishment their religions decreed. He thought before it was all over that he had definitely been left waiting for a far longer while than he had the first time, but at last the sexless figure returned, grudgingly opening the door just enough to let Raven enter.

"She is, as I attempted to warn you," the figure muttered, "very busy indeed. So busy that you should be honored that she would agree to see you at all. I pray you, do not think to keep the Lady Ardis away from her duties for long."

Raven frowned thoughtfully. For all the condescension, this certainly sounded like more than mere officiousness! Just what was going on in the Church these days? *Could this have something to do with the fire?* he wondered in wild surmise. "I'll try not to bother her for more than a few— Ah. My Lady Ardis."

To his dismay, the woman looked far more weary than before, far more harried, face pale against the brilliant scarlet of her robes, keen gray eyes troubled. The odd, sexless creature vanished as abruptly as if it had never existed. "Raven. If you've come to tell me about the fire at St. Bede's, be assured I already know."

"Ah well, yes," he admitted, "that was one of the reasons I'm here. But do you also know—"

"That it was the result of sorcery?" she nodded. "Yes, I do."

He felt a little deflated. "I guess a mage like you would."

But she was not finished. "It was my charm, after all. What touches my magic, touches me. I also know that the sorcery was almost certainly originally aimed, no matter how indirectly, at the Duke of Kingsford." She waited, watching dispassionately but carefully, to see his reaction.

"How could you know that?" he replied, startled. "I mean, we only guessed—"

"A recoiled spell has a certain *feel* to it. And what else could it have been recoiling *from* but the charm I'd given you to shield the theater? It *is* Duke Arden's theater, after all." She paused, eyeing him speculatively. "The Duke, as I think you've come to realize, has some very powerful enemies."

"Oh, yes," he replied glumly. Indeed, after that little interview with Regina and the Duke, he knew far more than he wanted to. "But . . . Lady, if you knew about the sorcery—" He paused, not certain how to continue without giving offense.

"Why didn't I do something to stop it?" she completed for him.

Raven blinked, feeling a little chill slipping up his spine. These sudden answers were growing just a bit too eerie for him! "Can you read minds?" he asked, only half in jest.

Lady Ardis smiled the thinnest ghost of a smile. "Hardly. That is *not* an ability most mages are granted. You needn't fear I will pry out all your mysterious Gypsy secrets."

"Then how . . . " he began.

She produced a dry husk of a chuckle. "Come now, given the path of our conversation and your expressions, I could hardly miss guessing what your next question was going to be." She lifted one elegant eyebrow at him. "You are not nearly as mysterious and inscrutable as you think you are, Gypsy Raven."

"Of . . . course." He wasn't sure he believed her, even given the disclaimer. How could she have known he was coming to tell her about the fire—and more importantly, how could she have known about the plot to undermine Duke Arden's authority?

"Ach, Raven!" The woman let out her breath in an impatient sigh. "I think you are under a number of delusions, and I don't know what Talaysen may have told you about me."

"That you are a truly pious woman," Raven said frankly. "And a truly powerful mage."

"For the first, I try to be," she answered just as frankly. "For the second, yes, I am. I don't believe in false modesty. But I am only human, Raven! I am *not* infallible. If I'd had any idea that the curse-casting was going to go beyond simple accidents, *I* would have done more than I did. By the time the curse rebounded, it was too late."

"But you know who did it?" he asked hopefully.

But she shook her head. "I had my suspicions about the fire and the one or ones who might have caused it—but by the time I reached the scene of the fire, all traces of its creator had been cunningly erased."

"Yet there wasn't anyone suspicious around?" he replied. "Not even at the church?"

"No." Lady Ardis paused wearily. "Such magics—and their erasure as well—are possible even when the mage isn't nearby. The criminal could have been any-where—and anyone with magic. He needed only to have the same connection with St. Bede's that the Duke has with the theater for the curse to rebound the way it did. It could even have been a *patron* of St. Bede's, and not anyone among the clergy."

"But it was probably someone with magic who's within the Church," Raven said daringly, and Lady Ardis raised an eyebrow in warning.

"All that was left," she said, "was a rapidly fading, totally useless aura of sorcery about the ashes—useless because I already knew dark magery had been used, and that was all the aura revealed to me."

"Lady Ardis," Raven began warily, "that fire really was the threefold result of a recoiling curse, wasn't it?"

She nodded, and Raven threw up his hands in disgust. "You already know everything I was planning to tell you! Except . . . do you know about Regina Shevron?"

"The Duke's mistress?" Her carefully neutral tone made *him* frown, but she shook her head. "No, Raven, don't give me that wary look. I am not disapproving either of the woman or of what she is. Regina Shevron is a good, kind-hearted soul who truly loves Duke Arden; she would never do a thing to harm him, and since he loves his city and his people, she would never do a thing that would distract him from his duties. And the Duke could do worse than wed her. If, of course, such a thing was possible."

"He . . . isn't going to be able to wed her. Ever." At Lady Ardis's surprised glance, Raven reluctantly told her about Regina's impulsive, heartfelt oath.

"Ah," the Lady murmured. "That *is* unfortunate."

"Can't you do anything?" he pleaded, wondering if somehow Lady Ardis could undo what had been done. Give special dispensation from the oath. Or something.

"What? She swore that oath before the One. Who am I to deny it?" Lady Ardis shook her head sadly. "I'm afraid there's nothing that can be done."

"Why did I even think to bother you?" Raven asked. "I've wasted both our times."

"No. You came here with all goodwill. And kindness is never a waste of time. Especially not when it comes from a profound longing to help others." She paused, a smile touching her weary face for the first time. "Why, look at this: I've embarrassed you!"

That was true enough. Hoping his face wasn't red, Raven grinned ruefully. "I hardly think of myself as an altruist."

"You're a better soul than you realize. Or want to acknowledge," she added wryly. "Ach, well, Raven, the doorkeeper wasn't exaggerating: I do have much work to do. Thank you for coming here."

He bowed and turned to leave, but Lady Ardis added softly, "Wait. Take this comfort away with you:

Both I and the other mages in the Justiciary are fully alerted to an enemy within the Church. I can swear to you that there are no false mages within *our* ranks. And I assure you, we will be watching, both over the Church as is our duty, and over Duke Arden and those he cares for, which is our pleasure—and where we can act, believe me, we shall."

As Raven walked back across the bridge through the oncoming evening, he barely noticed that the city—the serious side of it, at any rate—was settling down for the night. Below him, the lanterns at stem and stern of the docked riverboats turned them into so many golden fairy crafts and made the water glitter with reflections, but he spared the sight barely a glance. Headed back towards the boardinghouse, he was lost in thought and very far from content.

Too many unsettled matters here, too many maybes and not enough conclusions.

Ah well. All might, as the saying went, yet be very well.

But although he was preoccupied, his senses were still perfectly sharp. And his instinct for self-preservation was equally sharp.

He was being followed.

Raven turned and glared, not at all in the mood for an encounter. Whoever was stalking him was hidden in shadow, but he was caught for a moment in the flickering light of one of the rare street torches before he moved into the shadows himself. His fierce, dark, one-eyed face must have looked close to demonic in that uncertain, ruddy glow, because he heard a sudden gasp and the sound of running feet, moving away. With a grim, satisfied nod, Raven moved on, and was left undisturbed for the rest of his walk.

By now, the hour was very late. Raven crept into the boardinghouse as softly as he could so he wouldn't wake anyone, a little disconcerted at how easy it was to enter. But then, he admitted drily, what self-respecting thief would think there was anything worth stealing in this ramshackle place? Slipping into the kitchen, the Gypsy Bard lit a candle with flint and steel so he could put together a dinner of bits and pieces of meat, cheese, and bread, which he gulped down in silence. Brushing off crumbs, he stole upstairs, wincing at the loud creaks of the rickety stairway and the creaks from the floorboards.

Raven had just reached his room, hand on the door, when a sudden shrill little scream from Magpie's room brought him fiercely alert, heart racing.

Magpie! he thought wildly, and forced the door open —

— and stopped short in the doorway, feeling very foolish. There wasn't a sign of anyone in the room save Magpie herself, curled up in bed like a child, sound asleep.

Asleep and, it would seem, dreaming most foully. Without warning, she screamed again, and the sound of it wasn't that of a woman, but of a terrified child.

Nightmares out of the past—oh, poor child, Raven thought and, overwhelmed with a sudden surge of pity, he called her name gently to wake her. At the sound of his voice, she sat bolt upright, staring wildly.

But she doesn't see me, Raven realized. *She's still asleep.*

"Magpie," he murmured, taking a few steps into the room and touching her gently on the shoulder. "It's all right. You're dreaming, and you can wake up. Come now, wake up. Magpie!"

She came awake with a wild gasp; caught sight of his face in the moonlight coming in the window. "Raven! Oh—I—"

"Hush, now" he soothed, patting her shoulder awkwardly. "It was only a dream. Just a simple nightmare."

"I—I know. I . . . "

To his utter astonishment and embarrassment, he saw her turn and bury her face in the bedclothes, shoulders shaking. She was weeping, his strong, tough Magpie! "Oh . . . don't," Raven said helplessly. "Please, Magpie, don't . . . "

At last, not knowing what else to do, Raven sat down on the bed beside her, and pulled her gently into his arms. She snuffled on his shoulder for a time while he realized with an odd, happy little shock just how pleasant it was to hold her, to feel her warm and soft in his arms. Just then, he knew, he wouldn't have minded going on holding her forever. . . .

But then suddenly Magpie was pulling back, sniffing, scrubbing her face dry with a hand, blowing her nose on a scrap of linen, and the strange, gentle moment was gone.

"S-sorry," she said, her voice thick with embarrassment. "I don't usually . . . "

"Hey now, I've had a few horrific nightmares myself!" He tried to make his tone light to reassure her.

"Yes, but . . . " Magpie shook her head in disgust. "It wasn't just bad dreams bothering me," she admitted. "Though the One knows my mind's been upset enough to cause nightmares enough. Raven, I . . . I've been afraid to sleep lately."

That was not the sort of thing he expected to hear from *her*! "But why?"

She wouldn't meet his gaze. "I never thought I would react like this. I mean, I've faced an awful lot of dangers in my life so far, but—but nothing has ever scared me like this."

"The fire?" he asked hesitantly. "I didn't think you —"

"Oh, Raven! I'm not afraid of something as normal as fire. As . . . normal fire," she amended.

Raven straightened in sudden comprehension. "It was the magic!" he exclaimed. "That's what's got you so terrified, isn't it? I *thought* you were looking rather—ah—green, when we talked about the magic! I bet you've never had to come up against magic before, have you?"

"No." She brushed her tangled hair back from her face, eyes fierce. "Not really." Magpie paused. "You probably think that's impossible. You probably take things like that for granted, being a Gypsy."

He frowned, stung. "'Gypsy,' my dear, doesn't always equal 'sorcerer.'"

"Oh, I know that," she said in an embarrassed rush, "I didn't mean to insult—but you *are* more familiar with such things as magic, you have to admit it."

Raven shrugged. "It's difficult to exactly take magic for granted. But yes, I will agree that Gypsies are more at ease with such things."

"Then all those stories I've heard about Gypsies—" she began, haltingly.

He laughed. "Contain about as much truth as all the stories you've heard about Deliambrens! Let's just say we have a wider view of what constitutes natural than most other folk. And yes, I've seen spells worked before, both for good and harm, though," he added sharply, "my people refuse to make use of the darker side of such things."

But such frankness only frightened her again. Seeing her shiver, Raven hesitated, trying to find the right words to make her calm again. "Magpie, I won't be stupid enough to brashly tell you there's nothing to fear. But . . . magic's nothing more than a tool. Just because you can't see it being used, the way you can see a swordsman swinging a sword, doesn't change that fact."

"But that's just it!" she wailed, sounding for all the world like a terrified child. "You *can't* see it!"

"Ach, Magpie . . . my poor, down-to-earth Magpie," Raven murmured. "What a brave young woman you are."

That took her completely by surprise, startling a little of the terror out of her. "I'm not brave!" she replied.

"No?" Maybe she couldn't see his smile in the darkness, but surely she heard it in his voice. "What made you stay, then?"

She hesitated a long while. "I was afraid to leave," Magpie said at last, in a small voice.

Eh? "I don't understand."

"Raven, you know something of my past." She shook her head, and her long, fine hair brushed his hand. "I *always* run away from things. The only way I could survive this long was by running from anything that threatened me."

He laughed. "That's not exactly a foolish policy. I've done my share of running, too!"

"You don't see my point. I've *always* run. All my life, every time I had to face a challenge, I've always run." She swallowed convulsively. "I was afraid that if I ran this time as well, I—I was never going to stop running. You know, clichéd though this sounds, there really does come a point at which you have to take a stand. You have to face down the villain, or the evil, or—" Magpie broke off with a shaky little laugh. "Listen to me. I sound like a recruiting officer."

"I'll be happy to enlist," Raven said with a grin and a sharp salute, and was rewarded with a more genuine laugh. "Magpie, you are one of the bravest people I've met—No, don't you dare start arguing. You are—yes, I'll throw your words back at you—you are facing down something that's scaring you silly. You are refusing to give in. And if that, my dear, isn't courage, I don't know what the word means."

"Oh, I . . ." She faltered.

Greatly daring, he placed the tips of his fingers over her lips, silencing her. "Wait. Let me finish. I know the idea of the unseen is frightening. But hey now, the *wind* can be a deadly force, and you're not afraid of the wind, are you?"

She sighed. "No. Of course not. But the wind doesn't have an intelligent mind controlling it. The wind doesn't pick enemies to eliminate."

"Well, not as far as we know, anyhow," he replied. "But we don't know everything. Magpie, this may sound like I'm changing the subject, but you keep telling me I shouldn't keep secrets that can affect us all. Well, I ran two different errands today. First I went to see Regina in the Duke's palace."

"By yourself?" she said, with surprise. "Without an invitation? And they let you in?"

"Oh, thank you!" he said, with cheerful sarcasm, pleased to hear her voice returning to normal. "I didn't think I looked *quite* so disreputable!"

Magpie giggled in spite of herself. "I didn't mean that the way it sounded."

"Ah. Well, at any rate, there I was in the palace . . . "

He went on to tell her what had happened there. "If that's supposed to comfort me," Magpie said dryly, "it doesn't."

But she did seem calmer than before, and Raven continued, "After that, I went to see . . . someone important. The same one who gave me the holy medal. That someone assured me powerful folks are watching out for us, and I, for one, believe it." He reached out to close a gentle hand on hers. "That—ah—Personage told me enough to assure me that the Personage knows all about our little group. That *includes* you. You are not alone, woman. Remember that. You are not alone. And," Raven added with a smile, "if things get too bad, remember you always can have that proverbial shoulder to lean on."

She sniffled a little, and rubbed her eyes on the back of her hand. "Thank you," she said simply.

"Are you all right now?" he asked, as gently as he could.

She nodded. "Yes. I think so."

"Good." Raven patted her hand, and got to his feet, fighting back a sudden yawn. "Go back to sleep, Magpie. We have a full day's rehearsal ahead."

"You . . . don't have to go." It was said so softly Raven almost wasn't sure he'd heard it. Looking down at her face, soft and lovely and defenseless with sleepiness and spent emotion, he fought a quick, fierce battle with himself. No, dammit, it would be all too easy to take advantage of her right now. And Magpie deserved better than that.

Raven sighed. Wondering wryly, *Why do I have to turn honorable* now? he told her as firmly as he could under the circumstances, "Yes, I do. You're tired, and I—am *trying* to be a gentleman. Difficult a concept as that is for me."

She giggled, and he knew with relief that she had taken that for the joke he meant it to be.

"Good night, my dear Magpie," he said, instead of all the things he *wanted* to say.

As he was closing her door behind him, he heard her murmur, "Thank you," but wasn't at all sure if it was in gratitude or regret.

CHAPTER EIGHTEEN

BROODING

The Duke of Kingsford paused to survey this smallest portion of his domain. The tiny, quiet room in the heart of the ducal palace was plainly furnished, containing but the one chair and table. Its walls were paneled in sleek, amber-hued wood that had been polished till it glowed in the candlelight with elegant warmth. One of the Duke's ancestors several generations back had ordered an intricate pattern of roses painted on the ceiling, and that pattern had been carefully renewed every few years: it was the traditional "under the roses" design that was supposed to ensure privacy.

Interesting superstition, Duke Arden thought wryly, glancing up at it. *Too bad it doesn't work.*

More to the point, the room was soundproof, which was more likely to ensure privacy than any painted flowers, and the Duke himself had gone over the elegant paneling within the hour to be sure no one had bored any neat little spyholes in the wood. As far as Arden could tell, all his servants were truly his, but he certainly wasn't naive enough to believe that even the most seemingly loyal of men couldn't be bought.

A wonderful system we have here in Kingsford, he mused sardonically. *If someone isn't working for me, he could be in the pay of the King, the King's foes, my foes, the Bardic Guild, the Church—*

Ah yes, the Church. Arden had no doubts about the existence of the One, and he liked to believe in the concept of divine justice. But that didn't mean all the priesthood was as honest—or believable—as its doctrine. The Duke smiled grimly, remembering that one slimy priest who had lectured against the theater and, indirectly, against him. Had the man been acting alone, out of some misguided attempted at personal gain? Or was he part of a larger plot? Was that plot a matter of secular politics, or sacred? Who could say? There was just as much plotting and conniving in the Church as there was in the royal court, and it was every bit as convoluted and nasty.

Particularly nasty, if they were now making use of dark magery. Assuming, of course, that all the things that knave of a Raven had told him were true.

Raven. Arden's smile thinned. Amazing, the rush of jealousy he'd felt at the sight of this other man, this stranger, this *handsome, romantic* stranger, standing there in Regina's private suite as if he belonged there, fairly radiating that just too theatrical innocence.

Dammit, I know Regina would never betray me. And yet, and yet . . .

Arden shook his head impatiently, angry at himself. These stupid doubts and fears rightly belonged only to pimply-faced adolescents!

If only Raven hadn't looked so—so very rakish! So

devil-may-care and dangerous, as if he had stepped straight out of one of his own ballads to carry off the fair prize—

Ah well, that wasn't just. The man couldn't help how his ancestors had shaped him. The Duke acknowledged that a great deal of his reaction was due entirely to the fact that women surely found that narrow, swarthy face intriguing, what with its exoticism and hints of peril and the unknown. Oh, and the mystery of that black eye patch, as well.

Mystery, bah!

Probably lost the eye to some angry husband who— No! I am not going to start acting like a jealous fool! I am the Duke of Kingsford, I am an adult, and I— Ah, Regina, life would be so much simpler if I had never met you.

So much . . . emptier.

May the One help him, he had never intended, never even considered, falling in love with her. What, a nobleman love a commoner? An actress, no less, a woman with who knew how sordid a past? What a ridiculous idea! No one who had known him before he had met her would ever have considered such a possibility.

Least of all, myself.

Of course he had been struck speechless by his first sight of that sharp, elegant beauty.

I'd need to have my manhood checked if I hadn't been struck! Arden thought drily.

But even then he hadn't thought it more than simple, uncomplicated lust. He'd wanted her from that very moment, and felt no shame about it; many a man, noble or not, had his lowborn mistress on the side. And Arden had never doubted Regina would willingly become his mistress, not with all the comforts and social advantages he could offer her. She was too practical a woman to deny herself that. It was to be a simple business arrangement of sorts. She would join the list of others who had occupied the special suite in the west wing; she would grace his bed when he called and his arm when he chose—he would give her every comfort and luxury she could wish, and retire her with honor when he tired of her.

But somewhere along the way things had changed from mere business to—to—Arden shook his head in wonder. What had he done to make Regina love him? *Him,* not the Duke, not the fine clothes and riches and social status—*him!* While he . . .

Ah, ridiculous, truly ridiculous, this passion in a mature man. Particularly in a man who'd never known such a thing before. How could he? Dukes belonged to the world of dry, dutiful marriages, careful arrangements made for the best possible political gain. Try though he would, Arden had never been able to feel more than a polite, bemused affection for his late wife, his poor, fragile Amelia, a true child of aristocrats, gentle and bloodless as a flower. When she had died of fever five years back, he'd felt vaguely guilty and most decidedly relieved.

Poor shallow thing. While you lived it was like being haunted by a pretty, pastel, humorless ghost. I imagine right now you're up there somewhere using those pathetic little sighs and oh-so-weary glances to tell the One you don't quite approve of the way the Hereafter is designed.

Ah well, she'd been a good soul in her proper, bland way. But after Amelia's death, Arden had told himself enough was enough. He had never wished to find another wife, despite the need for an heir. He certainly had never dreamed he might find true love!

Love? Love was a thing for beardless boys, romantic maidens, and ridiculous ballads. Love was not something I wanted or needed.

As well deny the summer its warmth. Ridiculous or not, love this most certainly was, just as hot and wondrous as the Bards sang. Even though the cold, proper, aristocratic side of him was still in shock over what had happened to him, Arden knew he really didn't care what Regina was, he didn't care what she might have been or what she might have done to survive before he'd met her. He didn't care about anything but Regina herself, and Regina's love for him.

How could Fortune be so damnably cruel? Waiting till now to show me a glimpse of wonder, then hitting us both with harsh reality.

If only she had been born of noble blood or, for that matter, he of common blood, they could have wed without a single eyebrow being raised. But because things were as they were —

Why did you do it? he asked her silently. *Why swear that terrible, foolish, permanent oath? And why oh why did I let my stupid jealousy force you into it?*

The softest, most discreet of knocks brought him sternly alert, all softness banished. It was the Duke of Kingsford, not the lover, who snapped out, "Enter."

The one who slipped soundlessly into the room was a slim gray shadow of a man, most anonymous of face, who bowed bonelessly before the Duke. "My lord."

"Well?" he demanded harshly. More harshly than he had intended, but the shadow-man did not appear to notice.

The gatherer of information—*Be honest,* Arden told himself wryly, *the spy*—shook his head. "I entered the Cathedral as you bade, my lord Duke, and not a soul there suspected I was aught but a minor cleric. I wandered innocently about, listening, watching."

"And?" Arden persisted. It was the man's single fault that every bit of information must be *elicited* from him, and accompanied by altogether too much description.

"And yes, the place was, as you conjectured, all in a stir, much more than is the norm. It would seem," the spy added carefully, "two sects within the Church are quarreling, very possibly with magic involved, and quarreling quite seriously."

Arden blinked. This was not necessarily good news. "About . . . ?"

The spy sighed. "Ah, my lord, though no matter how carefully I sought the heart of the quarrel, I could learn nothing. Save the usual: both sides seek what all folk wish."

Arden raised a brow at the spy's cynicism. "Power, you mean."

The spy bowed gravely. "Indeed, my lord."

And let us hope the Lady Ardis ends up the winner over all. Honest, that woman, pious without being prudish about it. She led the Justiciars without becoming a tyrant, while ensuring that her fellows got every bit of authority and credit that they deserved, and that took a deal of work. And quite a powerful mage, he'd heard, though of course he had never seen her show more magic than was politic. Were she to unleash her full powers on her enemies, or his for that matter —

Oh, that's a tempting thought. Dare I ask her?

No, she would never condone anything that might be interpreted as misuse of her magic. A pity. A pity, too, that he couldn't, being a lay nobleman, interfere in Church politics to aid her.

The Duke sighed ever so softly. "Ah well. The end crowns all, as the saying goes, and things will be as they will."

"Would you have me return to the Cathedral, my lord?" the spy queried mildly.

Arden considered that for a moment. "Yes," he said at last. "But be wary, particularly if they're using magic in there. Don't risk more than you need to." His frown was not for the spy, but for the need to use him. "All men can be broken, and I would not have anyone learn what we know."

"I shall be wary, my lord." The spy bowed, and started to leave.

"Wait." Arden held up his hand to forestall him. "Remember that a mage can have more ways than the direct ones to uncover a man's intentions, and his past. Leave nothing behind—not even footprints, if you can help it. Give them nothing to use to get at you if they should come to suspect you."

"Of course, my lord." The spy's voice held a touch of surprise and admiration.

"Go, then."

He waved the spy away and waited with well-schooled patience for the next. The Duke scheduled his appointments with his intelligence-gatherers very carefully. He timed the visits of each with enough leeway so that the second would appear only after the first was safely out of the palace. He had not obtained his power and kept it without being wise in the ways of security. It wasn't generally a good idea to let one spy learn of the existence of another.

Ah, here came the new knock on the door. Arden sat back in his chair. "Enter."

The second spy, who entered with humble demeanor and bowing obsequiously, was of the merchant class. He was a round bundle in his brocaded blue robes, his pink, well-scrubbed face smooth and plump and cleanly shaved. He was far less at ease in this secondary role of espionage than was the gray, shadowy fellow, for whom the secret gathering of information was a passion. Bowing yet again to the Duke, his hands clasped across his plump belly, the merchant murmured, "My lord Duke."

Arden dipped his head a polite fraction. "Good day. And what news have you?"

"Very little that *is* new, I fear." The man took a deep breath and continued in a rush of words, "Your threat of raised taxes does not sit particularly well with the merchants."

"I expected as much," Arden muttered. "Idiots."

"Uh, that's as may be, my lord, but I fear that they refuse to see the need for any alterations in the present systems. Most particularly, they see no need for change in the way that fires are fought."

Arden just barely bit back a sudden angry oath. "Only because improved methods will cost them money! They gave me just the same argument about schooling for common-born children or better houses for caring for the sick! Why can't they, just once, surprise me and look further than their own fat purses? Let a fire start—and in this hot, dry weather that's all too likely!—and we'll see how quickly they change their minds, the short-sighted—" He broke off abruptly, forcing his temper back under control. "Well, anger gains us nothing. I shall deal with this. Go on. What else?"

The merchant eyed him nervously. "Not much else, my lord. The Church, as you know, continues to place its small restrictions on the common folk. Of course they grumble, but what can they do? None of the restrictions are quite enough to cause genuine unrest, and none, as yet, have the pressure of secular punishment behind them."

"No. Of course not." Church folk were masters at controlling public thought and knowing exactly how hard and where to push. It was one thing to declare something to be "sinful" and decree a penance for it. It was quite another to declare it illegal. And yet, often as not, the former had all the force and the authority of the latter! *Here's another wish that Lady Ardis triumph!* "Thank you," he said shortly. "You may leave."

The merchant bowed, then scurried off. Arden settled back in his chair with a sigh. The Church he could do nothing about, no matter how often he wished it— but his city —

There were times when he rather wished he *could* burn down a good portion of Kingsford (without causing any harm to anyone, he added hastily), get rid of that dangerous, unsanitary maze of wood and thatch and replace it with nice, clean, nonflammable stone.

I can imagine the uproar about their purses if I mentioned anything like that to the merchants!

Ah well. Nothing to do right now but wait for his third spy, the timid, very minor noble who was his insidious little informant in the King's court. No one noticed him—and therefore, no one paid any attention to what he overheard. And he never acted on any of it, so no one thought that it mattered. Very useful . . .

But to his uneasy surprise, the one who entered next was no nobleman but a very nervous servant. "Your pardon, my lord, b-but you have a guest."

"Do I?" he said in surprise. "Who the devil is it?"

The servant swallowed nervously; everyone in the Ducal household knew how he hated to be disturbed at his "conferences." "The—the Lord Menden, my lord, newly arrived from the King's court."

"So-o." Now what did *that* overblown fop want? Or was he, perhaps, sent directly from the King—or, more likely, from one of the many factions forever looking for advancement? Duke Arden got to his feet, stretching luxuriously. "The day has grown too warm for indoor meetings. I will meet him in the rose garden."

"Now, my lord?" the servant asked, hopefully. Everyone in the ducal household *also* knew how irritated these "conferences" made him.

Arden shook his head. "Eventually. Bring him whatever refreshment he wants, and send that idiot Guild lute player out there to entertain him. It will do the man no harm to cool his heels for a time."

But of course when the Duke finally decided Menden had waited long enough, Arden went out to the rose garden showing every appearance of distress.

"My Lord Menden! How can I ever apologize enough for having kept you out here in the heat of day, and for so long! But . . . pressing business, my merchants of Kingsford are most obdurate. . . ."

Menden glided smoothly to his feet, tall and so slender he seemed just this side of gaunt. Towering over the Duke, the sun picking out gleaming highlights in his golden hair, he was the essence of court fashion, not a plume drooping or a ruffle out of place even in this hot weather. He waved a languid hand. "Oh, believe me, my lord Duke, I do know."

The Duke gestured politely. "Come, my lord, walk with me if you would."

The two men strolled together for some time, making the idlest of chat, Arden pointing out this rose or that. "Now, this elegant beauty is one I call the Scarlet Empress. A hybrid, of course, but it seems to be throwing good seed." He glanced suddenly up from the flower, surprising just the hint of dislike on the narrow face. "Ah, but my roses are boring you! Tell me, my Lord Menden, what brings you to Kingsford at this time of year? I fear you've come too late for the Faire."

"Ah, the Faire." Menden waved a scented handkerchief in disdain. "*Such* a noisy, crowded affair, all those disgustingly *common* folk bumping into one, stepping on one's toes, breathing that dreadful *garlic* into one's face. No, my lord Duke, I haven't missed any of that at all."

Since the Faire was the pride and joy of Kingsford, the veiled insult could hardly be ignored. But Duke Arden let it pass. Better that Menden think him too dull to notice the slight, or too weak to dare counter it. Either would make the man underestimate him.

"What, then, my lord?" he asked bluntly. "Why are you here?"

Fanning himself genteelly with the scented handkerchief, Menden continued after a moment, "It's hardly seemly for one of noble birth to admit such a thing as this, but I fear I had some . . . business to enact in your city."

It was just barely possible; Menden's father had lowered himself enough to make the family a good deal of money in the fabric trade, though Menden tried to hide that rather scandalous fact. "It happens," Arden said dryly. "Even within the Church."

"Indeed, indeed," Menden replied languidly, without any visible reaction to the bit of bait the Duke had cast out. "But it would hardly be seemly of me to visit Kingsford without stopping to pay my respects to its lord and master."

"The King is that," Arden reminded him flatly—and quickly. "I do but serve his bidding."

"Of course." Menden managed to put a world of doubt into those simple words. "Ah, but my lord Duke, I hear that you have a most fascinating new hobby these days!"

The Duke managed to look both arch and puzzled.

"Have I? What hobby are you speaking of? Surely not my roses—"

"You jest, my lord!" Menden said with a hollow laugh. "I refer to your theater, of course, to your Company! What a *marvelous* thing that must be. I know I would *never* have had the nerve to lend my good name to a troupe of *actors*. But then, you have always been a far more daring man than poor, cowardly me."

Why you sniveling little—No. Calm. Don't let the fool see how his barb had struck home. Smiling thinly, because he took his theater company seriously, just as he did his patronage of all the arts, Arden decided to be blunt. Perhaps the novelty of the approach would startle something out of the man.

"Well," he asked, "Why, my Lord Menden, are you trying to goad me?"

"I, my lord?" Menden was the very picture of innocence.

Raven does it better, Arden told him silently, and added, just as archly, "Or are you merely trying to cadge a free ticket from me?"

The common audacity of such a thought left Menden speechless for a sputtering while. At last he stammered out, "My—my lord, believe me, I—I never—I wouldn't—"

"But you *would* like to see the play, wouldn't you?" he continued. "Perhaps in a full dress rehearsal? I'm sure you will quickly see that this is true patronage of the arts, as valid as commissioning a painting or a statue."

Menden considered this solemnly for a time. "I do believe I would," he said slowly. "If it's not too much of an intrusion, of course."

"No intrusion at all." *You couldn't have made your wish more blatant if it were a royal order. And who, I wonder are you spying for? The King, to let him know what I'm about? The Church? Or—Oh, damn, you could be here from half a dozen instigators, from the Bardic Guild right down to the Fabric Weavers' Guild!* "So be it, my Lord Menden," he said smoothly, with well-fabricated pleasure. "We shall visit the Company today."

And I hope your envy chokes you!

The slim, shadowy man who prided himself on being the Duke of Kingsford's finest spy moved silently back through the city streets towards the Cathedral grounds. But as he passed a narrow alleyway, a hand shot out to drag him in. The spy twisted about in his captor's grasp, slender, deadly dagger ready to strike.

But all at once he . . . could . . . not . . . move. "So," hissed a voice, "you are the false cleric, the infiltrator who would pry out secrets that don't concern you."

He knew that voice . . . his memory brought forth an image of its owner dressed in clerical scarlet. But when he tried to turn his head for proof, the invisible, sorcerous bonds clamped down on him ever more fiercely.

"No," his captor whispered. "You shall not see me. You have already learned too much, my friend. And I fear you shall not learn anything more, other than this: Death."

No! He couldn't—he wouldn't— Not like this, not so simply— He had to learn who was killing him, gain this one final bit of information. The spy fought his bonds with all his will, beginning to turn, slowly, painfully slowly . . .

But all at once the air was far too thick to breathe. The sorcerous bonds suddenly released him, but he still couldn't draw air into his aching lungs. The spy fell, choking, clawing at his throat. . . .

And at last he lay still.

❖   ❖   ❖

"You intend to *walk*, my lord Duke?"

Menden's face showed such blatant horror at the thought that Arden grinned. "Why, of course, my lord. I often walk about my city. Keeps me in touch with the common folk. And walking, the physicians all say, is very so good for the health! Come, come, my lord, you live such a sedentary life at court. A little exercise will do you good."

He set a brisk pace, forcing Menden, despite the lord's longer legs, to hurry after him.

But suddenly Menden flinched, then recoiled from the entrance to an alleyway in disgust. "Phaugh! You should have word with your street cleaners, my lord! Walking didn't do that fellow much good at all."

Arden glanced at the crumpled gray form that had been his spy in the ranks of the Church only a short while ago, and only by the greatest effort of will managed to keep the cold horror from showing on his face. Bending over the lifeless body, finding not a mark on it, he knew without the slightest doubt that this could only be death by sorcery.

And whoever killed you, my poor, luckless friend, could only have known you were one of mine, and meant for me to find you. A warning, sure as the One's sun shone in the sky. *But from whom? And where will the killer strike next?*

Suddenly so thankful to the Lady Ardis for the protective medal that hung about his love's throat that he could have wept, Arden straightened, face a determined mask. "A pity," he said in a perfectly cool voice, thinking wildly all the while that the acting he was doing would surely make him eligible for a role in his own Company. "This was a youngish man, too. No sign of illness on him; perhaps it was his heart that gave way."

Menden's greenish pallor could not have been feigned. "Perhaps . . ."

He turned with a false cheer and a hollow smile. "Ah well, let us not allow this sorry sight to depress us, my lord Menden. All that lives must die."

"You—you aren't going to just *leave* him there, are you?" The foppish lord had a handkerchief pressed to his mouth, and his eyes were wide with distress.

Well, well, Menden, if that isn't genuine shock I see in your eyes, you're a better actor than I. And that had most definitely been genuine surprise the man had shown when they'd first come across the body. *So now, at least you aren't working for my enemy. My sorcerous enemy, at any rate!*

"Squeamish, my lord?" Arden asked, deliberately casual. "Don't worry. The street cleaners will deal with him, as you noted. The body is still warm; he must have met his end before they had a chance to tidy him up."

Menden's pallor increased.

So now I have impressed you with my callousness, and my ruthlessness. Good. Go and tell your master, whoever he is. "Come, my Lord Menden," he continued, with a flourish, as if a man did not lie dead behind them. "The theater waits."

Menden regained his composure midway through the first act. By the middle of Act II, he had begun making witty little remarks in the manner of recent court fashion, which meant that each clever word was edged with the most delicate malice.

Disappointed, are you, Arden wondered, *because my Company turns out to be professional? Because you don't have any succulent, scandalous, or treasonous gossip to take home to your master? Who, I think, must be either our good King or someone highly placed in the Bardic Guild. Yes . . . I imagine it probably is the Guild. They never have quite forgiven me for not using their musicians.*

Determined not to rise to Menden's bait, Arden listened politely to all the nasty, clever little things the man had to say, and said nothing in return.

It wasn't easy.

"Ah, look!" Menden exclaimed with overdone delight as Regina made her entrance in Flora's piecemeal gown. "Is that not your mistress, my lord? How splendid she looks! Why, one could almost mistake her for a lady, instead of a common—"

Down on the stage, Regina started as a shriek sounded from somewhere up in the better seats. Wondering what could possibly have gone wrong now, she managed to stay in character till the play's end, then hurried down to meet Arden. He drew her aside, smiling as slyly as the cat with the cream.

"Arden, what—"

"My dear," he cut in smoothly, "I meant to introduce you anew to Lord Menden. But he, poor fellow, is temporarily indisposed."

Indisposed? I think not! She narrowed her eyes with sudden suspicion. "What did you—"

"Me? Not a thing." Arden's cheerful innocence was not quite as convincing as Raven's. "He suffered the silliest accident while watching the play."

"Was that he who shrieked?" she demanded. "Is he hurt? Arden, *what did you do?*"

"Why, I told you: nothing! Poor Menden was enjoying the play, or at least I think he was, judging from his clever little remarks about the story. The actors." Arden's eyes narrowed just a trifle. "You. His witty little remarks were oh, so amusing. Then all of a sudden he just . . . lost his balance and slipped off his seat. You know how those chairs are designed to fold up when they aren't in use?"

She pressed her hand to her mouth to stifle a laugh. The idea of foppish Lord Menden, trapped by what Crow called "the man-trap chairs" —She rounded on Arden with accusation in her tone. "You didn't."

Arden shrugged. "Ah well, in his struggle to get back on his feet, he must have hit the seat in just the wrong way. The seat folded up at an inopportune moment— and pinched him in a *most* unfortunate place. I doubt he'll be sitting in comfort for quite a while."

"Arden!" Regina exclaimed in scandalized delight.

He beamed at her. "Now, my dear, if you are quite finished rehearsing for the day, a most splendid dinner awaits us."

Grinning broadly, the Duke of Kingsford bowed graciously to his lady, and led her from the theater, with all the care and dignity as if she had been the King's own daughter.

CHAPTER NINETEEN

THE PLAY'S THE THING

Magpie sighed, surreptitiously wiping the perspiration off her forehead with the back of her wrist. Three days of complete dress rehearsal now: three days of dry, still, relentless heat. At least she didn't have to wear full costume, like the actors. As the Duke's musicians, they would wear his summer livery, which was suited to this weather.

I don't know how they stand it. I swear I've seen the makeup melting off their faces.

Mercifully, even with the footlights giving off a fair amount of heat, they could rehearse indoors, in the shade. Several street urchins had replaced the little Tilsani as "pigeon boys"; their job included opening louvers beneath the edge of the roof to bring in a fresh breeze from high above the sweltering streets. Outside, she knew, tempers were flaring, and the city's guards had their hands full with arguments and fistfights and the occasional knifing.

If only it would rain!

The heat wasn't helping her, either. Between its oppression and being perpetually on the alert, sure disaster was about to strike, she felt as flat and worn out as the little rug in her room.

She wiped her forehead again, this time not caring who saw, and closed her eyes for just a moment. This heat made her so sleepy—and yet, once she reached her bed at night, made it impossible to fall asleep. . . .

"What the *hell* do you think you're doing?"

Magpie started so sharply at this sudden angry voice she nearly fell off the stage. Oh, not *another* quarrel! Turning wearily to see who it was this time, she froze, staring. It was Regina, the usually unflappable Regina, Regina the Duke's mistress skilled in diplomacy, who was screaming like a fishwife at an actor costumed as one of the prince's servants.

Tears stood in her eyes, and Magpie honestly could not have said if they were tears of anger, frustration, or despair. "You fool! You idiot! You tore my gown!"

"It wasn't my fault!" he shouted back. "If you had been on your mark, where you were supposed to be, nothing would have happened!"

"I *was* on my mark!" she cried. "*You* weren't! And now look at this hem. *Look at it!* Your big, clumsy foot tore off the whole edging!" Her makeup streaked as tears poured down her face. "It's going to take *hours* to mend this!"

"Clumsy!" the actor retorted. "You great cow! I'm not the one who was—"

"Oh!" Regina screamed. "A *cow* am I? And you're calling *me* a liar as—"

"Stop it!" the Manager shouted, rushing onto the stage to separate the combatants before the quarrel came to blows, and more damage was done to the precious costumes. "Both of you stop it, right *now!*"

"But he—" Regina wept.

"She—" the other combatant shouted.

The Manager stamped his foot over the hollow trap-door, making it boom, and silencing them both. "Listen to you! Listen! You sound like two stupid little children fighting over a toy!"

The two actors gasped at that, stared, gasped again. But under the Manager's fierce glare, they couldn't find anything to say.

"Regina!" he snapped, turning towards her. "You have much more stage experience than Arnold. You know very well that the decorations on these costumes are meant to be taken off and on quickly! It won't take more than a few moments to mend that stupid flounce."

"And you, Arnold!" he continued, turning toward the actor. "You have experience enough to know that *you* are not the important person on the stage at this moment—the leading lady is! If *she* is off her mark, it is up to *you* to make certain to allow for that! One day, when *you* have a lead role, others will be doing the same for you! Furthermore, if she was *not* off her mark, it was doubly necessary for you to have been on *yours.* The leads rely on you to know your business so that they can do theirs without having to make allowances for amateurish mistakes!"

The actor hung his head. And slowly the tension faded out of both of them.

Regina sagged. "You're right," she admitted reluctantly. "Accidents happen. I shouldn't have lost my temper like that."

"Me, neither," the other actor agreed. "It's this damned heat. Puts everyone on edge. If only it would *rain!*"

"Amen," everyone muttered. There had been far more than the normal run of slip-ups and missed cues lately, and too many of these ridiculous, increasingly heated quarrels over who had stepped on whose lines or gotten in whose way.

"Everything will all be all right on The Day," the Manager declared—and earned himself a barrage of impatient glares from everyone who'd had to listen to him repeating that same traditional actor's litany over and over again for the last few days.

"It will be all right on The Day," Raven mimicked dourly. "If we last that long."

Magpie turned to him. "You're feeling the tension too."

He shrugged. "I'd be dense as marble if I didn't. Gods, I wish I was as *cool* as marble! I'm beginning to wonder if we're going to make it to Opening Day without one member of the Company killing another."

"Huh. I'm beginning to wonder if Opening Day for this play will ever come at all!"

"It had better! The Manager told me today that we're doing a brisk business in advance ticket sales. And not just those one-copper-cent standing room spots, either: the tiers are filling up as well, even the most expensive seats."

Magpie shook her head. "It'll never happen. We're caught in some sort of—of sorcerous time loop. That's it. We're going to have to go on rehearsing the same thing forever and ever. We're trapped, and this is hell."

"Well, if that's to be our fate," Raven said with a grin, "at least I get to spend it at the side of one of the loveliest, most charming women I've ever met."

"Who, Regina?" she asked, without thinking.

He rapped her lightly on the nose with the tip of his bow. "No, you sarcastic little idiot—you!"

She couldn't help herself; she blushed. "Oh, right. Of course. You flatterer, you say things like that to every woman you meet."

He never flinched. "Ah, but this time I mean it!"

"Huh." But as Magpie turned away, pretending to be insulted, she couldn't keep from smiling. Yes, Raven flattered women as easily as he drew breath, and probably would as long as he lived. Any compliment coming from him had to be taken with more than the proverbial grain of salt. But even so . . . who knew? This time what he'd said just might be for real. Maybe not quite *everything* was working so badly after all!

The musicians were all crowded into the common room in the boardinghouse this busy morning, fixing clothes or makeup, testing instruments or simply pacing nervously about, getting in the others' way. Nightjar, kohlstick in hand, said to no one in particular, "I can't believe the day is finally here," and surreptitiously edged Finch—or possibly Verdin—aside so she could peer into the mirror and finish applying the kohl to her dark eyes.

"*I* can't believe we sold out—sold out completely— almost a week in advance," Finch—or Verdin—replied, neatly edging her way back into place, and obscuring Nightjar's view again.

"Oh curse it all," Jaysen yelped suddenly, "I can *not* get these ribbons to fall right! Stupid fashion—what difference does it make what we look like, anyway? It's not as if anyone's actually going to see us!"

"Don't you intend to take your bows with the rest of us?" Raven asked wryly. Jaysen stared at him in wide-eyed panic for a moment, considering that, then yelped anew, "Please! Someone give me a hand with this!"

Linnet, who had been hovering on the stairway, watching the stir with amazement, hurried down to draw Jaysen into a corner, her eyes warm, smoothing the ribbons with a gentle hand. "There. That's better." She drew back, studying him, smiling. "My, how handsome you look! I—I wish I was coming with you. I'd love to see you perform."

"I bet," Nightjar murmured blandly, and Magpie nearly choked.

"You can," Jaysen told Linnet, earnestly ignoring the others' laughter. "I can get you into the theater, you know that."

But Linnet's bright eyes clouded, and her lower lip trembled just a fraction. "Oh, Jaysen, no. You know I can't leave Mother for so long, not now. Sh-she's so very ill. . . . "

Jaysen sighed. "That's right. I'm sorry."

"He should be," Nightjar said in Magpie's ear. "I've gone over that woman, you know that, trying to find a way to help her with my healing spells. I can't do a thing for her. Linnet *has* no choice."

"Yes." Magpie had spent a few late nights sitting around the kitchen table, giving Nightjar a chance to let out her frustration at the spells' failure. "The disease is too well established. There's a limit to what magic can do, right?"

"I know that!" Nightjar said impatiently. "That wasn't what I meant."

Magpie cocked an inquisitive eyebrow at her. "What, then?"

Nightjar lowered her voice. "Well, I've done my best to pity her; I mean it's not a nice way to die, the slow, strength-leaching way she's going. But in the process of trying to help her, I've seen more of her mind than I wanted." There was no doubt of the expression on the Gypsy's face: distaste.

"What do you mean?" Magpie asked, startled by such an odd expression on the face of a Healer who was speaking about a patient.

The corners of Nightjar's mouth turned down for an instant in a disapproving frown. "Just that our Madame Shenna turns out to be a small, selfish little soul who kept her daughter bound to her as a virtual servant till sickness allowed poor Linnet a chance to breathe for herself. When Madame Shenna dies, it's going to be a blessing for Linnet, not a curse."

Magpie sighed. "At least Linnet has Jaysen now."

They both watched as Jaysen and Linnet, oblivious of everyone else, snatched a quick, shy kiss. "Yes," Nightjar said gently. "That she most certainly does."

"Hey, hey, women," Raven snapped, brushing past them, bright ribbons flashing from his sleeves, bright sash fluttering about his lean waist. "Enough primping. Time's a-wasting, and all that!"

Magpie and Nightjar exchanged wry glances. "Stage fright," the dark woman said succinctly, and gave Raven the most elegant of oriental bows. "We hear, oh lord and master, and obey."

Raven grinned. "And a prettier lot of slave girls a master never had."

"Slave girls!" Magpie echoed indignantly, and tossed a wadded-up ribbon at him.

He caught it deftly, unfurling it and tying it with hand and teeth about an arm. "I wear your colors with pride, my lady. Now, come, come, *come*, everyone. To the theater!"

They scurried off together, following Raven's nervously excited lead. For once, Magpie thought, it was good to see yet another clear, sunny day: they wouldn't lose any theatergoers to bad weather. The theater loomed up before her, and she stopped short, heart

starting to pound, staring up at the banner flying overhead, announcing to all the world that the Duke of
Kingsford's Company was here and ready to perform.
And a little shiver of pure delight raced through her,
cutting through the ordinary pre-performance nerves.

Let it go well, she prayed to whatever gods of theater there might be, *oh, let it all go well!*

"Look at that!" Finch—or Verdin—whispered,
peeking around the curtain screening the musicians'
alcove. "The house is filling up. I mean, *really* filling
up!"

"We knew that," Raven muttered. "The Manager
told us the show was sold out, remember?"

The second twin crowded in beside the first. "Ooh,
and look at all the fine nobles! I never saw so much silk
and satin in my life! And look, look, there's the Duke
himself!"

"Well, of course he's there, you silly," the first twin
chided. "You'd hardly expect him to miss Regina's performance, would you? Ooh, look at that fine lady, the
one with all the jewels!"

Magpie couldn't stand it. She had to steal a peek,
too. Carefully, she pulled back the edge of the curtain,
just enough to let her see without being seen. But it
was not the silks and satins of the wealthy and powerful
that caught her eye, but a particular group that occupied a high tier like a shadow of ill omen. "Raven!" she
whispered. "Come here, hurry."

He was at her side in an instant. "What is it? What's
wrong—Ah. Priests."

She shivered, looking up at the rank upon rank of
sour-faced men in ecclesiastical black and clerical gray.
"A whole tier of them. Raven, I don't like this."

"Me, neither. And look at that, there, there, and

there." He pointed others out to her. "Priests are scattered all through the house." He hesitated, wary as a wild thing. "Well . . . I suppose even priests enjoy a day out. Maybe this is some sort of Church outing."

"You don't believe that any more than I do." Magpie eyed them uneasily. "Besides, they don't look like they're enjoying themselves. Staring grimly ahead like that."

He shook his head, and squinted his single eye. "I think they're . . . meditating."

"Or maybe spell-casting," she corrected.

"Or hunting," Raven said shortly.

"For Regina?" Magpie cried in horror. "Oh, Raven, what if they're trying to catch her casting her—her glamorie?"

"That's probably exactly what they're trying to do. That's why they're meditating. It's a passive kind of magic, rather than an active spell. Trying to *see* something rather than to do it." Raven glanced over his shoulder to where the actress waited backstage, pacing nervously to and fro, muttering her opening lines to herself over and over. "I only hope she behaves herself."

"Musicians. Musicians!" It was the Stage Manager, looking as fierce as Magpie had ever seen him. "Stop that spying! Do you want the audience to see you?"

Guiltily, Magpie let the curtain fall back in place, and the Manager nodded.

"Places, everyone!" Somehow he managed to alert everyone with that sharp whisper, even over the loud chattering of the audience just beyond the curtains. "It's time to begin!"

To Magpie's relief, everything really did seem to be all right on The Day. The Bards were all playing

together better than she'd ever heard, flawlessly on
pitch and on cue. The actors were moving through
their roles with fresh zest, almost as though they were
actually living their characters' lives, and for the first
time. Regina was so charming and believable a
Flora/Florian that for a moment Magpie was terrified
she was amplifying her performance with glamorie.
But no, after a time she realized that Regina was simply showing off her own talented self, enrapturing the
audience without the slightest need for magic.

What a wonderful, wonderful actress! Magpie
thought with just a touch of envy.

Act I passed without a moment's trouble. The audience laughed at all the jokes, hissed at nasty Sir
Verrick, and wept with Flora over her sudden fall in
fortune. When she declared herself Florian and set out
to bravely find her own way in life, the house exploded
with delighted applause.

During the brief interval, the Bards checked instruments, retuning a string or the tone of a drum, then
grinned at each other, shaking hands, giving various
signs for good luck. Regina, on her way to Costuming,
passed close enough to wave at them, giving them the
little hands-up signal that meant "Good job!" to anyone
familiar with street language.

Now if only the second act goes as smoothly. Magpie's thought was partly a prayer. Surely, for Regina's
sake, whatever saint that looked over players would
pay attention!

And the prayer was answered. Act II went as lightly
and sprightly as a spring day. The audience once more
laughed where they should, sighed where they should,
and applauded each clever turn with fresh delight.
When Regina first appeared in Florian's tunic and
breeches, there were more than a few appreciative

whistles, but those who tried to yell out obscene suggestions were quickly shushed by their neighbors. Magpie risked a glance at the priests, sitting like so many dull black and gray stones.

Bet they don't like the idea of a woman in breeches. Too bad, fellows! Nothing in the laws against it, not here in the theater, and not outside. There's too many farm women who have to wear breeches for the heavy work for you to get a law made against that.

Nothing magical for them to seize upon, either. Regina had, indeed, completely enchanted the crowd, but she was doing it on charm and acting skills alone.

And during the interval before Act III, Magpie saw all the priests rise like an ebony wave and silently leave the theater, clearly disappointed. For all their trying, they hadn't been able to detect the tiniest bit of magic at work here. Regina was safe.

And so was the Company.

Magpie sent a gleeful thought of ill-wishing after them. *May you never find enjoyment in anything, you old black sticks! You wouldn't know a good time if it bit you on the—*

"Good-bye and good riddance," Raven muttered, and Magpie gave him a quick grin.

She could hardly contain her excitement. "One more act to go. We're going to do it, Raven, we're really going to do it!"

But his face looked so troubled she added in sudden uneasiness, "What's the matter?"

"Nothing," he said shortly. "But it's not wise to tempt Fate."

She wrinkled her nose at him, now as full of elation as she had been full of tension. "Oh Raven, don't be —"

But now it was *he* who was the gloom-spreader. "Hush. Let us congratulate ourselves only when this is all over."

Superstitious Gypsy, Magpie told herself, and glanced over the score for Act III, preparing herself for the tricky little glissandos in the first scene. Soon, Raven notwithstanding, the play would be over. And then, by the One, they would celebrate!

Act III started precisely on cue, and continued precisely on cue, running so perfectly it sent little shivers of delight through Magpie. Now they'd reached her favorite point and she could stand and watch Regina-as-Florian gather the bits and pieces of her gown. She heard for the first time an audience sharing her pleasure in the clever writing and acting, enjoying the ripple of amusement running through the house.

But out of the corner of her eye, she saw Raven suddenly stiffen, missing a note, and hissed to him, "What is it?"

He shook his head. When the music allowed him to lower his bow, he whispered to her, "Could have sworn I saw that scrawny little priest running around backstage, the fellow I chased off his street corner a few weeks ago."

She frowned in puzzlement. "What would *he* be doing here? All the other Priests left."

Raven shrugged, and evidently decided to dismiss it. "Must have been mistaken. Hey, don't miss your cue!"

Magpie raised her flute and began to play, but Raven's words troubled her. It couldn't have been the Priest, she told herself. Raven must have seen one of the stagehands; it was shadowy back there, easy to mistake one face for another, even when you had two good eyes and not one. The play was almost over now, the prince about to go hunting for his own true love. Surely nothing could go wrong now.

Ah yes, here we were, the big dramatic climax: the prince had at last realized that Flora and Florian were

the same person. The music swelled up to a grand crescendo as, with a joyous cry of recognition, he pulled
his one true love into his embrace —

And a scream rang out from the back of the house.

"Fire! Fire! Run for your lives!"

"Oh dear One," the Manager breathed, staring in
horror, "No! Not this, not now!"

But all in an instant, smoke began billowing up from
all sides. Then, with a sudden savage roar of air, a wall
of the theater burst into flame.

CHAPTER TWENTY

FIERY FLIGHT

"Fire!"

Terrified screaming rang out above the roar of the flames. There was panic at the edges of the theater, confusion in the middle, where the groundlings could not see the fires around them. But the panic spread as quickly as the flames —

The actor playing Sir Verrick did the only sensible thing to be done. He sprang up to the front of the stage, and shouted, in his most penetrating voice, "Fire in the theater! Everyone, leave immediately! Make for the exits! *Now!*"

He gestured towards the exits in the rear, and the milling crowd took instant direction from him. "You've got to get out of here!" he cried.

At his direction, the audience stormed for the exits. Screaming people pushed and shoved their way to the back of the hall, some leaping down from the tiers, all of them running, hunting for the way out —

"They're blocked!" someone yelled in terror.

The panic spread through the crowd along with the word. "The exits are all blocked!"

"We can't get out!"

"We'll all die!"

Shrieking in mindless fear, surging back towards the stage, the crowd quickly fell from a mass of people to a mob, mindlessly charging this way, and that without direction. They milled like a flock of terrified sheep, knocking people off their feet, trampling them, crushing them against walls or seats. But in the middle of all the horror, Raven found himself noting with an odd bit of calm that rather amazed him that even with the flames hungrily licking at the walls all about, the air remained still relatively clear. There was very little smoke for all the flame; and the flames themselves were not as high as panic made them seem. And he thought fiercely, *That means we still have time, we're not dead yet!*

Someone has to do something— He looked around to see no one taking the lead. *Hellfires. I guess it's me.*

The Company remained frozen in place, transfixed by the same terror that had turned the people in the audience into maddened beasts. *First, get their attention!* Raven yelled at the other musicians, "Start playing, all of you! I don't care what! Play anything, as loudly as you can! And you," he shouted to the actors, "all you start singing along, now! I don't care what you sing, on tune, off—just sing!"

The music rang out, bright and bold as if the theater was not a death trap, all the disparate tunes somehow fitting together, melding into one melodic whole, challenging mindless fear.

But the mob wasn't going to calm, not unless they could find a way to escape; the way they were

trampling each other, they weren't even going to need
the fire to kill them!

Somehow, so suddenly it seemed magical, the Duke
was up there onstage with the musicians, disheveled
and sweating from what must have been a savage journey across the theater from the tier where he'd been
sitting. His fierce expression told Raven that *here* was
the leader he'd been hoping he wouldn't have to be.

"Stagehands!" he shouted sharply. "Get those stage
doors open! *Now,* dammit! Get the trapdoors open,
too, all of them—*hurry!*"

His was the voice of someone used to command,
and trained to be heard over the racket of a noisy
Court, and the stagehands obeyed him without a second thought. *"Here!"* he roared to the crowd, and
again, with almost superhuman force, *"Come you here!
To me! This way! You can get out, this way!"* And taking that as her cue, Nightjar began playing a martial
charge. The other musicians followed her lead, and the
actors onstage started to gesture wildly.

Raven's first thought was simple amazement at the
power of the man's vocal cords. His second was a surge of
astonished panic, because the mob was obeying! They
stopped swirling frantically about as if they were caught in
a whirlpool—and headed straight towards the stage.

By now the fire had crept up the wall to the height
of the first tier of seats. The raging flames threw waves
of hot orange light over them, dyeing their skin a
demonic red, reflecting off their wild, terrified eyes,
turning them into strange, terrible, fire-eyed monsters.

Powers, they'll crush us all!

But they came up to the stage, and could not seem
to get it into their heads that they had to *climb* it! They
ran up against the wooden barrier like a storm wave
encountering a breakwater.

"Keep playing," Raven hissed to the others. "Nice, cheerful march music like . . . like . . . " Damn, oh damn, he couldn't think of a title to save his life—literally to save his life— "'Lord Baltin's March!'" he cried in triumph. "All of you, play 'Lord Baltin's March!' Follow my lead. Keep it brisk, light, *loud!* All you actors, sing along. *Hum* if you don't know the damned words! Just mark the beat, everyone, especially, you, Crow, like this, like this, clearly, *clearly!*"

The power of music . . . please, let it work, let it work. . . .

The regular, insistent beat thrummed out, over and over, working its way into the collective mob mind, overwhelming panic by the force of sheer repetition.

I'll never want to play this piece again, never, Raven knew, *but if only we can keep it going long enough . . .*

"This way!" The Duke reached out to drag a woman up onto the stage by pure strength, and all but dropped her down the open trap. "Come on, all of you! This way is out to safety! Keep going," he shouted down at the woman, "follow the passageway out," then grabbed a man and shoved him towards the stage doors. "That way. Keep going, keep going, you can all get out." He pushed a second woman down the trap, dropped her child down after her into her waiting arms. "That's the way, keep moving down there. Don't stop, dammit! Stagehands, keep them moving, keep them moving, yes, right, good."

And, "Keep playing," Raven told his makeshift orchestra, "just keep playing!"

All around them, the crackling, roaring flames were surging up, hungrily devouring wood and paint and fabric, dazzling, spectacular, terrifying, engulfing the walls, the tiers, headed towards the roof.

Oh Powers, if we don't get out of here soon, the whole thing is going to come crashing down on our heads! But we can't—the people—we've got to get them all out!

The Duke, aided by the stagehands, was tirelessly continuing to funnel people out, some through the stage doors, some through the traps, his voice a never-ending stream of forceful command.

But now at last that commanding voice was beginning to falter. The Duke was forced to pause more and more often to cough. They were all starting to cough; the air was rapidly growing worse, rapidly growing too thick to breathe. Smoke was swirling in towards them now, a dense, roiling gray mass through which the licking flames, blazing orange, were muted, looking like the most incredible theatrical effects.

The flames of hell, Raven thought foggily, staring at it with blurring, watery vision, playing on and on, half-hypnotized by the horrific sight and his own growing claustrophobic terror, playing on and —

"Raven. Raven! Dammit, Raven, come on!"

It was the Duke, grabbing him savagely by the shoulder.

"The others—"

"They're all out. We're the last ones. Come on!"

A sudden roar made Raven glance wildly up. "Look out, the roof—"

He and the Duke dove frantically together through the trap as flaming hell came thundering down over their heads. They hit the ground, staggered, ran together through the tunnel under the stage, arms over their faces, struggling through smoke so dense Raven's lungs ached with the effort to breathe. His good eye was watering so badly by now that he could hardly see where he was going. Powers, he wasn't going to be able to find his way out, he was going to die down here —

But suddenly the Duke's arm was firm around

Raven's shoulders, guiding him, and then helping hands were pulling at them both, dragging them out into open air and a wild tangle of people fleeing in all directions. Raven gasped as the sunlight hit him like a blow. Sunlight! Surely it had no right to be so bright out here, so cheerful after that fiery horror?

For a moment Raven could do nothing but cough and cough; his throat was raw, his chest aching with the need for a good breath, his lungs afire with pain —

But then, at last, he could drag in lungfuls of wonderfully clear air.

He closed his eye, and sagged down where he was, simply breathing, ignoring all else. Someone called frantically, "Raven!"

In the next moment, Magpie all but threw herself into his arms, openly sobbing. "Raven! Oh, my dear! I thought you weren't going to make it, I thought you wouldn't get out in time!"

"The Duke helped me," Raven managed to gasp, then twisted about to stare up at the theater.

Flames were soaring out from what had been the roof, towering into the sky in bloodred ribbons, engulfing the whole building. Raven heard Finch and Verdin give little twin sobs of horror at the sight of pigeons that had been too terrified to fly trying to escape too late; fire-singed wings couldn't support them, sending the birds tumbling helplessly to their deaths.

The air was rapidly heating to the point of pain. "Hell of a place to stand," Raven said. "Back off, everyone! Walls could come crashing down any moment."

"Arden!" It was Regina, a weird, wild-eyed figure in Flora's ballgown, now so covered with ash it was uniformly gray. Her hair had come loose from its pins, swirling about her head like black smoke. "Where is he? Where's the Duke?"

"Here." Outlined against the flames, Duke Arden looked like a grim-faced specter, his gray beard and hair darkened to dead black by soot, his face and clothes soot-streaked as well. "They were bolted!"

"What—" she said, uncomprehendingly.

Duke Arden snarled. "The doors! They were all bolted from the outside!"

Raven stared at him in shock. Obviously someone had decided that subtle measures for getting rid of Duke Arden weren't going to work, so he'd taken the direct approach! *Even if it meant murdering a whole theaterful of innocent folk in the process—Damn him, whoever he is, damn him to the deepest hell!*

"No . . . " someone moaned suddenly. "The wind . . ."

Raven craned his head back as a powerful blast of air nearly staggered him, sending his hair whipping fiercely about his head. And sending the flames roaring skyward. "Not now," he gasped. "Oh please, no. We don't need wind now."

Someone somewhere was ringing the fire alarm, sending the harsh, terrifying sound roaring out over the city.

"Hurry, dammit," the Duke muttered to the myriad fire brigades of his beloved city. "Hurry! There's not much time!"

But the narrow streets were still crowded with the fleeing audience; the fire fighters might, indeed, be on their way, but they could hardly get through the crush. To Raven's horror, he saw the wind catch at the licking tongues of flame, tearing them from the theater in a blazing shower of fire-drops out onto the roofs of nearby houses—wood-shingled roofs cracklingly dry from too little rain. They caught in an instant, fire roaring up with terrifying speed.

"We've got to get the people out of there!" Nightjar yelled, and hurried forward, closely joined by the other musicians and the actors. She banged on the door of the first house, then the second, running from house to house, screaming warnings. Alarmed heads poked out, then stared up in horror.

"Don't try to fight the fire," the Duke shouted at them. "Just grab what you can and get out! Get out, dammit! Get to the river!"

The fires were already racing down from the roofs to the buildings themselves, eating savagely at wood and plaster, swirling down to the ground with horrifying speed.

"We're going to have to go in there!" Nightjar cried in agony. "And tear folks out by force!"

But all at once a panicky stream of people were racing from the burning buildings, their arms full of prized possessions. Some bore clothes, chests, books, whatever they could carry; a wide-eyed, white-faced child clutched her doll to her, and one straight-backed, proud old woman, helped by a deferential young man who must be her son, determinedly bore a terrified canary in its cage.

"Towards the river!" the Duke told the refugees. "Don't run, just keep moving."

"Oh no," Regina moaned. "Arden, look."

The firestorm was leaping from roof to roof like a demonic thing, and everywhere it touched, it sparked new flames.

"The wind!" the Duke groaned. "The damnable wind! Where are those cursed fire fighters?"

The irony of being so near the river touched them all: the wind was driving the fire away from the water, and without water they couldn't do a thing about it.

"Come on," Raven cried, "we've got to get everyone out!"

They knocked on doors, yelled in windows, tore shutters off with desperate strength to get into houses where no one answered. The actor who played Sir Verrick came staggering out of one house with a lame boy in his arms; the child had presumably been left at home while his parents went to work. The man dumped him on a cart loaded with possessions being pulled by a whole family. When they, wild with panic, would have shoved the boy off again, the actor roared at them savagely, "Leave him, and by the One, you die by my own hand! Get to the river, *go!*"

The whole world seemed to have turned to flame; there was no escape from the savagely hot, dry air, and bits of scalding ash raining down on everyone. "It's spreading," Nightjar sobbed. "Oh, the people, the poor people!"

"The boardinghouse!" Jaysen screamed in sudden new horror. "The fire's heading towards the boardinghouse—Linnet!"

He dove into the fleeing mob of refugees, who were hurrying as best they could towards the river, frantically pushing and shoving his way past people who were too maddened with fear to let him through.

He's like a fish swimming upstream! Raven thought wildly. *This is ridiculous, nothing we've got in that boardinghouse is worth this struggle, this danger. Linnet—oh, surely Linnet has enough sense to get out on her own!*

But Madam Shenna would not. Madam Shenna was too frail to even get out of her bed. When the other musicians started after Jaysen, Raven found himself following. They wormed their way into the mass of people, ducking a man carrying an armful of brocade, twisting past two people bearing a rolled-up mattress between them, dodging carts loaded with whatever panicky folk had managed to snatch from their burning homes.

"We're never going to make it!" Raven panted, every bit of formerly latent claustrophobia within him roused and screaming at being trapped in such tight quarters with only his narrow field of vision.

"We will!" Jaysen screamed back.

Lovestruck idiot! Raven thought, but kept going for all his panic. Damned if he was going to let the boy prove the braver!

The mob pressed relentlessly riverwards, heedless of these idiots trying to go the other way. With a startled little shriek, Magpie was shoved right off her feet, disappearing from sight. Raven and Nightjar grabbed blindly at her, by sheer luck catching her by the arms and pulling her back up again before she could be trampled. "Thanks, heroes" she gasped, eyes wild.

Raven didn't feel particularly heroic. In another moment, he knew, he was going to turn and run, back to where there was some open place where he could *see*, where he didn't have to be terrified that a spark would put an end to what was left of his vision altogether. There was no rest, no way to get out of the mob's way, no way to get even one clean breath, not with the walls of fire pacing them, blazing up on both sides of the narrow road. Fire-drops rained down on them so that they had to constantly beat out sparks in hair or clothes.

I can't go on, dammit, I can't—

And then they'd made it, they'd reached the boardinghouse at last —

And the musicians were just in time to see the ancient, rickety building burst into flame like a great torch.

"No . . . " Jaysen moaned, cringing back from the

heat with the others, arm raised to shield his face.

Owl, Sparrow sheltered tightly under his arm, came staggering out of the burning building to join them, eyes wild. "I tried to get Linnet and Madam Shenna out," he gasped. "Madam Shenna couldn't—wouldn't go, and Linnet wouldn't leave her, and I—I didn't dare wait any longer, not with Sparrow here."

"Linnet!" Jaysen screamed. "Linnet, where are you?"

Her face showed whitely at one window for a second; then she disappeared back into the boardinghouse as the window was engulfed in flame.

"Linnet!"

"Jaysen, no!" Raven grabbed at him as he started forward. "Don't— You can't—"

But the young man tore savagely free from Raven's grip and raced into the blazing building.

"Jaysen!" Raven shouted helplessly. "Ah, Jaysen . . ."

The musicians waited, surrounded by horror, watching horror, as the long seconds passed. "We can't stay here," Magpie cried. "We've got to get out before the fire cuts off our escape and— Oh, no, no!"

With a terrifying roar, the roof of the boardinghouse came crashing down into the flames.

CHAPTER TWENTY-ONE

FIREBIRDS

For a moment all the musicians could do was stare in mute horror at the flaming ruins of what had been the boardinghouse.

"The One have mercy," Owl murmured at last, hugging Sparrow to him as though he'd never let the boy go. "The poor lad! No one could have survived that. Jaysen has to be—"

"Wait, look!" Magpie screamed, pointing at a dark shadow in what was left of the front doorway of the house—a shadow that moved, and raised a hand in entreaty. "There's someone in the doorway— He's alive! Jaysen's alive! And he's got Linnet!"

The musicians raced forward, dragging the staggering Jaysen and Linnet away from the fiery doorway out into the open. Linnet, her fair skin red and scorched, her yellow hair disheveled and singed, was sobbing without tears. "She wouldn't leave. Mother wouldn't leave."

Raven glanced up at the ruins and shuddered. *At least it would have been quick. Quicker than the death her disease promised her.*

But there was no time for pity, not while the world was erupting into fresh hell all around them. New waves of refugees were pushing past the musicians, sobbing, screaming, cursing, some of them richly clad, some with nothing but the clothes they wore, some of them barefoot and bedraggled. Finch and Verdin gasped as one at the sight of one wild-eyed man who wore only a hastily tied house-robe but had a rich bolt of silk slung over his back, and hurried to block his path. The bolt was aflame at one end—and in a moment, he would set not only himself afire, but everywhere he passed!

"Get out of my way!" he screamed.

"It's on fire!" one twin yelled at him, and the other added, "The bolt's burning!"

With a choked sound that could have been either a curse or a sob, the man tossed the flaming mass from him and hurried off empty-handed. The whole weavers' district roared up into flame, fueled both by the dry wooden houses and the flammable fabrics and dyes within.

And next to it is the even more flammable painters' district, and the tanners' after that. Powers, if the fire spreads that far, the city will go up like a volcano!

"Come on!" Raven cried. "If we don't get out of here now, we're not going to get out at all!"

He dove into the flood of refugees, Magpie's hand clutched tightly in his, though Raven wasn't sure if that was for her comfort or his. The mob pressed in all around them, stifling and hot. At least the struggle wasn't so terrible now that they and the refugees were all going the same way—though in this maze of streets there wasn't anything like one clear direction.

Behind them, a new, deafening roar of flames told that the fire had reached the painters' district. Raven heard Nightjar gasp and glanced up to see that the clear sky was now tainted a smoky bloodred, a terrible haze behind which the sun glowered like a great, orange, demonic eye.

"The end of the world," someone moaned. "It's the end of the world."

"Hell, no!" Raven shot back. "Not while we live!" He aimed a savage blow at a man who'd started to sink to his knees in despair. "Get up, damn you! Move!" As the man staggered to his feet again, Raven shoved him roughly forward. "Keep moving! All of you, keep moving!"

The wind still blew, relentlessly, hot as a demon's breath, hurling the firestorm further and further. "How far is it going to spread?" a woman wondered.

"Not far enough," a man retorted. "Let it burn the rich, that's what I say. Let 'em stew in their marble halls!"

"Hey, now," another man protested, "the Duke's a good man. Let it burn the *foreigners,* that's what I say! An' th' Buggies! Them things that ain't human! Let 'em all burn!"

Oh, right. Blame the foreigners, Raven thought bitterly. *That's intelligent. Blame anyone who's different from you, you bigoted idiot.*

"Look out!" Magpie screamed.

A wall of flame came crashing down, the whole blazing side of a house, engulfing the street ahead of them. Magpie buried her head against Raven's chest as screaming people were buried beneath the flames. One man tore free, yelling in wordless panic, his clothes blazing, and Nightjar and Owl pounced on him, rolling him in the dirt till the flames were out. But he lay still, not moving even when Nightjar shook him, then checked his wrist for a pulse.

"Too late," she said bitterly. "He must already have breathed in too much fire to live."

"This way." Raven pulled Nightjar back to her feet. "Down this street, hurry."

"But I can't—the people—" Her Healer's eyes were wild with anguish. "I can't just leave them—"

"You can't save anyone else if you die!" Raven told her bluntly, and gave her a shove down the street. "No fire down this way." *Yet.*

Joined by a new swarm of refugees, the musicians staggered on. With startling suddenness, they were out in the open, out of the tangle of narrow ways and burning houses, gasping at the sudden change. Ahead of them was a paved square Raven couldn't remember having seen before, the far side as untouched as ever, the near side smoldering, the other two fierce with flame.

"Look!" Magpie cried. "The Duke!"

Duke Arden had requisitioned himself a horse from somewhere. Not, Raven realized, out of some ridiculous sense of snobbery but so that he could be easily seen, like any true war leader. It was no fine steed, only a shaggy-ankled cart horse, but somehow he made it look a true warhorse as he rode back and forth, calling orders to the fire fighters who had made it this far. Some of them, far too few, were operating the strange new water-wagons, sending repeated jets of water hissing onto the flames, others were using the more familiar water-syringes to squirt out quarts of water apiece.

But it's not enough! Raven saw. *The fire's gotten too good a hold. Oh damn, and now the wind's changing, blowing from a new quarter!*

He watched in stunned disbelief as it tore great flakes of fire up into the air for what looked like a good league, hurling them across emptiness till they at last pitched down on houses far from the original fire, sparking them, too, into flame.

Duke Arden also saw what was happening, and must have despaired, but nothing of that showed on his fierce face. His savage gaze focused on the musicians and the horde of refugees. "You, all of you, we have a bucket brigade started at the north side of the square. Get going. *Now!*"

His shout cut like the crack of a whip. Raven, fiddle case slung over his back, found himself before he knew it as one more body in the line, a familiar figure to his left —

It was Regina, the dark, tangled masses of hair tumbling down her back, her stage finery torn and tattered as a beggar's rags, hitched up to leave her legs free. For all that, Raven thought with a bittersweet stab of delight, she was still so fiercely beautiful his breath caught in his throat.

Ah, Regina, you should be up on that horse with your Duke. But then, I can't see you standing idly by while your city burns.

Regina gave him the weariest echo of her gamine grin, then shoved a leather bucket brimming with water into his hand. He passed the heavy, slopping thing on to the man beside him—Owl, as it happened—then waited for the next bucket to come up the line.

And the next.

And the next.

It went on forever, another kind of hell. Hot wind slashed at him, ash flew into his eye, sparks singed him. He fell into a rhythm, trapped by it as he had been by his own music back at the theater. His back began to ache, and his hands, his sensitive musician's hands, to blister. And still the buckets came.

Be lucky if I can play a note after this. Be lucky if I'm alive to play a note! Wonder how Regina can be holding up. Women are tougher than we men like to imagine. He glanced up, and just barely kept from crying out in despair. *Oh Powers, this is never going to work; the fire's spreading too fast!*

The water-wagons and water-syringes were wonderful inventions, but there weren't enough of them, and their resources were finite. As the streams of water began to falter and fail, other daring fire fighters dashed into the narrow maze of streets with fire-hooks attached to long poles. They used these to pull down the blazing shingles on buildings that hadn't yet fully caught fire, and smother the flames before the buildings themselves could be engulfed. Duke Arden was everywhere on his terrified cart horse, calling encouragement to the men, heartening them as best he could, riding up and down the lines with scant regard for his own safety.

But no matter how hard the men worked, the wind drove the fire further and further into the city.

"It's no use, my lord," Raven heard one of the fire fighters call wearily to the Duke. "The best we can do now is try to pull down enough houses to form a firebreak."

Duke Arden shuddered slightly, then nodded. "Do what you must."

Raven's bucket was taken from him. A pole was thrust into his hand instead. As he stared up the length of it to the wicked hook at the end, a fire fighter told him, "We're going to start tearing buildings down from there—" he pointed "—to there. You don't need any real skill. Just reach up, hook a ridgebeam of a building, and pull like a demon. Then get out of the way fast. Got it?"

Raven wanted to say, *I can't, I'm a musician, not a fire fighter!* But then the sound of a woman's frantic screaming drove that thought from his head as he ran forward with the rest of his hastily recruited band.

A young woman was standing trapped on the ledge of an attic windowsill, fire blazing behind her, a baby in her arms. "Help me!" she shrieked. "My baby, help him!"

Oh Powers, she was holding the baby out over open space, she was going to drop him!

"Don't!" Raven yelled, then raced forward as the woman, too reckless with fear to heed his shout, let the baby fall. He dove into place just in time to have the solid little weight land squarely in his arms, staggering him. For one wild moment he found himself staring down into solemn baby eyes, young enough to still be blued over, amazed that the little thing wasn't even whimpering. Then someone was taking the baby from him and shouldering Raven aside as the fire fighters dragged a ladder into place and brought the woman down to safety.

Raven was shouldered aside again, the fire-pole slammed back into his hand. "All right, you're a hero," a fire fighter told him with a world-weary grin. "Congratulations. Now go to work. We have buildings to dismantle."

Not sure if he wanted to grin or curse at the man, Raven obligingly raised his pole at the indicated building, on the burning side of the street; the side behind him was still untouched by flames.

A good place to start a firebreak; widen the street so the flames can't leap the gap.

It took him three tries—it wasn't easy to maneuver a pole that was over three man-lengths long—but at last he got the fire-hook caught firmly about the ridge-beam. A second fire-hook joined his. Raven glanced quickly at the man beside him—a stocky, soot-smeared fellow, no one he knew—then a fourth and fifth hook joined the first two.

"Now!" someone yelled, and they began to pull.

At first Raven was sure it wasn't going to work. He was going to ruin his hands for nothing. But then, with almost alarming ease, the ridgebeam shifted. Raven and the other men leaped hastily out of the way as the whole house came clattering down like a child's toy into a mound of fiery timber. As fire fighters set about dousing the flames, Raven was directed to the next house, and the next.

This isn't too bad, he thought, even though he was beginning to ache in every muscle, *this is almost easy. Doesn't say too much for the way houses are built about here; no wonder the fragile things are such targets for fire. Or were, anyhow. But we should be able to knock down enough of them to make a firebreak and —*

"Damnation!" someone shouted, and Raven whirled about to see that the cruel wind had lifted new flakes of fire from beyond the fireline and dropped them onto the as-yet-untouched side of the street, sparking new flames.

"All right, everyone get out of here," a fire fighter yelled, resignation in his voice. "This whole place is going up."

Raven ran with the others as flames shot up behind him.

All that work for nothing. Damn and damn and damn!

He came out on what at first he thought was another open square. Then, as pain shot up through the soles of his shoes, Raven realized he was standing on the not-quite-dead ashes of what had been a series of now completely destroyed storage shacks. On the far side, a row of women equipped with heavy folds of burlap were methodically beating out the remaining flames. Raven hastily sprinted across to safe ground before his feet were worse than just a touch scorched, and came to rest, panting, beside the last of the women. A familiar woman.

"Magpie!"

She spared him only one quick glance, brushing her tangled mass of hair back from her face with a filthy hand, her eyes fierce with exhaustion, her face flushed from the heat and streaked, like everyone else's, with soot, then went back to beating out flames. Raven looked quickly about for a way to help her. Ha, wait, there was a good-sized hunk of burlap someone must have dropped, back there beyond the fireline.

"I'll be right back," Raven told Magpie, and hurried off to get it. As he snatched the heavy fabric up (wondering where the women, especially slender Magpie, had gotten the energy to keep flailing away at the fire), sudden shrill screams made him whirl.

Oh Powers, no!

A new surge of wind had brought the fire back to vicious life all about the women. Most of them were running for shelter like so many deer, but to Raven's horror he saw that Magpie, through surprise or just plain weariness, had waited just a second too long to run—and a sudden shower of sparks set her wild mass of hair on fire!

Raven never stopped to think, *This is impossible, I can't possibly reach her in time.* He leaped across the distance separating them in one superhuman bound, catching Magpie to him, smothering the flames with his bare hands, not even feeling the pain, then threw his arm about her and practically carried her out with him to safety at the river's edge. He didn't even stop there; he let momentum carry them both into the water, into the blessedly cool, safe water. They tripped, and fell together, came up together, and discovered that the river here was no more than waist-deep. He helped her to stand.

Ach, and we both look like singed, half-drowned rats!

She seized both his hands in hers, gasping at the damage that had been done to them. "Raven, your hands—"

"It's nothing," he said, quickly. "Are you—did the fire hurt you?"

She shook her head, staring up at him. Her hair was a wet, frizzled, smelly mop, her face was still flushed and dirty, and with a sharp laugh, Raven hugged her to him as if he would never let her go again. Magpie drew back, but only to pull his face down to hers and kiss him with all the fierceness of the fire around them.

"Hey, you idiots!" a fire fighter called from the far side of the river. "You want to die? We're evacuating the area. Get out of there!"

Raven and Magpie drew back with a gasp, realizing the fire had nearly encircled them. "Hell of a hot passion we've got!" Raven said with a flash of wry humor.

"Hope it doesn't make an ash of us," Magpie retorted, then shrugged in apology.

"Can you swim?" he asked.

She nodded. "Well enough. You?"

"Terribly." In fact, he'd never had occasion to learn. "But what the hell, it beats burning!"

With that, the two of them, still clinging hand in hand, dove deeper into the river. Before Raven could even start choking on water, willing arms reached down from one of the boats that had been ferrying refugees out of the city, pulling him and Magpie both up onto a deck that reeked of fish but was most wondrously fire-free. Together with an exhausted crowd of fire fighters, they were carried across the river to safety.

All the refugees who'd managed to escape were here on the far side, milling about, hunting family or friends, lying collapsed in exhaustion, or just standing stock-still and blank-eyed in shock. As he scrambled out onto the muddy bank, Raven looked up to see the old lady he'd seen fleeing with her canary; now she was sitting as composed as any queen on an upturned box, the canary's cage on her lap, the canary, dusty but very much alive, bouncing busily about, a happy little golden bit of life.

Good for you, he told them silently, *good for you both!*

"One have mercy," Magpie murmured, her face a horrified mask, and Raven turned to look back across at Kingsford. He drew in his breath in a sharp hiss of disbelief.

I never dreamed the fire could have spread so very terribly far.

He'd lost all track of time during the struggle, and only now realized that the day was nearly over. In the deepening gloom, the flames could be seen all the more clearly, burning so fiercely they turned the darkness light. Homes, shops, churches, all were on fire and flaming at once, burning themselves into Raven's mind as one continuous arch of fire, a malicious bloody inferno that burned up against the sky, staining the first thin clouds a ghastly red.

"It really does look like the end of the world. . . . " he murmured.

"Don't think that!" Magpie said sharply. "Never think that!"

He glanced down at her, then put his arms about her, wincing a little at the soreness in his hands. "It can't be the end, not with you here," Raven told her. "And if that sounds too stupidly romantic, blame it on the fact I'm weary enough to sleep on my feet."

"Ah yes, me, too." But then Magpie stiffened. "There's the Duke, poor man."

Duke Arden, still on his cart horse, was riding restlessly back and forth on the river's bank, plainly wishing he could still be back on the other side, fighting the fire. His eyes blazed with pain for his city. "Where is the Church?" he cried hoarsely. "Their mages could put an end to that horror. Damn them, *damn them, where are they?*"

A glint of scarlet caught Raven's eye. For one horrorstruck moment he thought it was the fire, demonically managing to cross against the wind to this side of the river. But then he realized what he saw coming out of the twilight was a scarlet robe, another.

The mages of the Justiciary Brotherhood were finally here. Raven stared fiercely, as they loosed whatever magic they could. Even though he knew they were stinting none of their strength, he envied, admired, hated them, as every fire fighter must be hating them, for doing so easily what he and all the fire fighters had fought in vain to do. Some of the mages cast their will upon the air, thickening it, crushing the flames to death beneath it. Others, eyes shut in savage concentration, shouted out strange, sharp Words, thrusting out their arms, willing Power to blast apart burning houses to form wide firebreaks over which no flame could reach. Still others sent water in great, glittering arches up out of the river to crash down on the flames in huge, hissing, billowing clouds of steam.

"Back across the river," the Duke ordered wearily.

"They can only do so much. It's up to us to finish off the fire."

Slowly men and women dragged themselves back to the boats and across into the city, Raven among them, too tired to wonder why he'd involved himself yet again in this fight that wasn't his.

Stupid to stop now, he thought vaguely. *Will have wasted all my energy for nothing if I do.*

And all trace of conscious thought slid away from him. He no longer felt the pain of his seared palms or the ache of exhausted muscles. There was only the endless, endless rise and fall of arms beating out the last flames, tearing down the final crackling timbers, smothering the embers, doing it over and over and over. . . .

Someone was shaking his shoulders, taking the fire-pole forcibly out of his hands. "Raven. Enough. You can stop now."

The Duke's voice was so cracked and hoarse it was barely recognizable. Raven heard it through such a fog of exhaustion that for a moment he couldn't seem to understand what was meant. Was it over? Was this hel-lishness finally over?

But he no longer had an implement in his hands, and the Duke was gone, vanished into the smoke-filled darkness. Staggering, Raven made his way back to the riverbank with the others, literally falling onto the deck of a waiting boat. Ferried back to the far side of the river, he barely managed to drag himself ashore and up out of the mud, then crumpled where he stood, asleep before he hit the ground.

CHAPTER TWENTY-TWO

PHOENIX RISING

The morning dawned bleak and gray, the sky dead and dull over a world of ashes. Raven woke gradually, blinking up at a sky still hazy with smoke, his body warm on one side, chilly on the other. Slowly it came to him that he was lying on grass damp with dew, and that the gritty taste on his lips came from ashes still sifting down —

From the fire? Aie—the fire!

No, no, the fire was out, and this was the empty land that had, once upon a time, held the Kingsford Faire.

How impossibly long ago that seems!

The warmth, he realized suddenly, was coming from Magpie, asleep at his side, one arm thrown protectively across his chest, and he smiled and gently raised a hand to stroke her poor, scorched hair—then froze, examining that hand in wonder.

Amazing. Not a blister, not a mark. Fresh, healthy skin that didn't pull even when he tried a fist.

Well now, someone must have come by here in the night and worked a minor healing spell on me, bless whoever it was. Nightjar?

Possibly. At least he hoped it had been she, because that meant she'd gotten out of that hell safely. As had, he prayed to Whoever might be listening, all of the Company.

Oh please, let it be that most of the city's population had come to safe harbor, for that matter.

Raven sat up very carefully, not wanting to wake Magpie, and glanced warily around. The plain looked like the site of a bitter battle, with exhausted refugees sprawled wherever they had fallen. Belongings lay in untouched heaps. No looters here. That would come later, Raven thought cynically.

To his left, a small family group, father, mother, and son, ragged as homeless wanderers, huddled about a small campfire, their one blanket pulled taut about all of them. To his right, a man wandered disconsolately, staring into each face he passed, till at last he sank to the ground, weeping. A woman rose wearily from where she sat and pulled him against her, rocking him gently in her arms, and Raven turned away, suddenly flooded with memories of the horrors he'd seen. A little girl met his glance with the steady gaze of the very young, clutching what he at first thought was a doll. Then the small pink thing moved in her arms, and Raven realized it was a cat. Almost all its fur had been singed off, but the animal didn't seem to be particularly bothered by that; it joined the child in staring at him, feline arrogance in every naked pink line of it.

Life, Raven thought with a smile, *fierce, silly, wonderful life.*

Turning, he froze in sudden shock at what he thought was a heap of bodies, then let out a soft sigh of

relief. Those weren't corpses lying so close together
but living folk. *His* folk. Jaysen and Linnet, curled up
together like two puppies and sound asleep; neither of
them seemed more than a bit scorched. Raven felt a
wry, gentle smile touch his lips at the innocent sight of
them.

He straightened. Someone—officials of the Church,
he assumed—had erected a few tents during the night,
and presumably that was where the more seriously
injured were being tended. Scattered all along the
bank of the river were alarmingly bright splotches of
scarlet: the Justiciary mages, Raven realized after a
startled moment, so drained of strength they'd collapsed to sleep where they'd stood.

Ah, and there is Duke Arden. And, Powers be
praised, Regina with him.

The Duke was standing, merely standing, looking
out over the city, defeat in every line of him. Regina's
arm was about him comfortingly, and the two clung
together as though each was the salvation of the other.

As I guess they are, Raven thought, and glanced
down at Magpie, astonishing himself at the warm
surge of— Yes. Nightingale had been right with her
prediction back however long ago it had been. It was
love, it was indeed.

Just then, Magpie came awake with a start and a
shout, hand reaching blindly for him.

"It's all right," Raven soothed, crouching beside her,
taking her into his arms and stroking her poor,
scorched hair. "I'm here, my love. We're safe. We're on
the other side of the river."

Magpie sat up, starting to run a hand through her
hair, then stopped, feeling the short, frizzled ends, dismay on her face. Raven chuckled.

"Don't worry, it's not as bad as it feels." He kept his

voice down, not wanting to disturb the folk who were still sleeping. "You kept most of it. And a careful trimming should give you quite a fetching new look."

"Of course. Singed street rat. Very fetching." But she was smiling, and at last he understood how much of her jibing covered unease, unhappiness, and fear of her own feelings. "It's thanks to you that I have any hair left at all. Or any life, for that matter."

"Ah, well," Raven muttered in embarrassment. "I could hardly have let you burn."

Magpie shuddered, the smile fading from her face. "Others weren't so lucky."

"Love, we all did our best," he said, as much for his own sake as hers. "No more could have been done."

But she stared out over his shoulder, at the smoke that hovered over the blackened remains of the city, and shivered. "I know, I know. What happened, happened. I . . . just can't get some of those horrible, horrible images out of my mind."

"I know," Raven said softly. "Neither can I."

They sat for a time in silence, arms about each other. Then Magpie sighed and pulled away. "We can't put it off forever. Let us see what's left of Kingsford at first hand."

He sighed. "If we must."

Getting to their feet, they stared out across the river at—desolation, at the ruined stumps of walls and heaps of charred timber that had once been houses. They could see frighteningly far over the city, because there was nothing left standing for so much of it, nothing tall enough to block vision. Ash lay over everything, turning the city to a uniform dull gray. The horrifying wind had at last died away, but wherever a stray current of air touched, swirls of that ash would dance up for a time like dingy gray ghosts, then spread back down over the ruins again.

"I . . . how could anything be quite this bad? This is worse than anything I could have imagined," Magpie breathed.

But Raven was determinedly picking out those places that were relatively intact. "At least part of the city's still standing. See? The stone houses are still more or less erect. And the ducal palace doesn't seem to be too badly damaged."

"I'm sure that's going to be a great comfort to all the homeless," Magpie said drily.

"We have kissed away kingdoms and provinces," a quiet voice quoted behind them, and Raven and Magpie turned sharply to see the Manager standing there, his solemn face as lugubrious as ever, but a glint of relief in his eyes at the sight of them.

"Ha, you made it!" Raven cried.

"So did you, I see. As did most of the Company, as far as I could tell." He rubbed his red-rimmed eyes, and left behind a smear of ash. "Your musicians are all still alive."

"And unharmed?" Magpie prodded.

The Manager hesitated just a moment too long. "Ah well, mostly," he admitted warily.

"Mostly! What do you mean?"

"Your drummer, the one you call Crow . . . he's a hero. Raced into a burning building to rescue no less than three children from death by fire. He moved so fast they were quite unscathed. Unfortunately," the Manager added reluctantly, "he wasn't quite as fortunate."

"Powers!" Raven exclaimed. "Is he—did he—"

"He's alive." The Manager's tone suggested they not ask further. "But I'm afraid he was rather badly burned. He's in the nearest tent, that gray one."

As one, they started for the tent.

The Manager held out a cautionary hand. "Wait, I doubt that you'll be able to talk with him; he was sleeping when last I saw."

"We can at least see him!" Raven argued. "We're not the same clan, he and I, but——well——Gypsy to Gypsy, maybe he'll know I'm there."

The Manager shook his head at what he plainly thought superstition. "So be it. Come, I'll take you to see him."

The tent was crowded with makeshift cots full of the injured. Weary priests and lay healers made their way down the narrow aisles, casting healing spells and soothing pain. On the nearest cot lay Crow, most of his hair singed short, what was left curling tightly about a face that looked very young and vulnerable in sleep. His wiry body was thick with bandages. Raven snagged a passing priestly mage, a plump, harried, middle-aged man with gentle eyes.

"Is he going to be all right?" he asked urgently. "Is he——will he——"

"Ah, you're another of the musicians, aren't you?" the man said, his tired eyes lighting with recognition.

"Both of us are, yes," Raven said impatiently. "But is Crow going to be all right?"

The mage smiled wearily. "Yes, the One be praised. Some folks' bodies accept healing spells the way plants take to sunlight. And the healing spells set upon him by that woman musician——Nightjar? Is that her name?"

"Yes," Raven said warily, but the priest only shook his head in blatant admiration.

"A nice talent she has, a nice talent indeed." The priest smiled so warmly that Raven had to relax. "And a true gift for knowing exactly how and when to use it. Well, her spells had already set your friend on the road to healing by the time we'd found him. A pity she claims to have no religious vocation, because that Nightjar was a true selfless wonder, here, there, tending everyone she could possibly tend, wearing herself out to the point of exhaustion. Finally we had to set a sleep spell on her so she wouldn't kill herself!" He looked fondly over at another cot, three or four rows away. "If I had been a layman and had a child, I would have been proud to have one like your Nightjar."

"There she is, over there," Magpie whispered, and Raven nodded.

The mage patted Raven on the shoulder. "I've added to the work she started. Your heroic young friend is going to be just fine. Now please, I have far too many other patients to tend."

"Ah, of course," Magpie said. "Thank you."

But Raven paused. As soon as the priest was out of sight, the Bard bent over Crow, remembering traditions from his childhood. Not quite believing, not quite disbelieving, he traced a Gypsy sign for luck and health on the drummer's forehead with a finger. To his immense relief, Crow smiled in his sleep.

It worked! He knows I'm here. "Ach, Crow," Raven murmured in the Gypsy tongue, "all along I never thought you were much of anything; forgive me for belittling you. Sleep and heal, hero."

"Raven," Magpie whispered.

He nodded, and followed her out into the open. The Manager stood waiting, face closed, and Raven asked hesitantly, "I . . . don't suppose you managed to save any of your plays?"

The man's sad face lightened. "All of them."

In that inferno? "But—how?"

"Didn't you know?" The Manager actually chuckled. "It's standard practice for playwrights to register a copy of every play with the Church and keep that copy in their vaults for safekeeping. Never saw the need for it before, not really. Now I am most thankful I followed that practice! I promise you, as soon as things, ah, settle down a bit and we can manage to rebuild a theater, even if it's merely a tent, *A Twice-Told Tale* will finally see the light of day!"

"I don't think that's going to happen in such a hurry." Magpie hugged her arms to her as she looked out over the plain. "So many refugees," she murmured, and shuddered. "So many folks without homes or *anything*. Yes, the weather's warm and dry right now, at least there is that. But how is the Duke going to feed them all? Where are they going to be housed? What's going to happen to all of them? And when winter comes, and the cold and snow—"

"The Duke will answer those questions," said a familiar throaty voice—a little more throaty and rough than before.

"Regina!" The two women fell into each other's arms, chattering busily in relief while Raven and the Manager exchanged wry male glances. Regina had somehow managed to wash her face and bind up the remains of her costume into something like a service-able set of clothing. And, as always, she looked magnificent.

More like the survivor of a fire in a play, than a real survivor of a real fire.

"Oh, but my dear," Regina said at last, "your *hair!*"

Magpie flushed, raising a defensive hand to it. "Dreadful, isn't it?"

"No, no, not at all! If you combed it out, here and here, trimmed away all the singed ends and maybe tied it back with a ribbon . . . " Regina stopped and shook her head. "Listen to me. Talking fashion at a time like this. Duke Arden sent me to find you. We've accounted for all of the Company by now. We were . . . we were lucky. We only lost two actors, an extra I don't think you really ever met, and . . . Kedrin."

"Kedrin?"

Regina blinked fiercely. "He . . . he played Sir Verrick."

"Oh, Regina," Magpie cried in pain.

Raven bowed his head, giving the man a moment of respect and prayer for his spirit; thinking of how he had last seen him, standing firm and shouting directions at the mob in the theater. *He was braver by far than I—*

"He was terrified of growing old, did you know that? Terrified of getting too feeble for the theater and ending up in some shabby, lonely boardinghouse room. Well, n-now he doesn't have to worry." Regina caught her breath, a slow, tender smile forming on her lips. "He died a hero, saving others, so I guess he's up there somewhere, acting in perfect performances where— where trapdoors never stick and props never break!"

Magpie choked back a sob, and Raven felt his eye burning.

Regina wiped her eyes fiercely. "Ah well, that's not what I came hunting you to say. The Duke is about to make a proclamation, and I think he'd like to see some friendly faces there."

Duke Arden had climbed up onto an upturned crate, heedless of the perfect target he made for any who saw him as a scapegoat. *Not,* Raven thought wryly, *that he looks particularly noble.* The Duke was as worn and soot-stained as the rest of them, his face haggard with strain and grief. As a crowd gathered slowly about him, he began simply, his voice painfully hoarse from overuse. "I'm not going to offer you any foolish platitudes. You've all been through hell, you've lost more than I could ever dare imagine, and I—I grieve with you." Such sincerity was in the ragged voice that not one of the weary, bedraggled refugees even tried to argue.

The Duke took a deep breath, then tried in vain to clear his voice. "I'm also not going to insult you with a lecture. Instead, let me tell you what's already been done. This morning I sent off a messenger to the King, to tell him of our plight and ask him for royal support in the immediate form of food and the long-term form of money and materials for rebuilding. The Church mages have already agreed that the Church will provide tents for shelter until we can build more lasting shelters. I promise you that every coin available in my coffers and—" he shot a sharp glance at a huddled group of merchants "—those of the Council will be turned towards the rebuilding of Kingsford."

"When can we go back into the city?" a woman called out. "See if anything's left?"

"I can't give you an immediate answer on that," he replied. "I wish that I could, but I cannot lie to you."

"But—"

He held up a hand. "As soon as the mages declare it safe, I and a crew of workers are going back across the river to assess the damage. Once we're sure the fire is totally extinguished and the buildings left standing aren't in danger of collapse, you will be allowed back across."

"Sure, great, we can't go home," a man yelled, "but that's not going to stop looters!"

"Anyone found looting," the Duke said flatly, "hangs. *My* personal militia will be the first across, with orders to string looters up on the spot."

"But what *caused* the fire?" a woman hugging a child to her cried out. "Was it a judgment on us?"

The Duke sighed, and suddenly seemed to have all

the burdens of the world descend upon him. "This is the hardest. It was, as far as I can tell, a bungled assassination attempt on me. Someone thought to be rid of me by burning me in my theater. That same someone thought nothing of sending an audience full of innocent people with me. No divine retribution—or, for that matter, foreign intervention—was involved. Look you, all of you, the worst has already happened, and we have survived. I am still your Duke, if you will have me lead you still."

A few ragged cheers sounded at that, and Duke Arden frowned. "Well? Am I? Shall I?"

"Yes!" The chorus was stronger now.

It was enough for *him;* Raven saw that clearly even with only one eye. But it was not enough to raise *their* spirits for the long struggle to come. So now the Duke turned all of his formidable charm upon his people. "Come, now, such feeble voices don't belong to such brave folk! Am I your Duke?"

This time the roar of assent made Raven grin. *Shrewd, oh, shrewd, my noble friend! You've made yourself one of them and their leader at the same time!*

"My voice, as you hear," Duke Arden continued, "is not going to endure much more of this. Let me simply vow this before the One and you all: By the Grace of the One, I will live and die with you, and as your Duke, I will fight to the last breath of my lungs to keep you from further harm." He paused, shading his eyes with a hand. "Ah, I see high officials from the Church approaching now. If you will excuse me, friends, I shall go discuss our survival with them."

He jumped down from the crate as the cheers rang out again, more bravely than before. His gaze stopped on Raven and Magpie, and he gave them a quick grin. "Come with me. I want unaffiliated witnesses."

Raven bowed. As the scarlet-robed Church officials

came nearer, he whispered to Magpie in surprise, "The Lady Ardis!"

She shot him a quick glance. "Is *that* your mysterious friend?"

Raven shrugged. "Talaysen made me promise not to talk about her. It's a little late to worry about that now."

Ah, how worn the Lady Ardis looked now, wan and grim and as terrible as an executioner. *Like someone*, Raven thought uneasily, *who's been fighting a sorcerous battle. And won.*

"Duke Arden," she began formally. "Please accept my sorrow for all your people."

"I'm sorry, Lady," the Duke said, just as stiffly. "Words are easy, and I can't accept them. With the Church's aid, the fire would never have spread so far. But without it—we were doomed. *Where were you?*"

She winced at that cry of pain. "Believe me," the Lady Ardis said grimly, "if we could have helped you sooner, we would have done so. There was . . . internal trouble in the Church. Trouble that detained us until it was almost too late."

"Ah." Understanding blazed in the Duke's eyes. "Trouble that had something to do with the cause of the fire."

The faintest wry smile touched her lips. "I can't discuss Church matters here and now, as I'm sure you can understand. Let me just say the trouble has been dealt with. *Permanently.*"

Raven wasn't quite satisfied with that. He spoke up boldly, as if he had as high a rank and name as the Duke. "Our theater-hating priest really was involved, wasn't he? And sorcerously, to boot."

Her keen gray gaze flicked to him. "Clever Gypsy," was all she said, but it was a clear enough answer for Raven.

"Then I *did* see that sly little under-priest running

about backstage!" he cried, ignoring the disapproving glare from the Duke. "He wasn't the mastermind, but he must have been the actual arsonist!"

"What would you have me say?" Lady Ardis asked drily. "As I said, the trouble has been dealt with. And I am now," she added without a trace of boasting, "the High Bishop and Chief Priest of Kingsford."

"So, now!" Duke Arden said. "That's all well and good, and I am truly pleased to hear it. But what are you going to do for my people?"

Ardis was prepared, it seemed. She took a deep breath, and looked the Duke straight in the eyes. "First, I offer the shelter of the Church to all who have lost their homes. Those who prefer not to stay in the tent city are welcome to live within the Cathedral grounds for as long as need be. There are many tents stored here for use during the days of the Faire; we will appropriate them for as long as they are needed. Second, we shall send out word to our neighboring Cathedrals to see that food and clothing from all the outlying districts is sent to those in need. Third, I hereby vow before the One that the coffers of the Church will help rebuild Kingsford." Now her tone turned wry, rather than grim. "Let us say that in the course of dealing with the trouble, I learned some— interesting facts. If those facts are to remain within the pale of the Church, it will be necessary for the Church to think and act upon its ancient duties to all people."

"Thank you," the Duke said simply, and went to one knee in deepest reverence. The Lady Ardis placed a gentle hand on his soot-stained hair in blessing, then told him, "Rise, please. Thanks to what our good Raven has told me, I have learned there is still one matter that needs to be resolved."

As a puzzled Duke Arden got back to his feet, Lady

Ardis looked straight at Regina. "It is unfortunate that Regina Shevron perished in the fire. She was a good and brave lady."

As both Regina and the Duke blinked at her in complete bewilderment, Lady Ardis continued, "However, my lord Duke, I would like to introduce you to the lady who has been helping you all night—the Honorable Lady Phenyx Asher, my very own dear cousin, and quite noble enough to be anyone's wife. And—" she flicked a little water from a flask at her waist at Regina "—I so baptize thee and swear to verify."

With that, she turned her back on both of them and stalked away, leaving stunned silence in her wake. Raven just barely stifled a whoop of laughter. *Why, that sly creature! She just neatly worked around Regina's vow by making her—by word and action of the prelate of the Church, no less—a new person, born into the nobility. Now the Duke can wed her after all!*

The Duke had just realized that, his weary face all at once radiant with joy. "My dear Lady Asher," he said with a gracious little bow. "I am so pleased to meet you. Will you consent to wed me?" As Regina stared at him in shock, he laughed weakly. "It is a poor enough duchy you are getting for your pains. It will take years and every coin in the coffers to get Kingsford back to something like the state it was. I fear there will be no costly dresses for you or fine jewels till we have rebuilt it."

Regina was shaking her head in disbelief. "You're getting a poor enough dower with me—no money—no land—"

He stopped her words with a kiss. "You have all the dower I want. Honesty, courage, wit, beauty, and love. *Will you marry me?*"

"Oh my dear, what do you think? *Yes!* A hundred times *yes!*"

With a wild laugh, the Duke swept her off her feet, whirling her dizzyingly about.

"I wish I'd written that," the Manager muttered, and Raven laughed, only now realizing that he'd had his arm about Magpie all this while.

"You know," he said to her, voice trembling just a bit with sudden tension, "I think this kind of thing is contagious."

"What is?" she asked warily.

He laughed at her wariness. "Oh Magpie, my love, don't be dense! As the Duke said so forcefully, *will you marry me?*"

She stared at him blankly for a moment. "Oh—" she said. "Oh! Oh my dear, my very dear—b-but I don't have any dower at all!"

He tossed back his head in a loud roar of laughter. "Hell, woman, I'm a Gypsy! What sort of dower do you think *I* have? Magpie, dearest, I don't have anything but the clothes on my back—and my fiddle, of course."

"But—but—Raven," she protested weakly, "You're getting shortchanged! I don't have courage, wit, or beauty!"

He laughed at her. "You have wit enough to keep me working to come up with snappy retorts, beauty enough to satisfy me—even with that silly, frizzy hair— and as for courage—well, cowards are simply people who have forgotten they are brave."

"But—" she continued to protest.

He followed the Duke's lead, and stopped any further objections with a kiss. "Yesterday and today you remembered. Don't forget again. Now, one more time: *Will you marry me?*"

Her brow wrinkled. "It's not going to be a peaceful life together, I warn you that."

"If I wanted peace, I'd have joined the Church."

Raven stopped short, blinking. "Does that mean you've accepted?"

"*Yes!*" she cried, with a smile as dazzling and joyous as Regina's. "As Regi—as the Lady Asher put it, *a hundred times yes!*"

"I wish I'd written that, too," the Manager moaned in an agony of envy.

Raven grinned at him. "Make free of it with my blessing!" he said—and then took his Magpie into his arms and kissed her more completely than he had ever kissed a woman in his life.

And she returned the favor with fervor.

A timeless moment later, Magpie nibbled his earlobe gently, then whispered, "There's only one thing I need to know before we wed?"

Uh-oh. "Hmm?"

"Just how *did* you lose that eye?" Her face was alive with curiosity.

Raven grinned. At long last, he would be able to tell someone the truth! No matter how ridiculous it was. "Ah well, no secrets between husband and wife. You know how a mother's always saying to her son, 'Be careful with that stick or you'll poke your eye out'?"

Magpie stared at him blankly for a moment, then burst into laughter. "Oh, oh, dear, you didn't! Oh, poor Raven! How—how *ignominious!*"

Her hilarity was just too infectious. Arm in arm, laughing like idiots, they strolled along together.

"After all," Raven gasped out as people stared at them as if they'd gone mad, "we're Free Bards. We follow no rules but our own. And laughter, my dear, my own true love, is a fine way to start our life together!"

"If we shadows have offended,
Think but this, and all is mended,
That you have but slumber'd here,
While these visions did appear.
And this weak and idle theme,
No more yielding but a dream,
Gentles, do not reprehend;
If you pardon, we will mend.
And, as I am an honest Puck,
If we have unearned luck
Now to scape the serpent's tongue,
We will make amends ere long;
Else the Puck a liar call:
So good night unto you all.
Give me your hands, if we be friends,
And Robin shall restore amends."
                    —William Shakespeare
                A Midsummer Night's Dream,
                            Act V, 1